EXECUTIONER

REIGN OF BLOOD

EDWIN MCRAE

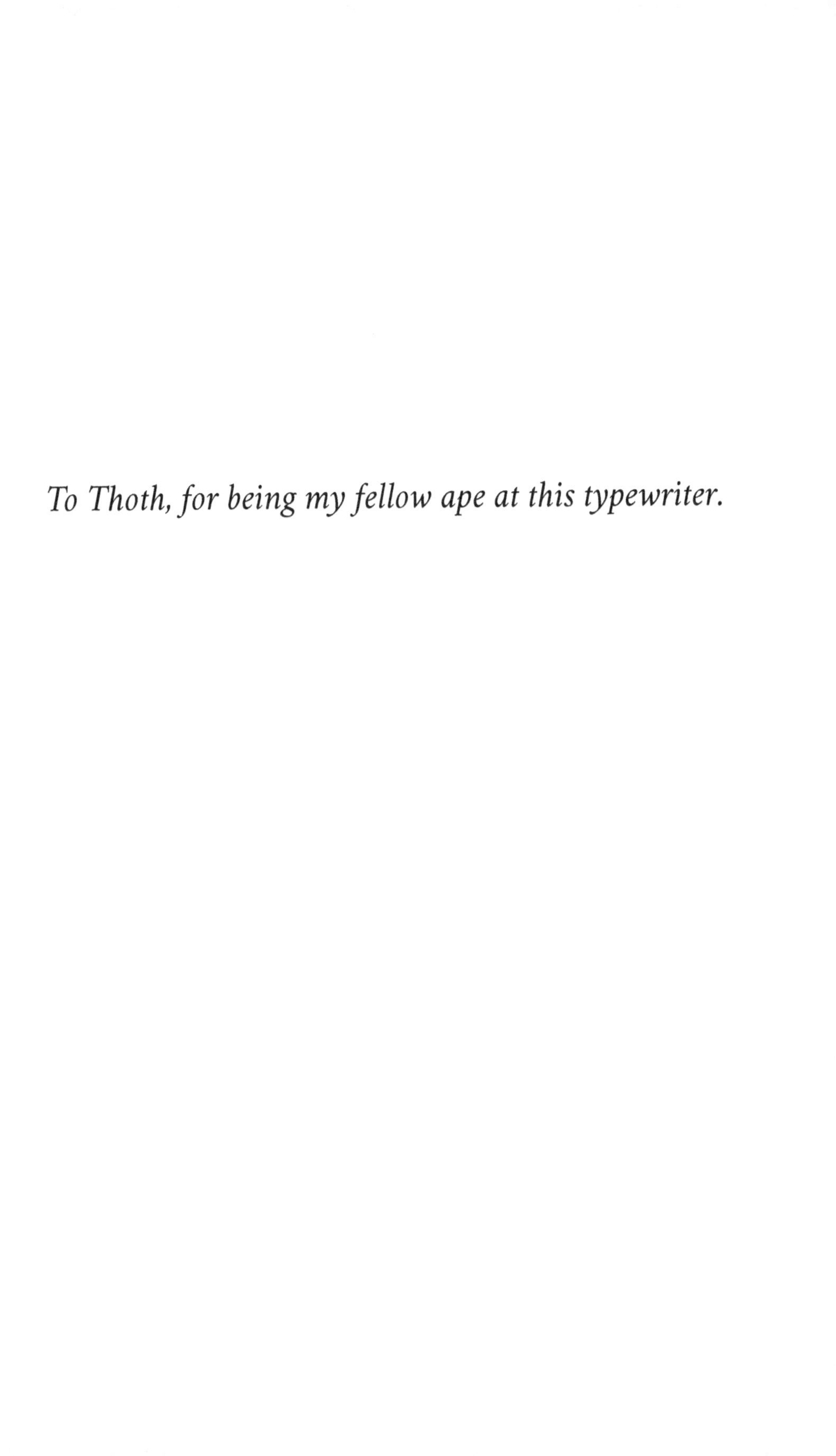

To Thoth, for being my fellow ape at this typewriter.

1

[KARINA]

Karina drummed her long nails on the arm of her chair, just to get under the soldier's tattooed skin. She was doing a passable job of masking her frustration, but the inquisitor noted the slight tightening of the muscles around the soldier's eyes.

The inquisitor offered a final "thrum thrum" for good measure and then made a point of inspecting those same nails, turning them this way and that to see if there were flaws in the paintwork. Her assistant had done well this morning. The man must have stayed off the booze last night, as instructed. He'd be hanging by his hands for an entire day otherwise.

The soldier rocked back and forth on her feet

and cleared her throat a little, as if that was going to nudge Karina towards making her point and letting the woman go. No, no, that would never do. Karina was in control here, not this platinum-haired ox with her muscles and tattoos. Karina eased her own plump form deeper into the chair. The brawny bitch needed to remember her place. She was a soldier and Karina was an inquisitor. And never the twain should meet, at least not eye to eye.

"So let me get this right," ventured Karina, keeping her voice low so that the soldier had to strain to hear her. That was another trick of the power trade. Never demand attention. Make others work for what you have to say. "You've had a dozen casualties in as many days and you are no closer to breaching the temple grounds?"

The soldier's frown deepened as she nodded.

"I'm sorry, I didn't quite catch that."

"Yes, Madam Inquisitor. Twelve casualties, twelve days. The creatures living in that temple, well, they're territorial as fuck."

Karina tapped her index nail against the table. "Language. You're not speaking to your fellow grunts here."

"Apologies, madam," muttered the soldier without an ounce of sincerity.

"You've tried a concerted push?"

"Yes, madam. Day three accounted for half our losses."

"I see." Karina sighed her disappointment.

She knew it wasn't the soldier's fault. Karina had seen the beasts with her own two eyes. Strangely humanoid yet with more limbs than they had any natural right to possess. Tails equipped with potent stingers. Fangs, claws and heavy scales that offered ample protection from archers. A peculiar hybrid of primate and scorpion. She would very much like to capture a few for study and experimentation, but that would have to wait. First they needed to get into that temple. By all accounts the Altar of Khorlvah was in there and she intended to have it.

"In that case, time to put the demon to work. Bring him into the courtyard."

The soldier's frown deepened so much that she looked almost comical, like she had just taken a bite out of a lemon. "I'm not sure we can-"

"Is this because of the warlock?" Karina interrupted her, keeping her voice deceptively soft, like she was expressing some sort of sympathy for the other woman.

Karina watched as the soldier swallowed

hard, her tension obvious in the muscles of her neck. "Yes, madam."

"Are you afraid of our demon?"

The murderous flash in the soldier's eyes was brief but telling. "No, madam."

Karina eyed the woman for a long moment, summoning the soldier's stats as she did so.

Sergeant Maribella of Credence
Class: Reiver Warrior - Level 6
Progress to Level 7 = 735/1000

Body: 18
Body +2 Class Modifier: 20

Mind: 11
Spirit: 11

HP: 120
EP: 66

Skills
Blade of Doom (Tier 4)
Horse Riding (Tier 4)
Authority (Tier 2)
Vigorous Healing (Tier 4)
Sword Storm (Tier 2)

Karina had personally believed every word of Captain Serik's endeavors, the Helm of Supremacy and Garland's pet warlock. It all made perfect sense based on what she knew of both the Barrens and the workings of the Garland druids. But one had to be thorough, just in case the subject forgot to mention something important. And yes, that lovely combination of high health points and Vigorous Healing had made Miss Maribella quite the delightful subject indeed. Karina fought the urge to lick her lips. She didn't want to give the *sergeant* mixed messages.

"You should be afraid of him. Were it not for that collar of mine, he'd butcher us all like chickens in a pen." She dismissed the sergeant with a flick of her fingers. "Make sure he's well fed and watered before you bring him in. And give him a bath. He's easier to deal with when he's been pampered a little bit."

The sergeant saluted, turned on her heels in one crisp motion and strode stiffly out of the room, her scarred left hand resting on the pommel of her sword. The reivers flanking the doorway both saluted, even though the woman wasn't an officer. That bothered Karina, truth be told. As did the woman's Authority Tier 2 skill. The sergeant commanded a good deal of respect from the soldiers. In the long run, she was a threat to Karina's own authority. For now she was useful, being one of the few reivers to survive a sojourn into the Barrens. But once her usefulness came to an end, Karina had plans for the resilient Sergeant Maribella.

Karina dwelled on that enjoyably dark thought for a moment as she stood and stretched. She made a point of never standing while in close proximity to Maribella, nor anyone else of that height and stature. Being a head shorter and several heads wider, Karina carefully avoided any mistaken perceptions of power based on physicality. Meat was meat at the end of the day, plentiful and consumable. Mind and Spirit, they were the only attributes worth nurturing, and those she had in abundance.

She smoothed her black robes and gave her hair a quick once-over in the mirror, tidying away any loose strands. Then she practised her iciest glare a couple of times. The demon was likely to get mouthy and she would need to put him back in his place. A cold stare and tweak of his collar should do the trick. Karina took one last look at herself and was pleased with what she saw. An inquisitor from head to foot. A figure to be feared, even by demons.

2

———————

[ARIX]

The pain clasped him around the throat and billowed over his body like a barber's gown soaked in acid. Arix raised his hands in supplication.

"Fine, fine, you win!" he wheezed through the collar's searing stranglehold. "I'll delve your fucking dungeon!"

You have received the "Bloody Devotions" quest.

Secure the Altar of Korlvah for Inquisitor Karina. Clear the area of hostiles. Reiver soldiers must be able to remove the altar from the Bloodstone Temple without casualties.

And when I'm free of this collar, Karina, I'll be showing you some right bloody devotions. The thought was a deep red splash across his mind, one that dripped slowly down the inside of his skull like the opening titles of a b-grade horror.

"There's a good demon."

The pain stopped as his gown of agony dissipated. The woman's plump-lipped smile was as frosty as her pale blue eyes. Arix could feel those eyes boring into him, drilling, poking, daring him to meet them in defiance. He knew better. Instead, he looked at the sergeant as she dumped his gear at his feet and backed away.

"Anything real special you want me to fetch, Madam Inquisitor?" he asked. Arix was testing to see if she'd seen the quest notification too.

Karina smirked and tapped her smooth neck with a long fingernail. "We both know what I want. Clear that temple of nasty creatures and you may consider yourself in my good books."

"You'll let me go, yeah?"

The woman's laughter was melodious, even pleasant. Karina sounded like she had a good singing voice. She ewas probably a soprano in the Virgins of Vigilance Junior Choir before growing up to become a professional sadist.

"No, my darling demon, but I promise not to

kill you slowly just for the fun of it. Not tonight, at least."

Arix focused on doing up buckles rather than dwelling on what Inquisitor Karina had put him through these past few days. She had managed to turn a simple respawn into a source of sweaty, gut-churning dread.

He secured his black leather armor, hooked his bolt case into his belt, and clipped his crossbow into place on his back. Arix then picked up his battle axe and gave it an experimental twirl. It didn't matter that he was doing it under duress. It felt good to have a little adventuring to do.

He turned to Karina and snapped off a sharp salute. "If everything goes tits up in there, madam, would you be so kind as to have your minions grab my gear?" He gave the sergeant a lascivious wink. He knew it was a good one, that wink, because he'd practised it to perfection in his web cam. "You want me to stay all sturdy and potent for you, yeah?"

Pain pulsed through the collar, driving him to his knees. It lasted only a moment but it was far sharper than before.

"What the fuck you do that for?!"

"Don't distract the help."

With the few shreds of dignity he could muster, Arix got to his feet and turned towards the ancient ruin. It loomed over him, a mass of corrupted stone and time-worn reverence. He rested his axe on his shoulder and walked into the temple's lengthening shadow. He didn't look back or offer any parting witticisms. His captor clearly wasn't in the mood for chitchat today, and if he was honest with himself, neither was he after several days of servitude and the kind of debasement that even his Tube Trolls would struggle to put into words. Not to mention that he'd searched his digital ass off to find this *Reign of Blood* Easter Egg, only to get clapped in irons the moment he stepped through the gate. Yeah, he was in the mood to seriously murder some shit.

The first candidate obliged by dropping from the roof with a hiss and roar. Its fang-filled maw was drenched in blood and it still clutched a tattered human leg in one claw. Arix had interrupted lunch. Judging by the boot on that severed leg, reiver was on the menu.

The creature crouched down on all fours and Arix watched with morbid fascination as a segmented tail rose up from the thing's hindquarters. He waited and watched the patterns of muscle tensing and contorting at the edges of the tail's armored plating. He identified the telltale twitch of impending attack and spun to the right. He held his axe close on the first revolution, then extended and braced it on the second. The wide blade crunched into the fleshy gap between two of the creature's bone plates and he felt a brief resistance before the axe sliced clean through. Arix then used the remaining momentum for a third revolution, redirecting slightly so that the blade of his axe was buried in the side of the monster's skull even before its dismembered tail hit the dirt.

You have killed a Level 3 Tomb Tyrant.
Your XP reward per party member = 15 XP
Your party currently has 2 members.

The thump of limp meat upon clay almost covered the light scuffling of approaching vengeance. Not for the first time since his arrival into *Reign of Blood*, Arix thanked his passive Fox Ears skill. Without looking, he knew there were three of them, all Tomb Tyrants, coming at him from different directions. He took a deep breath, closed his eyes and listened, focusing on the increasing volume of each scuffle. Two were ahead of the third. It would probably escape the initial onslaught, but even a glancing blow would make it falter long enough for him to follow up with a killing blow.

He waited a fraction of a second longer and shouted, "Clean Slate!" The axe did the rest, sweeping in a perfect circle like the big hand of a clock, using his body as the dial. He opened his eyes to enjoy the ribbon of steel light that always followed his axehead whenever he cast this spell. He savored the explosion of blood and viscera as the blade disemboweled the first beast, took the reaching claw off the third and buried itself between the ribs of the second. The tomb tyrant's bone-festooned hide offered as much protection as a piece of cold toast to Clean Slate.

Arix ignored the tortured screeches as the first monster tried to retrieve its entrails from the clay floor. He yanked his axe free of the second creature and raised it just in time to block the descending stinger of the third. Using the full power of his legs against the monster's heavily-muscled tail, he shoved the stinger aside and reversed the axe into the creature's snarling face, driving the punch-spike into one of its red-rimmed eyes. The tomb tyrant shivered as the spike skewered its brain and then it dropped to the ground like a fresh-born calf.

He put his boot against the dead beast's skull and wiggled the spike free. It came away with a squelch and Arix was happy to use it one more time to silence the nerve-scratching howls that 'Misery Guts' was still producing.

You have killed three Level 3 Tomb Tyrants.
Your XP reward per party member = 45 XP

Arix wasn't sure what fucked him off more. Was it the fact that Karina could use the collar to kill him where he stood, no matter where he was? That she controlled his resurrection point so that he always returned to her like a smack-addict to his dealer? Or was it that the collar made him permanently partied with her so that she was always leeching off half his XP?

He shoved those fuming thoughts aside and forced himself to survey his surroundings, keeping his breathing low and soft so that Fox Ears could do its thing. For the moment he was alone and standing in what looked to be the Bloodstone Temple's entrance hall, a dull red vestibule where devotees once gathered before shuffling into the main chamber to worship.

While relatively intact, the decorative statues were distorted in unnerving ways. A winged woman reached up out of a pit of raging fire. Human figures gathered around her. Their misshapen stone bodies reminded him of the melted chocolate santas he'd tried to save by putting them in the freezer. Their faces looked frighteningly like Edvard Munch's *The Scream*. To him it didn't look like the statues had been carved that way, rather that the stone had indeed melted a little before mysteriously resetting in its new and warped shape.

The devs wanted this supposedly ancient city to look like it had suffered a cataclysm. It was all bollocks, of course. About as real as instant coffee. Arix eyed the winged goddess one more time. Well-made bollocks though. He'd give them that.

A gaping archway led into the gloom-drenched chamber of worship beyond. Arix wondered if there were more tomb tyrants in there, or perhaps something a bit meatier. He would dearly love to drive his axe down the middle of that inquisitor cow, chop her into halves like a butcher bisecting a carcass of beef. He touched his fingertips to the metal collar and winced as it sparked, sending a painful warning through his fingers and neck. Through the collar, Karina could pinpoint his whereabouts at any time. If he tried to run she'd simply strangle him to death and he'd resurrect back at the reiver camp. He'd pay just about anything for an anti-curse or nullify magic spell right now. He wasn't holding out much hope, but perhaps he'd find something in this temple.

Arix crossed the chamber to the archway but stopped just before the threshold. Something wasn't right. The inside of the arch was decorated with symbols, hieroglyphs almost, and the air within the entranceway had a peculiar weight to it. As an experiment, he returned to the scene of carnage behind him and picked up the severed tail. He crossed to the archway again and lobbed the tail into it. The air within the archway flashed once, like the beam of a flashlight passing over a dusty mirror. There was a sharp hiss as the tail blackened and exploded into dust.

Damn, thought Arix. That would've been a bit shit.

He looked up at the archway and murmured "Truelight" under his breath. The archway glowed with chill, blue light. Three of its engraved symbols shone brighter than the rest. A circle with a jagged tail. A zee on its side. A three-pronged fork.

"Circle, zee, fork," he said out loud. His voice echoed eerily through the deathly quiet chamber.

Nothing. He tried saying the other five combinations of those words. Nothing. He gritted his teeth and let out a growl of frustration. He wasn't a fan of puzzles but they seemed to be a necessary evil in RPGs. He personally preferred the games where you just slaughtered stuff and worked on your character build, like the first edition of *Reign of Blood*. That was still his favorite, even now. Still, it looked like this version was determined to test his puzzle-solving skills so he would have to humor the designers this time.

He tried drawing the symbols in the air, starting again with the circle, zee, fork combination. He smiled as his fingertip began to glow. "ET phone the fuck home." He drew shapes in the air like a kid with a sparkler on Guy Fawkes Day. No sooner had he drawn the sideways zee, preceded by the fork and the circle, the air within the archway shimmered and the malevolent curtain of magic drew aside. Cursing himself for not thinking to bring two bits of tyrant in the first place, he went back, picked up the severed claw, returned to the archway and tossed the claw through. It landed with a light thump on the other side. So far so good, but he still braced himself for instant powdered death as he took the fateful step himself.

On the other side of the archway, he let out a sigh of relief and took a moment to absorb his new environment. He realized that it was the archway's deadly magic that had given this chamber of worship its gloomy appearance. The room was actually filled with light that poured down from the intact stained glass windows in the roof high above. Their imagery was warped, much like the statues in the entrance hall, producing an abstract smear of color that hurt Arix's eyes. He looked away and took in the rest of the room.

It reminded him a little of Salisbury Cathedral with all of its dwarfing magnificence. Stone pews lined a wide, central aisle. The aisle led to another winged woman with flames for legs, a much bigger one this time. Once again, she was surrounded by worshipping figures, warped and weird. It was strange that the winged woman wasn't misshapen in any way. In fact, to Arix's eyes she was oddly sexy for an object of worship, leaning more towards anime than avatar. He chuckled as he thought of the environment artist, a patina of lustful sweat on his brow as he fashioned this colossal wet dream out of pixels and code.

At the woman's fiery feet sat an ornate box that looked like a coffin, a masterwork of gold and carved wood. The latter should have rotted away centuries ago. Arix would hazard a guess that it was either petrified or preserved by some magical imbuement. From the description Karina had given him, this coffin was the Altar of Khorlvah.

Peachy. All he had to do was secure the area and call in the sergeant. She'd have her reiver grunts carry the thing out to Karina and he'd get a pain-free night for a change. Of course, as Arix had come to expect in these games, that was going to be easier said than done.

The vaults above echoed with scuffling and screeching. Arix unclipped his crossbow and loaded the top and bottom barrels with bolts. Now was his chance to *really* work out some frustration.

3

———————

[MARK]

Mark's "Volcanic Bastard" sword carved through the creature's abdomen, leaving a sizzling trail of green hemolymph and sundered chitin behind it. The lion-sized insect waved its remaining legs pitifully in the air and then fell still.

To his left, Braemar crushed two more of the oversized beetles under a cascade of ancient masonry. Mark flinched, remembering his own experience of being 'squashed like a bug' beneath stone and mortar. He turned to his right and winced a little at the pain in his thigh as he shifted his weight. His insectoid opponent had managed to take a chunk out of his leg before becoming properly acquainted with Volcanic Bastard.

He found Vari looking at him, her eyes bright, a faint smile on her lips as she murmured her spell. Warmth flooded across his leg, staunching blood, knitting muscle and stitching skin together. Soon only a memory of injury remained, a blood-stained puncture in the steel cuisse Citadel had forged for him.

Vari's Mend Flesh has healed you for 30 HP.
HP: 126

He made a mental note to find some better leg armor. Then he willed Volcanic Bastard into 'Cooldown' mode, returned it to the sheath on his back, and took a moment to survey the carnage. It consisted mostly of rubble and crumbling ruins, decorated with splatters of insectoid gore and fragments of midnight-black chitin.

Your party has slaughtered five Level 3 Pit Scroungers.
Your XP reward per party member = 50 XP
Your party currently has three members.

He pointed down the wide avenue they'd been following through the Barrens. It was lined with looming buildings that might once have rivaled the architectural wonders of Venice. Now they were distorted echoes of their former selves. The avenue ended in a vast edifice that looked to have been a government structure or major temple.

"That big building down the end, let's head there. Might be some interesting stuff in-"

He was interrupted by the wet screech of a shellfish being torn apart. He remembered that sound all too well, from the times his ex-wife would demand that he take her out to her favorite seafood restaurant. He always ordered the vegetarian nachos.

The smell was another unpleasant reminder. He pressed the back of his hand to his nose and turned to Vari. The figurist was crouched over the splayed innards of the giant bug she'd just cracked open.

"Woah, Vari. That thing reeks."

Vari nodded absently as she poked and prodded various viscera with her dagger.

"Judging from the contents of its stomach," replied Vari, her voice soft with fascination, "this thing was primarily a carrion eater."

"Then why did they attack us?" slurred Mark, his mouth now thick with nausea-induced saliva.

"Probably being territorial. We may have wandered into their scavenging ground."

"So there's more of them around?" asked Braemar.

Vari nodded. "Might be a nest."

She shrugged off her pack, opened it up, and took out a small lidded ceramic bowl and a pair of forceps. With a deft slice of her dagger, she cut a yellow sac out of the gooey mass and dropped it into the bowl.

Mark tried to keep the disgust out of his voice. It was cool with him that Vari was unfazed by stuff like this, but it didn't change the fact that it was pretty gross. "Um, that's an interesting choice of trophy, Vari."

Vari winked at him. "I'm going to make it into a hat for you."

"You're too kind."

"I know."

"No, seriously. What are you doing?"

Vari cleaned her dagger and forceps with a few large leaves she plucked from something that looked like a rubber tree plant. "Practising my Physik Perception and nabbing a nice, juicy ingredient for a potion I'm working on." She tucked the bowl and forceps away in her pack. "It's an acid sac. These insects disgorge acid onto their food, much like a fly does, to break it down before eating. It's a pre-digestion process."

Braemar's suddenly pale face was a striking contrast to the red frame of his hair. "We'll end up drinking that thing?"

Vari nodded, her expression deadpan. "Bile is a base ingredient for a lot of potions."

The druid's pallor took on a green tinge. "Even the essence potions you've given me to drink?"

"They didn't taste too acidic, did they? I try to balance the flavors, make them as palatable as-"

Braemar shook his head and pressed his hands to his belly. A sheen of sweat broke out on his forehead. "I think I'm going to sick."

"Hold on then," urged Vari as she took another bowl from her pack. "Let me collect some."

Braemar blinked, taken aback. "You want to collect my-"

"Of course. I can't brew essence potions out of water and kind wishes. I usually have to make myself throw up." She shrugged. "Unpleasant but necessary, you know?"

The druid's Adam's apple worked up and down like a busy elevator. Mark laughed, took the bowl from Vari and pressed it into Braemar's hands.

"Come on, mate. Do as the lady says. We're in the middle of the damned Barrens. I reckon we'll need all the essence potions Vari can make for us."

Braemar stared at Mark for a wide-eyed moment and then fled around the corner of a gutted building. Retching sounds followed.

Mark put his arm around Vari's shoulders. "You, my darling, have the strongest stomach of anyone I've ever met."

Vari smiled up at him and picked a scrap of chitin off his chainmail. A blob of insectoid goop trailed the fragment, stretching out until it snapped like a string of melted mozzarella. "I'm not the one who ends up covered in blood and gore half the time."

Mark shrugged. "That's adventuring for you."

He looked at Vari, and for a brief moment he felt scared for her. She was vulnerable, but not in the emotional sense. The figurist had been through a lot during her time with the inquisitors. Rather than damage her, those experiences had served only to make her more resourceful, more resilient. But on a purely practical level, thick cloth wasn't going to save her from a pair of sharp mandibles and she certainly wasn't going to be able to take anything down with that dagger of hers.

"Speaking of which, we need to get you guys some proper adventuring gear."

Braemar groaned as he shuffled back around the corner, having conveyed the contents of his stomach into Vari's bowl. He passed the bowl to Vari with trembling hands.

Vari smiled kindly as she secured the lid and slid the bowl into her pack. Then she looked to Mark, one eyebrow raised.

"What do you have in mind, Mark?"

He gestured at Vari's dissected beetle. "If these things have been scavenging around this place for a while, even since this city fell apart, they might have collected some interesting stuff over the generations."

Vari nodded. "Makes sense. They would've hauled whole corpses back to their nest so they could consume them in safety. Whatever was on those corpses might still be there."

"Exactly," said Mark with a grin. "So let's go bug hunting."

Then he realized what he was saying. Hunting, tracking, finding a needle in the proverbial haystack, that's what Dayna had done for them. For the dozenth time he saw the reiver sergeant's dagger in his mind's eye as it sank up to the hilt in the soft flesh under Dayna's chin.

"Mark?" asked Vari softly. "You okay?"

He nodded and sighed. "Just thinking how handy Dayna would be right about now. It's all well and good saying 'let's go bug hunting', but I wouldn't have the faintest idea where to start."

Braemar cleared his throat. "Um, I could give it a shot."

Mark tried not to let the skepticism show on his face. "Have you been learning a few ranger skills on the quiet?"

"No. If we were in the forest, I'd be bloody useless. But here's different." He swept the stark surroundings with a freckled hand. "A lotta dirt and dust, not much vegetation. I can use my Earthcraft skill to see where dust has fallen, naturally or otherwise. I can tell if soil and stones are where they should be or if they've been disturbed by something." Braemar crossed the battlefield, giving Vari's dissected beetle a wide berth, and knelt down to inspect the ground. "These little hollows, they're not due to the natural sedimentation process, and there's no sign of water erosion or subsidence. They were made by the beetles and the dust has blown over them."

Mark clapped his hands together in impressed applause. "I reckon even Dayna would've found that impressive, Braemar."

Braemar stood and shook his head. "Nah, she'd have called me a fucking amateur and pointed out exactly how many beetles had passed through in the last few days, where they came from, where they were headed, and probably even what their bloody names were."

Mark forced a smile and tried to ignore the nagging of guilt in his gut. He'd replayed Dayna's death in his head too many times and never once had he come up with something he could've done differently. "Well, let's face it. Dayna isn't here and some trail is better than none. Lead the way, good sir."

Braemar did as he was bade, watching the ground as he headed off towards a squat line of ruins. To Mark they looked to have been a row of terraced houses. He and Vari followed at a short distance so as not to disturb the earth or distract their druid from his work.

It wasn't long before the beetle trails led them

into a relatively intact townhouse. Judging by the worn carvings framing the entranceway, and the grand stone staircase leading from the foyer up to the second level, this had been a residence of wealth. To the right of the staircase, tucked into the gloom, Mark could just make out a large and misshapen mass. He drew his sleeping Volcanic Bastard and woke it up. The blade flickered, as if Mark had blown across the coals of a dormant fire, then took on the iridescent mottle of molten iron. The sword's warm light picked out the jagged boundaries of the pit beetles' nest, an organic coagulation of clay, rotting wood and withered vegetation, held together by a waxy yellow resin.

"Looks like it might burn," whispered Vari. "You could set it alight with your sword, or use that fire breath of yours if you didn't want to get that close."

Mark shook his head. "Might damage any loot these scavengers have collected. Braemar?"

"Yeah, Mark?"

"No bringing the roof down, please. Remember what happened to the Helm of Supremacy."

"And to the man wearing it," added Vari.

"No worries," answered the druid. "Got another spell I picked up at Level Six. Haven't had a chance to try it out yet. If you can draw them out, I should be able to soften them up a bit before they reach you."

"Sounds good. Let's give this a shot then."

Mark raised his glowing sword and advanced towards the nest. The firelight made the sharp shadows of the nest dance like gnashing teeth. Mark knew he was about to wake something huge and ravenous, a gigantic boss beetle of some kind. He glanced back at Braemar and Vari. If that happened, he would give them as much time as he could to get the hell out before he became bug food. At least he would wake up after the subsequent nightmare. They wouldn't.

As he neared the nest, he brought up the description of the Doppelganger spell.

Doppelganger

Creates an illusion of image, scent and sound that is an identical copy of the caster.

Tier 1: The doppelganger can appear up to 10 meters away and lasts for one minute.

"My darling wife aside, I tend to prefer my own company."

- Zevryn the Everborn

Good, he thought. Scent was important here. Though the pit beetles had eyes, he wasn't sure how well they would see his illusion within the gloom of their nest. But they would definitely pick up his doppelganger's smell with their antennae.

He whispered "Doppelganger" and focused on the beshadowed maw ahead. His own likeness flickered into existence instead. Mark was taken by surprise, realizing he'd not seen himself in a mirror lately. The warlock before him was much broader and significantly more athletic than real-life Mark. His wavy brown hair was an unruly mane reaching almost to his shoulders, and he cut quite a striking figure in Garridar's Ironhide and travelling cloak. He was no longer the noob, dying with a ranger's arrow through his neck. Nor was he the self-pitying bastard, dragging his sorry ass through each and every day, aching to be back in FIVR where he could have his precious mini-break from his real life. The Mark before him was a warlock, a man of might and magic fighting for what he believed in. He rolled his eyes, a bit embarrassed with himself. That last bit was OTT, but it still felt bloody good.

His observation was rudely interrupted by the pair of mandibles that snapped shut around his doppelganger's waist with such power they would've sliced the real Mark in twain. The boney clack echoed around the once-grand foyer and was followed by scratching and rustling as the giant beetle scuttled out of the nest. It was much larger and more heavily clad than the scavengers they'd met outside. A soldier bred to defend the nest.

As the first soldier beetle was followed by a second, and then a third, Braemar shouted "Erupt!" at the top of his lungs. His voice echoed only once before the rocks answered his call. One beetle saw its leg sundered from the tibia down as the rock it was standing on became the fantasy equivalent of a land mine. Stone fragments played drum tattoos across carapaces, and in two cases, punctured and ruptured compound eyes.

As the dust swirled around them, all three insects reeled in shock. Mark raised Volcanic Bastard, ready to make brutal use of their discombobulation.

"Mark!" yelled Vari. "Aim for the spiracles!"

"What's a spiracle?" he called back.

"Little openings along the beetle's flanks. They're for breathing."

"Barbequed beetle on a stick?"

"That's right!"

Mark laughed as he closed the distance to the first beetle. The giant insect was still shaking off the shock of Braemar's rock blasts. One of its bulbous eyes was a deflated mass of sinew and viscous goo. Through the dust he spotted the creature's abdominal spiracles, small holes that opened and closed like the mouths of goldfish. He leveled his sword at the nearest spiracle, took aim, and thrust forward with all of his might. The smouldering sword sank into the orifice with the ease of a skewer going into a roast chicken. Steam gushed from the hole, followed by a stream of bubbling hemolymph. The soldier beetle let out a hiss, its entire frame shuddered, and then it collapsed to the ground.

Mark hauled Volcanic Bastard free of the carcass and spun about in time to see another soldier beetle bearing down on him. Its mandibles were splayed wide, revealing a set of four finger-like palps that would happily chew him up once the crushing mandibles had their way. He dove to the left, rolled, and came back up onto his feet. The beetle struggled to halt its lunge, scrabbling for purchase on the dust and gravel under its tarsal claws. With its flank thus exposed, the beetle was a sitting duck for Mark's puncturing thrust. Once again the sword found the opening of a spiracle, plunging deep into the insect's abdomen, cutting and cauterising the creature's innards. The insect thrashed in agony, so violently that Mark was knocked sideways by the weight of its armored body. He lost his grip on his sword and tumbled in an ungainly heap into the dust. Mark heard a resounding "crunch" as he landed. His forearm was bent beyond tolerance by the force of the fall and the weight of his own body. The pain didn't hit him straight away but he could feel it building beyond the numbing fog of shock.

You have suffered 25 HP in damage!
Your left forearm is broken.
HP: 101

"Vari! My arm!" he shouted as he scrambled to his feet. The welcome words, "Sculpt Bone", swam through the gathering clouds of pain. Warmth washed down his arm, followed by the unnerving feeling of bone shifting of its own accord beneath his flesh. The encroaching agony receded and Mark waggled his fingers in relief.

Vari of Karajan has healed you for 25 HP.
Your left forearm is fully mended.
HP: 126

"Quagmire!" bellowed Braemar. Mark looked up in time to see a pair of mandibles plunge into a pool of mud rather than into his body. Another soldier beetle entered the battle from the nest and made a beeline for Mark while the fourth beetle, the one with the splintered leg, had positioned itself between him and Volcanic Bastard. The sword was still imbedded in its victim's abdomen. The healthy soldier was extricating itself from Braemar's quagmire and the injured beetle was sizing him up with its one remaining eye. The thing's other eye was a milky pulp shot through with shards of shattered stone. Unarmed, Mark knew he would last about two seconds against the healthy beetle and maybe four against the injured one. He had to get to his sword.

"Ethereal Flesh," he murmured.

Muddied mandibles snapped harmlessly through vapor that had been his body only a moment before. He flowed beneath this beetle and onto the second beetle. Then he repeated the movement, passing underneath the insect so it would have to turn around to attack him. Mark mustered his vapors by his beloved sword and made himself whole again. With a grunt of effort he pulled Volcanic Bastard free and parried the mandibles that now sought to tear him apart. Once, twice, he blocked the insect's desperate attacks. Then he saw his opening. He ducked under the remains of the beetle's injured leg and brought his sword sweeping up into the join between its thorax and its abdomen. Aided by its heated fury, Volcanic Bastard clove the beetle clean in half.

Mark rolled away from the final beetle's attack, staying close enough to strike when he came back to his feet. The insect moved too fast for him to aim for the spiracles so this time he focused on the legs, lopping them off, one by one, as his opponent tried in vain to turn around. Once all three legs on one side were gone, the defeated soldier flopped helplessly onto the ground and Mark was quick to put it out of its misery, toasting it from the inside out. He turned to the nest, sword raised, expecting another wave of defenders. The structure remained silent.

Your party has defeated four Level 4 Pit Soldiers.

Your XP reward per party member = 53 XP

After several long seconds of stillness and silence, Mark turned to Vari and Braemar and smiled at them through the settling dust.

"Anyone up for a bit of looting?"

4

[MARK]

Mark knelt over the armor he'd just dug out of a pile of bones and assorted detritus. The steel was pitted with corrosion here and there, but nothing some polishing wouldn't fix.

Breastplate, cuisses and greaves. Compared with Garridar's Ironhide, the Breastplate of the High Legion was nothing to write home about, but the cuisses and greaves were a definite improvement on Citadel's handiwork.

Cuisses of the High Legion
20% reduction in damage caused to the upper leg.
20% chance to prevent total damage to the
upper leg.

10% reduction in upper leg muscle fatigue.

"An empire begins with a pair of sturdy legs
and a willingness to march."
- Commander Ezra of the High Legion

Greaves of the High Legion
20% reduction in damage to the lower leg.
20% chance to prevent total damage to the
lower leg.
10% reduction in lower leg muscle fatigue.

"Forget ceremony. A soldier stands on tender
flesh
and brittle bone."
- Commander Ezra of the High Legion

Both cuisses and greaves were engraved with
the symbol of a hand grasping the sun, an image
of unbridled ambition. Mark suspected that same
ambition had come crashing down upon this once
grand city. The thought sparked an old memory,
one of being glued to the television, watching re-
plays with horrified fascination as the twin
towers fell. He shook off the morbid thought,
picked up the breastplate, and passed it to Vari.

"Here, my lady. Something to prevent that gorgeous heart of yours from being skewered by an arrow."

Vari smiled her thanks and pointed at the straps. "A little help, please?"

Vari settled the breastplate in place over her chest, as Mark buckled the straps across her back, enjoying the moment of closeness and the warm, appetizing fragrance of her hair. For some reason, Vari's scent reminded him of the beautiful sourdough bread his mum had baked in the oven every Saturday morning.

"Comfy?"

"A little tighter, please. I'm not as chesty as you seem to imagine."

Mark tightened the straps another notch. "Just didn't want to squish you," he murmured.

Vari turned to him, placed her smooth palm to his cheek and drew him closer. "You can squish me any time you like, darling." Her whisper tickled his ear and sent his pulse-rate through the roof.

"Oh shit, sorry. I'll just..." mumbled an embarrassed Braemar. Mark and Vari both laughed as they parted and turned to the druid. He'd been exploring the back chambers of the nest and had returned with a long ebony staff. It was shod at each end with silver.

"Nice stick," complimented Mark. "Magic?"

Braemar nodded. "Yeah, faster casting speed and packs a bit of a wallop as well. That's if I manage to hit anything with it."

"I can give you a few pointers on that, mate" offered Mark.

"Thank you. That'd be great."

"No worries. And try these on for size."

Mark picked out a pair of dark brown boots from the rest of the items he and Vari had recovered and passed them to Braemar. The remaining items consisted of another Breastplate of the High Legion along with another cuisse and greave, both missing their partners. There was an assortment of jewelry and a few valuable ornaments, stuff that could either be sold or melted down for use in the forge.

Braemar's eyes widened as he saw the stats on the boots. "Really? Boots of the Firmament?"

With the haste of a kid plundering a Christmas tree, Braemar sat down and pulled the boots on. He then nodded with both satisfaction and more than a little wonder. "Perfect bloody fit. Who'd have thought it."

Mark had to bite his tongue, knowing that the game was resizing items automatically. He could tell without putting them on that his new greaves and cuisses would be just the right size for him. Vari's breastplate had definitely shrunk a bit as he fastened the straps for her.

Braemar stood up and rocked back and forth a couple of times, heel to toe, pleased as punch with his new acquisitions. "Good Spirit boost too, especially for earth-based spells. So I reckon-"

The druid left the sentence unfinished as he crunched across the floor and passed the ebony staff to Vari. Surprised, Vari accepted the staff and ran her fingertips along the smooth ebony.

"You're sure?" she asked Braemar.

The druid shrugged. "Someone's got to keep healing our warlock here. Poor man's a bit accident prone."

"Cheers for that, Braemar," replied Mark. "Next time I'll let you take point with the giant bugs, eh?"

"I'm alright, thank you," answered Braemar with a wry grin. He gestured with his thumb over his shoulder. "There's something else you two should see as well."

"More loot?" Mark wondered hopefully.

Braemar tugged at his beard, something he tended to do when he was feeling unsure. "Don't know, to be honest."

They followed the druid down a short tunnel. It had been molded by beetles out of a mixture of resin and the bones of scavenged meals. Mark could make out more than a few humanoid bones in there. The tunnel ended abruptly at a ruptured wall. The masonry spilled into a huge, vaulted room. A single shaft of light poured down from the broken roof above, illuminating the otherwise darkened chamber.

"The beetles obviously broke into here but there's no sign of them beyond the rubble. No resin, no scavenged remains," observed Braemer. "The room's clean."

"Seems strange," offered Vari with a frown. "All this space on their doorstep yet they didn't make use of it."

Mark stepped through the hole and onto a floor that had been painstakingly tiled with an elaborate mosaic. Now faded with age, it was difficult for Mark to make out the exact details. He walked around the chamber, piecing the image together. Figures stood before a glowing orb that dominated the center of the room, their long-limbed frames casting even longer shadows. Within the heart of the larger orb sat a smaller one engraved with swirling, runic engravings. With a start he realized that he recognized those symbols.

"Wait, aren't those-"

"Pretty similar to the ones in Citadel's tunnels," Braemar finished for him.

Mark knelt by the orb, getting a closer look. "Not similar. *Exactly* like the ones at Citadel." He reached out to touch the patterns.

"Are you sure you should do that?" worried Vari.

Mark winked at her. "If it blows my hand off, you can grow me a new one, can't you?"

Vari rolled her eyes. "Maybe in a level or two. For now I'd just have to strangle you to death so you could resurrect in one piece."

"Ah, the things we do for-" The final word caught in his throat.

Inside him, a part of Mark was hauling on the rein and yelling "Woah, horsey!" First of all, he and Vari hadn't known each other that long. Yes, they'd made love in the mountain tarn, and a few times since at Citadel. Mark couldn't question that he had some serious feelings for her. But part of his brain, one that had the word "Sensible" melted into its grey goo, kept pointing out that Vari wasn't 'real'. She was an AI, an NPC, a character in a virtual reality game. Falling in love with Vari was the equivalent of falling in love with the Google Maps girl.

"Friends," said Vari, completing his sentence for him. Her expression was neutral, unreadable.

The heat of anxiety prickled across his shoulders and up his neck as he opened his mouth to explain himself. Not that he had any idea what he was going to say.

"Vari, I-"

Vari's dark eyes widened with alarm and she pressed her finger to her lips. She'd heard something, and now Mark heard it too, a soft scraping and the dry trickle of falling dust. He caught movement out of the corner of his eye, the sinuous unfurling of a shadow.

He jumped to his feet, put himself between Vari and the shadow, and shouted, "Second Skin!", just as the shape exploded into fragments of fast-flying darkness. Sharp shadows rattled against his magical barrier and tumbled to the floor. He glanced down and tried to focus on the objects. They were spines of some sort, their tips glistening with moisture.

To his left, he heard a sharp scuffing of leather

against stone. He turned to the sound and was horrified to see that it was Braemar. The druid lay flat on his back. He shuddered and thrashed, in the grips of a seizure. Bubbles of froth formed on his trembling lips and his eyes were wide with fear. While the spines had been aimed at Mark, the spread had been wide enough to catch Braemar. Two spines jutted from his left shoulder, having pierced the heavy cloth of his robe. Another pair had sunk into the bare skin of his left arm.

Vari rushed to the druid's side and plucked the spines from his flesh, being careful not to touch the moistened points with her naked fingers. Then she slipped her hand down the neck of his robe so she could place her palm over his heart. She closed her eyes and whispered "Purify Blood". For a moment nothing happened. Vari's brow wrinkled as she pushed harder to inject her spell into Braemar's veins. This time his body responded. The convulsions stilled, his jaw relaxed and Braemar opened his mouth to gasp in a welcome lungful of air. Vari opened her eyes, relief palpable on her face, and Mark let out the breath he'd been holding.

Then he turned his attention to the massive shadow creeping across the tiled floor towards him. Legs moved in a sickly Mexican wave, too many to count, propelling the worm-like body with unnerving speed. Mark noticed fresh spines sprouting up through skin that glistened with venomous moisture. Now it made sense why the Pit Beetles had stopped their tunneling at the ruptured wall. This was the territory of an even deadlier aberration.

The sleek, eyeless head broke open to extrude a long, pale tongue. A wet appendage reached out and tasted the air, perhaps trying to work out the type of prey that had wandered into its abode. Mark drew Volcanic Bastard and woke its inner fire. He wasn't about to give the creature time to grow a fresh set of quills. If any of those poisoned spines hit Vari, they were all done for.

"Arcane Edge!" he shouted as he charged across the mosaic. The monster seemed to sense his approach. Its tongue lashed out, a cracking whip of sticky flesh that wrapped around his chest and belly, crushing the breath from him like a boa constrictor. He pressed Volcanic Bastard against the rubbery flesh and began to saw at it, hoping to cut through before its tongue dragged him into its gaping maw. Mark got a frightening glimpse of pale muscles undulating like waves on a fleshy sea. Its head had parted wide enough to swallow him whole.

"Mark! Let it pull you in!" Vari shouted behind him.

"What?!" Mark hollered back. "Why?"

"The central nervous system is at the back of the head. Puncturing that will kill the thing straight away."

The monster's maw was closing in fast and Mark was running out of air. His ribs screamed, his lungs burned, and black spots danced in front of his eyes. He forced his foggy brain to compare the length of his sword against the length of the monster's head. Too short by roughly a meter, even if he fully extended his arm.

An image rose up from the encroaching blur. A battered helm tumbled from a saddle to land in the leaf litter of the forest floor. He nodded to himself and reached out with Volcanic Bastard to the full length of his trembling arm. His vision was closing in like the end of a Warner Bros cartoon. Yet still he waited, another long, agonizing moment, as the monster's tongue hauled him beneath the reeking canopy of its upper jaw. With the last scraps of breath he wheezed, "Mind over Matter". Volcanic Bastard flew from his fingers and dove into the rippling sea of flesh before him.

Steam gushed up around its hilt, scalding his cheeks and forehead.

You have taken 5 DMG in light burns!
HP: 121/126

He screwed his eyes shut and gritted his teeth against the pain. Then he was falling, the monster's limp tongue cushioning his impact on the tiles like a rubber mattress. The crushing pressure was gone from his lungs and he took in a welcome lungful of pungent air.

You have slain a Level 9 Horripede.
XP reward per party member = 30 XP

Your Mind over Matter spell has reached Tier 2.
Tier 2: Move an object of up to 50 kilograms of weight.
The object can be moved at the speed and distance of a person with Body 15 throwing the object naturally. Accuracy is dependant on the caster's Mind score.

"There is no boundary between Me and That. Our world is a reality that we alone create."

- Zevryn the Everborn

Mark extricated himself from the beast's tongue and turned to see Vari helping Braemar to his feet. "Feeling better, mate?"

Braemar nodded and offered him a weak smile. "Bit shaky still, but I'm coming right. Sorry I wasn't much help there."

"No worries at all. Vari had it covered." He crossed the floor, gave her a fierce hug and pressed his lips to her forehead. "Thank you," he murmured against her warm skin.

"Yuck!" Vari answered with a laugh. She gently pushed him away and proceeded to wipe tongue slime from her clothes and breastplate.

"Sorry about that." He looked back at the dead Horripede. "How did you know about the nervous system thing?"

"Physik Perception. It's Tier Four now so it gives me a pretty good idea of anatomy, human or otherwise."

"Damn, that's one useful skill."

"Thanks. The weirder the creature, the harder it's going to be for me to see what's inside it, but at least this Horripede made basic anatomical sense."

Mark grinned. "You're like an MRI of Doom, Vari."

"I have no idea what an MRI is, but I'll take it as a compliment." She beckoned him closer. "Now let me fix that handsome face of yours. You look like a fright."

Mark touched his fingers to his cheek and winced as he felt the blisters. Vari placed her cool hand against his jaw and murmured, "Mend Flesh". The heat faded from his face.

"All better," she said and patted his cheek.

He smiled his thanks and crossed to the creature's carcass to pull Volcanic Bastard out of its head. Then he checked the perimeter of the chamber to make sure there weren't any more nasty surprises lurking about. The place was clear and there was just one other way out, through an ornate archway that sported the same scrollwork as the orb in the room's center. Once again, they were the same as the decorations he'd first touched to light up the tunnels beneath Citadel. It looked like this building and Citadel had been constructed by the same people. Even the architecture and stonework looked familiar now that he had a proper chance to inspect it. He walked over to the small orb at the heart of the chamber, knelt down beside it and touched his fingertips to the engravings. Liquid silver spread through the scrollwork, a glowing filigree that filled every groove and eventually framed the orb so that it gleamed like a freshly minted coin.

You have discovered a Waypoint!
Your XP reward per party member = 15 XP

Waypoints were used by the former denizens of these lands to travel with speed and ease about their empire. This network has not been used for many hundreds of years. Each Waypoint must be awoken independently.

You have access to one other Waypoint situated in The Citadel.
Would you like to travel to The Citadel?

Y/N

Mark stood in the centre of the Waypoint and held out his hands. Both Vari and Braemar shot him quizzical looks but Mark simply smiled.

"Come on you two. Let's hold hands and do a victory dance."

A wary Braemar glanced at the glowing circle. "On that thing?"

Vari elbowed him in the ribs, making the druid flinch. "How about a little trust, Braemar?"

She crossed the space and clasped Mark's hand. The warlock beckoned to the druid. Braemar shook his head, sighed, and took Mark's hand. Mark held his friends' hands tight as he mentally clicked "Y".

5

[BRAEMAR]

Braemar likened the waypoint experience to a bag of beans. In particular, the bag of beans he had when he was a kid. His counting beans that he took to school each day. First he was shaken to see if he would make a satisfying rattle. Then he was emptied out and divided into types. Painted Pony beans for meat. Yellow-eyes for organs. Red Kidney beans for blood. White Kidney beans for bones and Black Turtles for brains. Then he was counted and arranged into an orderly pattern. He just hoped that the kid doing the ordering was going to get it right.

He let out a sigh of relief, one that was echoed back to him by Vari and Mark. Vari's olive face was bright with delight while Mark's was a squeamish grey. He was surprised to find that he felt fine. Just a little anxious still. Perhaps his contribution to Vari's 'vomit fund' had been a blessing in disguise.

Mark stepped down off the waypoint and took a deep breath to steady himself. "It's times like these I wish I hadn't watched the transporter accident scene in *Star Trek: The Motion Picture.*" The warlock put on a strange, nasal voice. "Enterprise. What we got back didn't live long, fortunately."

Braemar had no idea about the rest of it, but the last part rang true enough. He too was happy to be in one piece. He tried to dispel the dregs of his anxiety by concentrating on their new surroundings. They were in a circular chamber with a high ceiling. Every stone was covered in curling runes that glowed faintly, giving off enough light for him to see the bronze door that seemed to be the only exit. It was tarnished green with age and there was no handle or opening mechanism in evidence.

Mark approached the door and gave it an experimental shove. It was shut tight, most likely barred from the other side.

"Sid?" he called out.

"Mark?" Sid's voice rang through the chamber, his pitch raised a little with surprise. "Where are you?"

"Inside you, somewhere. We seem to be locked in." The warlock stamped his foot against the stones. "Can you feel that?"

"Feel what?"

"I stamped my boot on the floor."

"Try it again?"

Mark did so. "Anything?"

"Nothing. I can't feel that part of the fortress at all. It's numb. Jump up and down a bit, see if you can wake it up."

Braemar tugged at his beard again. It helped him to think, and this time it paid off. "I think I can do a bit bloody better than that."

Vari and Mark looked on with curiosity as Braemar knelt and placed his hands against the glowing stones. "Tremor", he ordered, mentally tethering the spell to Tier 1 so it wouldn't bring the roof down. The ground shivered like something alive beneath his fingertips. There was a soft rumble, like distant thunder, and a few trails of dust trickled down from the stones above.

Citadel's delighted voice cut over the dying murmurs of the little quake. "My, my, now *that* was stimulating!"

"Uh oh, Braemar," warned Mark with a wink. "I think you've started something."

Braemar felt his face grow hot and he tugged at his beard again while he tried to think of a response. He was grateful to be saved by a dull scrape at the door. A clang followed as a bar was pulled back. The door swung wide with a spine-shuddering creak and two sets of antennae poked into the room.

"Hi, girls," greeted Vari with a wave. The cockroaches seemed to understand her and wiggled their antennae.

"How do you know they're girls?" asked Braemar.

"See the pair of short antennae-looking things at the far back of the abdomen?"

"Ah, yeah."

"They're called cerci. Male cerci have around eighteen segments to them. Females have around thirteen."

"Shit, Vari. That's pretty insightful. Did you pick that up using Physik Perception?"

Vari nodded. "We'd all be Horripede food without it."

Braemar shuddered as he remembered the pain of those spines stabbing into his flesh, the fear as his muscles contracted of their own accord, paralysing him. "You're not bloody wrong there."

They followed the cockroaches into a dust-laden tunnel that wound its way beneath Citadel. The tunnel eventually popped out through a secret door in Vari's alchemy lab. Vari eyed the construction of tarnished bronze and stone that made up the door's veneer and shook her head in disbelief.

"I've spent hours in here and not once did I notice anything strange about that wall." Vari looked up, as was her habit when addressing Citadel. "Did you know about this, Sid?"

"Alas, no," was Sid's answer. "My guess is that the passageway and chamber haven't been utilized since well before my time."

Mark raised an eyebrow at that. "Could mean that this fortress was built around the same time as the city in the Barrens, and by the same people too."

"I reckon you're right there," agreed Braemar. "The masonry techniques are the same. The architecture is pretty similar. You see it in the archways most of all. And judging by the signs of aging, the stones here were laid a bit later than those in the Barrens, but only by a century or so."

Mark nodded, clearly impressed. "Wow, mate. You really know your stonework."

Braemar felt rather chuffed at the compliment but did his best to shrug it off and hide his pride behind his beard. Too much attention made him uncomfortable. In many ways he preferred spending time among rocks. They were calmer, less demanding. He enjoyed his time with Mark and Vari, there was no doubt about that. And he felt like he was doing something important, something that would help his people in the long run. But sometimes he just wished he was back in the limestone hills he grew up with, exploring caves, finding fossils and raising the occasional golem. A quiet life, stress free and painless. Maybe when all this Chasms of Corruption stuff was done, he'd head back there.

"The waypoint may not have been used since that civilization fell over," suggested Mark.

"Waypoint?" asked Sid. "I'm not familiar with that term."

"It's a type of portal that I seem able to activate as a warlock." He pointed back down the secret tunnel. "Although, judging by the fact that the door was barred from the fortress side, others must be able to use it as well. Best keep an eye on the place in future, in case we get unwanted visitors."

"I now have an uncomfortable case of pins and needles all the way from here to the portal," Sid complained.

Braemar felt a pang of guilt. Maybe he'd overdone it by using Tremor. "Shit. Sorry about that, Sid,"

"Oh, not to worry, Braemar," Sid assured him. "Better to feel something rather than nothing, and once it settles down, I should be able to sense if someone uses the waypoint and traverses that corridor."

"Come on," said Mark. "We've got some loot to haul." He headed back down the secret passage, waving for Braemar and Vari to follow him.

The teleportation back to the Barrens was less discombobulating the second time around, although Mark still looked a bit on the pale side.

"Don't worry, Mark," Braemar reassured the warlock. "You'll get used to it."

"Bloody well hope so."

They returned to the beetle nest, treading carefully in case other beetles had come home. The place was mercifully empty. They gathered up the jewelry and ornaments, whipped them back to Citadel via the waypoint, and were soon back in the ruins, standing before a darkened archway, the only other exit out of the Horripede's former den.

Mark led the way again, Volcanic Bastard drawn so that it cast a dull red glow over the passageway ahead. They were well clear of the terraced houses now, wending their way through a much larger structure. The place smelled of acrid dust and a faint hint of something foul.

"What is that smell?" asked Vari, wrinkling her nose.

"Sulphur," Braemar replied.

"Reminds me of Rotorua," said Mark. "It's a town back home that was built on an active thermal area. Steam rises up through the town from thermal vents and there is a permanent rotten egg flavor to the air. Whenever I visit the place, I get a headache for the first twenty minutes until I get used to it again."

"No offense to your people, Mark," ventured Braemar, "but who in their right bloody mind would build a town on a volcano's caldera?"

Mark laughed. "Yup, that's a really good point."

The large building had a religious tone to it. Braemar figured they were inside some sort of temple complex. Small chambers sprouted off the central corridor, each one empty except for some broken pottery and oxidized bronze utensils. The other contents had decayed into dust long ago. In the temple's heyday, it must've been where the monks or priests ate and slept.

There were numerous stone carvings and engravings along the passageways and inside the chambers. Most were indecipherable, but one stood out among the faded iconography. It was a naked, winged woman rising up from a bed of flames. He pointed it out to Vari and Mark.

"That image mean anything to you two?"

Mark shook his head and Vari furrowed her brow as she took a closer look.

"Actually, yes," she said. "I've seen similar statues in Credence, the reiver capital."

"Part of a reiver religion?"

"No, in the catacombs beneath the city. Credence was built on the bones of something else."

"Then the people who built this place may have built Citadel *and* the ancient town underneath Credence. How far away is Credence from here?"

"About a week's ride. But I've seen similar things in Karajan too."

"How far away is that?"

"A couple of month's journey at least."

"Braemar, have you seen buildings like this in other parts of Garland?" asked Mark.

The druid twisted the tip of his beard between his fingertips, creating a copper spike. "Other than Citadel, no."

"Still, quite the empire these people had then. Getting up near Roman Empire size."

Braemar enjoyed hearing about Mark's world, and for a brief moment wondered if he would ever get to see it. "What's a Roman?"

"Sandals, swords and a severe case of superiority complex."

Braemar offered Vari a wry smile. "They don't sound all that different from reivers."

Vari smiled back. "Sandals would actually be a great idea. You should smell it when a bunch of reiver soldiers take their boots off."

Braemar shook his head. That was one experience he'd rather do without.

They rounded a corner and were greeted by some welcome sunlight. The passageway opened out into a cobbled courtyard, the centerpiece of which was a towering fountain. It'd been a long time since the spouts had run with anything but dust. The basin was filled with stagnant rain water and algae.

"These Romans," wondered Braemar. "Do they still inhabit your world?"

"Yes," answered Mark, "but these days they concern themselves with coffee and fashion rather than conquest and fascism."

"You need to tell us more about your world, Mark." Braemar noticed an edge to Vari's tone. It wasn't just a suggestion, but Mark didn't seem to notice.

"To be honest, Vari, I wouldn't even know where to begin."

There was frustration in Vari's eyes as she placed a hand on his shoulder. 'It's alright. There's plenty in my past I'd rather not dwell on either. Just tell me the good bits of yours one day."

Mark's eyes took on a faraway look. "Lemon cheesecake. Baked. With berry coulis."

"Sounds bloody good," commented Braemar. "What's the recipe?"

"Cream cheese, crumbed malt biscuits, sugar, some lemon juice and vanilla. That's pretty much it."

"Got all of that back at Citadel. I'll bake one for us when we get back, eh?"

Mark's grin stretched from ear to ear. "Mate, you're a baker?"

"My father is. I helped him out in the mornings, before my druiding lessons." It felt embarrassed to admit this, but it was true. "I bake a lot better than I..."

He trailed off as he noticed something odd about the cobblestones. He pointed at one near his right boot. "These stones are showing stress fractures."

Mark and Vari peered at the cobblestone but clearly didn't see what he was seeing.

"Means there was a tremor nearby," explained Braemar. "Quite recently too."

"Like what you did back at Citadel?" asked Mark.

Braemar nodded. "A bit bigger. Could be natural."

"But might not be?" wondered Mark.

He sniffed the air. The stink of sulphur had grown stronger. "Could mean a chasm's opened up nearby."

Update for the Chasm of Corruption Quest. You have unlocked the Cracks in Reality Subquest.

A small chasm has opened up in the vicinity and is leaking corruption into the area. Seal it before the chasm grows any larger.

Special Requirement:
Druidic Elementalist specializing in Earth Magic.

"Huh, well look at that, Braemar," commented Mark. "You got a special mention."

"Meant for any bloody druid in the area," excused Braemar. "Just right time, right place, I guess."

He staved off further embarrassment by pointing across the courtyard, in the direction of the mountains. Their snowy peaks were just visible over the top of the ruins. Braemar found them reassuring, a reminder of the natural world in this graveyard of ancient humanity. "We head that way long enough, we'll fall right into the thing."

"Lead the way, mate," agreed Mark. "Try not to drop us into a plummeting, screaming death, eh? I'll recover. You guys won't."

Braemar shuddered, reminded of the close call he'd had with the Horripede. He feigned a tone of confidence, hoping it would rub off on how he actually felt. "The stones will give us fair warning. They're good like that. They hate bloody surprises about as much as I do."

He walked across the courtyard, quietly wishing he was back in those limestone hills right now. Denniston had told him that he had potential far beyond his humble aspirations, that he should join the warlock's quest to see what he was truly made of. Perhaps granite instead of soft, comforting sandstone. The druid's anxiety was a lump in his throat he just couldn't swallow. He really didn't want to end up like Denniston.

6

———

[ARIX]

You have slain seven Level 3 Tomb Tyrants.
XP reward per party member = 105 XP

Arix winced as he tugged up his leather armor. There was a bloody gash just above his hip and blood ran in a steady stream down his leg.

Warning! You are suffering from bleed damage!
Bleed rate = 1 HP per second.
HP: 41/75

"Justice Prevails," he murmured at the wound. The gash sparkled with a faint blue light and closed up like a zip. He watched with satisfaction as the HP countdown stopped and then reversed, counting upwards until it reached the current maximum of 75.

Arix went about retrieving his crossbow bolts, plucking them from the skewered tyrants with a twist and a squelch. He gave each bolt a flick to remove the worst of the gore and wiped the rest away on the tuft of coarse hair that sprouted from each tyrant's head. He tucked the bolts away in their case, gave his axe a quick wipe on the closest tyrant and then had a proper snoop around the chamber to see if there was any loot worth procuring. There were plenty of trinkets, forged from silver and gold, but they weren't much good to him at the moment. The reivers would relieve him of anything valuable as soon as he got back to camp.

But he did find something he could use in the meantime. It was tucked into a brass sheath that hung on the back of the Altar of Khorlvah. He unhooked the sheath, took hold of the leather-bound handle and drew the blade. Bright steel gleamed, embellished by a splash of rainbow from the stained glass windows above. The edge was a cruel curve, designed for slashing throats, and the pommel sported a tiny version of the winged woman.

Blood of the Lost

+20% to base dagger damage.
30% chance of inducing internal hemorrhaging in an organic enemy.
+30% accuracy when thrown.
Will return to owner if in line of sight.

"We might be lost yet our blood will always find its way home."
- Ishka the Devout

Arix nodded his satisfaction as he slid the dagger back into its sheath and tucked the sheath into his belt. Then he pulled up his character sheet to see how many more experience points he needed to reach Level 6.

Arix the Damned
Class: Executioner - Level 5
Progress to Level 6 = 475/500

"Fucking hell. Seriously?" Twenty-five pissant little points. Two more tomb Tyrants would do the trick but a quick study of the rafters above confirmed that he was alone. He sighed and went back to his sheet.

Body: 14
Modified Body: 15 (+1 from Dusk Leather Armor)
Mind: 15
Spirit: 11

HP: 75
EP: 55

Skills
Axework (Tier 4)
Horse Riding (Tier 2)
Arbalist (Tier 3)
Acrobatics (Tier 2)
Climbing (Tier 3)

Spells
Buzzard Eyes (Tier 2)
Fox Ears (Tier 2)
Hound Scent (Tier 1)
Chopping Block (Tier 1)
Truelight (Tier 1)
Clean Slate (Tier 2)
Justice Prevails (Tier 2)

There'd been no notification of completion for the "Bloody Devotions" quest so he figured there were a few tomb tyrants still lurking about nearby. Just not in this chamber anymore. It was a blessing in disguise that Karina would also be waiting for that quest completion notification. That meant she wouldn't be so quick to pull the trigger on him, to strangle him to death for simply taking longer than she expected. It bought him some time, if not space. Karina could use the collar to measure the distance from his location to wherever she was sipping wine and soaking up his XP like a fat, well-manicured leech. But she couldn't use it to spy on his circumstances. That meant he could explore the temple some more, hopefully find something that might help him. He would have to make sure he didn't wander too far from the reiver camp or inadvertently kill the last tomb tyrant in the area. At most he had until nightfall before Karina would get suspicious and summarily execute him.

Not for the first time, Arix fantasized about clipping the collar around the inquisitor's thick neck and giving the order that would leave her blue-faced and gasping. She might even beg for mercy as life drained from her eyes. *He* was the executioner after all, not her.

He cut the clinging thought free and made a beeline for the closest archway. It was tucked in behind the statue of the winged woman and led into a wide tunnel. The walls were lined with effigies of the same winged woman. Each time she posed in some religiously epic scenario. Sometimes she blessed people, other times she punished them, but every time she had been rendered in an alluring style. Desperately sexy and utterly unattainable. Whoever these priests had been, they certainly loved their romantic soft porn. No, he reminded himself. It's the *Reign of Blood* artists who love their romantic soft porn. Don't start losing yourself in the fiction, Arix.

He stepped into the tunnel and froze as something impacted the floor behind him, so hard that it sent vibrations up his legs, all the way to his knees. Arix unclipped and shouldered his crossbow in one smooth motion. His eyes looked for a target, a vulnerable spot, while his brain tried to comprehend what he was looking at. Slavering fang-filled maw. Check. Stinger-tipped tail, poised to impale him. Check. Armored hide. Check. Heavily-muscled limbs that ended in leathery hands and cruel claws. Check. It had all the makings of a tomb tyrant except it was bigger than all ten of those dead tyrants put together. Judging by the cracked flagstones beneath its hands and feet, the creature had dropped from the vaulted apex of the shadow-clad ceiling above.

He wasn't sure how he'd missed her, especially with his Buzzard Eyes ability. "I love a good game of hide and seek, darling, but you're s'posed to count to twenny before coming after me. Thems the rules."

The creature scowled at him then glanced at her dead minions. When her gaze returned to Arix, he could swear he felt the waves of heat emanating from those red-rimmed eyes. The roar that followed buffeted him with a gale of hot, fetid air and thundered through the temple, a storm of pure, feral ferocity. Arix breathed out through his nose, slowly emptying the air from his lungs and the stink from his nostrils as he took a bead on the monster's left eye.

"Sorry about the kids, mum, but you shoulda taught them better manners."

He pulled the triggers on his crossbow. Click, click, went the mechanism. The twin bolts streaked through the air and struck flesh with a pair of dull, wet thuds. The monster snarled as she lowered her claws from her face and plucked the bolts from the back of her hand with the delicacy of a nail technician picking dead skin from a cuticle.

"Fucking brilliant that is." Arix clipped his crossbow onto his shoulder, turned on his heels and sprinted down the tunnel with all the speed his 15 Body points could muster. Winged women blurred past and Arix knew he was moving far faster than his RL meat could ever manage. Sure, he worked out at the gym three times a week and jogged every other day, but in here, in *Reign of Blood*, he felt like Usain bloody Bolt. Yet it was all he could do to keep ahead of the monstrosity at his heels. One misstep, one hesitation and it was going to be a one-way trip into a new world of gastric acid and shit. Stone shattered behind him as the giant tyrant powered through tight archways and loose rubble like they were bits of sandcastle.

He ran until every breath felt like he was sucking on a car exhaust pipe. Still the monster kept right on his tail. He slid around corner after corner and sprinted down corridors that were all the same size. He would've given his left virtual bollock for a single crawlspace or sewer pipe, but the game developers didn't seem up for the trade. His legs had turned to lead. He was on the verge of stopping in his tracks to embrace a quick death when he rounded one last corner and found salvation from his personal hell.

The warrior was bathed in a blue aura and had a glowing red sword in his hands. Judging by his widely-spaced feet and strong stance, this guy had heard the monster coming and knew a thing or two about sword-fighting. To the warrior's right stood a red-headed, robed fella and a dark-haired woman. Though she was dressed in garb that reminded him of Karina, she had neither the pallid skin nor the tattoos of a reiver. All three looked at him with alarmed suspicion. Arix couldn't care less. No, he didn't know them from Adam but they were human and had 'adventuring party' written all over them. To Arix, two out of three was a pretty bloody good result under the circumstances.

"Incoming!" he hollered with the last of his breath as he skidded to a halt, unlimbered his axe and turned to face the marauding monster behind him. He gulped in as much air as he could while the giant monster took stock of the sudden shift in odds.

The red-headed guy didn't give the creature time to work out any kind of battle plan.

"Quagmire!" he shouted and repeated it twice more in quick succession.

The stones beneath the monster's bulk melted into a soup of mud and sand. The great beast howled as she sank up to her elbows and knees in the filthy porridge.

Arix and the warrior made eye contact, exchanged a knowing look, and charged. The warrior skidded to a halt at the quagmire's edge, drawing the creature's attention with his ember-wreathed sword while Arix ran up a partially toppled pillar nearby and leaped onto the thing's armored back.

"Keep it busy," yelled Arix to the warrior. "I'll-"

He cut his sentence short as the monster's stinger descended towards him. Arix rolled inside the stinger's arc, found his feet and lashed out at the tail with his axe. Metal met scales and the axe blade bounced back with a clang. Such was the shock of vibration that it almost jarred the weapon from his hands.

"Shiiiiiit!" was all he could manage as he windmilled one of his arms like an off-balance surfer about to wipe out. Below, he heard a squelch and a thud as the monster freed one of her hands and swatted the warrior away.

"Sculpt Bone! Mend Flesh!" yelped the dark-haired woman.

Out of the corner of his eye, Arix saw the warrior get up and shake off what should've been a rib-cracking blow. He regained his balance and smiled. The woman's a healer, he thought. Thank fuck for that. Arix looked up to see the long tail rear up, ready to strike again. This time *he* wasn't the target. Judging by the angle, the monster was going for a softer target. Carrot-top. Thankfully, the healer saw the danger too.

"Mark! She's going for Braemar!"

The warrior responded with a shout. "Terrifying Manifestation!"

Beneath him, Arix felt the monster shiver. Her muscles contracted and locked, freezing her in place like a hare caught in headlights. Whatever he'd done, the warrior had bought Arix a moment's window and he wasn't about to waste it. With the two-step-leap technique he'd been taught for heading by his grammar school football coach, Arix launched into the air, axe raised above his head. Near the end of his descent he shouted, "Chopping Block!" and brought his axe down upon the vertebrae that linked the creature's tail to her hindquarters. The resulting crack resounded off the chamber walls as the axe blade severed sinews and snapped bones. The great tail, nerveless and limp, toppled to the floor like a felled tree.

Your Chopping Block ability has increased to Tier 2.
Tier 2 activation cost = 12 EP

Behind him Arix heard the warrior shout, "Get off! We're going to try something!"

Arix didn't need to be told twice. When the stinger had fallen, it had jammed between two hefty rocks. As the beast tried to tug it free with its body, Arix used the dead appendage as a makeshift tightrope. With his axe held as a balancer, he ran along the taut tail, reaching the ground just in time to feel a wave of heat burst across his back. Startled, he dove and rolled to put out the fire he imagined was now crawling up his spine. But as he came back up to his feet, Arix was met with a rather impressive sight. Where once there'd been a swamp of sand and soil, now there was a pool of lava that glowed and bubbled.

With three of its limbs caught in the searing gruel, the monster could do nothing but howl in agony as flames spread up her flanks. She tried to haul herself out of the cauldron with her one weakened arm, but the warrior cut off that escape route at the elbow with a swing of his sword. Arix saw that the blade's fierce radiance perfectly matched that of the lava pool. Somehow, the warrior had used that sword of his to turn Carrot-top's quagmire into a molten death pit. The monster gave a final, shuddering sigh and collapsed in a steaming heap.

You have slain the Crypt Queen.
XP reward per party member = 100 XP
Please note that your party now consists of five
members.

**You have completed the Bloody Devotions
quest.**
XP reward per party member = 30 XP

Un-fucking-believable, Arix cursed inwardly. Karina the Cow just got served a whole bucketload of free XP for putting this torturous piece of shit around my neck. 'Justice Prevails' my ass. That's just not fair.

**Congratulations! You have reached Level 6 as
an Executioner.**
Progress to next level = 605/1000

You have been awarded 2 Attribute Points.
You may choose one skill to instantly upgrade by one tier.

The notification made him feel momentarily better until he realized what was about to happen. He rushed over to the three adventurers, the words already tumbling out of his ash-dry mouth.

"Outside there's a reiver bitch what's going to choke me to death in about ten seconds! I'm going to resurrect in chains and she'll spend the evening sipping wine and torturing my ass." He tapped the collar. "I need solutions, people. Now!"

The warrior nodded and looked to the carrot-top. "Braemar? Does your Sculpt Earth skill extend to forged metal?"

The man's beard was long enough to waggle a little as he shook his head.

"Vari? Got enough essence left for a Mend Flesh spell?"

The healer smiled. "Plenty."

The guy's hazel eyes meet his. "Sorry, mate. This is going to hurt."

Arix dropped his two attributes into Body and upgraded his Justice Prevails skill to Tier 3.

The first boost would give him a health buffer. The skill upgrade would give him some backup should the healer's spell not work. Then he put on his best 'I don't care' face, an expression he was rather proud of as he'd worked bloody hard on it. From the pursed lips to the fractionally raised right eyebrow, it was almost perfect, capable of hiding even the deepest hurt or inappropriate enthusiasm.

"Just fucking hurry, yeah?"

The warrior nodded, raised his sword and placed the edge to the collar. Patterns of molten metal shifted and swirled along the blade. Arix felt the heat coming off it. It reminded him of the time he woke up with his face half-cooked by the bar heater he'd passed out next to. The collar soaked in the sword's heat, becoming as hot as a branding iron, burning into his skin and flesh. This was worse than anything Karina had put him through and he would've screamed had his vocal cords not been fused together.

Then it was over. The smoking collar rang in defeated indignation as it hit the ground. Arix heard Vari utter the merciful words, "Mend Flesh". Blissful coolness swept over his cauterized neck, washing away the pain as it molded his flesh back into its natural shape.

"Cheers," he wheezed with vocal cords now unfused. "Got any water?"

Braemar passed him a flask and Arix gulped down the lukewarm contents like it was champagne at his one-millionth follower party. In fact, Arix thought it tasted a damn sight better. He passed the empty flask back and then performed a goal kick on the sundered collar. He struck it just right with the toe of his boot so the thing got some decent air before plopping into the pool of lava. He then turned and grinned at his new friends.

"The name's Arix the Damned, and I am so fucking happy to meet you."

7

[KARINA]

Nothing. No red blip in her mind's eye indicating Arix's presence. No measure of distance. No comforting leash tethering her to the demon. Not even a scarlet splash to note his death. Just a wall of black nothing. She opened her eyes and gave the sergeant her 'Don't say a fucking thing' look. The sergeant was smart enough to nod and divert the conversation to practical matters.

"Shall we take the altar back to camp, Madam Inquisitor?"

"Yes, and tell your men to be *very* careful. Any scratches or dents shall be repaid tenfold upon their naked backs."

"Understood." The sergeant turned to the

gathered company of soldiers. "You heard the lady! Get the altar onto a trolley and haul it back to camp. Drop it and your ass is grass!"

"Poetically put, sergeant."

"Thank you, madam."

Karina knelt beside one of the tyrant carcasses while the soldiers got to work. The sergeant joined her, a scowl of distaste on her scarred face.

"Ugly things, aren't they, madam."

"Quite the contrary, Maribella. They are creations of sheer imaginative beauty."

The sergeant looked surprised at that. "Someone made these things?"

Karina nodded. "Most certainly. Creatures like this haven't simply evolved like jackrabbits and jackals. A good deal of thought and effort has gone into this design."

"Where are the creators then?"

"Long gone. Taken by the cataclysm that reduced this magnificent city to rubble." She drew a brass syringe from her physician's belt, plunged the needle into the tyrant's stinger and drew up a tubeful of mustard venom. "My research indicates that they attempted something quite ambitious, something that was meant to be a great leap forward in their civilization."

Maribella eyed the soldiers who were carefully working up the edges of the altar, placing stones underneath to make a gap for the ropes. "The altar's part of that something?"

"Yes." Karina pulled up the quest notification and mentally pushed it at the sergeant. "It's time you saw this."

Maribella blinked a couple of times as the words materialized in her vision.

You have received the "Altars of the Breaking Dawn" quest.

Three altars were forged by the civilization that once inhabited these barren lands.

The Altar of Korlvah, Goddess of Hope
The Altar of Agrovesh, Goddess of Fury
The Altar of Solmora, Goddess of Despair

"When three altars are blessed by the Waters of Life, all shall witness the Breaking Dawn."
- Ishka the Devout

"All shall witness the Breaking Dawn? What does that mean?"

"Good things for those who embrace it. Bad things for those who don't."

"A weapon?" asked Maribella. A spark of naked ambition flickered in her blue eyes.

I'm going to have to watch this one, thought Karina. She has ideas above her station.

"Definitions are the domain of your betters, sergeant."

A sullen shadow extinguished the spark. Maribella clearly didn't like being reminded of her position in life, but she had the good sense to obey protocol nonetheless. "Yes, Madam Inquisitor."

Good, thought Karina. That was the stick, now here's the carrot.

She stood, stretched her back and then offered the sergeant a sly smile. "Of course, is not the desire to better ourselves the very cornerstone of this great empire of ours?"

The sergeant mirrored her smile and Karina noticed her shoulders relax. "Glory to the Great," recited Maribella as she slapped her palm to her breastplate.

"Glory to the Great," agreed Karina. She pointed to the Altar of Korlvah. "Once the altar is secure, give the order to break camp."

"Yes, madam. Our destination?"

"Names are irrelevant in this forgotten city. Their meanings died on the lips of their makers. Suffice to say that we have another temple to visit."

"Deeper into the Barrens?"

The sergeant did well to hide her anxiety but it was as plain as day to Karina's trained eyes. "Indeed. What's our current personnel count?"

"Two hundred and thirty-seven, not including you or I."

"Five percent losses so far. That's within acceptable parameters."

A blush of anger reddened Maribella's cheeks and neck. "Do you have a number in mind that you would consider unacceptable, Madam Inquisitor?"

"For the Breaking Dawn, sergeant, there is no such thing as an unacceptable number."

"I see."

"I certainly hope so, especially now that our demon is missing in action."

Maribella raised an eyebrow but had the good sense not to delve further. "In that case, may I make a request, Madam Inquisitor?"

"Be careful what you wish for, sergeant."

Maribella hesitated, as if second-guessing herself, then pressed on. "Let me to take the demon's place. Let me clear the way to the other altars."

Karina eyed her for a moment as she ran a quick cost-benefit analysis in her head. With the demon now at large, there were only two people capable of handling the horrors this ruined city would throw at them. Judging by her stats, her prior experience and cool-headed nature, the sergeant was one of them. The other, of course, was Karina herself. She'd not had the chance to flex her alchemical muscles on this expedition and they were starting to feel decidedly cramped. She looked from Maribella to the soldiers who grunted and huffed as they transferred the altar into the waiting trolley. Karina swept her hand across the scene.

"And leave this lot to their own devices? They're too good at getting themselves killed. Without the necessary leadership, we might return to a charnel house."

The sergeant blinked, not quite understanding. "Madam, but you-"

"Will be coming with you," Karina finished for her. "Your body might be willing but your mind is weak. These Barrens are beyond a simple sword-swinger, no matter how skilled in the arts of murder."

The sergeant held Karina's gaze for a long, chilling moment. Karina held her breath, wondering if Maribella would rise to the bait, reveal her anger and unsuitability in one foul burst. If that happened, she would continue to search the rank and file until she found the correct level of by-the-book ambition she was looking for. Karina didn't believe in loyalty. She needed someone she could control, some clay she could mold into an extension of herself. Only then could she be confident that the job would get done.

Maribella broke eye contact and let her gaze drop to her boots. "My sword is yours, madam. Just tell me where to stick it."

Karina felt a surge of relief. She liked being right first time. "Excellent, *Captain* Maribella. I knew I could rely on you."

Maribella looked up, her eyes now glistening with excitement. It warmed Karina's heart to see someone so easily manipulated by the promise of power.

"Which of your corporals can we safely promote to sergeant and leave in charge of this zoo?"

The freshly appointed captain turned to the busy soldiers and pointed out a stout, flaxen-haired man with a braided beard that reached down to the top of his bulging belly.

"Corporal Gunder. I fought with him in the Karaji Highlands. He's got his head screwed on right and he's well-liked by the ranks."

"Then go tell *Sergeant* Gunder that he's in charge of maintaining the camp and protecting the altar. While you're at it, pick out six capable fighters, preferably those who are either too stupid or too emotionally damaged to feel fear."

"Are we talking about 'acceptable losses' here?"

Karina smiled her approval. Her new captain was fast on the uptake. "Yes, but good ones. We don't want to lose them too quickly."

"Yes, Madam Inquisitor." Maribella turned to go.

"And captain?"

She turned back to Karina, her expression stern but her eyes bright with pride. Yes, Karina thought, I've judged this one correctly. She'll do pretty much anything for me now, for the gratitude and the glory.

"Yes?"

"If the soldiers feel inclined to speculate on the whereabouts of our lost demon, tell them that he has met a rather sticky end. His remains have likely been consumed by those creatures he so carelessly failed to slay."

Maribella's eyes narrowed a little. "I look forward to making that true."

"So do I, captain," agreed Karina. "So do I."

8

Vari brought up her latest notification while she waited for the silverbeet to boil.

Congratulations! You have reached Level 7 as a Figurist.
Progress to next level = 1078/1700
You have been awarded 2 Attribute Points.

Spell Selection
You have 5 magical spells available for selection.
You have 2 spell slots remaining.
Inner Strength (Cast cost = 7 EP)
Calming Influence (Cast cost = 8 EP
Discombobulate (Cast cost = 8 EP)

Heightened Awareness (Cast cost = 9 EP)
Scarlet Fever (Cast cost = 9 EP)

She swiped the notification aside and brought up the descriptions for Heightened Awareness and Scarlet Fever.

Heightened Awareness

The recipient gains significant improvements in the acuity of their core senses and incremental improvements their sixth sense.

Tier 1: Lasts for up to one hour. Recipient has a 30% chance of sensing danger and a 20% chance of sensing a hidden person or creature's presence.

"Ignorance is an endless well of pain."
- Abigail of the Blessed Touch

Scarlet Fever

The figurist's victims will suffer a raging fever that reduces their Body and Mind scores by 5 points and causes 1 HP damage per second.

Tier 1: The caster can infect up to ten victims

within her line of sight. The fever lasts for 30 seconds.

There was a wicked glint in Vari's eyes as she slotted Scarlet Fever into place. She was tempted by Heightened Awareness, seeing the obvious benefits, but then she'd hoped to slot in Calming Influence at her next level up.

Calming Influence

The recipient(s) levels of pain, anger, anxiety, stress and depression are significantly reduced for a limited time. Symptoms will return unless external causes are resolved.

Tier 1: One recipient at a time only. Effects last for one hour.

Vari lifted the pot of silverbeet off the fire so that it could cool and then slotted Calming Influence into place. Chasms of Corruption had been a rocky emotional road and it was only going to get rougher.

She dropped one attribute point each into Mind and Body and gave the lentils a stir before tasting them. They needed more seasoning. She added a little more salt and pepper from the paper packets she kept in her pack, gave the lentils another stir and then set them aside to cool beside the silverbeet.

The beet had been growing wild and lush in one of the neighboring chambers, flourishing in the sun and rain that poured in equal measure through the ruptured roof. Judging by the temperate climate, the Barrens had once been a land of plenty. Its fertile ground sheltered from storms by the mountains above. Perhaps it could be a land of plenty again if they could find and destroy the corruption that still plagued this place. The Barrens had a sordid history, that much was clear from the creatures they'd encountered so far. While the pit beetles had been natural enough, an understandable growth in size to fill a vacant niche in the local ecology, the Horripede and the Crypt Queen represented something entirely alien. Creatures of creation, not evolution.

Vari felt a chill run down her spine. She remembered the muffled howls and screams that breached the walls of her old quarters in the figurist compound. It was no accident that the inquisitors had housed them next door to the cells. They wanted their figurists to 'acclimatize' to their duties, to become numbed to the symptoms of their craft. Pain and suffering were the unfortunate but necessary side effects of their work. 'Growing pains' some inquisitors even called them, through lips curled in such a wry and dismissive way that even now Vari instinctively clenched her fist, ready to punch those smug smiles right off their callous faces.

"You finding this all a bit weird too, Vari?" asked Braemar.

Vari nodded. He'd read her wrong, but Vari understood that her dark thoughts were as much a product of the present as they were of the past. She looked to where Mark and Arix were sitting together, hunched over like two conspirators whispering about acts of treason. She could make out the rumble of their voices but none of the words. Mark hadn't spoken to her since Arix's arrival. That was over an hour ago. There was something happening that she didn't understand, something that made her feel more different from Mark than she'd felt at any time since they'd met.

"Any idea what Arix was talking about? What did he mean when he called Mark a 'player'?" wondered Braemar. "Player of what? I've never seen Mark with a lute or pipes or anything like that. And you and I have both heard him sing."

Vari rolled her eyes. "How is it possible to miss *every* note by a quarter tone?"

"No idea."

Braemar poked at the fire with a stick, shifting the embers to help the lentils cook evenly. "What's a bloody 'Enpeesee' when it's at home? Arix was pointing at us when he said that."

Vari shook her head. "Your guess is as good as mine."

"Arix mentioned resurrection. Guess that means he's some sort of warlock? Maybe 'Enpeesee' is just a word they use for non-warlocks?"

Vari shrugged and took another look at their huddled figures. She focused on Arix, willing his details into her mind's eye. While her Sculpt Bone spell had risen to Tier 3 during their battle with the Crypt Queen, her Physik Perception had reached Tier 4 earlier, during the battle with the Horripede.

Level 9 Horripede
HP: 200

That's all she'd seen at the time, along with the location of the creature's central nervous system and a few other basics about its anatomy. She didn't want to use this new ability on Mark and Braemar. It would feel like an invasion of privacy. But Arix, he was a different cauldron of eels. Vari didn't yet know why, but she felt a growing determination to find out.

Arix the Damned
Class: Executioner - Level 6

Body: 17
Mind: 15
Spirit: 11

HP: 75
EP: 55

"He's not a warlock. He's an executioner."

Braemar's eyes widened in shock. "Shit a brick, you can see that?"

Vari raised a hand to stave off his next question. "It's a new ability, and no I won't use it on you."

The druid relaxed and poked at the embers again. "In Garland, executioners went the way of the monarchy. Been over a hundred years now since anyone's lost their head over a crime. In fact, there's not been a serious crime in Garland for as long as I've been alive."

That surprised Vari. Robbery, murder and rape were all too common in Karajan, even before the reivers took over. In Credence, crime was a daily occurence. Figurists weren't allowed to walk the streets without a military escort.

"Who rules in Garland now? And how do they keep the peace?"

"The Council of Druids, but they don't exactly 'rule'. Everyone just gets on with enjoying life. No-one's rich, but no-one's poor either."

"Pretty much the opposite of Credence then. Karajan too. You're either fat or starving. Not much in between."

"That was Garland a hundred years ago. The king died and didn't leave any heirs. There was a civil war between two cousins. Thousands died. Then the druids led the people against *both* cousins, locked them up and threw away the key. Those two men owned most of the country, so the druids used that wealth to build farms, waterways, schools and so on. 'Desperation breeds destruction', that was the druid motto. So they got rid of the desperation, and a hundred years later, most people are pretty happy with their lots."

"Happy people don't commit crimes?"

Braemar shrugged. "Garland's not perfect. We

still have our fair share of assholes, but now being a prick is a luxury, not a necessity."

"Total opposite of Credence then."

"The reivers still have executioners?"

"Available for hire on every street corner."

"You're exaggerating, right?"

"Only slightly," Vari confirmed with a wry smile.

She lifted the lentils off the fire, gave them a final stir and set them down to cool beside the silver beet.

Braemer rubbed his thumb against his lips as he thought. "If what Arix says about that collar is true, he's no friend of the reivers."

"Doesn't make him *our* friend," snapped Vari, more sharply than she intended.

The corner of the druid's eye crinkled as he looked out at Arix and Mark. It was the only way Vari could tell he was smiling. The rest of his expression was lost in red hair.

"You're starting to sound like Dayna."

Vari had to admit that she was feeling a bit like Dayna right now. Her inner walls were right up and she was ready to defend them."

"Sorry. Guess I'm feeling a bit on edge."

"That makes two of us."

Something occurred to Vari then, and it

seemed like the perfect time to ask. "Your Council of Druids, they summoned Mark somehow?"

Braemar's eyes flicked to Vari but quickly slid from her face, falling back to the fire. It looked like he was trying to work out how much he was allowed to say. "Yeah, it's an old ritual." A smile crossed his lips, a forced one. "Probably why Mark ended up in the middle of nowhere. It's not something we druids have had much practice with."

Vari bit her thumbnail a couple of times and then gestured in Arix's direction. "The inquisitors must have their own version of that summoning ritual."

Braemar nodded. "Arix's accent is different but their way of speaking is pretty similar. Perhaps Mark and Arix come from the same place? Same world, at least."

"A world you and I know absolutely nothing about."

Braemar shrugged. "I try to think more about what I do know rather than what I don't." He pointed at her ebony staff propped up against the stone wall. "How's that staff working out for you?"

Vari smiled as she reached over and picked it

up. As she lay it across her legs, its stats popped up of their own accord.

Ebon Staff of the Dusk
20% increase in casting speed.
+20% to staff base damage during daylight or darkness.
+50% to staff base damage during twilight.

"Day and night are stale illusions.
Everything changes and dusk has the truth of it."
- Desir the Leaden Heart

She stroked the smooth, dark wood with her fingertips. The silver caps gleamed yellow and orange in the firelight.

"Looking forward to hitting something with this," she remarked with a fierce grin. She pointed the staff at Mark and Arix. "Maybe those two if they don't get over here before their dinner gets cold."

The druid snort-laughed as he stood. "I'll tell them."

He walked over to Mark and Arix, and while Vari noticed that Mark acknowledged Braemar with a smile and a thank you, Arix barely even registered his existence. She slapped her staff into her palm a couple of times, hard enough to feel the sting, and then leaned it back against the wall.

Soon they were eating her lentils and beets around the fire. Correction, thought Vari, three of us are eating my lentils and beets while one of us is wrinkling his nose at his plate like he's been served stir-fried insult on a bed of boiled contempt.

"Something wrong with dinner, Arix?"

"No offense, luv, but it's missing a vital in-gredient."

"I can add more salt if you like."

Arix shook his head. "I was thinking of some-thing more...meaty. Don't happen to have some bacon tucked away in your pack, do ya?"

It was Vari's turn to wrinkle her nose. "No, I don't."

Arix looked wistfully into the gathering dark-ness. "Wonder if I've got me enough time to raid that reiver camp? They had some lovely pork cutlets I fancy swiping."

Braemar looked from Vari to Arix, back to Vari and then down at his plate. Mark forced a laugh, trying to ease the growing tension. "You've only just escaped from them, Arix. How about we leave them alone for awhile?"

Arix shrugged and shovelled a forkful of lentils into his mouth. Vari noticed he'd already exiled his silverbeet to the very edge of his plate. She supposed she should be thankful that he was polite enough to not simply throw it into the fire.

The executioner pointed his empty fork at Vari. "Mark's given me the skinny on your backstory, Vari. Spare me the optionals. But I'd love to hear what you make of the inquisitors."

His dismissive tone was really getting under her skin. She resisted the urge to Sculpt Bone one of his fingers. "I wouldn't know where to start."

"Ever heard of Inquisitor Karina?"

"Jesus, Arix," snapped Mark. "Ever heard of manners? We're not doing in-game chat mode here."

Arix fixed Mark with a hard look. Mark held the man's gaze, finally forcing the executioner to look away and have another forkful of lentils. Vari felt a surge of pride for her man, pleased that he was standing up for them.

"Sorry," Arix muttered with his mouth still full.

"It's all good," Mark reassured him. "You've been through a lot." Mark gave Vari a half-smile and mouthed "Go easy on him".

Vari breathed in deep. Something about Arix

still rubbed her up the wrong way but she would try to keep a civil tongue with him, for Mark's sake. "Yes, I know Inquisitor Karina," she said as she exhaled, "at least by reputation."

"For being a sadistic bitch-torturess?" asked Arix, his eyes hard again.

"Sometimes, but mostly for her transmogrative work."

"Transmogrative?" asked Mark. "That's a new word on me."

"To use magic as a transformational tool. Karina specializes in living beings."

Arix raised a thick, black eyebrow. With his dark, stone-smooth scalp, deep-brown skin and jet eyes, Vari thought Arix could almost pass for a Karaji. But there was something different about his features. His broad jaw and nose set him apart from her people. He was the opposite of Mark with his pale skin, hazel eyes and mop of unruly brown hair. Arix was as tall as Mark too, if not a little taller, but he was an oak tree to Mark's slender willow. Braemar was right. Their accents were different too. While Mark's was a warm, reedy pipe, Arix's was a sharp and staccato bugle.

"That's code for 'she makes monsters out of people', yeah?" asked Arix.

The screams echoed up from Vari's memories.

Screams that curdled into bestial howls. She tried to ignore them. "Pretty much."

"No way," exclaimed Mark. "Hope we don't run into any of her pets."

"Far as I know," groaned Arix, "*I* was the only pet she brought with her from Credence."

"That's where they summoned you?" asked Mark.

"Yeah. Total fucking shithole."

"That we can agree on, Arix," admitted Vari.

Arix grinned. Vari was taken aback. He was actually quite handsome when he smiled. "And I forgot to say thanks for the food. It's good, even without bacon."

She ignored the uneaten silverbeet. "Thank you."

"How many reivers did Karina bring with her?" asked Mark.

"Couple of hundred at least."

Braemar sucked air through his teeth. "That's a fair bit."

Arix shrugged. "Mostly grunts. If not for the collar, I'd have sliced through them like butter, escaped ages ago."

Vari sincerely doubted that but tried to keep the skepticism out of her voice. "Do you know why they've come to the Barrens?"

"Not really. Karina made me capture something called the Altar of Khorlvah. That was before I ran into mummy monster back there. That name, Khorlvah, mean anything to you lot?"

Vari shook her head. Mark and Braemar followed suit.

Arix smirked. "Reminds me of Raiders of the Lost Ark. Nazis searching the ruins for ancient weapons."

Mark laughed. Vari looked to Braemar who simply shrugged. He had no idea what they were talking about either.

"So, Arix," asked Vari. "What's your backstory then?" She put quote marks with her fingers around 'backstory'.

His smile warped into a scowl. "Executioner class. Level Six. Summoned by reivers, tortured and treated like a slave for a few weeks. Nothing much to it."

"I mean, before you were summoned."

Mark was fairly tight-lipped on the subject of his world so Vari was interested to see what she could get out of Arix. Her hopes were dashed by a single glance from Mark to Arix. Clearly, they'd already talked about this.

Arix cleared his throat and set down his plate

by the fire. "Just doing what I do now, except I had an audience."

"An audience? Like a pit fighter?" She'd seen pit fighting in Credence. Reivers would drink and place bets while slaves killed each other in the ring.

"A gladiator slave?" He laughed and shook his head. "Nah. A business. Made good money too. People from all over the world would tune in to watch me play." He winced. "Fight, I mean."

Player. Play. These words were coming up more often. "What do you mean when you say-"

She was interrupted by a loud yawn. Arix stretched his arms and Vari heard several cracks as his vertebrae realigned along his spine. "Sorry, darling. Bit late for questions, innit. Past my bedtime."

Vari felt her lip curl all by itself. "Please don't call me 'darling.'"

Arix offered her an infuriating wink. "Sorry, luv." Then he stood and sauntered off to find himself somewhere to sleep for the night.

"Might do the same," added Braemar as he passed Vari his plate. "Thanks for dinner."

"You're welcome, Braemar."

As the druid headed off to bed, Vari gathered

up the pots, plates and cutlery and plonked them at Mark's feet.

He raised an eyebrow at that. "Guess I'm on dishes then?"

"There's a stream just through that archway over there. Just follow the silver beet plants." She kissed Mark on the forehead. "Try not to get eaten."

Mark caught her hand and pulled her a little closer. "Sorry, Vari."

"What for?"

"Arix, he's…"

"Just promise me one thing, Mark."

His eyes were wide and his lips were pressed into a thin line. He knew what was coming.

"When you're ready, you'll tell me," she whispered.

"Tell you what?"

"Everything."

She kissed him and felt his lips relax beneath hers. Then she gently pulled away. She didn't look back as she walked over to their sleeping spot, but she knew it'd be a while before Mark joined her. Arix's arrival had given them all plenty to think about.

9

[MARK]

Braemar's trail of fractures ended at a wide, open square. At its center, a towering winged goddess teetered to one side.

Her flaming base rested in the chasm that bisected the square from corner to corner. This statue was different from the others Mark had seen so far. Her softporn physique was encased in figure-hugging armor and she gripped a cruelly-pointed trident in her hands. She reminded Mark of Britannia, Great Britain's figurehead warrior woman.

"Looks like an old military headquarters," observed Arix. "That square was probably a parade ground." He scanned the parade ground with his dark brown eyes. "Can't see anything roaming about so that chasm's probably a mob generator. It'll kick into life once we get down there."

Mark winced. Arix had the mindset of a hard-core gamer, not a roleplayer. If he kept talking like that, Mark would end up fielding some very awkward questions from Vari and Braemar. He shot Arix a warning look. Arix rolled his eyes. Message received.

"What I *meant* to say, lady and gents, is that the corruption in the chasm won't wake up until we get close enough to sniff the stink of it," corrected Arix. His voice oozed exasperation.

Mark turned to Braemar. "You reckon you could close it from here?"

The druid shook his head. "Nope. Got to be pretty close for an Earth Sculpt of that size."

Arix scowled. "I get why you want to do this Cracks in Reality subquest. Probs some tidy XP in it for one and all. But what's your plan in the long run? Wander all over this place filling up cracks like a bunch of brickies?" He stretched out his arms to encompass the immensity of the Barrens. "In case you hadn't noticed, this place is fucking huge!"

"Do you have a better idea?" snapped Vari.

Her eyes were a shade darker than usual, a

shadow that Mark had only seen whilst in the midst of combat. It seemed his girlfriend had taken an intense dislike to their newest party member.

Arix grinned, a smarmy expression that only served to darken Vari's eyes further. "How about we go to Credence and rescue some gorgeous slave maidens from the clutches of them inquisitors? Plenty of XP going and those bastards will have some nice gear tucked away in their vaults." He pointed at Vari. "Our figurist even trained there for fuck's sake. Must know the place like the back of her hand."

Mark stepped between the two of them. "No mate, we're here to protect Garland from corruption. It's seeping through the mountains from places like this. These smaller chasms will lead us to the big one that's causing all the trouble. Once we close the source of the corruption, the others should dry up."

"So the main chasm's like a cracked sewage pipe and these smaller chasms are the puddles of shit what have bubbled to the surface?"

"Basically, yes. And you can either help us with this or..." He trailed off, leaving Arix to finish the sentence.

"Or I can fuck off?" asked the executioner.

Mark shrugged. "Not how I would've put it."

Arix looked from Mark to Vari and then winked at Braemar. "Bet there's plenty of gorgeous maidens in this Garland of yours, yeah?"

Braemar blushed. "Guess so. Depends what you're-"

Arix cut him off with a dismissive wave of his hand. "Don't matter. I'm not picky. Just as long as they're suitably grateful that I saved their fair land for them."

"That *we* saved their fair land," corrected Vari.

"Whatever, luv," said Arix as he turned to look out over the parade ground.

Mark placed a hand on Vari's shoulder. Her muscles were taut beneath his fingertips. He offered her an apologetic smile and her eyes lightened a little. She nodded, understanding that Arix was useful to them, for now. He gave her shoulder a reassuring squeeze and then joined Arix in surveying the grounds below.

He pointed out the half circle of an old stone grandstand in the closest corner of the square. "If Vari and Braemar put their backs to that, it should shield them from getting flanked."

"While we tank it out front," assumed Arix.

"Pretty much. We've just got to hold the line

long enough for Braemar to close the chasm. Once that's done, it's mop-up time."

"Hope whatever climbs out of that crack brings some juicy loot with it."

Mark shrugged. "Wasn't the case the last couple of times. Monsters only. No gear."

"Fuck me. Whatever's inside that chasm will probs come to life as soon as I hit ground level and start searching the buildings anyway."

"Yeah, that seems to be the way they work. The last big one we met was the Siren of the Lake and it only surfaced once I got close."

"Siren, eh?" Arix gave him a wink. "You get any before you put the bitch down?"

It was Mark's turn to blush. "I don't even know what to say to that."

Arix laughed and punched Mark in the arm. "Leaving people speechless is my thing, innit."

Mark rubbed his arm and heard Vari give a sigh behind him. Yes, it seemed they both agreed. Arix was turning out to be a bit of a dick.

The executioner seemed oblivious to their unimpressed expressions as he pointed down at the cracked stretch of paving between the grandstand and the chasm. "Best if I go in front, give me enough room to use my Clean Slate skill without accidentally taking your head off."

"Yeah, that'd be inconvenient."

"Speaking of which, we should set our resurrection points up here. If we go down we can at least get a bird's eye view of the battle before jumping back in."

"Alright, but we need to make the turnaround super quick. No time for screaming and wallowing."

"Fuck, what do you take me for? A noob?" Arix turned to Mark and prodded him in the chest. "I've just spent days being tortured by that twisted bitch of an inquisitor and I'm pretty ass-fuck furious about this whole not-being-able-to-log-off thing too." He feigned an apologetic look for Vari and Braemar. "Sorry. This whole not-being-able-to-go-home-thing. So don't you worry about me having a cry and a wank up here while you're all getting your guts torn out by monsters. I've got scores to settle with this place, and like it or not, you're all going to help me do that."

Arix scratched a hasty pentagram into the dust with the heel of his boot, stepped to the edge of the balcony and balanced there for a moment. "Let's do this before I decide to fuck off and leave your sorry asses to get banged by the beasties." With that he jumped off the balcony, hit the stones below and performed a roll as he regained his feet.

Mark shook his head and took a little more care with his pentagram, arranging it neatly with fragments of masonry. When he was finished, Vari smiled and pointed out some stone steps leading down from the balcony. "Shall we take the stairs like civilized people?"

Mark took Vari's hand in his and mirrored her smile. Behind them, Braemar chuckled as he followed them down.

THE FIRST CREATURE met the executioner's axe as it tried to crawl over the rim of the chasm. Mark got a glimpse of a sickly grey face and milky eyes before the axeblade split the legionnaire's helmet and bisected the head within. Three more heads followed the first, barely getting a peek over the edge before Arix decapitated them with a shout of "Clean Slate!" and a single sweep of his axe. Three were replaced by eight and Arix retreated from the chasm's edge as the eight multiplied to more than Mark could count at a glimpse.

He looked to Braemar. The druid was kneeling in the dust, his hands flat against the ground, eyes screwed shut in his beetroot face as he mouthed a stream of incantations. Mark caught Vari looking at him and flashed her a smile as the earth trembled beneath their feet. He desperately wanted to shout "Did the earth move for you too, baby?" but fought the urge back on the grounds that Vari would take it literally and they really didn't have time for his awkward explanation right now.

Your party has slain four Level 3 Corpse Soldiers.
XP reward per party member = 30 XP
Please note that your party now consists of four members.

It was nice to see that Arix's inquisitor 'friend' wasn't siphoning their XP anymore. He awakened the molten life within Volcanic Bastard, murmured "Arcane Edge" for good measure and charged into the fray. He cut through two corpse soldiers that were trying to circle around behind Arix. The undead fighters wore breastplates, cuisses and greaves. Mark made sure to aim for their unprotected bellies, cleaving through the mummified flesh and brittle bone, making four half-soldiers out of two. To Mark's relief, these weren't Walking Dead zombies that remained animate until their skulls were crushed. In un-death they fell to the same mortal blows that would've taken them in life.

Your party has slain two Level 3 Corpse Soldiers.
XP reward per party member = 15 XP

Arix grunted his thanks and finished dismembering his most recent pair of opponents.

Mark watched as Arix then proceeded to perform a startling piece of gymnastics. He planted his axeblade in the helmeted skull of a corpse soldier that was lunging towards him, then used the axe's momentum to swing himself up and over his foe like the lead weight on a metronome. As Arix landed feet-first on the ground, the axeblade pulled out with a spray of rotten greymatter. He brought it over in a perfect arc, and with such power, that it split the next corpse soldier in twain.

A rusted short sword snapped Mark back into the moment as it bounced painfully off Garridar's Ironhide. He huffed out his annoyance as he brought Volcanic Bastard to bear and removed the offending corpse's head.

Your party has slain five Level 3 Corpse Soldiers.

XP reward per party member = 37 XP

"Second Skin!" Mark shouted, and just in time as a spear came hurtling towards him. It fell in splinters to the ground along with fragments of his blue aura that dissolved like snow as they hit warm ground. He fired up his Second Skin aura again and heard "Justice Prevails!" to his left. Glancing over, Mark saw Arix's forearm glimmer with cold light as a nasty gash healed over. A blood-stained spear lay at his feet.

So the executioner can heal himself? Mark stored that observation away and made a note to mention it to Vari.

His thoughts were washed away in a wave of fear as he looked past Arix to the chasm. The ravine was narrowing rapidly, pulling together like the edges of a deep cut after one of Vari's Mend Flesh spells. Yet it still had a fair way to go.

In the meantime, it seemed an entire legion of corpse soldiers were making their escape, led by an officer in bronze armor. The big deadman bore a huge tower shield in one arm, held a longsword in the other, and wore a gleaming helmet with a bright, scarlet plume on its crest.

While pale as death, the officer was more fleshy than the others, still retaining much of his former stature and musculature. His creamy eyes gleamed with intelligence as he opened his mouth. Though no sound was uttered, his soldiers responded as if receiving a crisp order. Their ranks parted three ways, one group charging at Arix, one flanking him on the left and the other flanking Mark to the right.

He watched Arix meet the central charge with a flurry of axe blows, severing limbs and chopping off heads like a weedeater going through a patch of thistles.

Your party has slain three Level 3 Corpse Soldiers.
XP reward per party member = 22 XP

The undead officer seemed content to watch from the edge of the chasm, his blank eyes taking in the executioner's brutal efforts with cold detachment.

Mark turned to see that the two flanking groups had stopped and formed up in neat lines. Spears were raised in perfect unison, and judging by their angle, Mark knew where they were aiming.

"Braemar!" he yelled as he pointed at the spearmen. "Quagmires!"

No response. Braemar was flat on his back. Vari held his head with one hand while she poured an essence potion into his open mouth with the other.

"Variiiiii!" yelled Mark, his voice a chromatic slide from bass to tenor.

Vari looked up in alarm, saw Mark, and then her eyes widened even further when she saw the rows of spears and soldiers. "Sculpt Bone!" she shouted, three times in succession, snapping a trio of shin bones.

At the same time, Mark rushed the closest line of spearmen. He roared "Ignited Exhalation!" and felt the scorching wave of heat as it gushed out of his mouth. Flames swept across the line of mummified men and they went up like match wood. But not before their icy discipline saw their task through, launching half a dozen burning spears into the air.

Across the square, another wave of missiles took flight, minus the three whose owners were struggling and failing to stand on broken limbs. Vari's mouth made a perfect 'O' as she watched the deadly rain tumble down upon her. Braemar seemed to be recovering. He slowly rose to his feet, his hands rubbing at his eyes, utterly oblivious to the threat above.

Behind him, Arix had finished off the last of the soldiers and was moving on to the officer.

Your party has slain three Level 3 Corpse Soldiers.
XP reward per party member = 22 XP

Nearby, Mark heard sparking and crackling as the row of burning soldiers collapsed.

Your party has slain six Level 3 Corpse Soldiers.
XP reward per party member = 45 XP

"Mind over Matter," said Mark as he followed one of the spears with his eyes. He imagined it twisting like a march leader's baton in the air. The spear obeyed, somersaulting into its neighbors, knocking them off course. They clattered down around Vari. She was crouched down, arms over her head, making herself as small a target as possible. Other spears thudded headfirst into the dirt to her left and right.

But that was just one flight of spears. The others fell like burning rain. The clattering and thudding *almost* covered the sound, the sickening crunch, of a single spear driving into Braemar's eye and out through the back of his skull. A second spear skewered his thigh. A third impaled him through the chest. Mark knew the latter two didn't matter. Vari could fix a thigh, probably even patch up a punctured heart if she got to it fast enough. But nothing could bring the light back to Braemar's remaining eye.

He vaguely registered the yawp of triumph as Arix took the officer's legs out from under it and sent its rotting body plummeting into the chasm.

Your party has slain Captain Kren, a Level 5 Necrofficer.
XP reward per party member = 16 XP
Please note that your party now consists of three members.

Mark ran over to Vari, planted his boots and cut down one charging corpse soldier after another. He didn't look back, neither at Vari nor Braemar, as he strode over to the incapacitated deadmen and sent them back into the dirt where they belonged.

Your party has slain six Level 3 Corpse Soldiers.

XP reward per party member = 60 XP

Only when he was done, when there was nothing left to kill, did he lower his sword and shamble like a dead man himself to the corpse of his former friend.

10

[ARIX]

Your party has slain Captain Kren, a Level 5 Necrofficer.
XP reward per party member = 16 XP
Please note that your party now consists of three members.

Correction, thought Arix. *I* slew Captain Kren, thank you very much. Sure, Arix admitted, the others distracted a few corpse soldiers so I could bash the necrofficer without interference, but that was hardly worth an equal share of the spoils, was it?

It was a point he'd raised in one of his You-Tube shows, a call for RPG developers to get more granular with their XP systems. He was still rather proud of the title too. "The Massacre Meritocracy". It was a subject he was going to bring up again as soon he got out of this Easter Egg.

He tried not to think of all the money he was losing in his online absence. Nor how much Krissy would be freaking out about her comatose boyfriend. His FIVR life support was top notch and paid up for the year. He wasn't going to die in here, at least not literally, so there was no point in stressing himself out. It would only make it harder for him to find a way to log off.

Karina was the most likely option. She had made the door and lured him over the threshold. Clever bint she'd been too. In-game popups promising never-before-seen exclusive content, stuff that his fans would lap up like thirsty doggies. Well, the actual wording had been "Follow your destined path to the fateful door. Prove your worth to one and all. Glory to the Great." Typical fantasy RPG bollocks that literally meant, "Get your Easter Egg while it's hot!" At least, that's what he'd assumed.

Hopefully Karina could just as easily shove him back through that 'fateful door' and slam the fucking thing behind him. But getting to her meant wading through a couple of hundred reivers. That sergeant of hers wasn't to be underestimated either. He would have to do some serious leveling and looting before he was ready for that bloodbath.

He took a deep breath, raised his hand to wave the notifications away, and noticed the "Please note..." line for the first time. He glanced up to where he and Mark had set their resurrection points. Nothing there. He sighed and turned to look back across the battlefield. There was Mark and his AI fuck buddy, crouching over Brayden's spear-skewered body.

Braemar, he corrected himself. That was lucky. He'd have come across as a right wanker if he'd gotten the dead NPC's name wrong.

Arix paused to check that nothing else was going to crawl up out of the pit and took a moment to mourn the loss of Captain Kren's gear. A polish like that surely meant magic. He picked up the necrofficer's severed legs, pulled the steel cuisses and greaves off and shook out a few shreds of rotting flesh. They were light but looked like they could take some serious punishment.

Kren's Tempered Cuisses
25% reduction to damage sustained to the upper leg.

25% chance to prevent all damage to upper leg.
15% reduction in upper leg muscle fatigue.
+10% to knee attacks.

"I don't care if you've got balls of rock.
I've got a knee of forged steel."
- Captain Kren of the Imperial Guard

Kren's Tempered Greaves
25% reduction to damage sustained to the
lower leg.
25% chance to prevent all damage to lower leg.
15% reduction in lower leg muscle fatigue.
+10% to kick attacks.

"They say not to kick a man when he's down.
What a wasted opportunity."
- Captain Kren of the Imperial Guard

Arix donned his prizes then leaned over the edge of the chasm and snapped a salute at the murky darkness below.

"Thanks for that, Kren. "

Then hoping the worst of the weeping and wailing was over with already, Arix headed for Mark, Vari and the deceased Brayden. *Braemar*, he corrected and slapped his own face. Brayden was his sister's ex-boyfriend, a skinny ginger boy from Brighton. Nice guy. Way too nice for Venus.

He stopped short of the mourning pair and winced at the spear sticking out of the dead druid's face.

A quick death, at least. Hold on, what was he saying? A quick death? He tried to wipe his own frustration from his face with his hand. This Easter Egg was getting under his skin. Before him lay an NPC. It had ceased to function. Its script was done and its animations were frozen. Just like everything else in this world, from corpse soldiers to the gore-spattered rocks, Braemar was a nifty bit of code, nothing more.

He cleared his throat. "Look, sorry about Braemar, guys. I know he was your mate and all, but we should really be going." He scanned the ruins above them, searching for watchers. "It weren't exactly a quiet battle. Someone or something is bound to have noticed, and here we are, out in the open, sitting ducks for anyone with a spear to chuck at us. Brayden would testify to that, yeah?"

"Which is it?" asked Mark, his voice soft and hoarse. His eyes were rimmed with red.

"Which is what?"

"Which is it? Braemar or Brayden?"

Arix mentally kicked himself. "Braemar. Fuck, sorry. I've never been good with NPC names."

It was Vari's turn to look at him with bleary eyes. Her cheeks were moist with tears. "Why do you keep calling us that?"

He sighed in frustration. "Can we not do this here?"

Vari rested her hand on Braemar's leg. "We're not leaving him like this."

The figurist was never going to understand. She was a scripted character with no more consciousness than Captain Kren. Arix gave Mark his best pleading look, the one he used when he wanted fans to click on one of his affiliate links.

"Mate, come on. You know how this all works." He pointed at Braemar's boots. Judging by the fine leatherwork and their 'good as new' condition, they were magical items of some sort. "Take those boots and let's get the fuck out of here before we lose our healer too."

Mark's eyes narrowed and their rims grew a little redder. "Yeah, I know how this all works, and you have no fucking idea."

Arix resisted the urge to slap some sense into the guy. He was balls deep in this virtual world. So deep, in fact, that he'd lost sight of the horizon. He'd heard of people going 'native' in FIVR, or at least trying to. They wanted to believe in the fiction *so* badly that they ended up losing the plot entirely. If he could find a way out, and take Mark with him, he would even consider funding his RL therapy. 'Arix the Damned rescues fellow gamer from RL dislocation.' Yeah, it'd make for a great headline and a shit-ton of channel views.

"Alright, do what you got to, mate." Arix unclipped his crossbow and checked that he had two bolts locked and loaded. "I'll patrol the area, make sure you don't get jumped while you're paying your respects." While you're being a fucking fruitcake, he managed not to add.

Mark nodded, the ghost of a smile on his face. "Thank you."

"Don't mention it, yeah."

As Arix struck out for one of the taller buildings, a pair of notifications materialized at the edge of his vision.

Your party has failed the Cracks in Reality subquest.

Special Requirement Lost: Without a Druidic Elementalist specializing in Earth Magic, the Chasm of Corruption Quest is unachievable and has been removed from the quest log.

Arix smiled to himself. It looked like the game had as much time for faux sentimentality as he did. He shook his head. Fucking roleplay. Just a recipe for psychosis that was. The next notification made him smile even more.

Congratulations!
You have reached Level 7 as an Executioner.
Progress to next level = 1052/1700
You have been awarded 2 Attribute Points.
You now have access to Level 7 Executioner abilities.

It didn't matter how many times he leveled up, in however many games, he still felt that little rush of pride and excitement. And new skills and abilities were like new toys on his birthday.

Ability Selection
Bloody Retribution (10 EP)
Righteous Rage (10 EP)

Bloody Retribution
Reflects 50% of damage taken onto the damage dealer.
Base casting cost = 10 EP

Tier 1: The reflected violence effect remains in place for 10 seconds.

"Violence, like song,
is more fun when it's shared."
- Ezok the Butcher

Righteous Fury
Increases damage dealt by 100%.
Increases damage taken by 50%.
Base casting cost = 10 EP
Tier 1: Righteous Rage remains in place for 10 seconds.

"Vent your fury before it eats you alive."
- Ezok the Butcher

Arix decided he liked this 'Ezok the Butcher' geeza and dropped both attribute points into Spirit to make the most of his brutal new skills.

By this time he'd reached the tallest of the buildings. He clipped his crossbow to his back and scaled the ornate frontage, as quick and limber as a monkey. Yes, he could've gone inside and found a staircase, but Arix preferred to develop his Climbing and Acrobatics skills whenever possible. It was paying off too. He could feel his body growing more confident, internalizing the moves. He probably wasn't far off Tier 3 at this rate.

He clambered up onto the roof and took in the view. This building was a couple of storeys taller than most of those around it, and the vista it afforded Arix was nothing short of magnificent. Crumbling buildings and worn statues, dusty avenues and wind-swept courtyards. There wasn't much vegetation around, and what was there looked warped and stunted. The developers had carried this 'corruption' theme right through their whole design.

Arix wondered if they'd be cruel enough to add some sort of ambient corruption effect to the city. An insidious AoE that would eat away at his avatar, twisting and knotting the strings of its code until he turned into some virtual freak. It was enough to send a shiver down his spine. The reivers had muttered to each other about things like that, how the Barrens were tainted with sickness, how many a reiver expedition had disappeared in this city without a trace. One soldier had been stupid enough to voice that opinion in air shot of Karina. The man had wailed like a baby as the inquisitor proceeded to 'cleanse his mind' of such troubling thoughts.

Arix looked up at the sun, felt the warmth on his face, and let the chilling vision melt away. He'd been in these Barrens for a few days already and suffered neither a blemish nor a pimple. Surely, if there was a corruption mechanic in place, he'd have grown a tentacle out his ass by now.

Down below, Mark and Vari were constructing a makeshift stretcher from spears and breastplates. Arix glanced at the mountains and shook his head. He hoped they weren't planning to carry Braemar's dead weight all the way back to this 'Garland' of theirs. Judging by Vari's physique, her Body score wasn't that crash hot. Mark would try to rope *him* into stretcher-bearing duties. He sighed, supposing it wouldn't hurt to play along. The alternative was that he'd have to go after Karina by himself. Not impossible, but it'd be easier with a healer like Vari to back him up. Then he could spend his EP on offensive abilities rather than bucketloads of Justice Prevails.

He took a moment to scrutinize the area, watching for movement. The place was as quiet as a crypt. Other mobs were likely programmed to steer clear of the area so that the corpse soldier experience wouldn't get muddied by randoms.

He sat on the rim of the roof, dangling his legs over the edge. Watching Mark and Vari work together made him miss Krissy even more. Mark was bent over the stretcher, buckling up straps. Beside him, Vari reached over and rubbed the nape of his neck, running her finger tips up under the curly locks at the base of his skull. It was such a comforting gesture that Arix felt genuinely touched by the scene. It reminded him of the lazy Sunday morning he and Krissy had spent in the flat before he'd dived back into *Reign of Blood* and ended up here. Still in their PJs, they'd sipped coffee and basked in the bay window as the sun streamed in.

He *had* to get the fuck out of this Easter Egg, and when he did, he was going to sue the shit out of the *Reign of Blood* developers for this whole 'no logoff' nightmare. He'd been in here far too long for it to be a glitch. It was some weird-assed experiment. Mark might be happy to play the guinea pig but he sure as fuck wasn't having it.

Fury swelled within him and the ruins took on a cold and flat appearance. Arix the Damned was out for blood. Mark and his virtual pet were going to help. Karina was going to send him back into 'logoff land' or experience the wrong end of a branding iron. Torture wasn't Arix's thing, but in Karina's case, the ends would justify the means.

He stood, stretched and began his descent across the neighboring buildings, leaping from jagged wall top to fractured colonnade, broken balcony to sundered archway. He dropped down into the parade ground and rolled with the momentum. He luxuriated in each movement, feeling every inch the apex predator.

He curtailed his smile as he stalked across the cobblestones to where Mark and Vari had finished their stretcher and laid Braemar upon it. Instead, he put a suitably solemn expression in place. Today he was their sympathetic ally. Tomorrow they were going to help him whether they wanted to or not.

11

[MARK]

They took Braemar back to Citadel via the waypoint. The next morning, as the sun rose over the mountains, the villagers gathered with Mark and Vari to bury him.

Mark chose a site overlooking the quarry, with a lovely view up to the mountain peaks. Calder and a couple of his miners dug the grave while the rangers wrapped Braemar's body in cloth, as was the Garland tradition. Then the rangers lowered him into the grave while the senior ranger, Meredith, recited the Garland burial rights. Calder and his miners filled in the grave while Mark and Vari set a headstone in place. The headstone was made from a piece of limestone, carved by the wind and rain into a graceful shape. A bronze plaque, forged by Citadel and embedded into the base of the stone by Calder, provided a fitting eulogy.

> Here lies Braemar of Whitestone
>> A courageous druid and loyal friend.
>> A life given in service.
>> A life to be remembered.

After that, Mark and Vari tried to keep themselves busy, to fill the void that Braemar had left behind. Mostly they gathered alchemy ingredients in the forest, but they couldn't avoid the tension that now permeated the fortress. The rangers had encountered things on their patrols that had no business being in Garland. Small tribes of Cave Ghasts. Flocks of Mist Wraiths. Even a siren, encountered in one of the nearby lakes by fishermen who barely escaped with their lives.

Travelers were becoming more frequent at Citadel. Some journeyed there out of curiosity, some out of necessity. The former spun tales of strange beasts and desolate tracts of withered forest. The latter brought grim news of Garland villages laid waste by creatures of nightmare. When put together, the stories encompassed the full length of Garland's mountainous border with the Barrens. The only good news was that the reiver raids had stopped. Vari suspected it was just a side-effect of the rising corruption. The reivers were finding it increasingly difficult to get through the mountains. It wasn't worth their time and loss of life.

It took a couple of days for the weight of Braemar's death to ease from Mark's shoulders and another two days for Mark to regain the headspace to tackle this growing problem. In that time, an impatient Arix peppered him with questions about Citadel and Garland, and offered plenty of unsolicited town-building advice. The rest of the time, Arix entertained himself by collaring and cross-examining people.

Mark could tell that he wasn't genuinely interested in what the rangers or villagers had to say about themselves or their lives. His questions were pointed and erratic, more like an interrogation than a conversation. It was like the executioner was trying to exhaust each NPC's dialogue options, like he hoped to catch them out with a repetition or glitch and therefore prove that they were scripted. Mark interrupted whenever he could, inevitably exposing himself to Arix's variations on the theme of "When are we going back to the Barrens?". He found it ironic that the player was starting to sound far more scripted than any of the supposed NPCs.

So it was on the morning of the fifth day that Arix caught Mark by surprise.

"I didn't think we were at this point yet."

"What point?" Mark continued to brush his horse, removing smears of dirt from his pre-breakfast ride with Vari.

"AI that can mask itself as AGI." Arix was stretched out in a pile of hay, his hands clasped behind his neck.

"AGI? What's that?"

"Artificial General Intelligence. Software what basically thinks for itself."

Mark felt frustration building within him but he took it out on a particularly stubborn patch of caked mud. "What makes you think these people are masking anything?"

"I've followed the tech news, yeah. We're decades short of proper AGI. But limited AI, that's a different story. What them clever *Reign of Blood* fuckers is done, is got them algorithms to parse thousands of hours of dialogue. Means them NPCs got a ready line for everything, don't it. Don't know how they're sorting copyright and all that. Bloody sure I've heard some of them lines before in other games. Movies too. Probably scraping the internet for content, updating regular like. Yeah, that's what's going on."

Vari was all the evidence Mark needed to know that Arix was dead wrong, but he played along to get a better feel for Arix's perspective. "Isn't it usual practice for a team of writers to churn out a bunch of dialogue trees and casual utterances?"

"Yeah, but with these NPCs, their trees are like dialogue-fucking-thickets. Got to be an end somewhere but fucked if I can find it." He sat up, stretched and yawned. "The way I see it, this is some sort of prototype, innit." He fixed Mark with a hard look. "Ever been to the Garland capital?"

"Nope."

"Where you say you arrived again?"

"A small village, two days journey from here," Mark explained. "The village is gone now. The reivers destroyed it. The survivors were the first people to settle here in Citadel."

"Have you traveled beyond that village, further into Garland?"

Mark shook his head, a little embarrassed now. He'd vowed to protect Garland but didn't even know what most of the country looked like.

Braemar, Calder and various townsfolk had talked about other places in Garland, the beauty of the lakes, the fecundity of the croplands and orchards, the virgin forests and wildflower meadows, but he'd never seen any of it for himself.

"Beyond the Barrens?" pressed Arix.

"Where we met you, that's the deepest I've been."

Arix pursed his lips in thought. "Then between us we've only experienced from Citadel to the reiver side of the Barrens. The reivers talk about Credence. So does Vari. But I ain't never seen it. I popped up right in Karina's tent."

Mark set his brush aside and stroked his horse's neck. "Where are you going with this, Arix?"

Arix stood and dusted hay from his leather armor. "We've no idea how big this expansion is. Could be that it starts just before your dead village and finishes on the far side of the Barrens."

Mark shook his head. "Vari's homeland is at least two months' ride from the Barrens." He crossed to the stable doors and pointed out one of the rangers up on the wall. "Those rangers came from the Garland capital and it took them about a week to get here."

"Backstory, mate. Them rangers could've spawned out in the forest for all you know."

Mark scowled at Arix. "Braemar's home, Whitestone, that was near the capital too."

Arix folded his arms and leaned against the frame of the open stable doors. "Mate, you and I both know how NPCs normally work. They talk about far off lands to make the virtual world feel more expansive than it actually is. It's smoke and fucking mirrors."

"Look, 'mate'," said Mark with a sigh. "I don't pretend to know what's going on here, but I can assure you there's nothing 'normal' about this FIVR."

Arix winced and sucked air through his teeth. "Well, as much as you might *want* it to be different, Mark-"

"How about we postpone this debate until we get back from the Barrens?" He wasn't yet feeling ready for another round with the ruins but he couldn't think of any other way to shut Arix up.

The executioner grinned like the cat with its proverbial cream. "Now that's an offer I can't refuse, innit. When do we leave?"

"Vari and I will meet you in the library this evening for a planning session."

Arix gave him a double thumbs up. "I'll be there."

TRUE TO HIS PROMISE, Arix was already seated in the library when Mark and Vari entered. He raised his goblet of claret in greeting.

"Now this is what I call a tasty drop."

"Thank you, Arix," replied Citadel, his voice emanating from near the mantlepiece.

Mark imagined Citadel as a nattily dressed warlock, leaning against the warmed oak as he sipped at his silver goblet, his pinky finger extended just so.

"Garridar was a severe sort, prone to brooding," Citadel continued. "Yet he was a keen collector of Garland wines. Although, on hindsight, most bottles didn't stay 'collected' for long. That claret is one of the few that survived his rather unquenchable thirst."

Mark picked up a goblet from the giant cockroach that scuttled by, a silver serving tray perched on its back. He took a sip and sank into his chair with a sigh.

"Let's start with the obvious. Without Braemar, or a druid with his skills, we can't complete the Chasms of Corruption quest. Arix, you won't have seen that quest message so I'll-"

"Actually, I had a problem with that quest anyway," interrupted Arix.

"What? When did you see the quest description?"

"I saw the failure message. Sid filled me in on the rest."

"I didn't think you'd mind considering that Arix is now a member of your party," added Citadel.

"No worries, Sid, and thanks."

"My pleasure."

"What was your problem with the quest, Arix?" asked Vari, her tone guarded.

Mark reached over and rested his free hand on her forearm. He felt the tension in her muscles. Try as he might to ease her tension, her dislike of Arix showed no chance of abating. Arix seemed not to notice.

"The way I see it, the chasm was never the problem," explained Arix. "It's just the housing for whatever's fuelling and spreading the corruption, for what's making them smaller chasms and all. With them being monster generators, closing the chasm *might* kill whatever's inside, but there's no guarantee. What if the thing just goes deeper?

What if there's an attached cave system? Other chasms might open up as the corruption leaks to the surface. We might inadvertently make the source a shitload harder to get at."

Vari nodded with grudging agreement. "Like how the Ghast Queen was able to seep through the mountains. She consumed ore and then oozed through the resulting gap."

Arix grinned and snapped his fingers at her. "Exactly! Yeah, Sid told me about your Depths of Corruption quest too. You're not just a pretty face, are you, Vari."

"You know what it means to snap your fingers at someone in Karaji, Arix?"

"No, what?"

"For every word you offer in insult from now on, I shall cut off a finger or toe." She snapped her fingers at him and mirrored his grin with a sharper one of her own.

Arix raised his hand in supplication. "Alrighty, don't get your knickers in a twist."

"What are knickers and why would I twist them?"

"What are knickers?" Arix's smile took on a leery edge as he winked at Mark. "My kinda lady."

Mark felt his face go red and he offered Vari

an apologetic look. She didn't notice. Her dark eyes were now boring into Arix. Mark worried that she was about to break his fingers with a Sculpt Bone spell. He squeezed her arm a little tighter.

"We were talking about the chasms and corruption?"

"True true." Arix took a sip of his wine, savoring it for a moment before swallowing it down with an audible gulp. "In my experience, a well-designed quest is a guide, not an instruction manual. You can achieve the quest by achieving the goal. In this case, the goal is to destroy the source of the corruption. Closing the chasm might've done it, maybe, but it might be even better to lower Mark down on a rope and have him hit the thing a few times with that fiery bastard sword of his."

"Sorry to interrupt," interjected Citadel, "but might I query something about your theory, Arix?"

"I think it's pretty fucking watertight," said Arix, "but sure, Sid. Go nuts."

"Are you saying that the gods are fallible enough to create a poorly designed quest?"

"I was going to ask the same thing, Sid," added Vari.

Mark cringed. Arix was in dangerous existential territory here. Arix didn't seem worried though.

"Is that how it works here? The gods create your quests?" Arix looked around the room, pretending to search for the 'gods' behind the armchairs and up on the bookshelves. "Geezas and slappas in flowing robes serving up destiny like canapes on a silver platter?"

"Yes," answered Vari, unamused. "Mohkash of the Flowing Waters fishes our hopes and dreams from the rivers of consciousness."

"Urgred the Wise is our Garland equivalent," added Citadel.

Arix laughed. "In our world we call them the Developers of the Game. Right, Mark?"

"Regardless of where the quests come from," said Mark, trying to nudge the conversation away from gnarly metaphysical matters, "you're suggesting we have some room for interpretation, right?"

"Of course!" insisted Arix. "Where's the fun in just slavishly following quests to the final fucking letter? The prize is the prize. Doesn't matter how you take it." He leaned forward, cupped his hands around his goblet, and fixed them both with an intense look that made Mark squirm a little in his seat. It was the look of a pushy real estate agent about to close a deal. "I want to help you save Garland from the corruption, so-"

"Why?" interrupted Vari.

Arix raised an eyebrow at that. "Why what?"

"Why do you want to save Garland? You've only just got here. You don't know anyone apart from us and Citadel, and you barely batted an eyelid when Braemar died."

"I've talked to lots of people since I got here," defended Arix.

Vari and Mark exchanged an incredulous look. She'd seen Arix's style of 'conversation' too.

"Besides, I'm an adventurer," continued Arix, "like Mark here."

"You're nothing like-" began Vari but Mark squeezed her arm, imploring her to stop. He had a pretty good idea of Arix's motivation. Get back to reality.

On that front, Mark was in no hurry. He knew he was in hospital, and the New Zealand public health system was such that he'd get a good level of care. He had health insurance. One of the few things he could now honestly thank his ex-wife for. He wouldn't have bothered had she not insisted. If there was a question mark over his ongoing care in public, his insurance would cover private. His mum would sign the paperwork on his behalf.

He felt a pang of guilt as he wondered how his mother was faring. Theirs had never been an easy relationship. After his dad died, parental arguments morphed into mother/son arguments. Without his father around, Sandra wanted to re-shape him instead. She hoped to turn him from a "hopeless dreamer" into someone who was "going places". Now she could bemoan her poor fortunes and the tragedy of her talented son with all of his "lost potential". And he wasn't there to inconveniently point out the bald facts of his rather unremarkable life. Sandra would take comfort in signing the papers, in making sure the insurance company did right by him. She could console herself that she was still being an excellent mother while her 'troubled' son languished on life support, his head in proverbial clouds.

The irony of it was that Mark had become exactly the sort of man she'd wanted him to be. He had skills, respect, and even his very own castle. If she could get her head around the 'virtual' aspect of it all, she might even be proud of him.

"Arix wants to help and that's good enough for me," said Mark before Vari could start up again.

"Sorry, Mark," retorted Vari through gritted teeth, "but it's not good enough for me, not at all."

"Okay," soothed Mark, "but I want to hear him out all the same. Can you do that for me, Vari?"

Vari curled her lips, clearly tempted to argue further, but then nodded and put her other hand on top of Mark's.

"You were saying, Arix?" she prompted, rather coldly.

Arix shuffled forward on his chair and his right leg started into a steady up and down jiggle. The executioner seemed unaware of it but Mark wondered if it was a tell of some sort, an unconscious gesture that hinted at hidden anxiety or excitement. By contrast, the gamer's voice was slow and calm.

"Braemar's passing was a fucking tragedy. I didn't get the chance to know him, but from first impressions he seemed like a really nice guy."

He sounded genuine but Mark knew Arix was just saying that for Vari's sake. His right knee kept on jiggling up and down with enough energy to send tremors through the floorboards.

"But the real point is this," continued Arix. "His death has closed off just one way of skinning this cat. He were following stress fractures in the earth, yeah? That's how he found the chasm in the parade ground?"

"That's right," confirmed Mark.

"Okay, so none of us have that kinda smarts. But we have others. Like, who has spent more time in the Barrens lately than anyone else we know of?"

Mark realized where Arix was going with this. "Your inquisitor friend?"

"Exactly!"

Arix was about to snap his fingers at Mark but stopped himself in the nick of time. He winked at Vari and got a faint smile in return. Good, thought Mark, the first sign that Vari and Arix might learn to tolerate each other.

"I overheard that this is the first expedition she's ever *led* into the Barrens," Arix explained. "But not the first one she's been on."

His jiggling knee picked up the pace and the tremors in the floor grew stronger. Though his voice remained calm and collected, the knee told Mark that Arix was building up to something. "By the way some of them soldiers were talking, the last expedition didn't end well. She and a few grunts got out but there weren't much change from the fifty poor bastards what went in. Probably why she's got four times that number with her this time. And there's that sergeant what Karina treats like her lapdog. She's delved into them Barrens and lived to tell the tale too."

Mark felt a jab of adrenaline in his gut, one that spread its prickling wings right up his back. "This reiver sergeant. What did she look like?"

Arix looked up to the left as he searched his memory. Mark remembered reading somewhere that the left brain is for logic and memory and that the right brain is for creativity and imagination. A person instinctively looks up to the left when they're remembering a fact and to the right when they're making something up. So whatever Arix was about to tell him was either the truth or the executioner knew that little psych snippet too and was using it to cover his tracks. Mark wanted to believe Arix, but there was a mismatch between his voice and body language that was simply rubbing him up the wrong way. He wished, for a start, that the guy would stop jiggling that knee. It was distracting.

"She was one of them girls what look chubby but is actually a fucking beefcake," offered Arix.

"A cake made out of cow meat?" wondered a bemused Vari.

Arix gave her a wry grin. "Built like a brick shithouse."

Vari's confused expression was very cute and Mark had to laugh, albeit softly. "He means heavily-muscled."

"Oh, like a flesh boulder."

Now it was Mark and Arix's turn to look confused.

"It's a Karaji saying," explained Vari.

"Yeah," agreed Arix, almost succeeding in keeping a straight face. "I prefer to keep my flesh boulders in my pants, but if you Karaji like to have them roaming about the countryside, far be it from me to judge."

Vari looked to Mark for help. Mark rolled his eyes. "Arix is now referring to his testicles."

Vari wrinkled her nose in disgust. "Could we stick to the topic at hand, please?"

"Oh, I always keep my bollocks at hand, darling. Would be a tragedy to misplace them."

"Arix!" warned Mark.

It was Arix's turn to roll his eyes. "Fine fine, Mister and Missus Grimsby. This sergeant, she moves like a killer too, so I'd hate to think how many fights she's seen the better side of. The scars on her face and arms tell the same story."

"What color is her hair?"

"Are you kidding me? Reivers change hair

color more often than they change their underpants."

Vari nodded. "For once, Arix and I agree on something."

"Was it platinum?" pressed Mark.

"Yeah, actually, it was."

Mark looked to Vari. Their eyes met, and Mark could see that Vari was thinking the same thing. Arix was talking about Dayna's murderer.

"You two met this lady before?" asked Arix.

"Yep," answered Mark softy. "She killed a friend of ours."

"Then what are we waiting for? We kill the sergeant and capture her boss. Vengeance and info in one tidy package."

Mark clenched his teeth against the rising heat within him. It was tempting, to put Dayna's murderer in the ground, but this was about Garland, not revenge. In RL, his mother always labeled him too timid or accused him of being a chronic procrastinator. In RL, he was inclined to agree with her. Here, he'd been through too much for anyone to mistake him for timid. He looked over at Vari and took a moment to soak her in, her smooth chocolate skin, her dark, glistening eyes, her cascade of jet black hair. No, he wasn't timid or a procrastinator. He just had a lot to lose.

"Are you sure this inquisitor will know where the source of the corruption is?" asked Mark.

Arix shook his head. "No, but nothing's ever one hundred percent. I just think she's our next best hope. I mean, she's there to find artifacts, so she must have read up on whatever history there is of the place.

"Like the Altar of Khorlvah?" asked Vari.

"Yeah, but from what I heard, that's just one item on her shopping list."

Vari squeezed Mark's hand. "What do you think, Mark?"

He smiled. "I was going to ask you the same question."

She shrugged. "Over two hundred reivers, and we've both seen what the sergeant can do."

"Maybe we could take some of these rangers with us," suggested Arix. "Seems like there's more than enough to guard Citadel."

"No," answered Mark, a little too sharply. "I won't be responsible for any more deaths."

He looked at Vari, about to say more, but she silenced him with a frown. "Don't go thinking you're responsible for me, Mark. If I die out there, it'll be my own stupid fault."

"You go girl," quipped Arix.

Vari shot him down with an obsidian glare. "Be a good executioner and execute some restraint when it comes to voicing your false niceties."

Arix shrunk back into his chair and pressed his finger to his lips. "Forget I spoke," he squeaked, both knees now jiggling furiously. The floorboards creaked in protest, and that's when irritation turned into an idea for Mark.

"Did you hear all this, Sid?" he asked.

"I did, yes."

"Could you also hear Arix's jittery legs?"

"At first, yes. I had to withdraw my consciousness from the floor so I could concentrate on the conversation."

Surprised, Arix stilled his legs. "I'm a kinaesthetic. Movement helps me think."

Mark ignored him. "You can shift your consciousness around?"

"Within the confines of this fortress, yes."

"Sorry, bear with me here, but if I moved the fortress, would you stay with the land or travel with the building?"

The question seemed to catch Citadel by surprise and there was a long silence as he mulled over an answer.

"Um, I just want to point out," interrupted Arix, "that the longer we wait, the more chance Karina has of finding her other artifacts and fucking off back to Credence."

"If my theory plays out here, that may not matter," Mark assured him.

Arix didn't look reassured. If anything, he looked a little pissed off, like something he wanted very badly was slipping through his fingers.

"I am the stones of this fortress and they are me," Citadel finally answered. "I go where they go."

"Okay, cool. Then I have just two more questions. One, could you shift your entire consciousness into a single stone?"

"I...I actually have no idea," admitted Citadel. "I've never tried."

"Could you try now?"

"Alright. Give me a moment."

The fortress rumbled. The rafters, door frames and floorboards creaked, the sounds of an old house settling in for the night after a hot summer's day.

"Well I'll be." Citadel's voice, while the same tone and timbre, sounded much smaller. And rather than coming from everywhere at once, it seemed to be projecting from just behind Mark, near the study door. "I am now officially haunting the stone directly to the right of the door catch."

"That's really impressive, Sid," complimented Vari. "Your proprioception must be extraordinarily sensitive."

"I know the feeling," quipped Arix. "My prostate is extraordinarily sensitive too, especially when my girlfriend strokes it by putting her finger-"

"I'm referring," interrupted Vari, "to Sid's awareness of his own body."

"Yeah, it was a joke, Vari," answered Arix. "I know what proprioception is."

"A pity you don't know what a joke is," snapped Vari.

"Oi! Shoosh, you two," insisted Mark and he knelt so that he was at eye-level with Citadel's stone. He tapped the stone three times. "Sid? Can you feel that?"

"The first one felt like a hammer blow to the skull so I withdrew into the stone's core so as to dull the subsequent assaults."

"Sorry. We'll make sure you have a nice, comfy satchel or something for travel."

"Travel?!" squeaked Sid.

"Yes. I was hoping you'd come to the Barrens with us."

"Why?"

"Stress fractures in stone, that's caused by earth movement, right?"

"Mark!" exclaimed Vari. "That's genius!"

Mark blushed and his smile made his cheeks ache. Yes, he was feeling rather proud of himself.

"Oh, I see," said Sid. "You want me to sense the tremors that will lead you to the source of the corruption!"

"Only if it's not too much trouble for you, Sid."

"To feel fresh earth beneath me, to sense the contours of rugged new climes and exotic architecture? That would be simply astounding, Mark."

"So I can take that as a 'yes'?"

"Emphatically."

Mark stood and turned to Vari and Arix. "There we have it. The Chasms of Corruption quest continues."

Congratulations!
The Chasm of Corruption Quest has been reinstated in your quest log.

"Mohkash of the Flowing Waters agrees with you, Mark." Vari stood and hugged him. "I think Braemar would've been proud of you."

"Thanks, Vari."

He looked across at Arix and saw a flicker of anger cross the gamer's face before it was lost in a seemingly genuine smile.

"Well done, mate. Most astute."

Mark nodded his thanks, but inside he was wondering just how much he should really trust the executioner. His motive was painfully clear now. He had wanted Mark and Vari to help him hunt Inquisitor Karina because she was the only person who might know how to log him out of *Reign of Blood*. The fact that he hadn't just come out and said so, that was the troubling bit. Mark decided he was going to have to play his cards close to his chest where Arix the Damned was concerned.

12

[KARINA]

Karina pulled her kerchief up over her nose to block the putrid aroma of rotting flesh. Maribella seemed not to mind the stink. She was kneeling by one of the corpses, inspecting the dead soldier's armor.

"This gear's better than ours. Greaves, cuisses for everyone," Maribella ordered the assembled reivers. "Breastplates too for the scouts and archers."

"Begging your pardon, captain," answered one of the archers. She was a stocky young woman with scarlet hair that was shaved on the sides and tied up in a topknot. "Dez and I can't wear breastplates. Gets in the way of our draw."

"I know that, Tris. Strap the fucking thing to your back so you don't get knifed while aiming."

"Oh. Thanks, captain. Didn't think of that."

Karina allowed herself a smirk. Maribella had done as she asked. Two archers, two men-at-arms and two scouts, each as stupid or psychotic as the next one. She watched as her small troop salvaged armor from the withered bodies. The magic that had mummified and preserved them was gone. Most pieces had to be scraped out and then polished clean with dry dirt. Maribella offered her a breastplate but Karina pulled down the collar of her shirt to reveal the blue-tinted sheen of her chainmail vest.

The captain raised her eyebrows in surprise. "Can't say I've seen that metal before, madam. That something you inquisitors cooked up?"

"Indeed it is. Take high-grade steel and apply lightning to galvanise it. Skyforged steel, we call it. It's a time consuming and rather expensive process."

"How expensive?"

"A soldier's annual pay."

"Not too bad. Might start saving up."

"Per link, captain. Per link."

That produced a stunned silence and the

faintest twinkle of avarice in the captain's eyes. Karina cooled her down with an icy smile.

"The penalty for a non-inquisitor found in possession of skyforged steel is an extended period of suffering far beyond the point where the recipient begs for execution."

The harbingers of a scowl twitched at the corners of her eyes and mouth as Maribella turned to her soldiers. "Dez and Tris, find shooting positions and skewer anything that's not us. Kravel and Durk, with me. Serna and Colik, have a snoop around."

"Anything you want us to keep an eye out for, captain?" asked Colik. He was a wiry greyhead, not much different to the mummified corpses that lay about them. Karina wasn't sure how old he was, but he'd already shown himself to be as agile and tireless as a mountain goat.

"More of her," answered Maribella, pointing at the statue that languished in the chasm nearby. "Agrovesh. She's a war goddess," explained Karina. She encompassed their surroundings with a sweep of her hand. "This was the headquarters of the Vorasii Legion, once the mightiest army in the world."

"Guess they didn't know us reivers then," growled Kravel.

The others laughed while Karina offered them a patient smile. "Your tiny brain would bleed at the mere sight of the Vorasii Legion in full force, Kravel. Just feel fortunate that your eyes will only witness the fading epilogue of their once glorious story."

That got an even bigger laugh, but Karina knew it was because she'd said Kravel had a tiny brain. They likely didn't understand the rest of it. She felt a pang of loneliness, one she quelled immediately. Yes, she often felt like a stranger in her own culture, but that only made her stronger. You had to be far above it all to truly see the big picture.

"Be on the lookout for shrines, temples, anywhere these legionnaires would worship their goddess," she ordered.

"Yes, madam," confirmed Colik.

The grey goat and his lean offsider jogged off towards one of the larger buildings that bordered the parade ground. Judging by the majesty and ornate nature of the structure, it was where she would've started looking too. So far it seemed that the captain had chosen her people wisely. Half conscious yet highly capable. A perfect combination in a minion.

The archers left to take up their positions

while Karina led Maribella and the two lumbering men-at-arms over to the chasm. Kravel was as bulbous as Durk was tall. The pair reminded her of the bat and ball used in a game of Diamond. She found their muscled masses quite comforting. Plenty of metal-clad meat to hide behind should someone or something start shooting at her.

Although the depths of the chasm were submerged in inky darkness, Karina didn't think there was anything lurking beneath that midnight surface. Not at the moment, at least. She'd been honing her Sparks of Sentience skill since her first foray into the Barrens. The ability allowed her to sense the energy produced by the brain, human or otherwise. The larger and more active the grey matter, the more obvious the energy signature. Although the Barren's denizens weren't exactly what she'd call "intellectual giants", most still gave off enough energy to be identified up to a distance of about thirty meters, further if she invested some EP. Which is what she did now, probing deeper into the black, scouring it for signs of life. Nothing. The chasm had emptied its belly into the parade ground.

Karina left the chasm's edge and picked her

way through the battlefield, flanked by her human shields. Maribella brought up the rear.

The inquisitor pointed out the blackened line of burned corpse soldiers. "If I recall correctly, you saw the warlock breathe fire at Captain Serik?"

"As far as I could tell, madam. I was choking on my own blood at the time, so not totally sure I saw things straight."

"Well, judging by the burn patterns, these deadmen were all set alight within the same moment. If just one had been set alight, perhaps by a torch, we would see more variation in the char as the fire spread from victim to victim. Yes, I suspect your warlock friend is here in the Barrens somewhere."

Maribella scowled and there was a murderous glint in her eyes. "That fucker and his bitches massacred our company."

"Then I would be happy to facilitate your vengeance. Garland's conquest is long overdue and removing *that* obstacle would please our betters most mightily."

"Begging your pardon, madam, but I won't be taking anyone's opinion into account when I shove my sword through his bowels."

"The glory of our empire is built upon the

collective glory of its citizens, captain."

"Thank you, madam."

Karina crossed to a patch of bloodstained dirt. "One of them fell here." She knelt down and scrutinized the scene. She picked out a hair from the mess of dried grey matter and splintered bone. It shone a light copper when held to the sun. "Your report mentioned a red-haired druid?"

"Yes, madam. He created the quicksand that I fell into, and brought the wall down that crushed Serik."

"We don't need to worry about him then." She motioned to a spear lying nearby, its head caked in dried blood. "Regrettably, his death was quick and painless."

She stood and walked over to the other line of corpses. She nudged a broken leg with her boot, noting how the shin bone had broken without any sign of exterior force. "The Karaji Figurist snapped your forearm, did she not?" Karina noted the captain's involuntary shudder with quiet amusement.

"Yes, madam. Sculpt Bone spell, if I heard her correctly."

"You did, and it seems these deadmen suffered it also." She swept her eyes across the battlefield, confident in her summations. "Once we add the axe wounds into the mix, it would appear that the warlock and his companions helped facilitate our demon's escape. They came here, probably to investigate the chasm, and subsequently lost their druid."

"That means they're close," growled Maribella, her hand instinctively dropping to the pommel of her sword.

"Yes."

Your Mind's Eye ability has increased to Tier 4. Your chance of an intuitive leap when assessing a situation has increased to 25%.

Karina nodded with satisfaction. She'd spent too much time in the library and torture chamber of late, neglecting some of her more pragmatic abilities. It was nice to be in the field again.

"We should follow the warlock," urged Maribella. "Kill him and that Figurist bitch. Recapture the demon."

"No." Karina fixed her with a cool, 'remember your place' look. "We shall locate and recover the Altar of Agrovesh."

"We're going to let the demon escape with the warlock? Surely that's-"

"Calm yourself, captain, before you say something you will regret over many an agonising hour."

Maribella closed her mouth with an audible clack of teeth.

"Good girl. And rest assured that we shall make our amends in the fullness of time. Once we have all three altars, our demon and our warlock shall melt away like shadows before the Breaking Dawn."

As if on cue, a distant whistle cut through the tension between them. It was Colik, waving from the balcony of a tall, thin structure that leaned precariously against its more sturdy neighbor. Karina was reminded of a drunk propped up against a wall so he wouldn't topple over while he took a piss.

"He moves quickly for an old goat," remarked Karina, rather impressed.

"Colik spent most of his younger years as a mule for the starweed gangs in the Bardruls. The starweed got the better of him in the end. Only reason a patrol was able to corner the wily bastard. He chose to sign up rather than hang."

"Is he clean now?"

Maribella smirked and took a small pouch from one of her pockets. "Strict rationing. Keeps him useful and loyal at the same time.

"You know your soldiers well."

The captain shrugged as she tucked the pouch away. "Everyone's selfish, madam. If you want a bunch of people to work together, you've just got to get all that selfishness pointed in the right direction."

"Now there's a philosophy we share, Maribella."

The captain called in the archers and led their small troop over to the leaning building. Colik greeted them at the partially collapsed entranceway.

"Find something?" asked Maribella.

"Serna did, yeah."

"Is that why she's not here?"

"Afraid so. She was careful too. Just not careful enough." He pointed inside. "Come see."

After ducking and weaving their way through a rubble-strewn antechamber, they stepped out into a once mighty hall of worship. Now it was warped and cracked, teetering on the brink of collapse. The looming figure of Agrovesh was the only upright piece of architecture in the place. One upraised arm had punched through a ceiling that now rested snugly against her head.

An ornately carved door was set into the base block of Agrovesh's statue. That would be their most likely path to the goddess' altar, yet their way was blocked by a wide stretch of dark water. A thin bridge spanned the artificial lake. Serna floated beside it. She was face down, her outline made ragged by the creatures that now tugged at her leather armor and ripped small chunks from her flesh.

"Something got her when she knelt by the water to take a look," explained Colik.

"Those somethings?" asked Karina, pointing at the feeding monstrosities. They looked like a cross between a maggot and a tadpole, a coagulation of each animal's worst features.

"No. Big ugly thing. Like an asshole on legs. Tongue of a toad. Pulled Serna in real fast, before she could even bleat."

"A mother putting food on the table for her youngsters," concluded Karina. "Any other ways into this place?"

The scout shook his head. "Collapsed long ago."

Maribella pointed at the left hand wall, the one leaning against the neighboring building. The incline was steep but the various windows and carvings offered plenty of handholds and footholds for climbing. "We could all get across there."

"How long was the creature's tongue, Colik?"

"A few meters, I reckon."

"The creature's legs, toad-like were they?"

"Weirdest fucking toad I've ever seen, but yeah, it had the basics."

"Then it can likely jump, and once we take that tongue into account, it might just pick us off that wall like flies."

"Perhaps we should return to camp," suggested Maribella, "bring some engineers so we can rig up a suspended catwalk."

Karina shook her head as she took a small glass flask from her satchel. It was filled with cloudy water. Tiny, sinuous shapes flitted about inside.

Maribella curled her upper lip in disgust. "What are those?"

"Bloodworms. A waterborne parasite that burrows through the flesh until it hits a vein. Then it injects a venom that paralyzes its victim while it feeds and lays its eggs. After hatching, the offspring eat their way out, swim off to find another host, and the whole process starts again."

Her explanation drew four horrified stares. Durk's eyes remained blank and distant, probably because the dullard had only understood a fraction of what she'd said. Colik seemed equally unmoved, and Karina put that down to the starweed. It tended to burn the emotions away with extended use.

Karina smiled. "Needless to say, don't touch the water." She unstoppered the bottle and murmured, "Command Creature" under her breath. She expressed her wishes to the Bloodworms with a single, clear mental image and passed the bottle to Durk.

"Want me to tip this into the water, madam?"

"Yes, please." She looked to the others. "Tie a rope around Durk just in case our toad decides to grab him." She pointed at Kravel. "You be the anchor."

She motioned for Maribella to follow and moved to a safe distance so they could watch the show. The creature didn't disappoint. As Durk stepped to the edge of the water, a slimy, bloated head broke the surface. A gaping, wrinkled sphincter of a mouth opened and out shot a length of jaundiced muscle that lassoed the man-at-arms around the midriff. To his credit, Durk didn't flinch. In fact, he seemed oblivious to his plight as he upended the bottle into the water, his own tongue poking out of the side of his mouth in an almost cute expression of childish concentration.

The muscle and sinew snapped taut as the creature started to pull. So did the rope tied around Durk's waist. Kravel and the two archers hauled with all their collective brawn while Colik drew his shortsword and sawed through the monster's tongue. Yellow flesh parted and the reiver tug-of-war team tumbled backwards. The creature let out an almost puppyish whimper as it drew in its injured tongue, and then gave a shiver that sent out a ring of waves to lap at the lake's edge. The bloodworms were making themselves at home. The whimpering turned to agonized squeals as the monster thrashed about in the water, trying to rid itself of its new additions. Then it fell silent as the bloodworms filled its blood with paralyzing toxins.

Your party has neutralized a Level 11 Lakestalker.
Your XP reward per party member = 15 XP
Your party currently consists of seven members.

Durk giggled like a little boy as he got to his feet. "I just leveled up."

Karina raised an eyebrow at the captain who shrugged. "Too stupid to feel fear. I believe that's what you asked for?"

"He can go to the toilet by himself, can't he?"

"Thankfully, yes."

"Glad to hear it." She strolled over to Durk and gave him a companionable pat on the arm. "Well done. Now be a good boy and walk across that bridge for us. I want to make to make sure it'll take our weight."

"Yes, madam."

"Don't want us going for a swim with those nasty bloodworms now, do we?"

"No, madam."

Durk did as he was told and the bridge, though crumbling at the edges, proved sturdy enough for even his considerable weight. They crossed one by one, just to be on the safe side, and gathered outside the ornate doorway at the statue's base. An experimental shove from Colik proved it was locked and an inspection of the mechanism showed that it was sealed with rust.

"Durk and Kravel. Bash it open."

As the men-at-arms set to pummelling the door with their warhammer and mace, Karina folded her arms and looked up at the looming visage of Agrovesh. The second altar would soon be hers, and all of this war goddess' ancient fury with it.

13

——————

[ARIX]

Arix tried to contain his frustration as Mark stopped again, took the amulet from around his neck and pressed it gently to a cracked colonnade. The polished ruby glinted in the morning light, a happy twinkle in Citadel's eye as he got to work.

"Follow this street for roughly one hundred meters and then we'll check again," concluded Citadel after a moment or two.

Mark thanked him, slipped the silver chain back over his head and tucked the amulet underneath his armor.

As he and Vari followed Mark down the desolate thoroughfare, Arix tried to breathe through his impatience. Yes, he could still abandon Mark, go after Karina, but that meant taking on a reiver army all by himself. If he died, he'd have no-one to retrieve his gear. Then there was the very real danger of Karina finding his resurrection point and clamping one of those bollocks-shrivelling collars around his neck. No, he couldn't go through *that* again. For now he would have to bide his time and get in some serious leveling up as he helped Mark with his Cockholes of Corruption quest. After that he'd demand that the warlock to help him hunt down Karina.

It pained him no end to be stuck in this virtual prison while his real life went on without him. Krissy would be weeping at his bedside. His channel fans might be holding candlelight vigils as they awaited his return to the land of the living. He consoled himself with those soft-focus images as Mark stopped at yet another crossroads and laid Citadel on the fractured cobblestones.

"The vibrations are growing quite vigorous," reported Citadel. "I liken it to the feeling I had of woodworm in my timbers."

"Poor you, Sid," commiserated Vari. "I imagine it felt similar to boneworm."

"Boneworm?" asked Mark. "What's that?"

"A parasite you can pick up from eating contaminated beef. It bores through the bone and feeds on the marrow within. The inquisitors use them to wear down a subject's will power over a period of days, even weeks. Victims feel a deep, dull ache... a constant discomfort that prevents sleep and makes it very difficult to think about anything other than mental images of creatures gnawing at your insides."

"That sounds horrifically like the experience I had," said Citadel.

"Jesus," exclaimed Mark with a shudder. "How did you get rid of them, Sid?"

"It turns out that woodworm is vulnerable to the salivary secretions of cockroaches."

"You got cockroaches to spit on you?" asked a revolted Arix.

"Yes, and it was far preferable to having my internal tenders chewed upon. By the way, we need to go right from here. Tread carefully. I believe we're close to the chasm."

"Will do," said Mark as he picked Citadel up and put the amulet back on.

As they followed the right hand street, Arix marveled at the trust Citadel was putting in Mark. If Arix was a disembodied spirit able to possess buildings, he sure as fuck wouldn't trap himself inside a single gemstone. That was the solution Citadel had offered, to migrate himself into one of the amulets Mark and Vari had brought back from a previous foray into the Barrens. Sure, it was better than lugging a brick around, but what if Mark died and fell into the very chasm they were trying to clear?

He checked himself, realizing that he was falling into the same trap Mark seemed hooked by, the blurring of the virtual and the real. Citadel was just a scripted AI like Vari. It wouldn't upset Citadel one little bit because Citadel wasn't capable of being upset at all. Yes, he could *sound* upset, he could feign all of the symptoms and eloquently express his emotional discomfiture, but it was all bollocks. He was a soulless facade just like everything else in this make-believe world.

Take the figurist, for instance. She hadn't spoken to him on this trip so far, containing her communications to the occasional impassive glance. He didn't take it personally because Vari wasn't a person. She was a sophisticated piece of code written to drag hopeless romantics like Mark into La La Land so they would max out their credit cards on lust-induced microtransactions.

He moved up to walk beside Mark and did his

best to mask his inner vitriol. "Mark, when we hit this chasm, I'll take point while you stay back with Vari. You take out anything that gets around or through me."

"Good call."

The pain of guilt etched into the furrows of Mark's/ brow. Arix suppressed the urge to tell Mark to "snap the fuck out of it". Instead, he patted Mark on the shoulder.

"I'm sure Braemar would've wanted you to look out for Vari and Sid, mate."

"Yeah," Mark agreed. "He would've."

No, he wouldn't, thought Arix, because he was a mindless muppet made of pixels and script.

It occurred to Arix that he'd have to drag Mark kicking and screaming out of this game. Perhaps if he got one of Karina's collars and learned how to use it, he could kill Mark and then keep him subdued while Karina performed the necessary rites to send them back to RL. It was a "cruel to be kind" move, but Mark would thank him in the long run.

He smiled. It reminded him of the time his dad made him smoke a full pack of cigarettes. It was the day after his eleventh birthday. He puked his guts out and the head-spins and cold sweats had lasted the rest of the day and most of the next one. And the stink was something he'd never forget. To this day, Arix felt nauseous at a mere whiff of cigarette smoke. He thought his father was a right bastard at the time. He changed his tune when his old man died of lung cancer two years later. That was why his mum had stood aside and let it happen. She knew. His dad had tried and failed many times to give up 'the ciggies' and wasn't about to let his only son go the same way.

They walked in silence up a long series of marble stairways. They crested the rise and saw the chasm stretched out before them. It was far larger than the one the corpse soldiers had crawled out of. Much of it was obscured by the ruins of the palace it had sundered. Towers had toppled to form bridges. Basilicas had been cracked open like chocolate eggs at Easter. Arix rubbed his hands together. This once mighty center of glory and government was likely to be brimful of loot. Perhaps this Chasms of Corruption thing wasn't such a bad idea after all. Arix quietly prayed to the developers for a Battleaxe of Shit-fucking-upness and then turned to the others.

"Let's do this section by section, make sure we only aggro as many mobs as we can handle."

"Good idea," agreed Mark. "We should see if we can pull a few outer mobs first so we can find out the level range we're dealing with. If this place is out of our league we might have to find a smaller chasm to grind first."

Vari sighed. "Is this some sort of arcane language the followers of The Developers speak when they don't want anyone else to understand what they're saying?"

Mark laughed. "Sorry, Vari. 'Mobs' is our name for enemies. 'Grinding' is our name for doing something over and over, like killing a lot of the same mob. Through grinding we can get strong enough to take on something bigger."

A wicked smile crawling across Vari's face. "Like if I tied Arix up then stabbed and flesh mended him a few dozen times?"

"Wo, lady!" said Arix, taking a step back. "What did I ever do to you?"

Vari winked at him. "Just joking, luv."

Mark laughed even harder as Vari strode off down the steps, headed for the chasm.

Arix shook his head. "Remember that old 90s film with Michael Douglas and Sharon Stone?"

"Basic Instinct?"

"Yeah. Beware of ice picks." He set off after Vari, leaving Mark to stew over his words.

The warlock was clearly in love with Vari and that shit just weirded Arix out. Not that it was uncommon. Guys were falling in love with virtual girls long before FIVR. It was a one-way street to nowhere good as far as Arix was concerned. He sighed, realizing that he was just missing Krissy and should go easier on Mark. He didn't know anything about Mark's RL. Krissy would've reminded him of that had she been here.

He stopped and looked back up the steps at Mark. "Sorry, geeza. That was a bit uncalled for."

Mark's expression was implacable as he walked on past. "Yes, it was."

Shit, thought Arix. He was going to have to watch his mouth if he wanted Mark's help with Karina.

He followed the warlock down the steps, making a mental note not to openly criticize Mark's weird-assed fuck-bot relationship, at least not until he was at liberty to slap some sense into the bloke.

As they entered the first of the ruptured basilicas, Arix picked up a faint scrabbling of claw against stone. His Fox Ears skill was handy like that, a passive perception boon that enhanced his hearing far beyond natural human levels. Although it was a passive skill, he was able to switch it off during non-critical times so he didn't have to deal with a steady chorus of belly-gurgles, burps and farts from his companions. It wasn't that they were particularly gassy. Everyone sounds like a leaky gas bag when you have preternatural hearing.

He motioned for Mark and Vari to stop, put a finger to his lips to quieten them, and then closed his eyes so he could better focus his Fox Ears. He picked up the scrabbling again, this time accompanied by a low hum. It was off to their right. Two more sounded up ahead, either side of the path, and a fourth one behind them.

"Mark, put your back to Vari. You've got a mob directly behind you, another to your left once you're in position. I'll take the two up front."

"Okay." Mark did as he was instructed then murmured "Second Skin". Blue light formed an ephemeral crown on his forehead then cascaded down over his body.

"If they've got eyes, I'll try out my Blinding Malaise spell," offered Vari.

"Physik Perception too, please. It's real handy," answered Mark.

"Physik Perception?" wondered Arix.

"Allows me to spot anatomical vulnerabilities," explained Vari. "For instance, to slow you down I'd slash your hamstrings. They're the most vulnerable target on your legs."

"Good to know," he answered, a tiny bit freaked out that their bot-healer was sizing him up for weak spots. Doing his best to ignore the malicious glint in her eyes, Arix turned as he heard the scrabbling grow louder. "Look alive, geezas. Here they come."

Four misshapen figures crawled into view. To call them a hybrid of insect and human was to do both categories a disservice. To Arix they looked more like insects made out of various human parts. Head a cluster of skulls. Legs and arms twisted together to form limbs. And while many of the exposed bones looked ancient and yellowed, they were all held together by still-functioning flesh. Rib-cages and pelvises had been lashed together with dried intestines and the limbs retained much of their former musculature. As the creatures moved, they disturbed clouds of flies and the entire undead amalgamation wriggled with maggots.

Mark drew his sword and it burst into super-heated life. "Vari? Weak spots?"

"Whatever's controlling these things is nestled in the very center, behind multiple layers of bone.

See those green ropey things that look like veins?"

Arix peered at the closest monster with his Buzzard Eyes ability and saw what Vari was referring to. A network of slimy wiring reached up from within, weaving down into the limbs and onto the snapping jaws of those skull clusters.

"Yup. What about them?" he asked.

"Think of them as the strings on a puppet."

"Leading to the puppet master inside?" asked Mark.

"Exactly," answered Vari. "Cut those strings. The body should fall apart and expose the master within."

"Alright," agreed Arix. "Here we go."

The monsters launched their attacks simultaneously. Judging by the precise timing, the puppet masters were able to communicate with each other noiselessly, either through some form of telepathy or body language that was indecipherable.

Arix would've preferred to use his agility to run rings around these creatures, hack and dodge until they unwrapped like chocolates to expose their gooey centers. But that would mean leaving Vari exposed to attack and he wasn't about to risk that, not after what happened to the druid.

Not that he personally cared whether bitch-bot got whacked or not, but her healing abilities were handy and her death would probably reduce Mark to a useless, emotional mess. Arix didn't have time for that.

He met the first snapping jaw with a sharp uppercut from his axe, shattering the offending mouth. Then he ducked under a bone-taloned swipe and brought his axe-blade down onto the closest shoulder joint, targeting a tight bundle of dark green tendrils. The sinuous strands parted with a spurt of chartreuse blood that spattered over him. The fluid stank like urine but did him no immediate harm.

The bot knows her stuff, thought Arix. Then again, of course she does. The programmers coded her that fucking way.

He continued to duck, weave and chop, getting the better of his two opponents until one of them tore the cuisse off his right leg with one claw and skewered his thigh with the jagged end of a broken tibia. He growled his pain through gritted teeth while he made the most of the opportunity presented to him. He pivoted, felt the creature's bone grate against his own leg bone as it was pulled off balance. He roared "Chopping Block!" and drove his axehead into the cluster of skulls that served as a head. The blade shattered the grinning ensemble and sank deep into the creature's putrid mass. The blow sent the monster into a full-body spasm. There was a sickly snowstorm of rotting flesh and splintered bone as the thing's entire bulk disintegrated.

As Arix pulled his axe free, the monster's necrotic heart came with it. At least, it looked like a heart at first glance. Arix took in the grotesque picture of its suppurating flesh and writhing tendrils, and decided it was as far from being a heart as this fucked-up game was from being real. He drove his axe down once more, this time against the ground, and watched with nauseous satisfaction as the tumorous growth split open like a rotten pumpkin.

You have slain a Level 9 Flesh Nester.
Your XP reward per party member = 30 XP
Please note that your party has 3 members.

Only three? wondered Arix. For some reason the game wasn't including Citadel as a party member.

He shrugged, gritted his teeth, and hauled the shard of bone out of his leg. Vari shouted "Mend Flesh!" behind him. He expected it to be Mark she was healing but was pleasantly surprised as a warm tingling spread across his thigh. The hole in his flesh closed up and he had his mobility back just in time for the second Flesh Nester to descend upon him. He knocked aside the first couple of attacks, trying to open up a gap so he could go for the killing blow.

"Mark!" he shouted.

"Yup?!"

"The Flesh Nester, it's behind the skull cluster!"

Mark's answer was drowned out by a thrice-repeated cry of "Sculpt Bone!" from Vari. Arix heard a loud snap in the monster before him and the sound was echoed from the creatures fighting with Mark. One after the other, three skull clusters tumbled to the ground. With its shield of bone gone, it was a much easier matter for Arix to drive his axehead into the resulting orifice and bisect the puppet master within.

You have slain a Level 9 Flesh Nester.
Your XP reward per party member = 30 XP

Squelch, hiss. Arix turned to see Mark run his second opponent through with his volcanic sword. Squelch, hiss. It reminded Arix of the time he'd taken Krissy camping in Ireland. The sausages had made that same squelch when he'd slid them onto the skewer and that same hiss as they cooked over the campfire.

Your party has slain two Level 9 Flesh Nesters.
Your XP reward per party member = 60 XP

Arix checked his stats to see how close he was to Level 7. It couldn't be far away, surely.

Arix the Damned
Class: Executioner - Level 6
Progress to Level 7 = 972/1000

"Fuck me!"

"Something wrong?" asked Mark.

"Only twenty-eight XP off my next level." He scanned the area for more Flesh Nesters or anything they could kill for the measly 28 XP he needed. Nothing obliged.

Mark gave him a wry grin. "Then maybe now's not the best time to say that I just hit Level Eight. Tier Four in Swordplay too."

"Well aren't you the clever bastard," countered Arix. "Bet your mummy's right fucking proud."

Mark flipped him the bird but was still

smiling as he did it. Arix retrieved his Tempered Cuisse and looked sadly at the broken strap. "Well, that's a bit shit."

Vari took it from him and tucked it into her backpack. "One of the villagers will fix it back at Citadel. In the meantime..."

She crossed to one of the putrid meat piles and pushed it open with her ebony staff. Without showing even the faintest hint of disgust, she reached through the mass of writhing maggots and lifted out a pair of gauntlets. The chainmail gloves were slick with gore but still gleamed like they'd only been forged yesterday. She poured their contents of maggots and liquified flesh onto the ground.

Arix felt the gorge rise in his throat. "I can't wear them things."

"Why not?" asked Vari as she flicked a few strands of something unsavory from her fingers.

"It'd be like sticking my hands in a corpse," complained Arix.

"Have you never done that?"

"Of course fucking not!"

Vari rolled her eyes, took a flask from her bag and sprinkled a few drops of its contents into the gauntlets. Steam rose for a few seconds and then dissipated as Vari passed them to Arix.

He inspected them gingerly. "What'd you just do to them?"

"Potion of Purification. Go on, try them on."

Bracing himself to feel 'slime of putrefaction' and 'wriggle of fly larvae', Arix slid his hand into the glove. It was warm, dry and fit him like a...glove.

Jaravir's Handshake

Silver-forged Gauntlets
40% reduction in damage to the hands.
10% reduction in all physical damage received.
10% increased accuracy with two-handed
weapons.
10% increased damage dealt with two-handed
weapons.

"I make a promise with a handshake
and keep it with a fist."
- Jaravir the Bloodcoin

Vari salvaged and purified a helmet in the same fashion, handing it to Mark. It was a sleek thing with nose and cheek guards, and gleamed with the same silver forging as Arix's gauntlets.

"Something else from our dearly departed Jaravir?" asked Arix.

Mark nodded and recited the stats.

Jaravir's Icy Resolve
Silver-forged Helmet
+2 Body.
+1 Mind.
40% reduction in damage to the head.
10% reduction in all physical damage received.
Contains 'Petina of Frost' to keep the wearer cool during battle.

"Either your head stays cool or you lose it."
- Jaravir the Bloodcoin

"You're playing favorites, Vari," jabbed Arix, covering his twinge of jealousy.

"He's prettier than you," reposted Vari.

Arix didn't even bother answering that. "I'll scout ahead while you two finish looting. Don't want any more nasty surprises."

"Alright thanks, Arix," answered Mark as he and Vari bent over the next pile of rotting meat.

"Don't mention it," said Arix, simply glad to get away from the smell. It was even worse than London in summer, and that was saying something.

14

[MARK]

"This is the source of the vibrations," concluded Citadel as Mark popped the amulet chain back over his neck.

Mark took in the pulsating mess before him and tried his best not to chunder his guts out. The air was fat with putrefaction. Hands, feet and heads sprouted from the glistening bulk like flowers on a bulbous cactus. Thick green cords ran through everything, making the thing look like a gigantic cancerous tumor.

You have received a Chasm of Corruption Subquest.

Pit of Despair

Destroy this legendary creature, the Root of Solmora, to cleanse this area of corruption.

"And I thought the Ghast Queen was ugly," he remarked to Vari, his voice thick with nausea.

"Those poor people," was all Vari could say in response.

He put an arm around her shoulders and pulled her close. "Who were they?"

"Reiver settlers."

Mark noticed that some of the hands and feet were much smaller than the others, having once belonged to children. "This'll happen to a lot more people if we don't stop it. Reivers and Garlanders both."

And he *could* stop it. That was the difference here. He was a nothing back in RL. He wasn't a doctor driven by the death of his father to discover a cure for cancer. Nor was he an aid worker fighting poverty in the third world. He wasn't a policeman or an eco warrior or a therapist hauling others from the swamps of their own questionable decision-making. He operated a drone forklift by day and lay on his back playing FIVR video games at night. Here in *Reign of Blood* he felt every inch the hero he'd always dreamed of being. He wasn't just some sack of meat and blood hauling himself through another meaningless day. He was a warlock, fighting corruption to save the innocent, and he had the character sheet to prove it.

Mark of Citadel
Class: Warlock - Level 8
Progress to Level 9 = 1797/3000

Body: 18
Jaravir's Icy Resolve +2 Modifier: 20
Mind: 12
Jaravir's Icy Resolve +1 Modifier: 13
Spirit: 14

HP: 144 / 144
Modified HP: 160 / 160
EP: 112 / 112

Skills
Swordplay (Tier 4)
Horse Riding (Tier 2)

Spells
Terrifying Manifestation (Tier 3)
Arcane Edge (Tier 3)
Ethereal Flesh (Tier 3)

Avalar's Leech (Tier 2)
Ivara's Ignited Exhalation (Tier 2)
Doppelganger (Tier 1)
Second Skin (Tier 3)
Forge Anew (Tier 1)
Mind of Matter (Tier 1)

Having leveled up to 8 after their encounter with the flesh nesters, he'd received a rather surprising and welcome upgrade.

As a Level 8 Warlock, you have mastery over the magic that flows through your veins.

Transference

Transfer a Tier from one spell to another.
Requires a Mind Score of 16 and the consumption of one Spell Slot.

Even with the +1 Mind from Jaravir's Icy Resolve, Mark was only going to hit Mind 15 if he applied his two new ability points there. But Transference would be a bloody useful ability once he had it, so he dropped both points onto Mind. He would either have to wait until Level 9 to make the most of Transference or find another magical item that would boost his Mind score.

Perhaps Vari could even cook up a potion that would give him a temporary +1 bonus. In the meantime he brought up his spell list.

Spell Selection

You have 7 magical spells available for selection.
You have 5 spell slots remaining.
Cunning Linguist (Cast cost = 7 EP)
Brain Leash (Cast cost = 7 EP)
Lurking Inferno (Cast cost = 8 EP)
Crippling Lethargy (Cast cost = 9 EP)
Contagious Fervor (Cast cost = 9 EP)
War Cry (Cast cost = 10 EP)
Shroud of Shadow (Cast cost = 10 EP)

Alternatively, you may wish to save your spell slots for 'found' spells.

Mark figured he should pick out a spell now and earmark one slot for a spell he might choose to deal with a situation at hand. That would still leave him three spell slots to consume for Transference should he find a way to reach Mind 16.

Shroud of Shadow

The caster becomes invisible to the direct gaze of

the naked eye. The warlock can be seen in peripheral vision but details will be blurred.

Tier 1: Lasts for up to 30 seconds. Upon taking damage, the caster becomes visible once more.

"My wife wished I would disappear one day, so I did."
- Zevryn the Everborn

That sounded pretty bloody useful to Mark so he didn't bother investigating any further. He slotted Shroud of Shadow into place.

"What are you smiling about?" asked Vari.

"I'm a Level Eight Warlock now *and* I have a new spell to try it."

"I'm glad you can find something to smile about when faced with a horror like this."

Mark looked at her for a long moment, trying to work out if she was having a go at him. From his ex-wife, that comment would've been fair dripping with passive aggression. Vari looked up at him, wide-eyed and sincere.

"You really mean that, don't you?"

Vari nodded. "Of course I do. You've died in so many horrible ways. You've seen friends killed before your eyes. You've battled creatures that look like they've crawled straight out of an inquisitor's worst nightmare. Yet here you are, facing it all with a smile. You're either very brave or slightly crazy. Either way works for me."

Mark pulled Vari close, channeling his sudden love surge down through his arms and into a tight squeeze.

"Mark?"

"Yes?"

"Can't breathe."

"Oops, sorry." He relaxed his arms. "The helmet's boosted me to Body Twenty. Still getting used to it."

Mark's amulet coughed politely. "At the risk of interrupting this lovely yet somewhat macabre moment," said Citadel, "do we have a plan for destroying this abomination?"

Mark scanned his surroundings until he spotted Arix. The executioner was perched on the opposite wall now, peering down into the chasm. "We'll see what Arix has to say when he gets back, but I'm thinking that we bring the roof down on this thing." He pointed up at the remains of the basilica above them. While the dome looked like a partially eaten Easter egg, there was still enough masonry to crush the horror below them into a putrid pulp. "Arix climbs like a monkey so we'll see if he's prepared to clamber up there with one of Calder's explosives. How many did you bring, Vari?"

"Three."

"Okay, cool." He touched his fingers to the amulet. "Sid, would you be able to sense the weak spots around here?"

"I could certainly give it a try."

Mark took the amulet from his neck, crouched down and pressed it to the stone at his feet. The ruby sparkled for a moment. Citadel was exercising his powers of perception.

"Yes, there are stress fractures near where Arix is now. Calder's explosive should be enough to collapse that portion of the basilica. However, the angle of the falling rock will only partially crush the Root of Solmora. For complete obliteration, I would suggest blowing the base of that teetering goddess statue nearby, and also the colonnade across the way. The latter would bring down another sizeable portion of the roof."

A thin bridge crossed the chasm to the colonnade in question. It looked none too stable to Mark. "Will that bridge hold me?"

"Yes, although it'll collapse when the colonnade goes. We would have to find another way back as you are not endowed with Arix's rather remarkable climbing abilities. Never fear though, I will be able to feel the terrain out ahead of you, identify the correct passageways."

"Sorry, Sid, but you're not coming with me." He removed the amulet and placed it over a surprised Vari's head. "I'll reset my spawn point over this side." He unbuckled his sheath and handed Volcanic Bastard to Vari as well. "Worst case scenario, I'll die and resurrect nearby, but I can't risk you getting scooped up by someone or something before I get back to you."

"Might I remind you that I can transfer myself through architecture?"

"I know, but you'd have to be touching the architecture first, and I can imagine far too many scenarios where that isn't going to be possible. I'd feel much better if you were with Vari for this."

"You clearly have a more active imagination than I do, but I shall bow to your fanciful logic this time."

"Thanks, Sid."

Vari buckled Volcanic Bastard to her back and then handed Mark her dagger. "Not much good to you in a fight, even with Arcane Edge, but you could always stab yourself in the throat with it."

Mark gave her a wry grin. "Your kindness is unrivalled, my lady."

Vari remained solemn. "Whatever it takes for you to come back to me."

Mark cupped her face in his hands and kissed her on the lips. Then he pressed his forehead to hers so that her two eyes became one, like a cute cyclops.

"Then make sure you're safe so there's still a beautiful lady for me to come back to."

"On that note," said Vari as she gently pushed him away, "I'm not sure leaving me with Arix is what I would call safe."

"I shall be here too," offered Citadel.

"True, and thank you, Sid. No offense though, but Arix is a little more corporeal than you are and therefore more dangerous."

"Point taken."

"What is it about Arix that worries you, Vari?" asked Mark.

He felt like he already knew the answer. It was clear that Arix thought of Vari as an NPC, nothing more. Just a bunch of code and dialogue scripts. He didn't know this world yet, not like Mark did. Coupled with the fact that Arix was more of a hardcore gamer than a roleplayer, it meant that the executioner wasn't going to change his attitude anytime soon. Still, he wanted to hear what Vari had to say before he jumped in with his own opinions. He stayed quiet while she formulated the right words.

"It's hard to explain," began Vari, "but it's like he thinks I'm no different to the monsters, the 'mobs' as you call them. And it's not personal, I know that much. He was the same with Braemar and with the villagers back at Citadel. I watched him when he was exploring the place and talking to people. He didn't really chat to the villagers like you or I would. His manner was...I'm not sure how to explain it."

"He asked very direct questions and then cut the conversation short as soon as he found out what he needed to know?"

"You heard him too?"

"Yes, and I've also seen that kind of behavior before."

He's the sort of gamer who just wants the quest brief info and clicks through everything else. As much as he wanted to, Mark couldn't think of a way to share this knowledge with Vari and Citadel, not without depicting *Reign of Blood* as the game it actually was.

"I have to concur with Vari's observations," said Citadel. "He asked me many questions about the fortress and Garland, and did exactly as you say, cut my answers short and moved onto the next question. It was more of an interrogation than a conversation. To be frank, I find the man quite unnerving."

"I felt the difference between you and him straight away, Mark," Vari continued. "You actually want to connect with people."

"I second that," added Citadel. "You're really quite engaging, if I may be so bold."

"Thank you, Sid." Mark felt genuinely touched by that.

"Yes, and Braemar felt it too. Even Dayna, though she seemed determined to make it an uphill battle for you."

Mark nodded sadly. "We had enough of a connection to dislike each other, so I get what you're saying."

Vari looked at the executioner on the other side of the chasm. He hadn't moved, seeming content to rest and observe the pulsating mass below. "Arix seems to neither like me nor dislike me. Yes, he teases and provokes, but it's like he's playing with a toy rather than a person. I'm with Sid. He unnerves me. He lacks any regard for anyone but himself and you. The rest of us…"

She left the sentence unfinished but Mark knew where she was going with it. Vari was worried that Arix would turn on her and Citadel as soon as it made sense for him to do so. And she was probably right. It would be nothing for Arix to kill Vari and destroy Citadel. He'd seen plenty of instances where players had slaughtered whole villages of NPCs for the sheer brutal 'fun' of it.

In fact, many a FIVR had become famous by allowing you to play the bad guy, mowing down civilians with a car or machine gun like they were pins in a bowling alley. He'd been guilty of it himself, gunning down cops in a mall to try for a 'berzerk kill streak' or flattening a line of chanting hari krishnas with his stolen car to complete the relevant achievement. That part of gaming hadn't changed since Space Invaders. Virtual characters were there for the gamer's entertainment, nothing more.

But here, Mark could feel the difference. He didn't know how, but Vari felt truly alive to him. So did Citadel, Calder and everyone else he'd met here in *Reign of Blood*. Even the reivers. Yes, they had killed him and he had killed them, but it was far deeper than shooting space invaders. He wished Arix could see that, would take a moment to look more closely at this world. His mother had told him, almost every day, that he was too sensitive, a dreamer, an 'over thinker' who would stress himself into an early grave. His ex-wife had echoed that sentiment. Maybe, or maybe he could just feel things that other people couldn't. There was something intuitively alive about this virtual world, more than any other he'd experienced, and he sorely wanted Arix to understand that.

"This is going to sound strange, guys, especially since we're having this conversation beside that thing." He jerked his thumb at the monstrosity below. "Do you remember your childhood?"

Vari raised a dark eyebrow at him but it was Citadel who spoke up first. "In fact, I do remember a few bits and pieces. It's patchy, but I recall growing up in Garland, in a small village called Oakdale. My parents grew wheat for the local flour mill. I had a sister." His voice took on the slightest tremor. "She drowned in the river that ran through our farm."

"I'm really sorry to hear that, Sid."

"Thank you, Mark."

"So how did you go from being a wheat farmer to a warlock?"

"Head too high in the clouds to feel the dirt under his feet. I believe my father used to say that. Or perhaps my mother? I don't know. Neither do I recall how I came to live in the Citadel.

Ivara of the Dancing flame was the resident warlock at the time. Eccentric woman. I must have wandered there somehow and she took me under her wing."

Mark nodded in recognition. It sounded all very plausible, and all too like something a narrative designer would write into a character profile, so he decided to try something.

"Okay, you totally don't have to answer this, but here goes." He took a deep breath and exhaled slowly, trying to cool the heat of embarrassment that was fast spreading across his face. "Who was the first girl you fantasized about while masturbating?"

"Mark!" It was the first time Mark had seen Vari look genuinely shocked. It was a seriously endearing expression.

Citadel laughed. "It's alright, and I think I see the point of the question. Sorting reality from illusion are we Mark?"

"Trying to, yes Sid."

"In that case, *his* name was Albert. He had beautifully smooth skin that tanned to a luscious gold in the summer, a mane of gorgeous blond curls, an adorable lopsided smile and buttocks that could crack walnuts."

"Right, thank you, Sid."

"My pleasure, actually. I haven't thought of him in decades. I should frolic with that memory more often."

"Did you and he…"

"No, alas not. I quickly learned to despise the term 'just friends' with a passion."

"Yeah, it's not one of my favorites either, Sid."

"I gave a boy a blow job in return for a puppy," blurted Vari.

"What?!" exclaimed Mark and Citadel at the same time.

"She was a really cute puppy," she added, looking suitably abashed. "We were inseparable for six years, she and I. I buried her a few days before I was captured by the reivers. Dogpox. If she'd been alive that day, those reivers wouldn't have got anywhere near us. Tulip's nose was amazing, even for a dog, and reivers aren't renowned for their cleanliness."

"And the boy?"

Vari shrugged. "I caught him doing another puppy trade the next day, so I put highland senna in his morning goat's milk. Perhaps a little bit too much. The poor boy barely left the privy for two days."

Mark grinned. "Interested in alchemy from an early age, were we?"

"Of course," said Vari with a wry smile on her dark lips.

Mark folded his arms and looked across the chasm at Arix. He was on his way back to them, crawling across the inside of the basilica like a spider. The stories Citadel and Vari had shared wouldn't prove a thing to the executioner. This was just a game to him and he would dismiss it all as a far more intuitive narrative system than most, but a system all the same. Mark wasn't buying it. He'd read a bit about developments in AI, about machine learning. Google's AlphaZero beat the world's best chess computer after teaching itself to play chess for a mere four hours. Therefore, it was possible that Citadel, Vari and everyone else in *Reign of Blood* had lived their entire virtual lives in a matter of weeks of processing time. Days even. His mind boggled at the complexity of a system like that. It was no wonder the *Reign of Blood* developers had kept this version of their game a secret. It was a breakthrough that would be copied by every big game company in the world once it went public.

And if Citadel end Vari had indeed lived complete lives within this virtual environment, had lived, loved and lost just like people in RL, there was no reason to treat them any different. Their flesh and blood was made out of digits instead of cells but that was all that set them apart from Arix. In fact, he and Arix weren't all that different right now either. Though his body felt real, and certainly hurt like it was real, it was just a digital representation interacting with his own neural network.

It was at this point Mark wished he'd read more than the first chapter of that book on Cartesian Philosophy. Cogito, ergo sum. "I think, therefore I am." If it was good enough for Descartes, it was good enough for Vari and Citadel. Arix could go fuck himself.

"Okay, my friends, here's what we do," announced Mark. "We cleanse this chasm. Then we help Arix hunt down his inquisitor and make her send him home before he does this world of ours a serious mischief. In the meantime, we trust him about as far as we can throw him."

"I'd like to throw him into the chasm with that thing," said Vari with a wicked smile.

"He'd just resurrect and demand that we help him retrieve his gear."

"I know," she shrugged. "But it'd still be worth it."

Mark laughed as he gestured for Vari to give Citadel and Volcanic Bastard back to him. She obliged, clearly happy to be relieved of the dual responsibility.

"You guys are with me. Sid, are we okay to forget that statue over here? Will the roof fall be enough without it?"

"If you're happy to tidy up with Ivara's Ignited Exhalation and Volcanic Bastard," Citadel supposed.

"With you two helping me, no problem."

It was Vari's turn to give him a rib-cracking hug. Mark smiled to himself as he luxuriated in her embrace. He had no proof. Everything he'd just theorized was just that, a bunch of theories. But it felt real and right, and that's all that mattered to him now. He didn't care if he stayed in a coma for the rest of his days in RL. Maybe, one day, they'd pull the plug on him or he'd die of some hospital infection. In RL he was just as likely to die of cancer or a car crash anyway. At least here he could make something of whatever life he had left to him.

In here, he could be alive.

15

[KARINA]

The descent into the temple's bowels proved to be an intestinal labyrinth of twists and turns.

The journey left Karina doubly glad of Maribella's choice of scout. Colik had an almost supernatural knack for picking out subtleties in architecture, air movement and water flow. It was a faultless performance, marred only by the loss of Kravel. For all his skills of concentration and deduction, Colik was a little neglectful of his companions. He didn't think to point out the pressure plate that he intuitively avoided until Kravel stomped on it with his own oversized boot. The floor beneath the man-at-arms parted, dropping him several meters onto a bed of iron spikes. His meaty bulk, having served Karina so admirably as a human shield, worked against Kravel this time. His own weight drove the spikes through both armor and flesh, leaving him impaled and squealing like a stuck pig.

To the captain's credit, the woman didn't hesitate. She ordered Tris to put an arrow through Kravel's throat. It saved them all from the shrill screams and mercifully hastened Kravel's death. Karina decided she needed to deter Colik from further negligence by subjecting him to a bit of Brain Seeding. It was a technique she'd gained at Level 4.

Seed of Doubt

The caster may plant a vivid false memory in the subject's mind, one that causes compulsive rumination and exaggerates the associated emotions.

Tier 3: The memory causes a strong involuntary physical response in the subject, such as terror or euphoria.

"Rumination is the mill that grinds us into dust."
- Kerisk Bloodfinger

She glared into his bloodshot eyes and planted a memory of a particularly creative torture. It involved honey, fire ants, and a particularly sensitive orifice. Colik's face took on a taut cast and he could no longer look Karina in the eyes. But it had the desired effect. He pointed out every potential hazard from then on with almost painful eagerness.

Colik's fearful guidance eventually brought them to an immense underground chamber. Luminescent fungi lit the place with a pallid hue. The walls were decorated with bones and skulls, formed into swirling patterns of conflict and violence. Agrovesh presided over it all from the far end of the chamber, fierce and foreboding. At her feet sat an altar stained almost black with centuries of sacrificial blood.

Karina ordered the others to wait and muttered, "Sparks of Sentience". Low cunning twinkled among the luminescence. Camouflaged predators lay in wait.

"Captain. We have company. Seven creatures, hiding among the fungus."

Maribella acknowledged the intel with a nod and ordered the archers to her flanks. Tris and Dez readied their bows as the captain took it upon herself to be the bait. Sword in hand, she moved towards the altar with the grace of a cat stalking an unwitting rat.

The chamber's denizens reacted before Maribella got within a few meters of her target, bursting from their fungal hideaways in a shower of spores. At first glance, Karina took them for moths. Their velvety wings and fluffy abdomens gave that impression, but the likeness ended in long rows of jagged teeth and scythe-like claws.

They were quick too, but not as quick as Tris and Dez. Arms became a blur as the archers fired arrow after arrow in quick succession, intercepting each creature before it could lay a talon on their captain. The animals shrieked and fell to the stones where Maribella proceeded to separate heads from thoraxes with surgical precision.

Your party has slain seven Level 3 Mushraptors.
Your XP reward per party member = 35 XP
Your party currently consists of six members.

Silence fell as Tris and Dez advanced into the chamber, arrows nocked, their wary eyes searching. Had the mushraptors made a sound as they plummeted from the ceiling, the archers might have stood a chance. But clearly the monsters had learned from the sacrifice of their fellow broodlings. They came down like a velvet curtain, unfurling their wings at the last moment to convert their falls into swoops so sharp and low that Karina heard the dry shriek of their claws scraping across the stone floor. Dez got one arrow away before the mushraptor hit him with claws fully extended. He went down hard, his assailant latched to his chest. The mushraptor ripped the bow from him with two claws while digging in deep with its remaining four. Teeth closed around his throat, silencing his screams with a crunch and a gout of blood. Tris did a little better, felling two mushraptors in mid-swoop before a third took her legs out from under her. The archer's head hit the stones hard enough to knock her out. Unconsciousness spared the tender agonies of being torn limb from limb.

Captain Maribella fared the best, ducking, diving and rolling her way across the chamber. Karina watched with quiet fascination as the warrior woman maintained a steady pattern of dodge and counterattack. She seemed to have a knack for judging the creatures' flight patterns, putting herself between the lines and then cutting those lines with a swift strike of her sword. Several flying monstrosities tumbled to the ground before one got lucky, raking Maribella across the back of the legs with its claws. The captain crashed to the ground, and when she tried to stand it was clear that the attack had severed one of her hamstrings.

"Durk. Go get her."

The man-at-arms saluted, his long face split by a grin of innocent pride, and charged into the fray. He was an easy target for the Mushraptors but his armor proved impervious to their talons. Keeping his head down to protect his face, he scooped the captain up like she was no heavier than a child. In moments he was back, and as a group they retreated from the chamber and slammed the heavy door behind them.

Your party has slain six Level 3 Mushraptors.
Your XP reward per party member = 45 XP
Your party currently consists of four members.

Karina knelt beside Maribella and inspected her leg wound. The gash was already knitting together at the corners.

"What's your tier in Vigorous Healing, Captain?"

"Four."

"Then you'll be right as rain by the time we've had lunch."

"Lunch," grinned Durk. "Good idea, madam."

Karina shrugged. "It'll give me time to consider our options. We're not leaving without that altar."

"I'll eat on the go then," suggested Colik as he took a strap of dried meat out of his pack. "See if I can find us another way in, one that those beasties won't be expecting."

"Thank you, Colik. That would be splendid."

Colik scampered off down the passageway. Beside them Durk was already tucking into his rations with childish gusto. Karina had allowed him to recover and keep Kravel's share, so there was plenty to go around. She sat down beside Maribella and helped the woman remove her backpack. They ate together to the sounds of Durk's noisy chewing and gulping.

Karina mulled over the options in her mind. They could return to their main camp for reinforcements and take the chamber by force. Her men-at-arms could draw the creatures into attacking while her archers picked them off from the relative safety of the arched doorway. Yet that would all take time, and she wasn't sure that time was on her side. The demon knew she was after the altars and might have enlisted the warlock's help in tracking them down first. She had the advantage still, having studied the historical tomes and deduced where in this dead city the altars might reside. But the demon could always follow her trail. Out here they were sitting ducks to the likes of him. No. They needed to clear the chamber, find all of the entrances, and hold them while Colik went back to the camp.

They would still need reinforcements even to achieve that much, but Karina was confident she could manage with the materials at hand. She took the silver flask from her backpack and gave it a shake.

"Please tell me that's whisky, madam," said Maribella.

Karina smiled and shook her head. "Something far more potent."

"Alchemy?"

"Child's play. This is a far more mature art. It was developed right here in the Barrens, when this civilization was in its prime. This little tincture is the product of Biomancy."

"What does it do?"

"You're going to find out first hand."

The captain's jaw tightened with fear. "Sorry, madam, but I'd rather just wait for this leg to heal and try-"

"Seed of Doubt." Karina's voice was as quiet as an assassin's knife. Maribella stiffened as the spell sank its claws deep into her mind. "Let me explain just how sorry you will be, *Maribella*." She pushed the ripe seed deep into the captain's mind, tucking it into a fertile bed of nightmares.

Maribella was a woman who prized her strength and speed above all else. She reveled in the power of her body, so that's what Karina took away from her. She coaxed the seed to sprout and bloom into a flower of putrid flesh and numbing incapacity. Leprosy was rare among the empire's populace, having been studied and controlled by the inquisitors long ago. But it was still used for special prisoners, of a political nature usually, whose iconic images demanded a little degradation.

With a smile, Karina felt Maribella's mind draw back in horror from her own body as she watched it rot and disintegrate in her mind's eye. Once the inquisitor was sure the terror had taken firm root in Maribella's subconscious, Karina returned to herself and proffered the tincture to the now shivering captain.

"If you embrace your evolution, Captain,

those fetid dreams need never become your reality. Glory to the Great."

"Glory to the Great," echoed Durk between chews.

Karina gave him a speculative look, studying his eyes for any signs of intelligence. They were as blank as polished stones. His response had been one of habit rather than understanding. She gave him a 'proud teacher' smile and almost laughed at his foolishly chuffed grin. Whether physical or psychological, something had happened to Durk's mind, arresting his development. Battle trauma could do that sometimes. Then again, she really didn't need to know the reason. He was perfect the way he was, a useful and unquestioning tool.

For a moment she considered giving him the biomantic formula instead. He would be easier to command post-transformation, less likely to turn on her than the clever Captain Maribella. Then again, she doubted Durk could find his way out of a privy unless the door was labeled with a pretty picture. She didn't fancy having to be in that chamber with him, micromanaging his every move. She needed a loyal minion, not a dull puppet.

Maribella reached out for the flask with a trembling hand but Karina shook her head.

"Finish your lunch and focus on healing that leg. You'll need all of your strength for the transformation ahead."

The captain shuddered and a bead of sweat trickled down her pale brow, sliding along her scars like a barge negotiating a network of rivers. "It's going to hurt like fuck, isn't it?"

"A little bitterness makes victory all the sweeter, don't you agree?"

Judging by the look in Maribella's eyes, clearly not, but Karina honestly didn't give a shit.

16

[ARIX]

Arix leaped into the air as the ledge exploded into silicon shrapnel. He soared through the billowing dust, landed on the next balcony, performed a perfect roll and sprinted for the next ledge.

An avalanche of fractured masonry chased him around the curvature of the basilica as he jumped from platform to pillar top to statue. He stopped for a moment to catch his breath and glanced back at the damage he'd wrought.

Roof tiles rapidly gave way to sky as the once impressive structure tumbled into the chasm. Stonework and gravel struck the putrid mass of flesh below, sending up spouts of viscera into the air. Arix noticed a few warped figures stumbling across their queen's bulk, their boney claws scrabbling for purchase on the leviathan's oozing skin.

He launched himself forward as his former vantage point was lost to another cascade of stone. Ahead of him, at the other end of the chasm, a second explosion splintered the base of a mighty colonnade. It toppled and added its crushing weight to the ruinous deluge, bringing another hefty chunk of roof with it. With the basilica now collapsing both behind and in front, Arix had precious little room left to maneuver.

"Could've waited just a few more secs, Mark," he muttered to himself. "I'm not fucking Spiderman."

With gritted teeth, Arix blocked out everything else and focused purely on timing and distance. He'd played many a platformer in his day so this wasn't anything new, but if he put just one foot wrong now, he'd be right royally fucked. He ledge-hopped twice more and then began his descent, a series of drops that would take him to where Mark and the others were sheltering from the fallout. He landed and lunged into the alcove just as a mosaic the size of an SUV hit the attached balcony and reduced it to a cloud of jagged pebbles.

His roll stopped at the toe of Mark's boots. He lay on his back and thrust out his hand.

"A little help?"

Mark gave a faint smile as he took the proffered hand and hauled Arix onto his feet. Arix caught Vari's eye but the figurist met his gaze with a cold, impassive look. It figured. She probably didn't have a script for this situation so was falling back on her default settings. Say nothing. Stare blankly.

Arix loaded his crossbow as he read his latest notifications.

You have performed a remarkable feat of Agility.
Your personal XP reward = 30 XP

Your Acrobatics ability has increased to Tier 3.

He nodded with satisfaction and lined up the first Flesh Nester as its hazy silhouette appeared through the dust.

"Hey Mark, had we blown that statue as well, we wouldn't be facing this cleanup job," he pointed out. "Just saying."

"Yup, maybe," answered Mark as he drew his sword and brightened their gloomy hidey hole with firelight. "But let's just concentrate on killing these bastards, shall we?"

Arix leveled his crossbow at the approaching monster. He shattered a clacking skull with the first bolt and sent the second plunging through the decaying flesh to skewer the puppet master beneath. The creature shivered and stumbled, giving Mark the opening he needed to drive Volcanic Bastard into the bolt wound and cook the monster from the inside out. The amalgam of carcasses slumped to the floor and Mark sent it all tumbling into the chasm with a shove of his boot.

Your party has slain a Level 9 Flesh Nester.
Your XP reward per party member = 30 XP

"Mark?" Vari called out.
"Yup?"
"Save the next one for me."
"Righto."
Arix raised an eyebrow at Vari who ignored him. He shrugged it off and busied himself with reloading his crossbow. He'd just put the second bolt in place when another flesh nester made its

appearance. He repeated the process, shattering one of the protective skulls with the first bolt, stunning the flesh nester with the next. Mark followed up as before, giving the nestled monstrosity the hot poker treatment. This time he refrained from kicking the dead lump off the ledge. Instead, he offered the mound of carrion to Vari like a magician presenting a magic trick. The Figurist smiled and murmured "Puppeteer" under her breath.

Arix flinched and raised his axe as the flesh nester lurched to its 'feet'. He relaxed again as the notification rolled in.

Your party has slain a Level 9 Flesh Nester.
Your XP reward per party member = 30 XP

Okay, so this was new. The figurist could control dead bodies, or anything made out of dead flesh, it seemed. Just as well, because their next attackers came as a pair. He and Mark concentrated on their shooting and skewering routine with one of them while Vari's puppet and its opponent proceeded to tear each other to pieces. By the time he and Mark had finished with theirs, Vari had ripped her foe from its rotten refuge.

Arix looked at the shivering blob of life with

open disgust before he chopped it in half with his axe.

Your party has slain two Level 9 Flesh Nesters.
Your XP reward per party member = 60 XP

Arix wiped his axe head clean and turned to Mark. "Them devs went all out with the aesthetics when they designed this quest line," he said with a smile.

"I don't think the devs had a hand in it," argued Mark.

"Are you saying this shit's procedural?"

"Yeah, but not in the normal sense."

"What other sense is there?"

Mark sighed. The warlock clearly had something on his mind.

"Out with it, man. What do you think you know that I don't?"

"Boys," interrupted Vari, "could we please discuss this away from the mortified crowds?"

She pointed at a new pair of flesh nesters crawling up over the edge. Since Arix had been too busy chatting to load his crossbow, he shouted "Righteous Fury!" and let rip on his chosen opponent with his axe. To his left, Mark shouted "Arcane Edge!" and "Second Skin!" in quick succession before hacking away at the second creature with Volcanic Bastard. A little pain and a couple of Mend Flesh spells later and they were standing over two piles of offal that they happily shoved off the edge.

Your party has slain two Level 9 Flesh Nesters.
Your XP reward per party member = 60 XP

Arix looked down into the chasm and saw the source of this cadaverous onslaught. While most of the Corpse Queen was dead and buried under tons of rubble, a small portion of it remained and was squeezing another morbid horror out of something that looked like a leprous anus.

"Fuck. We missed a bit. Right where that statue would've fallen too. Why didn't you-"

"Let us not waste your precious blood whilst we weep over spilled milk," interrupted Citadel, his ruby flaring brightly. "I would recommend we now proceed as I previously recommended?"

"What previous recommendation?" Arix eyed the others with open suspicion. "You lot been talking behind my back?"

Mark did a bad job of looking innocent. "We did some forward planning while you were climbing about."

"Indeed," confirmed Citadel. "To prevent further division of the party, I proposed that Mark forgo the third explosion in favor of clearing up any dregs with his Ignited Breath ability."

Arix gave a grudging nod. "Worked well enough with them corpse soldiers. Got any rope?"

"Twenty meters," answered Vari, "in my pack."

"Then let's get down there. I'll mind the kids while you fire up the barbeque."

Vari sighed. "Is it fun for you to be completely incomprehensible, Arix?"

"Just have to be smart enough to know what I'm saying, luv."

He caught the coil of rope that she threw at his face, tied it to the only surviving statue, and snapped off a smug salute at the Figurist before abseiling into the pit. On the way down he chuckled to himself. Vari was getting under his skin and only real people were allowed to do that. If he wasn't careful, he'd start falling into Mark's trap. Hate can drag you into madness just as effectively as love can.

His feet sank into the squelching flesh of the Corpse Queen's body, making him extremely glad of his boots. He tangled with the freshly born flesh nester until Mark joined him. Together they put the thing down.

Your party has slain a Level 9 Flesh Nester.
Your XP reward per party member = 30 XP

Mark whispered "Ignited Exhalation" and proceeded to breathe fire all over the show. Arix noted with approval that he aimed for fatty deposits, the most likely spots to catch fire and spread the flames. The warlock repeated his spell until he'd exhausted his EP reserves and then began to attack the mob-generating sphincter with his simmering sword in a bid to cauterize it shut.

In the meantime, Arix fended off a couple of flesh nesters that had survived the rockfall. He sundered one with Chopping Block before getting stabbed through the side with a shard of bone. Within seconds, he heard "Mend Flesh!" echo throughout the chasm. He looked up to see Vari's dark face poking over the edge.

He should've felt grateful, he supposed, but then the NPC was just doing what she was programmed to do. It would've been like thanking his apartment's central heating for warming the bathroom floor. He missed that bathroom with its shiny copper taps and half-pearl tiling. He and Krissy had 'christened' the new shower only a couple of months back. Now here he was, spattered in stinking bodily fluids, chopping the shit out of a crawling coagulation of cadavers. Arix decided then and there that he would swear off *Reign of Blood* and every other dark fantasy or survival horror FIVRrpg when this was all over. He would focus on nice, clean racing and space games instead.

He finished his assailant off with another Chopping Block and then turned to Mark.

Your party has slain two Level 9 Flesh Nesters.
Your XP reward per party member = 60 XP

"You done?"

In that moment the warlock looked quite striking, his black armor in stark contrast to a backdrop of roaring flames, volcanic sword in hand and firelight flickering off his shining helm. Arix wished for the in-game snapshot function then. It seemed to have been disabled along with streaming and logoff. A crying shame. It was a seriously postable moment.

"Yup!" shouted Mark. "Let's move before the whole place goes up."

Arix followed Mark up the rope and tried to ignore the stench of burning flesh wafting up from below. It brought out some rather mixed sensations and thoughts. Salivating over a nicely seared steak whilst also imagining what it would be like to eat the carbonized fat off an old barbeque. He did his best to block out both thoughts and kept on climbing.

The notifications rolled in just as he hauled himself up over the chasm's edge.

Congratulations!
Your party has destroyed a Legendary creature, the Root of Solmora.
Your XP reward per party member = 300 XP

You have completed the Pit of Despair Subquest.
Destroy the Root of Solmora to cleanse this area of corruption.
Your XP reward per party member = 50 XP

A clump of neurons fired in Arix's head and released a memory from captivity. "Hey guys?"

"Yup?" acknowledged Mark.

"Just remembered where I've heard the name Solmora before. Inquisitor Karina mentioned it.

One of the altars she's after, it had something to do with this Solmora bint."

"That means the Altar of Solmora could be close by," suggested Vari. "Sid? If there was a hidden chamber around here, do you think you could find it?"

"I shall give it a whirl," answered Citadel.

Mark took the amulet off and placed it against the ground. The ruby twinkled as Citadel reached out into the surrounding structures. After a few minutes, Citadel gave a chuckle.

"It seems we're in luck."

"You found it?" asked Arix.

He felt a thrill of anticipation tingle through his body. He wasn't interested in the altar but he was definitely interested in what the altar could do for him. It was the bait he needed to trap an inquisitor.

"There is indeed a chamber," answered Citadel.

"Where?" pressed Arix.

"At the far end of the chasm."

His heart sank. "Shit. Buried underneath tons of rubble now, right?"

"The main entrance is, yes. There's another way in. It appears to be a chute of some kind that runs on a steady decline from the chamber into the lower portion of the pit."

"You know what that sounds like to me?" ventured Vari.

"A disposal chute of some kind?" wondered Citadel.

"Yes." She gestured towards the chasm. "No prizes for guessing what they were disposing of."

"Are we talking human sacrifice here?" asked Mark with disgust.

Arix nodded. "Yeah, that would make a nasty kind of sense. This thing was too big to be made up of a few reiver settlers. It's been growing here for a long time, since this city was supposedly alive and kicking."

"Which would mean that the Root of Solmora was older than the cataclysm that laid this place to waste?" wondered Vari.

Arix knew there was no such thing as the cataclysm or the so-called civilization that had inhabited the Barrens. It was all back story. The devs had created a tract of ruins, not a city. Still, it was an NPC's job to help suspend disbelief and he knew there was no point in trying to disillusion her. About as useful as trying to teach a dog to speak English.

"I would say so," he answered.

"Arix." Vari fixed him with an intent gaze. "Do you think Karina is trying to control these things? Could the altars turn the chasms into a tool that the reivers could use?"

He hadn't thought about it, but it made sense. "Maybe, yeah." Not that he really gave a shit what happened to this world once he got Karina to send him and Mark home. But it also made sense to play along so that Vari and Sid would remain cooperative. "All the more reason to find the Altar of Solmora before she does. Then we can lay a trap and nab her when she turns up to claim it."

"Let's do it," agreed Mark.

Hold on a sec, thought Arix. That was a bit too fucking easy. "What about this whole Chasm of Corruption quest? I thought you was all about finishing it."

Mark shrugged. "Maybe we're killing two birds with one stone here. If Vari's right, and the altars can control things like the Root of Solmora, then they could also be the answer to shutting down the corruption for good."

Arix grinned. Looked like things were going his way. "It's all pie in the sky until we have the Altar of Solmora."

"Yup," agreed Mark. "So let's head back to

Citadel, clean up, and plan our next move."

"Lead the way, warlock."

He and Vari trailed Mark as they followed Citadel's directions to the waypoint. Vari pointedly ignored him, but that was just fine with Arix. Mark's illusions were keeping him here so it was Arix's duty to disillusion him, for his own good. It was time to plan Vari's murder.

17

Karina ordered for Durk to bind the naked captain from head to foot. Maribella almost broke free during the transformation, before the pain subsided enough for her to regain some semblance of self control. Eventually the agony and terror drained from the captain's eyes, replaced by the steely glint of anger.

The inquisitor allowed herself a moment of pride. Maribella was strong, tempered by pain and a life of fighting. As long as her anger was directed at the appropriate targets, she'd be a fine weapon in Karina's arsenal.

You have successfully created a Level 6 Lycanthrope.
Your XP reward = 120 XP
Please note that your XP is not shared with your current party due to prior preparation of the Lycanthropic Formula.

She motioned for Durk to untie the captain's bonds. The soldier did so without even a hint of wariness, a foolish attitude considering the deadly nature of the beast he was unwrapping.

Maribella lay there for a moment, panting away the dregs of her trauma, her long tongue dangling over pointed teeth. Then she got to her feet and looked down at her fur-clad body with a mixture of wonder and disgust.

"My monthly waxing bill has just gone through the fucking roof."

Karina indulged her with a smile. "No need for that. You'll be able to transform back any time. Such is the power of lycanthropy. Tissue, bones and organs, they're all at your command now."

"Will it be the same each time?" The captain's words were thick and slurred as she struggled to adjust to the new configurations of her mouth.

"Think of it as growing pains."

Maribella flexed her claws. "Then I'll stay like this for a bit. Not keen to go through that again just yet."

"Wise choice, captain. And besides, you'll want to get the measure of your new body first."

Maribella performed a languorous stretch and then looked to the chamber door. "Yeah, got a bit of nervous tension to work off."

Karina clicked her fingers in Durk's face to get his attention. The man had been staring and gaping like a child in a lollie shop. He blinked and looked at Karina with those blank eyes of his.

"Yes, madam?"

"Get the door for the good captain, will you?"

"Yes, madam."

"Fucking balls of shit, what is that?!" The exclamation came from Colik at the end of the passage.

"Careful, Colik. You're still speaking about a superior officer. Show some respect."

Colik gulped back his next curse and tentatively approached. "Captain? Is that you?"

"Who the fuck else would it be, Colik?" answered Maribella. "If you're finished tripping over your own jaw, tell us what you found out there."

"Right, sorry. There's a spiral staircase, partly

collapsed, but we can get across the gaps with ropes. It leads to a balcony that overlooks the chamber. Puts us right beside where those mushraptors are perching."

In answer, Maribella leaped to the ceiling above them and latched on with her claws. The movement was effortless, as graceful as a cat. She released her hand grips and unfurled so that she hung upside down by her feet, dangling like a bat.

"I should be able to get the drop on them," she said. "Kill the little shits before they take flight."

Karina tried and failed to quell a grin of pride. "My my, captain. You've taken to this new form like a duck to water."

"Begging your pardon, madam, but I'm feeling a bit more useful than a fucking duck."

The grind of wood on stone jerked Karina's attention away from her beautiful creation. It was Durk, red-faced with exertion as he pushed open the chamber door.

"Close that, right now!"

"But you said-"

Karina sighed. Simple-mindedness had its drawbacks. "Close the door. We're going a different way."

"Yes, madam."

With a grunt he shoved the door shut and stood there, awaiting orders.

"Now salvage what rope you can from the captain's bindings." She looked to Maribella as the she-wolf dropped from the ceiling and landed on all fours. "Ready to move out?"

"Yes, madam," answered Maribella as she stood and stretched again, clearly luxuriating in her newfound strength and flexibility.

"You seem to be enjoying yourself, Maribella," observed Karina.

"I am, thank you, madam."

"A word of warning though. Don't forget yourself. You're not the first to receive the benefits of this formula, but you are currently the only living example."

"What happened to the others?"

"They lacked mental fortitude. Keep your wits about you, tame the beast within, and you'll do just fine."

"So this urge to tear Durk's leg off and eat it, that'll pass?"

"Not that I've observed, no."

Durk at least had the intelligence to flinch when Maribella patted him on the shoulder.

"Don't worry, big fella," Maribella soothed. "I've had lunch already."

Karina laughed as she turned to Colik. "Lead the way, scout. It's time to give our wardog some exercise."

"Wardog?" Maribella cocked her head, a very canine behavior that proved Karina's point.

Karina focused on Maribella and brought up her stats. She recited as she read.

Captain Maribella of Credence
Class: Wardog - Level 6
Progress to Level 7 = 825/1500

Body: 18
Wardog +12 Class Modifier: 30

Mind: 11
Spirit: 11

HP: 180
EP: 66

Skills
Blood-curdling Howl (Tier 1)
Fevered Regeneration (Tier 1)
Scented Pathways (Tier 1)
Acoustics (Tier 1)
Feral Fury (Tier 1)

Maribella nodded, impressed. "So I'm dual-class now?"

"Yes. Hence the higher XP threshold."

"Can I use my warrior abilities while in Wardog form?"

Karina shook her head. "The two classes are mutually exclusive. But I'm sure you'll find your new skills more than adequate. For instance, Fevered Regeneration will heal most wounds faster than your Vigorous Healing ability, even at Tier One."

"Most wounds?"

"Try not to get burned or cut by anything made of silver. Your body is now infused with lycanthropic bacteria. Fire will cauterize your flesh, temporarily killing the bacteria around the wound site. It'll take time for the disease to reinfect your tissues. And silver has potent antibacterial properties. Pure silver is particularly devastating."

Maribella growled with revulsion. "So I'm a walking sack of disease?"

"Indeed you are." She pointed at Durk and then at Maribella's pile of clothes and equipment. "Be a good packhorse and carry the captain's gear for her. She'll want to remain unencumbered for now." Then she looked to Colik. "Lead the way, scout."

Together they struck off down the passage-way, headed for Colik's alternative entrance into the Chamber of Agrovesh. The scout's route took them through a winding series of tunnels that left Karina feeling completely lost. At last they came to a spiral staircase and ascended to the point where the steps had crumbled away. Maribella took one end of the rope proffered by Durk and leaped across the gap with ease and remarkable grace. Lacking anything suitable to secure the rope to, she simply wrapped it around herself, using her own supernatural strength as the an-chor. One by one, Karina, Colik and Durk swung down into the ravine of shattered rock below and were pulled up by the freshly-minted wardog. Al-though the captain panted a little with the exer-tion as she hauled Durk and all of the gear onto the upper flight of steps, her disease-ridden mus-cles proved worthy of the task.

Colik then led the way up the remainder of the staircase to the promised balcony. It afforded an excellent view of the temple's rafters. Karina counted a dozen roosting mushraptors, hanging upside down like fuzzy peaches gone to rot.

"Ready, captain?" whispered Karina.

Maribella nodded, needing no further instruction. She jumped to the first rafter and then crept along it. When she reached her first slumbering victim, she grabbed it by the legs, flipped it upwards and tore out its throat with her fangs. The motion was smooth and almost soundless.

Your party has slain a Level 3 Mushraptor.
Your XP reward per party member = 7 XP

The other mushraptors didn't stir, oblivious to the predator now stalking among them. Maribella placed the carcass gently on the top of the rafter. Then with stealth and patience, the wardog plucked her prey one by one until the tree had been stripped clean of its fruit.

Your party has killed eleven Level 3 Mushraptors.
Your XP reward per party member = 82 XP

Maribella returned to the balcony and thrust her claw out at Durk. "Water. Now."

Durk obliged, handing over a canteen which the captain unstoppered and upended into her fanged mouth. Much gargling and spitting later, Maribella handed the empty canteen back.

"Are mushraptors not to your taste, captain?" asked an amused Karina.

"Like mushrooms and blue-vein cheese."

"That actually sounds quite appetizing."

"I prefer pork," said Maribella with a sly wink at Durk.

The big man gulped and grew a little paler.

"Save your appetite for a certain demon and his warlock friend."

"Yes, madam."

From the balcony they were able to descend into the chamber via a series of stone catwalks and steps that hugged the inside wall. When they reached the chamber floor, they found the archers still lying where they'd fallen, surrounded by the carcasses of the mushraptors they and Maribella had killed.

Colik knelt by Tris and closed her staring eyes. "Wonder why those things didn't eat Tris and Dez, or any of their own."

Karina took a closer look at one of the mushraptors, at its jagged teeth and sickle-like talons. "They're not carnivores. They eat fungus."

"Then what about the teeth and talons,

madam?" wondered Colik. "They did a good enough number on our archers."

Karina prodded a nearby fungus with a finger. It was like poking an overstuffed leather armchair. "They're for ripping through the outer skins of these mushrooms. The mushraptors were simply defending their territory, fending off would be predators."

"Seems coincidental," remarked the captain as she ripped a long tear in the closest mushroom with her index claw.

"What does, captain?"

"That their favorite food just happens to grow in the Chamber of Agrovesh."

Karina gave Maribella a hard look. The woman kept surprising her with her astuteness, and she wasn't yet sure if that was a good thing or a bad thing. She activated her Mind's Eye ability and surveyed the chamber. It only took a few seconds to confirm the captain's suspicions. At first glance the mushrooms appeared to have spread randomly from one wall to the other, but patterns soon started to form. The mushroom colony was at its most populous along the edges of a central aisle, like they'd been planted in neat rows bordering the walkways and then spread from there. At their highest density, the mushroom patch formed a thick half-circle around the altar. Once again, the original planting had been neat and orderly.

She knelt by one of the mushraptors. A quick comparison between the creature's swirling wing patterns and the chamber's engravings and carvings showed striking similarities. Either the artists had taken inspiration from the mushraptors or the animal's creator had taken inspiration from the carvers. Either way, these monsters were likely the chosen guardians of the Altar of Agrovesh, and that left her wondering. The mushraptors were all of a similar size and maturity. There was no differentiation between adults and juveniles, no obvious life cycle in process. That meant the twenty-five they'd just killed were all from the same brood. Same age, same parent. That left one last question.

"Where's the mother?" she queried out loud.

"Oh shit," responded Maribella. "Really?"

"Afraid so. Unless the young eat the parent, which does happen with certain species, something nearby laid a whole mess of eggs for this monstrous ensemble to hatch out of."

"Eggs to grubs to moths?" wondered Colik.

"Indeed."

"Some moths die after laying their eggs," offered Colik rather hopefully.

"To be on the safe side, scout, I think you should approach the altar while we take up battle positions."

Colik looked from Karina to the altar and back again.

"Is there a problem?"

"I'd rather run for it and take my chances with the captain, truth be told. Her claws should make quick work of me. Painless, kind of." He pointed at a nearby mushraptor carcass. "Mother of them things, don't know what it'll do to me or for how long."

"Colik?" Karina forced sweetness and understanding into her tone. "Listen to me very carefully."

"Yes, madam, I'll-"

"Starweed."

The effect was immediate. One moment, Colik was standing there, defiance in his eyes. The next moment he was curled on the stone floor in fetal position, trembling and whimpering.

Karina walked over to him, watched impassively for a count of ten and then said "starweed" again. Colik gasped like he'd just woken from a nightmare and slowly rose to his feet.

"I implanted that memory in that rather sludgy little brain of yours, Colik. Starweed withdrawal at its very worst. It takes a twenty year habit to produce withdrawal symptoms of that magnitude. I doubt you've ever been a heavy enough user to experience it for yourself, but I've seen it too many times. I captured that memory from a poor suffering fool in their final hours. And it does take hours, Colik. Hours filled with minutes that themselves feel like hours. So you can either do as I ask and brave the very small chance that you will be eviscerated by a giant mushraptor, or you can suffer for a seeming eternity until your heart gives out. What shall it be?"

Colik nodded, a faint smile on his face like someone had just offered him a choice between the garlic beef steak or the roast lamb. "Think I'll just go rest my ass on that altar for a bit. Legs are a bit tired, you see."

"You do that," agreed Karina.

As Colik approached the Altar of Agrovesh, Karina gestured for her wardog and her man-at-arms to form a barrier in front of her. No sooner had the scout plonked his grubby breeches onto the delicately carved slab, he and his seat vanished with a click and a screech of rusted iron. Karina pursed her lips, perturbed that her Mind's Eye ability hadn't identified a trapdoor. She clearly hadn't scored within her 25% chance of an intuitive leap.

With a beating of wings that sent a cloud of dust billowing towards them, the mushraptor matriarch rose up out of the open doors, a wriggling Colik clenched tightly in one of her claws. With a snap and a squelch that same claw reduced the scout to a limp sack of red pulp. She then shook the mess from her talon and issued a piercing shriek of rage at the sight of her massacred children.

Karina glanced at the captain, noting the wideness of her blue eyes, the trembling of the muscles at the back of her long jaw. She laid a hand on the woman's furry shoulder.

"False Courage," she murmured, and then dove out of the way as the matriarch swooped in to attack.

Durk wasn't as coolminded as Karina. Rather than dodge away, he raised his arms and screamed like a little boy as gigantic talons bore him to the ground and slavering jaws descended towards his bright red face. He would've lost that face, too, had the captain not sprung vertically into the air, timing her jump so that she dropped onto her target's back and buried her claws deep in the thing's thorax.

The giant mushraptor turned away from the prone man-at-arms and endeavored to shake the wardog off her back. Maribella hung on tight as she flapped from side to side, a flag on a pole during a ferocious gale.

"Durk!" roared the wardog. "Go for the legs!"

Durk scrambled to his feet, readied his shield, and charged the thrashing beast with his mace raised high. His first strike cracked one the monster's forelegs, causing it to crash to the ground in an ungainly heap. Maribella took the opportunity to crouch and dig, her claws tearing through the monster's flesh like a toddler's fingers through a birthday cake. The mushraptor shrieked again and struggled to stand. Durk got in first, bringing his mace down on another leg, sundering the exoskeleton with a resounding 'snap'. With only one good leg remaining on its right side, the mushraptor couldn't find its balance. Yet it still had one more trick up its sleeve.

The giant creature dropped to the ground with a thump and went perfectly still. For a moment Karina thought it was playing dead, one of nature's silliest survival mechanisms in the inquisitor's opinion. Then it started to heave and swell, and Karina had a pretty good idea of what was about to happen.

"Gas!" she shouted. "Retreat!"

Maribella wrenched something wet and glistening out of the creature's thorax before performing a two-stepped leap off the monster's abdomen. She landed in the mushrooms, sending a cloud of spores into the air. Durk, to his detriment, was slower.

As he turned to run, sinewy valves opened in the mushraptor's sides. Out poured a wave of sulphurous vapor. The gas was so thick that Karina lost sight of him for a moment. Then the big man stumbled into view, his shield and mace discarded, his hands scrabbling at his throat. One glance was all Karina needed to know that Durk was a goner. The glands around his neck were so swollen that there was no hope of him catching even the smallest breath. He looked pleadingly at Karina and took a trembling step towards her. The inquisitor felt a brief tinge of guilt, a moment where she felt genuinely sorry for this simple man. He'd wanted to please her, that was all, and now he was going to die for it. She extinguished the spark of empathy inside her before it flared into something inconvenient. She'd seen inquisitors go that way before, crippled by compassion. They were used as examples to harden the acolytes. The devotion of inquisition was a lifelong journey. There was no stepping off the path to entertain the misgivings of the conscience.

Karina made sure she looked Durk in the eye, sharing his terror until death finally took him. Then she scrambled clear as the gas cloud expanded and dissipated. After several minutes, the vapor was gone and a final spasm passed through the mushraptor's carcass.

Your party has killed a Level 16 Mushraptor Matriarch.
Your XP reward per party member = 80 XP
Your party currently consists of two members.

Maribella rose out of the mushrooms and shook spores from her fur like a dog shaking off water. Karina found it quite adorable. The captain caught her staring and cocked her head to one side.

"Something wrong, madam?"

"Not at all," covered Karina. She pointed at the slimy, organic lump that the wardog still held in her claws. "What's that?"

Maribella shrugged. "Brain, I think. It smelled important so I took it."

"You should keep trusting that nose of yours."

"Smelled the gas coming too. Thank you for the warning, though, and for the False Courage. I was quietly shitting myself before that."

"Yes, I noticed. You're welcome, captain." She glanced at Durk. The dead man's mouth was gaping wide. His tongue was blue and three sizes too big. "A shame about our pack mule."

Maribella barely spared the corpse a glance. "Maybe I should change. Put my gear back on."

"Let's have a look into the pit first, shall we? I want to know where my altar has gone."

"Yes, madam."

The wardog led the way and peered over the edge. Her 'huh' told Karina it was safe enough to look for herself. The altar had fallen roughly ten meters onto a mass of woven silk. The strands had proven strong enough to resist its not inconsiderable weight. Within the shrouds, Karina could make out forty or so oblong pupae and countless semi-formed mushraptors shifting sleepily inside them.

"Let's head back to camp," suggested Karina, "and fetch a salvage crew before this latest brood hatches."

"Good idea, madam."

"Oh, and captain, not a word to the troops about your alter ego. They may not grasp the full beauty of your transformation."

The wardog's blue eyes narrowed. "No-one's ever called me beautiful before."

"Let's just say that you've at last grown into yourself," said Karina with a smile. She pointed at the pupae below. "You've hatched out of your cocoon and spread your wings. Unfortunately, when we get back to camp, you'll be surrounded by grubs, not butterflies."

Maribella nodded and smiled, her tongue lolling over her sharp teeth. "Point taken, madam." The wardog looked to Durk's prone form and the pile of offal that had once been Colik. "It's actually kinda handy that mother mushraptor killed Colik and Durk before I had to. Not really the types to keep their traps shut about something like this."

There was more than a touch of pride in Karina's smirk. "A shame we didn't catch you earlier, captain. I think we could've made a fine inquisitor out of you."

Maribella gave her a fang-filled grin in return. "I'll pop behind the Agrovesh statue. Wouldn't mind a bit of privacy while I change."

"I shall cover my ears too."

"That'd be nice, thanks."

Karina did as promised, turning her back and pressing her palms to ears. The latter did little to muffle the piercing howls as they slowly turned into screams.

18

Mark dropped the trapdoor back into place with a *thunk,* closing off the rank atmosphere of roasted flesh that wafted up from the chute.

"Pretty dark in here," remarked Vari.

With a whisper of "Truelight", Arix lit up like a glowstick, bathing the chamber in a warm, golden hue. A statue of the Goddess of Despair loomed over them, her beautiful face marred with anguish, her delicate hands curled into claws. While her body had been carved from quartz, her eyes were obsidian orbs of the deepest black. The Altar of Solmora lay at her bare feet, an ebony coffin carved by the trembling hands of some tortured artist.

"Nice trick that," said Mark. "You're a human lightbulb."

"Bit more than that, innit. Look down."

The floor was made of hexagonal tiles, each engraved with a symbol that looked to Mark like kanji drawn by a goth. Thanks to Arix's Truelight spell, most of the tiles glowed a dull red of warning. The exceptions stood out like islands in a red sea.

"Truelight's actually a sense traps spell, eh?" mused Mark.

"Secret doors, too."

"It's not that I don't trust your abilities, Arix," said Vari, her distrust more than evident, "but maybe you should step on those tiles first?"

"Or Sid, maybe you'd like to check them out?" suggested Mark.

"Indeed. Touch me to the floor and I'll see what I can do," agreed Citadel.

"Fucking hell, you're a suspicious lot," said Arix, shaking his head.

"Better safe than sorry," answered Mark as he set Citadel down on the closest of the safe tiles.

"This is a false floor," reported Citadel, "suspended above a pit lined with steel spikes. The tiles engraved with the tree-like symbol are in fact pillars capable of supporting weight. I naturally can't see if those tiles have been identified by Arix's Truelight ability, but if there is indeed a correlation then the spell's accuracy would seem bonafide."

"See?" Arix stepped onto the first tree tile and bounced up and down a couple of times. "A little trust wouldn't hurt, you know?"

"Sorry, Arix," said Mark. "Just wanted to be sure."

The executioner shrugged and then picked his way across the safe tiles to the altar. Mark and Vari followed suit. It was only when they reached the altar that Mark noticed the book, a heavy, leather bound tome lying atop the engraved stone. From a distance he'd taken it to be part of the altar's warped construction. There was writing on the cover, but nothing that Mark could decipher, at least not without some arcane assistance. He flipped through the pages. The writing was the same on every sheet of yellowed parchment; intricate, beautiful, and utterly incomprehensible.

Vari peeked around his shoulder. "You feeling as illiterate as me right now?"

"Afraid so."

Arix sighed. "It's just a fucking book. Probably full of thees and thous about people we don't know and shit what doesn't matter coz it happened ages ago."

"I take it you don't stop to read tomes much?" wondered Mark.

"Shit no. Waste of good playtime."

"Do you click through the dialogues as well?"

"Sure do. If the info's not in the UI then it's TLDR."

"But the lore is where you actually find out why you're completing a quest, not just how."

"I complete a quest because I'll get an XP payload and some loot. What more reason do I need?"

"Not the romantic type then, eh?"

"Fuck you very much, warlock," scoffed Arix. "I'm plenty romantic. It's just that when I read a book I do it in my armchair with a nice drop of merlot. Got a cozy spot in the mezzanine that overlooks the Thames. Sunny too."

Mark laughed. "When I visited London I didn't see the sun for three weeks. When it finally broke through the clouds I just stood in it and grinned like a goon at the sky. The locals thought I was nuts."

"Sounds like a horrendous place," said Vari.

"Probably a fuckload nicer than Credence," retorted Arix, a little defensively.

"Anywhere is nicer than Credence," Vari pointed out. She turned back to Mark. "You don't have a language spell up your sleeve, do you?"

"Actually, yes I do."

He took a closer look at Cunning Linguist to make sure it was up to the task.

Cunning Linguist

Enables the spoken and written understanding of any language.

Tier 1: Allows for a solid understanding of the target speech or text. Enables good comprehension for 30 minutes. Subtleties such as humour and double meanings may be missed.

"The well-read warlock is the not-dead warlock."
- Zevryn the Everborn

Good enough. He dropped the spell into an empty slot and murmured "Cunning Linguist".

"Cunnilingus? What do you think it is? The karma-fucking-sutra?" Arix pressed his first and second fingers to his lips and waggled his tongue between. Mark didn't find it funny, and by Vari's expression, neither did she.

"Could you please keep a lid on it for a

minute, Arix?" he asked, failing to keep the frustrated edge from his voice.

"Fine, fine. Keep your hair on, Mister Prude." The executioner passed Mark a candlestick. "Light that so I can take a look around."

Mark took the candle, drew Volcanic Bastard and touched the blade to the wick. It flared instantly. As he tucked his sword away and looked at the cover of the book, the name of the language came to him. Vorasii. The title and the author byline shimmered for a moment before transforming in English.

"The Breaking Dawn - Sacrificial Rites by Ishka the Devout" he read aloud. "Ever heard of the Breaking Dawn, Vari?"

"Afraid not. So you can read it now?"

Mark skimmed over the first page and made a "tsk, tsk" noise. "The writing is pretty flowery."

"How flowery?"

"Like this." He cleared his throat and recited a particularly purple passage. "Thus shall the detritus of creation clamber from its abyss of despair. Thus shall the forsaken become the cherished. Thus shall the despised become the delight of those who would welcome the dawn."

"Too much starweed, I'd say."

"Starweed?"

"A narcotic herb. You smoke it. Most users just go starry-eyed and giggly, but some get long-winded and prophetic."

"Pathetically prophetic?"

Vari grinned. "Profoundly pathetic."

Mark laughed and kept reading. "From what I can gather, you were right on the money with your prediction."

"Are you calling me prophetic?"

"Wouldn't dream of it."

He caught her hand and pulled her in for a kiss. Some would think it odd to be flirting over a sacrificial altar, but he was a warlock, she could tear a person's flesh open with a mere whisper, and this was *Reign of Blood*.

Vari gently pulled away and tapped the book. "Eyes on the page, good sir. I want to know how right I am."

"Yes, ma'am." He read on, his mind grudgingly adjusting to the florid language. "Yup, this confirms that the Altar of Solmora is just one of three altars needed for the Breaking Dawn ritual. The others are the Altar of Khorlvah, Goddess of Hope, and the Altar of Agrovesh, Goddess of Fury."

"Agrovesh, she's the Karaji war goddess."

"Maybe inherited from these people, the Vorasii?"

"Could be, yes. Makes me wonder about the statue we saw, back where Braemar-"

"Where we lost Braemar," Mark finished for her. He put his hand on the small of her back and drew her closer. "The winged lady with the trident?"

She rested her head against his chest. "Different from how she looks in Karajan, but Fury and War seem to fit together."

"Shit." Mark's heart sank a little.

"What?" wondered Vari, looking up at him.

"If that was Agrovesh then her altar was probably nearby."

"Do you think we should go back for it?"

Mark shook his head. "Based on where Arix said the reiver camp was, chances are they've found it already, or at least locked the area down." He turned the page. "We're better off doing as Arix suggested."

"Ambush her here?"

"Let's just hope she doesn't bring her whole army with her."

He peered at the script, deciphering the next few passages. As he focused on them, the letters transformed from esoteric symbols into the

Roman alphabet. It was like Google translating a web page.

"Okay, so once the altars are bathed in something called the Waters of Life, nightmares incarnate will rise from the earth to 'end the nighttime of ignorance' and usher in the 'daylight of epiphany'. Sounds like corrupted creatures crawling out of chasms to me."

"Me too," agreed Vari. "And the Waters of Life means blood. At least it does in Figurist lore."

Mark sighed. Sacrifice of all kinds seemed to follow him around like a bad smell, even from RL into FIVR. His real life had been one big sacrifice to other people's dreams; bosses, ex-wives and mothers included. Now other people were sacrificing themselves for *his* dreams. Denniston, Dayna and Braemar. No, he admonished himself. Denniston, Dayna and Braemar all died for Garland. Not for him, and not because of him either. If he kept saying it to himself often enough, he might just start believing it.

"Something wrong, Mark?" Vari asked.

"We have to stop Karina from completing this ritual." It was true, but it was an evasion of the question. "If she gets full control of the Chasms of Corruption, Garland is in serious trouble."

"So is Karajan. No chance of freedom when

the reivers have that kind of power at their fingertips." Vari gently pulled away from Mark and fixed him with a hard look. "We might have just found our own solution to the Chasms of Corruption quest."

"Really?" Mark had a bad feeling about this.

"Whoever controls the chasms can close the chasms."

"What? We make the sacrifice? We complete the ritual?"

She pointed at the book. "All the instructions are there, aren't they?"

Mark flicked through the pages and found one that appeared to lay out the Breaking Dawn ritual step by step, starting with a detailed description of how the sacrificial subject had to be of Level 6 or greater, and how their throat would need to be slashed open, their body suspended upside down so that at least three liters of blood could be captured, one liter per altar. The callous precision of it all made Mark feel a little sick.

"I'll need to read over it all properly, but it looks like it's all here." He looked over at Arix who was working his way along the closest wall, using Truelight to look for secret doors. Mark waited until Arix had moved around behind the looming statue of Solmora before leaning in towards Vari, close enough to whisper. "Who would we sacrifice? The book says it needs to be someone of Level Six or over."

"Inquisitor Karina," Vari whispered back. "She has to be at least Level Seven if she's leading an expedition of hundreds."

"And if we don't manage to take her alive?"

She drew closer so that her breath tickled his ear. "Arix is Level Seven."

"Physik Perception strikes again?"

"Yes."

Mark grimaced, wishing she hadn't suggested what he'd already been thinking. "He has the luxury of coming back to life, too. But then again, so do I."

"You can't read the ritual when you're dead, Mark."

"I could teach it to you first. I don't think you'll have any trouble remembering it."

"No, but I'd have all sorts of trouble when it came to slitting your throat."

"It would be for Garland."

"Fuck Garland! I'm not doing that to you."

"Maybe I could do it to my-"

Vari stepped back and shook her head. "We're not having this conversation anymore!"

"What conversation? And why wasn't I invited?" said Arix, his radiance washing over them as he stepped out from behind the statue.

"Just talking about how we're going to capture Inquisitor Karina and sacrifice her," Mark explained a little too quickly.

Arix raised an eyebrow. "Why?"

"So that we can complete the Breaking Dawn ritual, take control of the Chasms of Corruption, and close them for good."

"You know how to perform this Breaking Dawn thing?"

"Yup, it's all in the book."

Arix looked suitably abashed. "I take back everything I said about reading in-game tomes."

"Really?"

The executioner's abashment dissolved into a mocking grin. "Fuck no. Why bother when I got lore nerds like you to do the reading for me?"

Mark gritted his teeth and exchanged a frustrated look with Vari. "Did your explorations turn up anything interesting, Mister Hardcore?"

"Mister Hardcore. I like that. Must see if the url is free when I get home. And speaking of which, I can see one little flaw in this genius plan of yours."

"What flaw?"

"Karina is the only person I know what can

get me out of this bloody fairytale. Now you're planning to off her."

"The druids who summoned me, they can probably send you home."

Arix stretched out his arms and spun in a full circle. "Hello? Druids? Be good chaps and come out where we can see you."

"They're in the Garland capital city, idiot."

"A place neither of us have seen. We don't even know if it-"

"It exists," interrupted Mark through gritted teeth.

For a moment Arix looked like he was going to argue. Instead he sighed. "Fine. Maybe it does. How long to get there?"

"A week from Citadel. Maybe more?"

"Fuck that and the horse it rode in on! I've got a beautiful lady and a successful business to get back to. I'm not traipsing halfway across this virtual landfill to find some druid what may or may not be able to wake me from this shit-eating nightmare." He strode up to Mark and pointed a finger in his face. "We'll capture Karina and make her send me home. After that, you can do what you want with the sadistic bitch."

Vari shrugged. "Kills two slugs with one boot if you ask me."

"Luv you too, darling," snapped Arix with a sneer.

Mark gently pushed Arix's index finger aside with his palm. "Alright then. We help you capture Karina, but only if you help us set things up for the Breaking Dawn ritual."

"Set things up? Like how?"

"We need all three altars together. That means we can't take her here."

"What?!" spat Arix. "I've just finished scoping out the best ambush spots! This place is perfect!"

"No, Arix. Not for us. We need her to take the altar. She'll be gathering all three of them together, and that's where we need to strike."

Arix shook his head in disbelief. "That'll mean cutting our way through her entire fucking reiver army."

Mark's many hours of the Murderer's Dogma FIVR came back to him. Lots of practice in sneaking and killing. "We'll do it guerilla style. Hit and run, whittle their numbers down until we're ready to strike at the heart of the camp and capture Karina."

"I could find you the best places to hide," offered Citadel.

"Shit, hi Sid!" exclaimed Mark with a start. "Sorry, forgot about you for a bit there."

"I've been resting this past while," explained Citadel. "All this terrain exploration makes me quite tired. I only heard that last bit about sacrificing an inquisitor to the Vorasii goddesses. I like the sound of it." He yawned and Mark was struck by the strangeness of the sound. Citadel had neither mouth or lungs for yawning with. It was probably an unconscious behavior, left over from his days of flesh and blood. "I'm off back to sleep. Give me a gentle tap if you need me."

"Night, Sid."

Arix had a faint smile on his lips. He seemed to be warming to Mark's idea. "We'll be grinding as we take the reivers down, leveling for when we hit the main event."

"Exactly." Mark looked to Vari, wondering how she'd react to what he was about to say. "How would you feel about providing potion backup rather than hands-on healing?"

She put her hands on her hips and fixed him with a dark glare. "You are not leaving me out of this."

"Wouldn't dream of it," he assured her. "What I'm thinking is this. That first waypoint of ours isn't too far from the reiver camp. You could pop back to Citadel and brew EP and HP potions, then bring them to us at the waypoint. Then you could patch us up for our next raid, and we could take the potions with us so we can fight on for longer each time."

"Feels like you just want to keep me out of the fighting."

He pressed his palms together. "I promise you, Vari, I'm not. We need your support, your healing and potions, otherwise we're screwed." He took a deep breath, trying not to think about how he would feel, the pain and emptiness if he should lose her. "We can die as many times as it takes, but you can only die once. I'm being brutally practical here, but…"

Vari dropped her hands to her sides and gave a reluctant sigh. "Yes, alright. It makes sense. But I'm coming with you when we take Karina."

"Wouldn't be the same without you," Mark agreed with a fierce grin. Then he turned to Arix. "Sound like a plan?"

The executioner looked at him for a long moment, his lips pursed in thought. Too long, thought Mark.

"I just need a yes or no. Unless you have an alternative you'd like to propose?"

For a moment Arix looked like he was going to say something. Then he just shook his head and grinned. "While I would love to stick around and see you drain the life out of old Inquisibitch, I have a date with my real life. Count me in up until that point. But don't worry, I'll make sure resistance is pretty fucking pathetic by the time you're ready capture Karina." Arix raised three fingers and pressed his little finger down with his thumb. "Scouts honor."

Mark laughed. "You were a boy scout?"

"Twenty-third Chingford Scout Group."

Mark simply laughed.

19

———————

[VARI]

Arix's search turned up the secret room. It sat at the back of Solmora's Chamber, tucked between two more equally tragic renditions of the goddess.

Vari watched Arix with suspicion as he picked out the most useful items from the assorted miscellania. There was plenty of gold and silver in the form of statuettes, candlesticks, and trinkets of various shapes and sizes. Had they gathered it all up and sold it in the markets of Credence, she and Mark could have retired to Karajan, bought a vineyard and hired people to tend it for them. They need never lift a finger for the rest of their lives.

Which got Vari to thinking about Mark's

mortality. Yes, he could come back from the dead, but could he age? What if she grew old and died while he remained forever young? She shuddered at the thought. What in Agrovesh's teeth had she got herself into? The slippery slope of those thoughts was thankfully cut short by an excited Arix.

"Oh happy days!" The executioner lifted an ornate ceremonial axe from its perch on the wall.

"Very pretty," commented Vari, "but can it actually hurt someone?"

Arix's grin broadened as he recited the stats.

Solmora's Bite
+50% to base axe damage.
+25% attack speed.
50% chance of inducing a melancholy that reduces the victim's damage dealt by 25%.
20% chance of inducing crippling despair that paralyzes the victim for 5 seconds.

"Despair is the fertile soil from which delight may sprout and bloom."
- Ishka the Devout

"And now something for the lady," Arix continued as he held up a silver-grey cloak.

Vari took it from him and marveled at the softness and lightness of the wool. The item's stats came to her of their own accord. She read them out for Mark's benefit.

Solmora's Blessing
+25% reduction to damage received.
+1 to Body.
+3 to Spirit.
+50% resistance to magical manipulation of the wearer's Mind.

"With clarity and purpose we find our way through the mists of despair."
- Ishka the Devout

"No point in casting Terrifying Manifestation on you, then," joked Mark.

"Not that you ever would," hoped Vari.

"Only on Halloween," he replied with a smirk.

"What's Halloween?"

"A festival we hold every year in parts of our world. A day for kids to dress up as monsters and threaten to terrorize people if they don't give them sweets."

"Sounds like an extortion racket to me," said Vari.

She'd seen plenty of those in Karajan. The reivers had plundered her land so badly that there was precious little remaining for her people. The less scrupulous Karaji had formed gangs to control what was left. The irony was that it was the oppressive ganglords that kept the Karaji from rising up to throw off the reiver occupation, not the reiver army. Vari had no doubt that the reivers knew that and fostered it. Inquisitors stalked Karaji, preaching law and order, truth and enlightenment, while turning a blind eye as the strong brutalized and butchered the weak.

Mark blushed a little. "Yeah, it kind of is when you think about it."

"So is Christmas," added Arix as he handed Mark a pair of black leather gloves. The knuckles were studded with silver skulls. "Ho ho ho."

"Thanks, Arix," said Mark as he slipped the gloves on and read out their stats.

Solmora's Caress
30% reduction in damage to the hands.
10% reduction to all physical damage.
10% increased damage dealt with handheld
weapons.
20% chance of inducing crippling despair that
paralyzes the victim for 5 seconds.

(Only effective if the victim's bare flesh is touched.)
Chance of crippling despair may be increased by 1% per essence point invested.

"The kindest touch becomes cruel
to the unrequited lover."
- Ishka the Devout

"Christmas? Ho ho ho?" Vari sighed. "What are you two talking about now?"

"Christmas," explained Arix, "involves a fat man in a red suit what sneaks down your chimney at night and gives presents to your children."

That made no sense to Vari, and as a young girl she would've been terrified if a fat man had snuck down her chimney at night. And one should never trust a stranger offering presents.

"What does he want in return?"

"Nothing."

Vari shook her head. "Fat men with gifts never want nothing."

"Apparently it's a reward," explained Mark, "for being a good kid all year."

"But threatening people to give you sweets, that's not good."

Arix and Mark exchanged a bemused look.

"Yeah," admitted Mark. "I hadn't thought of that."

"Neither," agreed Arix. "Being a kid in our world is a bit complicated."

"Sounds like it," concluded Vari. She shot Mark a wicked grin, knowing this would unsettle him. "We'll be raising our children in Garland, won't we Mark?"

Mark turned paler than she'd ever seen him, even in death. "Um, I, yeah, we could-"

She laughed and patted his arm, putting the poor man out of his misery. "See, I don't even need to dress like a monster to terrorize you." As Mark mustered a weak smile in return, Vari turned to Arix. The executioner was rifling through the remaining pile of magic items. They were mostly rings, bracelets, amulets and odd pieces of armor. "Anything else in there?"

"Not really. The armor is lower grade than what we have already, and these trinkets have just a smattering of elemental resists. Two percent Fire Resistance and shit."

"I don't see the point of jewelry like that," complained Mark. "Magical items take a lot of effort to forge, so why would you go out of your way to imbue something with a measly two percent Fire Resistance? That wouldn't even stop you getting sunburnt. Same goes for cursed items. What's the point?"

"Well, we both know how quickly an artist and a game designer can churn this shit out," responded Arix, "so it's the backstory here what's paper thin. You'd have to be a right bastard to put time and energy into a cursed item that pisses off some random stranger countless years after you're dead and gone."

Vari noted that Arix was making more of these strange comments about her world, treating it like it was some elaborate set for a play. The items were all props and the people were all characters. She also noted that Mark was countering those comments less and less, like he was beginning to accept the truth of them. Anger flickered inside her. Not at Arix this time. At Mark.

Her beloved warlock was beginning to pose more questions than he answered. She knew nothing about his world and how it related to her own. She knew nothing about his past before appearing in Garland. She knew only what she'd witnessed since meeting him. She had fallen for Mark the Warlock, but Arix was drawing out more and more of who Mark had been before, and if Vari was going to allow herself to fully love him, she needed to know who he really was first. If she didn't, she was just being a character in a play, oblivious to the world beyond the edge of the stage.

Arix plucked a sapphire ring from the pile and tossed it to Vari. She caught it one-handed and held it up to Arix's aura to get a better look.

"Pretty," she remarked.

Ring of Radiance

Produces a white light with a radiance equivalent to a burning lantern. The wearer can invoke the radiance effect by uttering "Illuminate" and stop the radiance with an utterance of "Extinguish".

The wearer can strengthen or weaken the radiance through force of will.

"Illuminate," said Vari.

The sapphire began to glow, emitting just enough white light to show up against Arix's Truelight spell. She willed the gem to grow brighter until it drowned out Arix's aura and forced Mark and Arix to shield their eyes. Satisfied, she willed the radiance down to an ambient level.

"Thank you, Arix."

"Got something else for you, too," said the executioner as he drew a dagger from his belt.

Vari felt a jab of adrenaline in her belly and she gripped her staff more tightly, ready to defend herself. Out of the corner of her eye, she saw Mark reach for Volcanic Bastard. Arix rolled his eyes, reversed the dagger and offered it to her, handle first.

"A little trust, come on," he insisted.

Vari felt a bit sheepish as she accepted the dagger and read its name and stats.

Blood of the Lost

+20% to base dagger damage.
30% chance of inducing internal hemorrhaging in an organic enemy.
+30% accuracy when thrown.
Will return to owner if in line of sight.

"We might be lost yet our blood
will always find its way home."
- Ishka the Devout

She nodded, understanding the weapon's significance. "This was made for the Breaking Dawn ritual, correct?" She passed it to Mark to take a look.

He raised his eyebrows in surprise. "Ishka the Devout again? Her name's on the book as well."

"A high priestess of some kind," suggested Vari.

"Yup. High Priestess of Solmora?"

Arix shook his head and pointed at the dagger. "I found that behind the Altar of Korlvah. She was probably high priestess of all three."

"Makes sense," said Mark as he passed the dagger back to Vari. "One sacrifice, one priest, one liter of blood per altar."

"Do you think it was Ishka who caused the cataclysm?" asked Vari as she cast aside her old dagger and slid the new one in its place.

"Guess we'll know more once Mark has finished geeking out over Ishka's tome," answered Arix.

"Oh, and thank you again, Arix," said Vari. "For the cloak, ring and dagger. You needn't have been so generous with the salvage." In fact, she wasn't sure *why* he was being so generous all of a sudden. He could've made good use of both the Blood of the Lost and the Ring of Radiance, yet he'd only taken the axe for himself.

"Ho ho ho," answered the executioner, his polished white teeth gleaming in his aura.

Vari found a smile tugging at the edges of her

own mouth. "If you try to climb down my chimney, Arix, I'll stab you in the ass with this dagger."

Arix's laughter echoed around the chamber. "Point taken, luv. Literally." He looked at the remaining loot. "Any reason for taking the rest of this junk? Not like we have vendors we can pawn it off to."

"Sid can extract the magic out of items when he melts them down," answered Mark. "He should be able to take several weak items and turn them into one strong one."

"Upcycling? Nice." Arix scooped the rest of the magical items into his backpack and shouldered it. "So we're headed back to HQ then? Might as well rest up while Karina finds and nabs this Altar of Solmora thingy."

Vari bit her lip and tried to read Arix's body language. It was possible that he was just enthusiastic about their deal, about helping them capture Karina so he could go home. He sounded genuine. He even looked the part. But there was something niggling at Vari. He was being too amenable, treating her like a real person rather than one of those 'en-pee-sees' he mentioned on occasion. It felt nice and weird at the same time. She remembered what her inquisitor mentor had told her.

There was no such thing as unconditional love, no such thing as loyalty. Everyone was selfish, and selfishness was the glue that bound people together. When one person's selfishness crossed with another person's selfishness, conflict ensued. Blood was drawn. When one selfish ambition nurtured another selfish ambition then society grew between them. That's what society was. A horde of selfish people accidentally helping each other to be selfish.

That same inquisitor had put Vari's hand in a fire to demonstrate the application of Mend Flesh. Vari learned a valuable spell and the inquisitor got to satiate his sadistic cravings. She supposed that's what the inquisitor had meant.

She eyed Arix as he led the way out of the chamber. Yes, that was probably it. They were helping Arix with his selfish desire. He wanted to go home. In return, he was helping them with their selfish desire, to be the saviors of Garland. Was saving Garland really selfish? Vari had to admit that it probably was. It was where she wanted to live happily ever after with Mark in peace and prosperity. She wasn't saving Garland for the Garlanders. She was saving Garland for herself. The end result was the same. Did it really matter what the reasons were? Vari didn't think it did.

THOUGH THEIR CONSTANT vigilance made it seem longer, it only took them a few hours to reach the waypoint. It was just as well too. The sun was setting and none of them were willing to brave the Barrens at night.

When they got back to Citadel, they shared a hot meal together in the library. Afterwards, Arix excused himself to go take a bath and then head off to bed. Citadel was happy to sink back into the fortress, to spread his mental wings and enjoy the various goings-on of the villagers within. More people were arriving every day, seeking shelter from the rising corruption that was destroying their homes and livelihoods. Calder had taken on the mantle of honorary mayor, seeing that everyone was fed, watered and applied to the work of building the village's capacity and strengthening Citadel's fortifications. He and Citadel worked closely together in this, and it was a partnership that both seemed to enjoy.

After she and Mark had shared a luxurious bath together, and dressed in fresh clothes, Vari led Mark to the top of one of the towers and dismissed the ranger on lookout there. It was time she and the warlock had a heart to heart. Mark look absolutely terrified by the prospect.

"You look like you've cast Terrifying Manifestation on yourself," she said with a laugh.

Mark relaxed, but only a little. "Sorry."

"Are questions really that scary compared to what we've faced in the Barrens?"

Mark hesitated then sighed as he turned to look up at the mountains. The sun was about to disappear behind the peaks and the first stars were twinkling in the clear sky.

"What scares me is that you won't like the answers."

"That's up to me, isn't it?"

He looked at her, anxiety in his eyes, and nodded.

"Then let's start with an easy one," suggested Vari. "What were you before you became a warlock? What did you do with your days?"

"I worked at a market that sold food and other goods. It was my job to unload the trucks and get all the stock ready for distribution out to the shelves."

"Trucks?"

"Wagons, basically."

"You unloaded the wagons yourself?"

"No, I controlled a drone forklift. Kind of like one of Braemar's stone golems. Big, strong thing made of metal rather than stone."

"And it did what you told it to do? Like Commander Serik did to those cannibals with his Helm of Supremacy?"

Mark laughed. "Pretty much, but I could only control the drone, not people or anything. It's more like how you can turn corpses into puppets."

Vari breathed a sigh of relief. This was going better than she'd anticipated. "Did you like your job?"

"I like being a warlock a lot more."

"You're pretty good at it, too."

"Thank you."

"But a wagon boy doesn't have to face danger, apart from the odd falling barrel. You didn't have to suffer death over and again like you do now."

His jaw tightened and there was anger in his eyes. "I was suffering death. Just a little bit at a time."

She took his hand and squeezed it until she felt his muscles relax. "What about your family? Your loved ones?"

He shrugged. "Only child. My father's dead

and my mother and I don't get along. I had a wife but that didn't really work out."

"Did you love her?"

"Thought I did for a while there." He sighed. "Don't think I even knew what love was, until..."

Vari felt a surge of warmth so sweet it almost made her sick. She desperately wanted to pull him close, to hold him and tell him that nothing else mattered as long as they were together. But she held back because she knew that simply wasn't true. There was a lot that mattered.

"Until us?"

He nodded but didn't look at her. He was struggling with something and Vari needed to know what it was. She took a deep breath and let it out slowly, trying to settle her own anxiety.

"Now for the hard questions. Are you ready?"

Mark turned to her, his eyes fixed on hers. "Fire away."

Her breath faltered and fear got the upper hand, spreading through her gut and bowels, clawing and scratching as it went. She didn't *want* to know the answer to this question. She *needed* to know.

"Do many people in your world know about my world?"

"Kind of."

"That's not an answer, Mark."

"It's complicated."

"Are you calling me stupid?"

He looked shocked. "Of course not. Never."

She forced a smile. "Then trust me."

"Okay. Yes, people know your world as the setting of a game called *Reign of Blood*."

"Reign of Blood?" Vari stifled a laugh. "Sounds like something a reiver would come up with."

"Yeah true. Kind of is, eh."

"And it's a game? What sort of game?"

"It's a thing called FIVR. Full Immersion Virtual Reality." His brow wrinkled as he struggled to explain it. "Remember when I cast Doppelganger into the beetle nest?"

"Are you trying to say that my world is an illusion?"

"Kind of."

"There goes that non-answer again." She squeezed his hand again, gently. "Please, Mark. Try, for me."

"It's like a vivid dream that people can enter, one that can be seen, smelled, heard and felt like it's completely real."

"Are there others here? Like Arix? Is he another dreamer from your world?"

"Yes, Arix is, but he's the only one I've met. It's

strange. In other versions of *Reign of Blood* there are thousands, even millions of dreamers. But not here. Not in Garland or the Barrens. Probably not in Karaji either."

"I've never met anyone like you before," confirmed Vari. "I don't know anyone who has, either."

"Sid has."

"The warlocks that came before you? They were from your world?"

"Seems that way. At least some of them."

He released her hand and gripped the battlement as he looked over the evening bustle below. Dinners were being cooked, children put to bed, final chores finished off while there was still light. Vari heard Calder's gravelled voice above the others as he sharply reminded a group of young men to pack their tools away before calling it a night.

"I'm starting to wonder if the previous warlocks were mostly developers, popping into this world to test their creation."

"Gods?" wondered Vari.

Mark shook his head. "No, very human. But yeah, to someone looking out at them from this world, they could seem like gods." A faint smile crossed his lips. "Gods who sit in swivel chairs all

day, staring at screens, clicking mouses and tap-
ping at keyboards. Pretty much like scribes or
monks, I guess. Just the tools are a bit different."
His smile grew stronger. "For some reason, this
version of *Reign of Blood*, your version, feels more
real than anything I've experienced in FIVR
before."

"There are other worlds in this...FIVR?"

"Yup, thousands. And it's not the land or the
buildings that look and feel more real. I've played
many games with this kind of fidelity. It's not the
monsters or the animals either." He turned and
looked at her. *Really* looked at her. "It's you and
Sid and Dayna and Braemar. Calder and Den-
nistan too. Even Serik and that murdering sergeant. You're like no NPCs I've ever met."

"En-pee-see? What is that?"

"It's actually three letters. N, P and C. It stands
for non-player character."

She was right then. She was in one of those
stage shows that traveled about Karajan, an actor
in a troupe. Except she hadn't known she was
playing a role and that her whole world was just
set decoration and props. But she didn't feel like
an actor, a non-player character. She felt like Vari
of Karajan. She felt like a little girl who had
grown up in a small highland village, a village

that had burned to the ground the day the slavers came. Her parents weren't actors and they hadn't screamed like actors as the reivers hauled them away, as gauntleted hands bundled her into a cage with all of the other children. She was there, experiencing it all. She knew firsthand what it was like to grow up in a slave camp. She learned how to keep her misery at bay by studying the cockroaches and flies, by dissecting the rats, mice and birds she caught. She came to know every sinew and bone in the weekly ration of roasted chicken.

And she shared it all with Mark, there and then. She told him how she'd caught the eye of an inquisitor and been initiated as a figurist. She dissected the bodies of slaves who had once shared her pen. She mended the flesh of slavers while villagers died with pitchforks and hatchets in their hands. She lulled her mentor into trusting her then slipped him a poisoned healing potion after one of his rabid creations tore a hole in his guts. She watched the inquisitor die, wide-eyed, frothing at the mouth. Then she stole what she could carry and ran.

She didn't tell him because she wanted to prove she was real. She told him because it all made sense. The world was full of cruelty and brutality, and before meeting Mark she'd accepted it, warts and all. Like the other slaves she bowed her head and got on with what little life could offer. Now she knew differently. This wasn't even her world. Someone else had made it from the comfort of their swivelling chair. They'd fashioned it to be cruel and brutal so that people could come here and strive to be kind and just.

"Kind and just? I wish players were really like that," said Mark somberly.

"You are."

"I haven't always been." As he spoke, there was more sadness in his eyes than Vari could bear to witness.

"What were you like?"

"When a child sees a broken world he breaks his toys to match it."

"Sounds more like Arix than you, Mark."

"Yeah, pretty much."

"Nothing pretty about it, Mark."

The sun sank behind the mountains and a cold wind rose to rustle the rusty autumn leaves of the forest. Mark drew Volcanic Bastard and lit the brazier with it. Together they huddled next to the fire and warmed their hands. Vari cupped Mark's face in her hands and drew him into a kiss. As their lips parted, she held him there, gently, and looked into his eyes.

"Is this really you, Mark? Am I here with you or with your character?"

Mark's smile was bleak. "There's a pile of meat, blood and bone in RL. Real Life. It looks like me, but I'm not there. My mind is here."

"Magic?"

"Technology. Same thing, really. I'm being looked after by my world's version of figurists. We call them doctors. And my mum will be making sure they do their jobs properly. She's good like that."

She stroked his cheek. "This body? You don't really look like this?"

Mark laughed. "I don't have abs in RL, but otherwise, this body is me, just in better shape."

"The Developers made this body for you?"

"Yup. Instant adult. Just add XP."

Vari dropped her hand from his face and folded her arms. "I had to grow up the hard way."

"So did I, Vari. Just not here."

He looked at her and his sadness was gone now. Instead, his eyes were full of wonder.

"What?" she asked him as she hugged her chest a little tighter.

"You're amazing, Vari."

"Why? Why am I amazing?"

"Because Arix is wrong. You're not an NPC."

She could feel anger welling up inside her now, and confusion. It felt like he was lying, like he was desperately trying to convince himself of something. And what made her angry was that she wanted to be convinced too.

"You're a player," she snapped. "I'm not. That makes me a non-player character, doesn't it?"

He shook his head. "NPCs are no different from your puppets, Vari. They look and sound like real people, but they're not. They follow a script. That's it."

"Like actors in a show."

"Exactly. But you, Vari, you've lived an entire life in this world. You're not just reciting a backstory, are you?"

Vari shook her head. "It would take a playwright an entire lifetime to write my backstory, to capture every detail and feeling I remember. It's impossible."

"Yes, you're impossible, or I would've thought so before coming here."

There was bewilderment gnawing at the corner of her sanity. She could feel it, a dark, hungry mass. But she wasn't going to let it in. She would do what she always did. She would understand it. She was a figurist, and it was a figurist's responsibility to study and make sense of life in all of its forms. Though he had deserved to die, there was much she could thank her mentor for.

"Where is here?" asked Vari. "Where is my world in relation to yours?"

"Inside a thing called a computer. A very big and sophisticated computer."

"What's a computer?"

"Think of it like a brain, but made of lightning and metal."

Vari tried to picture it but it was beyond her. Eagerness overcame her bewilderment. She would dearly love to dissect a brain like that one day.

"The Developers, they control the computer?"

"Kind of."

"I might have to Rend Flesh your testicles if you say 'kind of' one more time." She was joking, kind of.

Mark grimaced. "Sorry. To me, this version of *Reign of Blood* feels like it's been set up and then left to its own devices. Even the quests. They respond to what we do, not the other way around. It's like this world makes the quests up on the fly and just offers them for the sake of clarifying our goals. Yes, we get XP if we complete them, but nothing's stopping us from just ignoring them altogether."

She encircled his waist with her arms and laid her head against his chest. His heartbeat was a muffled thrum beneath his shirt.

"Like we could ignore the Chasm of Corruption quest?" wondered Vari. "We could ride for the Garland capital. I could earn us a good living as a healer."

"What would I do?"

"Let's see. You can breathe fire, turn into mist, create scary visions and move objects with your mind. Children's entertainer?"

"A nice change from monsters made of corpses."

Vari sighed. "Those monsters would turn up sooner or later, wouldn't they."

She felt Mark nod and then place his chin on the top of her head. "Afraid so."

"So we can't really ignore the quest, can we."

"Others might."

"Like Arix?"

"Yes. But you and I can't."

"No, my dear warlock, we can't."

She gently extricated herself from his embrace and looked up into his eyes. "Thank you, Mark. For being honest with me."

He smiled, but there was worry in the lines of his face. "You're taking this all incredibly well, Vari. I've just told you that your world is a game inside of a metal brain."

Yes, she thought, the bewilderment is there to tell me it's true, and it doesn't change a thing.

"I'm a figurist, Mark. I see inside bodies. I control corpses with my mind. Flesh knits together and falls apart at my command. We're all just made up of bits and pieces and we make what we can with what we've been given. And you know what?"

"What?"

"In RL, as you call it, you can die? Like, properly die?"

"Yes. I only get one shot there."

"Then you and I are not so different after all."

Mark laughed. "When you put it like that, I guess not."

She cupped his face once more, kissed him, then drew him down with her to the floor. It was warm next to the brazier, sheltered from the wind by the battlements. Warm enough to shed their clothes. Warm enough to make love beneath the star-filled sky and to forget that they were from very different worlds.

20

———

[KARINA]

"Search the chamber again. Leave neither nook nor cranny uninspected. If you miss anything, I'll be exploring *your* nooks and crannies with a hot poker. Have I made myself clear, Sergeant Gunder?"

The reiver gave her a crisp salute and went back to hollering at his troops with increased vigor. There was a shrill edge of fear to his bellowing.

With a start, Karina sensed Maribella's presence behind her. The woman hadn't been heavy-footed before the transformation but now she walked as if her boots were made of silk. She could feel the wafted heat of the wardog's breath on the side of her neck. A little too close for comfort. Unbidden came the savage image of canines puncturing her skin and tearing through her flesh. She excised the thought and cast it into forgetfulness, a technique she'd learned early in her inquisitor training. Then she waited a moment longer to ensure that her voice belied nothing of her moment of weakness.

"Yes, captain?"

"Begging your pardon, madam, but we have the Altar of Solmora. The quest is complete. What are we looking for now?"

Maribella was right. They'd both received the notification when the captain, in her wardog form, had simply leaped across the tile puzzle rather than bothering to solve it. Given time, Karina would've worked it out, having studied the Vorasii logographic writing system in some depth. But Maribella's transformation seemed to have made her as impulsive as she was stealthy. It concerned Karina that her wardog was exhibiting autonomous leanings. She would have to tame her, even break her, if Maribella didn't learn to rein in her independent spirit.

Gunder hadn't worried about solving the tile puzzle either. He'd simply ordered his engineers to build a bridge over it. Such was the way of the reiver empire, Karina supposed with a sigh.

Though she and the other inquisitors did their best to lend a little sophistication to reiver culture, at the end of the day they were a brutally practical lot. They weren't interested in delving into the greater mysteries of life and existence. They just wanted a quick and dirty fix so they could get back to their drinking and fucking.

Karina had known she was different from a very early age. While other children played in the mud, she snuck into the local commander's house to read his books. The commander had a mighty plum tree beside his house. Other kids would plunder it mercilessly, eating sweet plums until their bellies ached. Some were invariably sick, although they had the good sense to return to the street before doing so. The commander would've flogged any child found vomiting onto his floorboards.

Karina had ignored the plums entirely. Her point of focus was a far greater prize, a long branch reaching a window with a faulty catch. The bedroom beyond had once belonged to the commander's son, but the boy had never returned from the Karajan conquest. It hadn't been touched in years. It was a mausoleum for all intents and purposes, and Karina had to be careful not to disturb the dust as she crept through it.

She would sneak down the stairs, testing every step as she went in case it creaked and gave her intrusion away. Upon reaching the commander's library, she would pore over book after book, delighting in the few pictures she found, puzzling over the tightly packed symbols that no-one had taught her how to decipher.

Those symbols had remained a mystery to her until the day she was caught, until that fateful moment the commander offered her a deal. He would teach her to read, and in return, he would be allowed to take certain liberties with her young body. Karina had accepted the trade without hesitation. Here was a chance to feed her starving mind, to prove that she was more than a child playing in the mud and gorging herself sick on plums. Besides, the commander was gentle and impeccably clean. It could've been worse.

She learned and she read until one day it did become worse. Until the day that he hurt her and she was forced to hurt him in return with the carving knife she stole from his kitchen. After that, she ran - straight to the Hall of Inquisition in Credence. The commander possessed a full set of the Inquisitional Histories. By volume two Karina knew what she wanted to be. By volume seven she knew, without a doubt, that she could become it. She knocked on their door, passed their tests, and became an apprentice inquisitor by the end of the week. No-one connected the murder of a smalltown commander to this bright, young runaway who had mysteriously learned to read and write like an accomplished scholar.

Of course her mentors knew. They were inquisitors after all. But she'd proven her value. She was one of them.

"Madam Inquisitor?" prompted the captain.

"A book," answered Karina. "A tome with clear instructions for the ritual of the Breaking Dawn. Although Ishka the Devout frequented all three temples in her role as high priestess, Solmora was her favorite."

"The goddess of despair? Ishka must've been a barrel of laughs."

"Not really the done thing to crack jokes during a human sacrifice, so no, I don't think Ishka had comedic leanings."

"This book, it was definitely here?"

"This is where Ishka came to contemplate and write. It's the most likely place."

"Well, considering that charred mess outside is probably the work of the warlock and the demon, they might've picked up the book while looting this place," concluded Maribella. "One of the scouts found a secret chamber out back. Whoever was here cleared the place of anything valuable."

A cold fury gripped Karina's throat. "When I get my hands on those two, I'm going to use them to spearhead an entirely new torture practice. Something involving generous amounts of acid."

Maribella's expression was implacable. "Will you be able to perform the ritual without the book, madam?"

"Yes, but it'll take longer to prepare. I'm going to have to piece it together from the various historical accounts I have."

By now the Altar of Solmora had been lifted onto a sturdy trolley and was being rolled across the makeshift bridge. Unfortunately, the engineers hadn't properly accounted for the combined weight of the altar and the trolley. About halfway across there was a sharp crack as ropes broke and the bridge collapsed, spilling the altar, trolley and a half dozen soldiers onto the tiles below. As luck would have it, the altar landed on top of the safe tiles.

The soldiers weren't so lucky, plunging through the thin veneer of stone. Four of them died on impact, impaled through the vitals by the steel spikes below. The other two wailed for mercy.

Karina sighed. "Captain, please throw one of the engineers into the pit. Choose the most inebriated one as I suspect 'drinking on the job' is the primary culprit here. Then tell the others to construct a winch and pulley system so we can salvage the altar."

"And the soldiers, madam?"

"Leave the dead. See what can be done for the other two. If they can be saved, do so. If not, order the archers to put them out of their misery."

"Yes, madam."

The captain turned to go but Karina wasn't quite done. "One last thing. When we return to camp, I want you to inform Sergeant Gunder that he is to retain day-to-day command of the troop."

"While I protect the altars?"

Karina smiled, pleased that the captain was such a quick learner. "I want you to handpick the guards. Six shifts per day of four hours a shift. I want you to personally patrol the perimeter at night, in wardog form. You'll find your night vision more than adequate. Just don't spoil it by looking directly at any of the lanterns."

The captain's eyes narrowed a little. "Won't

the soldiers find it strange that there's a lycan-thrope prowling around the camp?"

"What lycanthrope?" asked Karina with a shrug of feigned innocence. "How can they know of such a beast if they never clap eyes on one? You should transform some distance from the camp, and gag yourself for good measure."

The wardog's lips curled back from her teeth but there was no hint of a snarl. "Yes, madam. Of course."

Karina studied Maribella for a moment as she tried and failed to decipher her expression. It un-nerved her a little, to find her own creation so unreadable. Perhaps the transformation had done more than twist Maribella's body. She would have loved to cage the lycanthrope, study her at leisure, but right now she had larger concerns at hand.

"I need to focus on reconstructing the ritual. You will buy the time. See this through, captain, and your future will be secure as a loyal and much rewarded servant of the Inquisition."

Maribella licked her chops, her wolven blue eyes bright with barely-tamed ferocity. "Glory to the Great," she growled.

"Glory to the Great," Karina returned, a little uneasily.

21

———

[MARK]

Mark made his way back from the reiver camp, his Tier 2 Shroud of Shadow in effect so he could take stock of the opposition without being noticed.

As he approached their vantage point, he scuffed his boots and kicked a couple of stones. He didn't fancy getting decapitated by a spooked executioner, but knew he needn't have worried as he heard the harsh whisper from above.

"Heard you the whole time, dipshit. Fox Ears ability, remember? Stop making so much fucking noise."

Mark shook his head. Arix had been on edge since they left the waypoint. Perhaps the stakes of this operation were getting to him. If they didn't capture Karina, or if she was accidentally killed, Arix's immediate way home was gone. They would have to travel into Garland and persuade the druids to send him back. Even then, there was a chance that the druids simply couldn't reverse the summoning. Yes, he could understand why Arix might be feeling a bit stressed out. He did his best to be quiet as he climbed into the sundered turret Citadel had chosen for them to hide within.

Arix shot him a suspicious glance as the warlock hunkered down beside him.

"What?" wondered Mark.

"How did you level that Shroud of Shadow up so fucking fast? It weren't nearly as good back at the waypoint. Now it's looking quite slick. Couldn't even pick you out with my Buzzard Eyes ability."

"You heard me though."

"Yeah, well lucky reivers don't got my sorta senses."

Arix fixed Mark with a steady, questioning gaze. Mark sighed. Looked like he wasn't going to be able to wriggle out of an explanation. Although he was prepared to work with Arix, for now, he didn't want to reveal *every* trick he had up his sleeve.

"I drank Vari's plus-one mind potion before scouting out the camp. Tasted like fermented apple juice and wild black currants. Pretty good for a first try."

"What's a Mind potion got to do with the price of eggs?"

"I'm getting to that. So I needed to boost my Mind score to 16 so I could use my Transference ability."

"Transference? What's that?"

"Picked it up at Level Eight. I can transfer a tier from one spell to another."

"Diamond! Wish I had that."

"Consumes a spell slot every time I use it though. Good for specialization, not so great if you want a flexible character build."

"So what was the tier trade you made?"

"Doppelganger. Make an illusion of myself. Tier One. Bit bloody pointless so figured I'd use it to give Shroud of Shadow a boost."

Arix elbowed Mark gently. "About time *Reign of Blood* added some features like that. Nice change from them fucking multichoice tests in the old version. My executioner class gives me new skills and spells on an odd level and allows me to instantly upgrade a skill on an even level."

"Cool. By the way, I was thinking about making another trade as well."

"Oh yeah? What?"

Mark smiled. Despite the fact that they were hiding out in an old turret overlooking a reiver encampment, and that Arix wasn't exactly his first choice in co-op buddies, Mark found himself enjoying this conversation. When not actually in FIVR, Mark liked to jump onto the forums to discuss and debate character builds. With the notable exception of *Reign of Blood,* he often had more fun chewing the fat over games than he did actually playing them.

"I'm sorely tempted to cannibalize both tiers of Avalar's Leech. It's life drain is pretty pitiful compared to Vari's Mend Flesh spell. I was thinking of putting them both into Ethereal Flesh to take it to Tier Five."

"What would that give you?"

Mark pulled up the spell description and read it to Arix.

Ethereal Flesh

Tier 5: Can move as a cloud at a Level 1 human running speed for up to 20 minutes. Mist becomes extremely caustic to organic material and corrosive to non-organic material.

The executioner's face puckered like he'd just bitten a lemon.

"What?" asked Mark, a little surprised by the reaction.

"Think about it. There would literally be a reiver inside you, screaming and dissolving."

Mark had to agree. It sounded quite gross when explained out loud. "Actually, if they're higher than Level One, they might escape and outrun me. That would leave the poor bastards horribly maimed until they either die or receive healing."

Arix shrugged. "It's not like these mobs feel pain, Mark. They might *sound* like they do, but it's just audio files of real voice actors screaming their guts out."

Mark felt the muscles tighten at the back of his jaw. Why did Arix have to go and spoil a perfectly nice conversation.

"Let's agree to disagree on that point, eh?"

"Whatever." Arix pointed at the reiver camp. "How's it look down there now?"

Earlier in the day, he and Arix had taken up this position and watched the goings on from a distance. Karina had ordered the altars to be arranged so they formed the three sides of an equilateral triangle. Torches had been placed and lit in the corners of the triangle. Beyond the torches, pairs of heavily armored reiver soldiers settled in to play cards or dice, each pair assigned to a specific altar. Six soldiers in all. The rest of the camp was quiet now, most of the troops having retired to their tents after a fairly raucous drinking session. The party had started up in one of the larger tents near the altars, going on for a few hours until a stout sergeant arrived to bellow at them like a panicked cow. The revelers dutifully slunk off to their beds after a brief chorus of, "Fuck you, Gunder". To his credit, Gunder wasn't having any of that, and gave several butts some resounding smacks with the flat of his sword. This produced yelps of pain from the victims and guffaws of laughter from the onlookers.

"Two-person patrols working the perimeter," replied Mark. "Quite a few, actually, so they can remain in sight of each other as they do their rounds."

"Bollocks. Any places we can take them without being seen?"

"Sid might know." Mark tapped the amulet lightly with his fingertip. "Anyone in there?"

"Yes, hello!" answered Citadel, a tad too emphatically. He sounded a bit caught out. "Sorry, dozed off for a bit there. What's the question?"

"Are there any places on the perimeter where we can off them patrols without getting caught with our knickers around our ankles?" reiterated Arix.

"If I catch your meaning correctly, Arix," answered Citadel, "then indeed there is. Over to your right, do you see a jumble of walls and rubble where a domed theater has collapsed?"

"How do you know it was a theater?" asked Mark.

"By the terraced stone seating. There's a partially intact proscenium arch as well. The patrols must skirt the edge of the theater and that puts them out of sight for several seconds."

"But if we kill one patrol behind the theater, the following patrol will notice when they don't reappear," complained Arix.

"Yes, but a few seconds is all I need if you can cover me with your crossbow," Mark assured him. "There's a large supply tent just inside the perimeter. I'm going to set fire to it."

Arix quirked an eyebrow. "You got some plan for getting out again without leaving a trail? Shroud of Shadow won't work. You'll still make tracks." He pointed at the camp. "You only got away with it the first time because they weren't looking for nothing."

Mark gave him a wicked grin. "Where there's smoke there's mist."

"Eh?"

"I'm going to use Ethereal Flesh, turn myself into mist, and use the smoke as cover to drift away."

"Now that's a nifty trick," said Citadel. "Very clever indeed."

"Thank you, Sid."

"Where to after that then?" asked Arix. "Do some hit and run attacks around the perimeter while most of them reivers are dealing with the fire? Bit risky, if you ask me. Would only take one wrong move from us and we'd be cornered by a whole marching band of the fuckers. Yeah, we've hidden our resurrection points, but it's going to be an uphill battle what with all our gear gone."

"Let Arix know what else we found, Sid."

"There's a river some one hundred meters from the theater. I felt footsteps on the closest bank, no doubt soldiers gathering water for the night."

Arix's face lit up with understanding. "When Sergeant Gunder sends some soldiers to get water to put out the fire, we'll ambush them."

Mark smiled. "I've seen it once before. The reivers will form a bucket team, single file, and they won't have their weapons drawn. They'll need their hands free for passing the buckets. We charge that line and kill as many as we can before they regroup. Then we fade into the ruins. We can keep rolling with that general technique, if it works, drawing reivers into the ruins, hitting and running until they're too scared to set foot outside their camp."

"A night of hide and wreak-fucking-havoc, eh?" asked Arix. He waggled his eyebrows like an evil clown.

"Pretty much."

"In that case," said Arix with a wink. "Care to make a small wager?"

Mark felt a prickle of anxiety down his back. He could hear the competitive edge in Arix's voice.

"What sort of wager?"

"If I kill more reivers than you, we get Karina to send you home as well. If you kill more reivers than me, I shut the fuck up and leave you to it."

The executioner just couldn't understand that this wasn't a game to Mark. Not anymore. He wasn't doing this for the XP or the bragging rights. These reivers weren't just mobs made for slaughter. If Vari was a living, thinking, feeling entity in her own right then so were all those reivers down there. Each one had been born screaming. Each one had suckled at the breast of their mother and skinned their knees while playing tag. They'd fought with sticks and pot lids until they were old enough to enlist. They had hopes and doubts, pride and fear, just like he and Arix. They could feel love, just like Vari.

Mark shook his head. "They're not just numbers on a fucking scoreboard, Arix. Those are people down there. Yes, they want to raise up all hell with those altars and then turn Garland into a slave state, but they're still sentient beings." He brushed his fingertips across the amulet. "Just like Sid here."

"Well said, Mark," agreed Citadel.

"And as for going home," continued Mark, "it's not happening. I'm a warlock, and like all the warlocks before me, I'm sworn to protect Garland, no matter what."

Arix sneered with frustration. "Are you listening to yourself right now? Do you have any idea how insane that sounds? This isn't the real fucking world, Mark! This is just some gamer's wet dream that you don't want to wake up from!"

"I'd love to stay and hear this riveting discourse," interrupted Citadel, his tone now subdued and tense, "but I think now would be a good time to return to my meditations. All this sensing of foreign terrain, it's all rather taxing, you know? Best I rest now so I'm up to the task later on."

"That's fine, Sid," Mark assured him, happy to give the poor guy the excuse to escape. "This is going to be a circular and rather pointless discussion anyway."

Citadel didn't respond. The ruby dulled and Mark could feel the amulet grow a shade cooler against his skin.

"Is that what you think of the real world, Mark? Circular and pointless?" growled Arix.

"Pretty much sums up my life. Yes."

"Fuck, that's depressing."

"Yup, it actually is. But I don't feel like that anymore. Sure, I had my moments when I first came here, when all that numb grey felt like it was going to bushwack me around the next corner. Like any minute someone was going to tell me to wake up and smell the shit. But now, nothing. I feel great, and it's all because this place gives me a sense of purpose."

"Then you just need to find a purpose in RL. I could help with that."

"How?"

"You're a fucking decent gamer, Mark. You've

got a talent for tactics and you don't know when to quit. I could feature you as a regular on my channel."

Such was Mark's anxious pricklings that they now felt like Sonic the Hedgehog was rolling up and down his back. "You're offering me a job as a streamer?"

"Okay, mate, breathe. You've gone all pale and sweaty. I thought you said you felt great now."

Mark held up a finger, wanting Arix to give him a moment while he got his shit back together. After a moment or two the prickling eased to a dull discomfort and he nodded, ready for the executioner to continue.

Arix raised an eyebrow but had the good grace to refrain from comment. "Yes, I'm offering you a job as a streamer. Full time and at a better rate than you're probs getting at your current job. What is it you do in RL? Sorry, realized I never asked."

"I operate drone forklifts at a supermarket."

Arix gave him a wry grin. "I can totally do better than that, yeah. The rate would go up depending on your viewership numbers too. I could even spot you the airfare to London, if you wanted."

Mark blinked at Arix in disbelief. Here they

were, in the middle of the Barrens, about to execute the wholesale slaughter of a small reiver army, and Arix was offering him a dream job. But all he could think about was Vari, Sid and what would happen to Garland if he didn't complete the Chasms of Corruption quest.

"Sorry, Arix. I can't."

The executioner sighed. "That's what I thought you'd say. So let's get down to the nitty gritty of it, yeah?" Though his dark eyes were wide with feigned sympathy there was a hard flicker within. "You've got a problem, Mark."

"What problem?"

"You've fallen in love with a bunch of dialogue trees and sensation code. No matter how much you want her to be, Vari just isn't real."

Mark shook his head as the dregs of anxiety melted away, replaced by a smoldering anger. He was grateful to Jaravir's Icy Resolve for helping him keep his cool, but still he could feel the heat rising, threatening to burst into flames.

"You don't know what you're talking about."

Arix scoffed. "Fuck's sake, you're talking to a professional gamer here. I've seen enough FIVR to know that this one's pretty flash, but under the hood it's no different to any other. It's digital make believe, innit."

"Yeah," admitted Mark, "it looks like that at first. But if you look closely enough, you realize it's so much more. This version of *Reign of Blood* hasn't been constructed. It's been…" He struggled to find the right word. It came to him, along with a memory, of picking wild herbs with Vari in the forest near Citadel. "It's been 'grown'."

Arix frowned and looked at Mark like he'd grown a second head. "What the bloody hell does that mean?"

"The devs have put all the parameters and assets in place and then they've just set the system running, for hundreds of virtual years if my theory is correct. Vari isn't an NPC, she's a fully autonomous AI who has lived a complete life in this place. She was born, Arix, not made." He pointed at the reiver camp. "Same goes for them. There are no backstories and scripts here. These people have personally experienced every single memory they have." He picked up a piece of masonry and held it up for Arix to see. "The devs didn't handcraft this ruin out of tile sets and shaders, this was a city that suffered a genuine apocalypse."

The executioner's frown deepened. "The *Reign of Blood* team don't got that kind of tech. No-one does."

"Not that we know of, but I think you and I have been pulled into a virtual experiment. They haven't gone public with it yet. They're probably still observing and testing to see if it's going to hold up when masses of gamers pour in here."

Mark shuddered at that thought. He knew plenty of ethical gamers, and he knew even more who weren't, many who would treat this place like their own personal orgy of sex and violence. He dearly hoped the developers would take that into account, perhaps profile people before they let them in. Then again, they'd let Arix in. Or had they?

Arix voiced his thought before Mark could finish it. "If your theory is correct, and that's a big fucking IF, then how did we get in here and why haven't the devs booted us out?"

"You've got a FIVR implant, right?" asked Mark.

"It wouldn't be FIVR if I didn't. Trodes have too much lag and there's no way you're getting me into one of them sensor suits. Makes me feel like I'm sausage meat stuffed into a strip of in-testine."

"I don't know how," admitted Mark, "but the druids must have found a way to access my *Reign of Blood* account and engage my FIVR implant.

It's like the system converted their summoning ritual into code."

"You're saying they effectively hacked your implant by dancing about naked in some Stonehenge?"

"I have no idea what the ritual looked like. I turned up somewhere else in Garland entirely, but yeah, that's the crux of it. Inquisitor Karina must have achieved the same thing. Her summoning ritual was converted into a hack."

"Okay, I'm humoring this weird-assed theory of yours for now, mostly just to understand the fucked-up shit what's going on in that head of yours," said Arix. "So answer me this, Mister Amateur Virtologist. Why us?"

"I'm just guessing here, but it probably has to do with our gaming behavior profiles. It's not something they would publicize, but I bet the devs track everything we do in *Reign of Blood*, and it'll all be tagged to our account. In their rituals, the druids and Karina would have asked for a certain type of person to help them. In my case, my play style suited the warlock class so I got picked, probably randomly, out of all the potential candidates in the *Reign of Blood* player database. Yours obviously suited the executioner class, so same deal for you."

Dark clouds had gathered over the Barrens and the moon was barely shining through. Arix leaned back against the wall of the turret and looked up at the sky. "I got an invitation from the *Reign of Blood* community manager, to an Easter Egg hunt. Looked completely legit so I followed the clues and they led me here."

"See? That was your summoning! That was Karina's hack."

"Maybe, but it's all conjecture at the end of the day. Where's your proof, Mark?"

Mark felt a flash of anger. Why couldn't Arix just believe him? He took a deep breath, knowing that an outburst would get him nowhere. Not to mention the fact that he'd call the entire reiver army down on their heads if he raised his voice.

"I only know what I've seen and learned from others," said Mark.

"Vari?"

"Of course, yes. We talk a lot."

"And it never occured to you that she's pro-grammed to be a one woman charm offensive? That she's an NPC what's been designed to heighten your sense of immersion?" The mask of false sympathy returned to Arix's face. "I'm not saying she's doing a number on you, Mark. It takes a person to lie to another person. I think she's just telling you what the developers want you to hear. It's a total mind fuck and you can bet your bollocks that my lawyer will be reading the *Reign of Blood* small print as soon as I wake up back in London."

Mark's burning anger was extinguished by a flood of dismay. What if Arix was right? Vari felt every bit the real girl, and he loved her more than he had ever loved anyone in his life. She was everything he'd ever hoped for in a woman, in a lover and friend. But he'd just told Arix that the developers would have their gaming behavior profiles. What if, from Mark's profile, the system had been able to predict more than just his most compatible character class. What if it was able to estimate his preferences in love and companionship? The main *Reign of Blood* world was vast and he'd interacted with more NPCs than he could ever hope to remember. What if every interaction had been recorded along with his biometric responses to each and every character? Could the system have constructed a perfect mate for him out of all that data? It was possible.

Frighteningly so.

Arix's expression took on a smug edge. "You know I'm right, don't ya."

It was Mark's turn to look up at the stars as he

resisted the urge to punch Arix in the face. That one comment had been enough to drain the dismay from his mind, as if Arix had simply pulled the plug. His anger filled the void.

"Where's your proof, Arix?"

Arix opened his mouth for a quick answer and found none forthcoming. He gritted his teeth and curled his upper lip as he struggled to come up with something. Eventually he said, "Thousands of hours of FIVR experience. Interviews with the developers. All the articles I've read on FIVR development and all the conversations I've had with other gamers. Not once have I ever come across an organically grown world full of artificial general intelligence."

"Ignorance isn't truth," snapped Mark. "Just because you don't know it, doesn't mean it can't exist."

"Look, Mark, here's the thing," said Arix softly. "You have feelings for Vari. I get that. I'm sure she's real convincing." He stretched out his arms, encompassing their surroundings. "I'll be the first to admit that this whole world is real fucking convincing, more than any other game I've experienced. But you need to take a good, long look at yourself, geezer, because I'm seriously concerned about your mental health right now."

"Fuck you, Arix."

Arix raised his hands. "Fair enough. That was crossing the line. But you've got to understand my position in all this."

"What position? That you consider everything I think and feel to be some crazy delusion?"

"No, I think that you're the victim of some very devious game design, and I *know* that I need your help to get home."

Arix reached forward and placed his hand on Mark's forearm. It felt like a tentacle to Mark, like the life-sucking tendrils the Siren of the Lake had wrapped around him. He fought the urge to shake Arix's hand off.

"So my offer still stands," the executioner continued. "You can come with me and have a career, a real life, or you can stay here in Neverland and play Peter-fucking-Pan." Arix's grip grew a little tighter on his arm. "I'll even track down your real body for you, make sure you're okay. You're in a hospital somewhere in New Zealand, right?"

Mark nodded, unable to speak, choked up by the emotions battling within him.

"I'll get word to you here, via the *Reign of Blood* devs. The risk there is that they might pull you out. It's totally up to you. I'll just leave you alone if that's what you want."

Mark's voice was a hoarse whisper. "I'll think about it."

"Good man." Arix's tentacle gave Mark's forearm a squeeze then retracted. "Now let's go kill some reivers. I think we've both got some tension to work off after that deep and meaningful."

Yup, thought Mark, and nothing would relax me more than driving Volcanic Bastard through your tiny, withered heart, Arix the Damned.

22

Arix put a bolt right between the reiver's eyes. The scout had been stupid enough to forget his helmet. The second one was wearing a helm with a nose guard. Arix shot her in the throat.

Your party has killed four Level 2 Reiver Scouts.
Your XP reward per party members = 40 XP
Your party currently consists of two members.

It was interesting to Arix that Citadel wasn't counted as a party member, even though he would be integral to the success of this operation. Without him they'd be stumbling blindly through these ruins, just begging to be caught. Perhaps Citadel was at the point where leveling was irrelevant. He was supposed to be several hundred years old. Perhaps the normal rules didn't apply any longer. Not that Arix really cared. He was more than happy to keep more XP for himself.

He loaded his crossbow while looking to where Mark had felled the other patrol behind the theater. As Arix watched, the warlock sprinted into the camp, making a beeline for the supply tent. His crossbow now locked and loaded, Arix took up a firing position and covered Mark's flanks while the warlock impaled a surprised reiver warrior who had chosen that moment to step out of his tent. The bearded reiver had a tankard in his hand having poured himself a sly nightcap. Guts and beer spilled onto the ground as Mark withdrew his sword and let the warrior fall.

Your party has killed a Level 3 Reiver Archer.
Your XP reward per party members = 15 XP

Arix heard a shout to his left. The next patrol had stumbled upon their former comrades. These two were men-at-arms, clad head-to-foot in armor. With no easy killshot available, Arix aimed for the legs, opting to wing them. His bolts punched through their cuisses and caused both soldiers to howl in pain as iron punctured their flesh. Arix found it almost touching to see the two bearded men throw their arms around each other, forming a comradely embrace to support each other as they limped into the camp.

In fact, it surprised him. He'd never seen mobs behave like that in any other FIVR game he'd played. That sort of intuitive scripting was far beyond what he'd seen in previous *Reign of Blood* versions. Maybe they'd expanded their dev team, added some behavior psychologists or something. A little voice at the back of his head wondered if Mark was right about this AGI malarky. He gave it a mental slap and told it to shut the fuck up.

Other soldiers popped out of their tents to see what the two wounded reivers were bellowing about. They were just in time to see Mark breathe a plume of fire into their supply tent. It hadn't rained since Arix's arrival in the Barrens. The dry canvas and rope caught fire immediately. The entire tent was ablaze in moments.

The more quick-witted soldiers drew their weapons and charged at this firebug of an intruder. Mark mouthed "Ethereal Mist" and melted away into a cloud of dark vapor. He was soon indiscernible from the black smoke that was now billowing up from the burning tent.

Arix ran towards the theater, following the route that Citadel had described to him, the one that would lead him to the stream. He rock-hopped his way across the rubble around the theater and then wove through a short stretch of streets, coming out at what had once been a wharf. A stone pier stretched out into the river, a stopping point for the trading barges and rowboats that would have plied these waters before the apocalypse.

He caught that thought and squeezed it to death. There was no history of river trade and no fucking apocalypse. That was all back story. This city had been a ruin since the first day it was constructed in the *Reign of Blood* studio.

He focused on his surroundings to prevent any further rumination. Using his passive Buzzard Eyes ability, he peered into the shadows. With Hound Scent he sniffed the air for any traces of danger. That's when he caught the faint whiff of dog hair and blood. He spun about, wide-eyed, just in time to catch sight of a shaggy shadow before it melted into the darkness. His Fox Ears picked up the scratch of claws on stone and the soft pant of exertion before they were lost in the rising din of the nearby camp. He was alone again. This particular Barren denizen had decided that Arix was more bite than it could chew. Just as well. He would be inundated with reivers in a minute or two. The last thing he needed was a random monster encounter messing up their carefully laid plans.

An old stone warehouse overlooked the pier. Arix clambered up one of its intact walls and perched on the edge of the collapsed roof. He loaded his crossbow and watched out for Mark. The warlock arrived soon after, coalescing into human form almost directly below Arix.

The executioner performed what he hoped was a convincing bird whistle. Not that he'd taken the time to observe the local avians to hear what noises they made. It would probably stick out like a ram's bollocks to any reiver acquainted with the native flora and fauna. Mark looked up, gave him a thumbs up, and ducked into the warehouse. There was no way to reach Arix's perch from the inside. The staircases were long gone. The warlock was just finding cover.

They didn't have long to wait. Soldiers burst out of the ruined streets and headed straight for the water. With much shouting, cursing and jostling, they formed a rough line and began the arduous process of filling and passing buckets of water. They'd clearly been roused in a hurry. While all had managed to don their weapons, most had neglected to wear their armor.

This is going to be easier than I thought, mused Arix as he took a bead on the reiver closest to the river. The bolt hit the woman between the shoulderblades. Judging by the way her legs crumpled beneath her, how she flopped haplessly into the water, the bolt had severed her spine. The man beside her died as he reached out for the bucket that the woman could no longer pass. Arix's bolt punched through his temple.

Down below, Mark charged out of the warehouse, shouting "Second Skin!", "Arcane Edge!" and "Terrifying Manifestation!" in quick succession. A half dozen reivers shrieked and dropped their buckets, some covering their eyes as if attempting to block out some horrific scene. Mark cut them down with Volcanic Bastard, dropping all six soldiers in as many strikes. The poor bastards didn't even try to run, so absorbed were they with their own nightmarish visions.

So much for all your talk of treating these mobs like humans, thought Arix with an inner smirk. He then clipped his crossbow to his shoulder, unlimbered his axe, and muttered "Chopping Block" before leaping off the wall. He targeted the biggest, ugliest and most heavily armored reiver in the vicinity, a hulking woman-at-arms who looked to be a couple of levels higher than anyone else there. He was rewarded with a metallic crunch as Solmora's Bite split her helm. Then came a mixture of screeching and squelching as the axe tore through chainmail and sundered flesh. The resulting halves toppled their separate ways, hitting the ground with a couple of wet thuds.

Your party has slaughtered five Level 1 Reiver Soldiers, three Level 2 Reiver Soldiers and one Level 4 Shieldmaiden.
Your XP reward per party member = 75 XP

Congratulations!
You have achieved Level 7 as an Executioner!
Progress to next level = 1752/3000
You have been awarded 2 Attribute Points.
You may choose one skill to upgrade instantly by one tier.

He dropped both AP into Spirit. He needed to be able to take these reivers down as fast as possible, especially the higher level ones. That meant utilising his special skills. He would need all the EP he could get his hands on. To that end, he spent his upgrade on Clean Slate, raising it to Tier 3.

An arrow stung him just below the armpit, punching through his leather armor but stopping before it punctured a lung. Another bounced off his cuiss and a third shattered against one of his gauntlets. The fourth stabbed into his shoulder.

You have taken 27 damage from two arrows!
HP: 109/136

He spotted the culprits atop the ruin of another warehouse. Four reiver archers. As he yanked the arrows out of his smarting flesh, three more archers joined the first four. He rolled to avoid the next wave of projectiles and sprinted towards Mark. The warlock was fighting the remaining members of the massacred bucket team. Mark felled two more soldiers before Arix reached him, but reinforcements were now spilling out of the streets and the next wave of arrows took out the warlock's Second Skin aura.

Your party has killed two Level 2 Reiver Scouts.

Your XP reward per party members = 20 XP

"Time to go!" shouted Arix.

"Second Skin!" yelled Mark, replenishing his protective aura before giving Arix a sharp nod.

They both ran for a row of small storehouses. Citadel had pointed them out as their best escape route. Arrows thudded into the ground and glanced off their armor as they zigzagged their way to safety. Once under the cover of the buildings, they rock-hopped across the rubble, aiming for a partially collapsed wall at the back. Arix's Acrobatics ability meant he could traverse this kind of terrain with ease. He took the lead, picking the most stable pathway so Mark could get to the exit without breaking a leg. They were carrying some of Vari's healing potions but it would take a Sculpt Bone to fix a snapped tibia. Arix didn't fancy hauling Mark's heavy ass all the way back to the waypoint. Then again, he could just kill him, collect his gear, and meet him back at the resurrection point. What were teammates for, after all.

He still had the image of a beheaded Mark in mind when they finally hunkered down at the back of the buildings. They listened to the ruckus as the reivers searched for them. Mark took the amulet from around his neck and pressed it to the ground. While the warlock conferred with his pocket pal, Arix kept a lookout.

And there it was again, the shaggy shadow. Wolven eyes glistened in the reiver torchlight. Its half-human, half-canine body was hunched over as it clung to the top of a wall. Their eyes met and then it was gone again. Arix had never heard of any *Reign of Blood* expansion that included werewolves, but this creature was definitely pissing in the corners of that ballpark. Then again, this Easter Egg had more new material than he'd ever seen in *Reign of Blood* before, so werewolves weren't exactly out of spec. Besides, this one seemed content to watch the fun. Perhaps it was waiting for a better time to attack, but surely it wouldn't risk getting caught by the reivers. Whatever the monster's motivations, there wasn't much Arix could do about it right now anyway. It would probably just pick off a reiver to eat while they were all trundling through the ruins in search of him and Mark. One less reiver for them to worry about. Still, he should mention it to Mark just in case the monster decided to be annoying.

"Hey, Mark."

"Yup?"

"We've got a monster trailing us. Hairy humanoid. Looks a bit like a werewolf?"

"Werewolf? Since when does *Reign of Blood* have werewolves? Or any kind of changling for that matter."

"Just what I was wondering. I haven't kept up with their dev diary, but I'm pretty sure the Creative Director was dead set about nothing sneaking in from the classic monster set. No vampires or werewolves. No giant spiders either."

"Yeah, I read that too. He was pretty bloody vehement about giant spiders. Most overused monster in RPG history apparently."

"He's not wrong," admitted Arix.

"This werewolf. Did it look like it was hunting us? Kinda don't need that right now."

"Strangely enough, no. It weren't giving off that vibe. Seemed happy just watching."

Mark shrugged. "If it leaves us alone, we might as well return the favor."

"Sounds good to me." Out of the corner of his eye, Arix saw the amulet sparkle.

"Sid. Are you awake in there?"

"I am now, although I prefer meditating while

you're dashing about the place. Makes me a little motion sick otherwise."

"Sorry, can't really be helped at the moment."

"Not to worry. Now, there's an archway in front of you," explained Citadel. "Follow that for roughly fifty meters and take a sharp left. Stop as soon as you see the fountain of Khorlvah. Ascend the steps to your right. Go all the way up and follow the roofline until you overlook a wide avenue. Make yourselves visible but don't move from that spot until your pursuers arrive."

"What about archers?" asked Arix.

"There is enough cover at the chosen vantage point to keep you safe. I cannot stress how important it is that the reivers travel down that street. There is a rather nasty surprise waiting for them."

"What sort of surprise?" asked Mark.

"A type of creature that remains dormant within the ground until it feels the vibrations of approaching prey."

"Will they come after us once they're done with the reivers?" wondered Mark.

"Most likely. It would be a good idea to move on rather speedily once these creatures engage the soldiers."

"Sounds like a plan then," said Arix, clapping his gauntlets together. "Let's go feed the locals."

Citadel continued to guide them as they went, reminding them of the directions until they reached the vantage point. He'd chosen the spot wisely. An attic had partially collapsed, leaving a clear view of the street but plenty of sturdy wall to cover them should archers shoot upwards from the street.

The warlock pointed at an intact turret across the street. "Can your crossbow shoot that far?"

Arix wondered for a moment what he was on about, but a quick look at the turret told the story. "Worried about them reiver archers getting the drop on us?"

"Exactly."

"I'll aim a little high, allow for the drop off," answered Arix, quietly impressed with how swiftly Mark could take in the surrounding area and spot potential hazards. "The archers tend to be lightly armored so my bolts should still punch through easily enough. I'm going to have to start rationing my ammo though." He rattled his quiver to make his point. It was only half full. "Haven't seen any crossbows among them reivers so there won't be no restocking either."

"I asked a couple of the rangers to make you

some more. It turns out most rangers have a fletching skill. Vari probably has a bunch at the waypoint already."

"You've thought of everything, haven't ya?"

"I wish." He pointed down at the dusty street. It was flat and featureless, devoid of anything that would indicate a lurking horror underneath. "Going forward from here, we'll lead them into natural hazards or hit them with melee. If we ensure there are two escape routes from each ambush site, we should be fine."

Arix nodded his approval. "You know your shit, Mark. That offer of mine still stands."

Mark scowled and shook his head. "We should just focus on getting through the night, eh?"

"If you're only staying because of Vari, you've got to-"

"Later, alright?" Mark hissed.

"Hey, just making the most of our spare time before the anti-cavalry arrives."

Mark ignored him and pressed the amulet to the closest wall. "How long until they get here, Sid?"

"Any moment now. Time to take in the show from the box seats, gentlemen."

They perched on the edge of the attic to await

their pursuers. As Citadel had promised, the reivers didn't take long to get there. Soldiers poured into the street below, a few scouts leading the way. As per Citadel's instructions, Mark had been careful to cover their tracks up to the roof. Arix and Mark held their positions until one of the scouts shouted and pointed up at them. A few archers among the group notched arrows, ready to fire until an older woman with a longbow barked something and beckoned for them to follow her into the nearby turret. The other archers obeyed, heading for the darkened doorway that would lead them upwards.

The first scream came from the front of the pack as a scout was dragged into the dirt by some unseen assailant. A second followed, also at the front, and the third was the older woman, her two hands on the doorframe, bracing against whatever had burst from the ground and seized her legs. She only held out for a second or two before her grip gave way and she was dragged, shrieking and flailing, into the dirt. The remaining reivers tried to run for it. Most only made it a few steps before being pulled down. One particularly athletic scout leaped up and caught hold of a windowsill. As she struggled to haul herself to safety, one of the creatures burst from the ground beneath her. It latched onto the stone wall with hairy insectoid feet, like a fly settling on a wall, and scuttled upwards with frightening ease.

This was the only clear view Arix got of the creatures. This thing's carapace shone like burnished copper, and though its basic shape was that of an ant, it had more legs and mouth parts than it had any right to possess. Two of those legs grabbed the struggling scout around the waist and drew her down into a gnashing array of mandibles. The woman was still bleating and thrashing as the monster peeled off the wall and performed a graceful backwards dive into its hole. An eerie silence fell over the street.

"Oh my god," whispered Mark. "Those poor bastards."

Arix shrugged. "If it was real, it'd be truly horrifying, yeah. Personally, I give it eight out of ten for monster design. Nine out of ten for execution. Overall score for the viewing experience, eight point five out of ten. If we weren't so busy, I'd be tempted to pop down there and take some of those things on. They look like they'd make a satisfying crunch under my axe."

Mark looked at him with disbelief. "I don't think I've met anyone quite so determined to ignore the truth that's right in front of their eyes." He pointed down into the street. "Could you not see their fear? Could you not hear the genuine pain in their screams?"

Arix took a deep breath and put on his understanding face. It was the one he used when his esports interviewees marched out that tired old trope about finding and following your passion. He'd met many a passionate failure in his day.

"A bit of a spell in reality will do you a world of good, geeza." Arix was saved from Mark's sour retort by a welcome notification.

By using the environment to your advantage, you have slain a force of reivers.
One Level 4 Archer, two Level 3 Soldiers, four Level 2 Soldiers and six Level 1 Soldiers.
Your XP reward per party member = 100 XP

"Twenty-nine reivers in total so far," said Arix. "Not a bad start, but there won't be any more coming this way, what with them ruptures in the ground. Let's double back and see who else is backing around in the darkness, begging for a horrible death." He laughed. "Just like a b-grade horror movie. The victims split up so they can cover more ground, making it a piece of cake for the monsters to pick them off one by one."

"That's right. We're the monsters," answered Mark darkly.

Arix clapped his shoulder in what he hoped was a good-natured way. "Rather be remembered than liked." Then he tapped the amulet with his gauntleted finger. "Hey Sid. You in there, chap?"

"Ouch."

"Sorry, but do you think you could sort us a way back to the perimeter?"

They carried on this way for several hours, drawing reivers into the ruins, leading them into traps, ambushing them in person when there were no natural or unnatural hazards at hand. Both he and Mark took several bad beatings and they died a few times too. Twice for him and three times for Mark.

The warlock's third death was Arix's personal favorite. A soldier broke the handle off his axe while cleaving through Mark's leg, amputating the limb just above the cuiss. Having no other weapon handy, the resourceful reiver pulled Mark's helmet off, picked up the warlock's severed leg and bashed his skull in with it. Arix could've intervened but Mark would've been a goner from blood loss anyway. The reiver was really performing a mercy killing. As payment for the entertainment, Arix gave the soldier a swift decapitation. Clean and painless.

Treating death as pretty much a given, Arix and Mark had committed to resetting their resurrection points regularly, and in each case the survivor managed to finish off the last of the opposition and retrieve the fallen one's gear before reinforcements arrived. During that time they returned to the waypoint twice to pick up crossbow bolts and fresh EP and HP potions from Vari. Although the figurist had recruited four rangers to help her guard the place, they took a new and painfully circuitous route each time to throw off any unseen pursuers.

When they stumbled one last time into the former Horripede's lair, Vari took one look at them and ushered them to the waypoint.

"You two look like cadavers. Three days old, without the benefit of cold storage."

"Okay, maybe you can head out in my place next time," offered Arix. He was barely able to keep his eyes open and wasn't in the mood to take any scripted crap from a bot.

Vari ignored him and hugged Mark, ignoring the blood and gore splattered across the man's armor. "Bath and bed for you, mister."

"And me?" wondered Arix. Not that he fancied having a threesome with the two of them. Neither were his type. And none of the rangers present were up to snuff either. Two were blokes and the girls had a weathered outdoorsy look that didn't really do it for him. He liked his glam girls, and Krissy was the glammest girl he'd ever fancied. Still, when in Rome... "Scratch that. You two aren't invited. I'll have a chat to those two village girls I met the other day. The blond sisters with the big-"

"What were their names?" asked Mark, his tone flat as a sword blade.

"Fucked if I know or care, frankly."

"I care," snapped Mark as he stood on the waypoint. "They live within my walls which means they're under my protection."

Arix gave him a mischievous grin. "I shall promise to treat them like the lovely people you believe them to be, as often and for as long as they want. I shall ask very nicely and will gracefully accept a 'no' should that be their misguided desire."

"Aaaaaanyway," exclaimed Mark, "we can only afford a couple of hours sleep. If we wait too long, Karina will decamp."

"She's not going to leave her precious altars behind," countered Arix.

"No, but she still has the personpower to shift them."

"Ninety-one soldiers," Citadel informed them. "Not including herself and Dayna's murderess."

"If I were her," mused Vari, "I'd stay put and try to complete the Breaking Dawn ritual."

"But we have the instructions," said Mark.

Vari shrugged. "She's an inquisitor, Mark. Her whole life is devoted to finding things out, no matter the cost. She'll work it out."

Arix rolled his eyes. He desperately wanted to clean up, fuck away the dregs of his adrenaline, and then get a good night's sleep surrounded by soft, warm virtual bodies. Krissy would understand. She knew she was the only *real* girl for him. He pushed the tempting daydream aside and embraced the ugly truth instead. Mark and Vari were right.

"Yeah, don't matter what way we slice it. We don't have a lot of time." He sighed. "Guess the sisters will have to wait."

"Poor them," muttered Vari.

Arix ignored her. "Okay, dibs on going through the bath first. Then a nap. Two hours, tops."

Mark nodded his agreement. "I've left Ishka's tome in the library. I'll have another quick look at it while you're cleaning up. Got to make sure we can actually pull this off when the time comes."

Arix offered him a wicked grin. "Just sorry I won't be there when it's time to slit her throat. I owe that bitch a nice, slow death for all the shit she's put me through."

Mark shot him an expected look of disgust, but Vari surprised him by nodding her approval.

"See? Vari knows what I'm talking about."

Vari shrugged at Mark's shocked expression. "Sorry, Mark, but you've not seen an inquisitor's work firsthand."

"Let's just get back to Citadel and rest up. We've still got a lot of work ahead of us."

Yes, Arix thought to himself, more than you've bargained for, Mark.

23

———

[MARK]

Mark sank into the steaming bath and let out of groan of bliss. He washed the blood and dust from his body, starting with his face and working his way down. The heat dulled the aches and pains in his tired muscles and the water eased the weight of the world from his shoulders.

He worried that he wouldn't be able to sleep. There was just too much adrenaline in his blood, too much purpose on his mind. He was *this* close to saving Garland from the corruption and creatures that terrorized the people who lived along these mountains. And from the brief chat he'd had with Calder while Arix was using the bathroom, the corruption was spreading deeper into

Garland. One traveler even talked of Mist Wraith sightings near the capital. Yes, things were getting worse and Mark felt that he was the only one who could put it right. Well, not alone, of course. He couldn't do it without Vari and Citadel. And then there was Arix.

Mark looked forward to sending the executioner back to his flash London pad and his streamer stardom. He didn't want to hear one more word about how he needed to wake up from his dreamland and embrace the real world. As far as Mark was concerned, the real world had dealt him a pretty shit hand so far. He sure as hell didn't owe it anything. In his short time in *Reign of Blood*, he'd lived a richer life than all of his years of RL put together. Out there he was just another guy, slogging away at a job he hated until the day a robot could come along and make him redundant. He was just another guy with debts he couldn't afford to pay off and friendships that bellied out at "What'cha up to this weekend?".

It sounded crazy, even to himself, but he would happily die in this place.

Like, properly die.

And maybe he would.

Maybe the hospital would write him off as a lost cause and pressure his mother into pulling the plug. She might decide to mourn and move on, like she'd done with his father. Mark couldn't remember the last time she'd mentioned him. Would his dad have told him to wake up and get back to reality? No, he didn't think so. His father's motto had always been, "If it makes you happy, do it." Not that he had exactly lived by that motto himself.

"Reality," Mark murmured to himself, "you and Arix the Damned can go fuck each other."

He pulled up his latest notification, figuring he'd do a little character building while he bathed.

Congratulations! You have achieved Level 9 as a Warlock.

Progress to next level = 3537/5000
You have been awarded 2 Attribute Points.

Spell Selection

You have 7 magical spells available for selection.
You have 4 spell slots remaining.

Brain Leash (Cast cost = 7 EP)
Lurking Inferno (Cast cost = 8 EP)
Crippling Lethargy (Cast cost = 9 EP)
Contagious Fervor (Cast cost = 9 EP)

War Cry (Cast cost = 10 EP)
Obsidian Plate (Cast cost = 11 EP)
Wave of Despair (Cast cost = 11 EP)

Please note that Wave of Despair has been unlocked because you visited Solmora's Shrine of Despair.

Your Swordplay skill has reached Tier 5.

Your Arcane Edge spell has reached Tier 4.

Your Second Skin spell has reached Tier 4.

Your Ivara's Ignited Exhalation spell has reached Tier 3.

The battle ahead was going to be fierce. There were still ninety-one reivers between him and the altars, and if Karina was the type of leader who kept back the best soldiers for her personal protection, they'd all be at least Level 3.

He shuddered as he thought back to his first encounter with the murdering sergeant, the agony of having his lung ripped from his chest by her serrated Blade of Doom. He hadn't seen the sergeant yet, but figured she was staying close to

Karina. He sighed and sank a little deeper into the bath. The water lapped at his chin. He was actually looking forward to the confrontation, to returning the favor and avenging Dayna's death.

He dropped both AP into Mind so that he could use Transference without needing a Mind boost from one of Vari's potions. And he figured it made sense to continue with his general fire theme. Volcanic Bastard, Ignited Breath and maybe Lurking Inferno?

Lurking Inferno

By scratching a fire rune into stone, earth or wood, the caster can create a combustion trap with a radius of three meters. The contained inferno will remain dormant until released on command or can be set to explode when a living creature breaches the trap's perimeter.

Tier 1: The resulting conflagration consists of natural fire. The flames can be extinguished with water or through smothering. The fire can be extinguished instantly by the caster.

"Like the human mind, fire only wishes to be free."
- Zevryn the Everborn

He and Arix wouldn't be able to go toe to toe with ninety-one veteran reivers. They would have to continue their hit and run tactics, and Lurking Inferno was the perfect ambush tool. Even better if he used Transference to upgrade it. To that end, he glanced at the spell's two tiers.

Tier 2: The resulting conflagration consists of pitch fire. Can only be extinguished through smothering. Can be extinguished instantly by the caster.

Tier 3: The resulting conflagration consists of arcane fire. Can only be extinguished through magical means. Can be extinguished instantly by the caster.

Mark cringed at the thought of burning people alive, but then had to check his own hypocrisy. He had quite literally burned a reiver commander's face off, on the very wall above this bathroom. Though he was loathe to admit it, Lurking Inferno was an ends-justifies-the-means kind of spell and one that would come in bloody handy in the battle ahead. Knowing it would just stress him out if he dillied and dallied over the various spell options, Mark used one of his four slots to pick Lurking Inferno. There wasn't much point in setting fires that someone else could put out, and he wasn't keen on leaving anyone smoldering and disfigured either. He used two more to cannibalize Avalar's Leech and boost Lurking Inferno to Tier 3. He immediately regretted his decision. Avalar's Leech was his only healing spell. He fretted about that for about a second and a half before giving himself a mental slap. No, Avalar's Leech was more like a blood transfusion than a band aid, and from an unwilling patient too. No, he was a warlock, not a lich. He dismissed this moment of shopper's remorse and focused on his next choice. With only one slot left, it made sense to choose one of the big spells. Either Obsidian Plate or Wave of Despair.

Obsidian Plate

The caster becomes encased in a full plate constructed of arcane obsidian. This armor will take twice the caster's HP score in damage before shattering. The caster retains full mobility.

Tier 1: Obsidian Plate will shatter of its own accord after 30 seconds if not forced to by damage.

Once the plate has disintegrated, this spell has a 30 minute cooldown period.

Mark curled his bottom lip over his top lip and gave a "hmmm" of delight. This spell effectively tripled his HP score, at least for half a minute. Pretty handy if he got himself cornered and had to hack his way out.

Wave of Despair
A wave of negative emotion emits from the player, affecting every creature capable of feeling emotion within the caster's line of sight. Affected creatures will suffer symptoms stipulated by the tier description.

Tier 1: 100% chance of inducing crippling despair in Level 1-3 creatures. Paralyzes the victim for 5 seconds. 50% chance of paralyzing Level 4-6 creatures. 20% chance of paralyzing Level 7-9 creatures.

While he was quite chuffed at having unlocked a spell through his own explorations, he placed Obsidian Plate in his one remaining spell slot. Wave of Despair would've been great at the beginning of this war against Karina's reivers, but now that many of her remaining soldiers were Level 4 or above, it just wasn't something he could rely on in the heat of-

"Mark?"

He sat up in the bath so fast that water slopped over the sides. There was alarm in Citadel's voice.

"Sid? What is it?"

"Someone has activated the waypoint. Judging by their gait as they walked down the passage, I believe it is Arix."

"Why didn't you lock the door on him?"

"Alas, the bar is on this side and I can only jam a door if it is already out of-"

"Was he alone?"

"I only noticed one set of footsteps, but he was walking more heavily than usual, as if he was bearing extra weight."

"Have you noticed anything missing?"

There was a moment's silence as Citadel checked. "Ishka's tome is gone from the library, but that wouldn't be enough to account for the weight difference."

"Dammit, I'm going after-"

"Wait, Mark."

"What?"

"I can't locate Vari. Everyone else I can account for, but-"

"FUCK!"

Mark burst from the bath in a shower of water and sheer panic. He scrambled to get his clothes and armor on, buckled his sword belt in place and was almost out the library door when Citadel called out to him again. "Wait!"

He skidded to a halt. "Sid, what is it? I have to-"

"Take me with you, Mark. You'll need all the help you can get."

"Okay, thanks, Sid. But before you go into the amulet, check one more time for Vari, just to be sure."

"I have already done so. The bed you share with her is empty and I cannot sense her presence anywhere within the fortress walls."

"Could she have gone outside?"

"I would have noticed."

"Any signs of a struggle?"

"No."

"Bastard must've snuck up on her. Knocked her out before she could put up a fight."

"But why, Mark? Why would Arix do this?"

"I have a few ideas. I'll tell you on the way."

The amulet was hanging on a hook on the library wall. Mark reached for it.

"Not that one," said Citadel.

Mark let his hand drop. "Sid, we have to-"

"I know, Mark. Believe me. This will only take a moment."

As if on cue, a cockroach scuttled into the library. Upon its back sat an elegant amulet rendered in silver and gold. A silver chain, delicately rendered yet sturdy enough for battle. A golden disc upon which tiny rubies had been inlaid to form a bright red sword. Mark took the amulet from the cockroach's back and pressed it to the wall. The rubies twinkled with life as Citadel passed into it. Mark slipped the chain over his head and felt the cool of the silver against his flushed skin.

Amulet of the Citadel
+2 Spirit

"Magic is the essence of a warlock.
Loyalty is the essence of a friend."
- Citadel

"It's beautiful, Sid. Did you make this from the loot we picked up in the Temple of Solmora?"

"I did, yes."

"Thank you, and I'm damned lucky to count you as my friend."

"Likewise, my dear warlock. Likewise." There was a faint tremor in Citadel's voice. "Mark, what if-"

"We're not going there, Sid. If my theory is correct, Arix needs Vari alive."

"Then let us make sure she stays that way."

24

[KARINA]

Karina slammed the book down onto her desk and stood so quickly that her chair toppled backwards. She gripped the book again and was about to repeat the act of literary violence when she was interrupted by a soft cough at the door flap of her marquee. Her sigh was almost a growl.

"What is it, Gunder?"

The hefty sergeant stepped inside and offered her a stiff salute. She didn't bother to return it.

"I'll have you know, sergeant, that I'm in the mood for gratuitous torture. You had best speak your piece and be quick about it."

While the man struggled to retain his composure, she brought up his stats just to make sure the solution wasn't staring her in the face.

**Sergeant Gunder of Credence
Class: Reiver Warrior - Level 5**
Progress to Level 6 = 367/500

She didn't bother with the rest. Level 6 or higher, that's what she needed to complete the Breaking Dawn ceremony, and she didn't have time to wait for this lout to level up. In fact, the way her luck had gone of late, Gunder would get himself killed at something tragically ironic like 499 XP. Captain Maribella was probably Level 7 by now but she'd not shown her traitorous snout since Karina had ordered her to patrol the perimeter. If she was alive, that was. As a combined force, the executioner and the warlock were proving to be quite formidable. Perhaps they'd gotten the better of her wardog. Or perhaps Karina was simply a far worse judge of character than she imagined.

"The demon has been sighted, madam."

"Oh good. Come back to slaughter more of your utterly hapless ranks, sergeant? Right now, I would consider that a welcome depopulation of the useless-fucking-majority!"

"He's not attacking, madam. He's waving a white flag and there's a woman with him."

Karina leaned forward on her desk, knuckles pressing into the wood. "The Karaji Figurist?"

"Judging from Captain Maribella's description, yes, madam. The demon says he wants to parlay."

It could still be some sort of trap, thought Karina. A way to get directly to her. "Any sign of the warlock?"

"No, madam, and I've had our remaining scouts circle around behind the demon to check."

"They all returned?"

"Yes, madam."

"But found nothing."

"No, madam."

"Then I think I need to have a chat with this demon."

THE EXECUTIONER HAD POSITIONED himself well. The terrace he was perched upon on had multiple exits, and the building itself was a rabbit warren of passageways. It would be impossible to cover them all with sufficient soldiers to impede his escape.

"Evening, Madam Inquisitor!" the demon called out in a cheerful tone. "I've brought some peace offerings, a book and a bitch to help you out with that Breaking Dawn ritual of yours."

The figurist was propped up against his legs, bound and gagged. Blood matted her dark hair but Karina could tell by her occasional twitch and thrash that she was alive. She brought up the woman's stats to be sure.

Vari of Karajan
Class: Figurist - Level 8
Progress to Level 9 = 2219/3000

Body: 12
Solmora's Blessing +1 Modifier: 13

Mind: 17
Spirit: 19
Solmora's Blessing +3 Modifier: 22

HP: 91 / 104
EP: 176 / 176

Skills
Alchemy (Tier 5)
Physik Perception (Tier 4)

Horse Riding (Tier 2)

Spells
Mend Flesh (Tier 5)
Rend Flesh (Tier 5)
Puppeteer (Tier 4)
Sculpt Bone (Tier 4)
Purify Blood (Tier 2)
Blinding Malaise (Tier 1)
Cleanse Infection (Tier 2)

Yes, Vari of Karajan would fit the sacrificial bill quite nicely.

"Show me the book," Karina demanded.

The executioner pulled it from his backpack and waggled it in the air. "Do you know how to read it?"

Karina gritted her teeth against his condescending manner. As much as she'd love to order her archers to cut the bastard down, she knew he would just resurrect nearby. And there was the chance that they would hit the Figurist. Unfortunately, the demon held all of the cards right now.

"Of course."

"Then here's a little something else to help kick off the negotiations," said Arix.

He took a sheathed dagger from his belt and

tossed it down to her. She picked it up, drew it and turned the fine blade in her hand.

Blood of the Lost
+20% to base dagger damage.
30% chance of inducing internal hemorrhaging in an organic enemy.
+30% accuracy when thrown.
Will return to owner if in line of sight.

"We might be lost yet our blood
will always find its way home."
- Ishka the Devout

She returned the dagger to its sheath and tucked it into her belt. "What is it you want?"

Arix laughed. "I've never been any good at this roleplaying shit so I'll get straight to it. I'm a real boy who wants to go back to his real girlfriend, his real career and his real triple-shot lattes."

"The demon wants to go back to his realm of debauchery?"

"Sure, lady. Whatever those algorithms of yours can understand. Just send me the fuck home."

The demon limbered his axe and leaned on it.

The threat was clear. He would execute the figurist if these negotiations didn't go to his plan.

"Is that all?" she asked.

"Not quite. But I think you're going to like this bit."

"How so?"

"Well, the warlock is going to come looking for his lady love, yeah? He's a real boy too, but the poor bastard's lost his grip on reality. So I think we should do everyone a favor, him included, and send him home too." He grinned. "Think you can do that, Inquisitor?"

"I can. Do you have a plan for capturing the warlock?"

"Oh, we won't need to capture him. He'll give himself up to save his brown-eyed beaux here."

"You're sure of this?"

"Sure as anything in this fucked up fairytale."

Karina pondered the situation for a moment and came to the conclusion that the demon was wrong.

"Tell me, Arix the Damned. How did you know that I would need someone of Level Six or higher to sacrifice for the ritual?"

"The warlock has this spell called Cunning Linguist. It allows him to..." Arix trailed off as realization dawned.

Karina enjoyed watching him deflate. "Yes, my dear demon. If he has read the book then he knows I can neither give the figurist up nor kill her prior to the ritual's completion. There is no room for bargaining here. He will come for his lady with the vehemence of a stricken lover." She sighed. "Our only hope is that I complete the ritual. Of course, if I am to do that, I will need some assistance in slowing him down." She shot Gunder a dark look that left the man visibly shaken. "You and he have already proved that my defenses are less than sufficient."

Karina almost laughed as Arix struggled to retain his composure. "Not a problem. We could...um…"

"Here's what we're going to do, demon," Karina interjected. "You bring the figurist and the book to my camp." He opened his mouth to protest. "I know there's no point in killing you," she cut him off, "as you'll simply pop up again somewhere annoyingly difficult to find. What I'm offering here is a partnership. I will offer you the services of my remaining soldiers so that you may capture the warlock before he becomes too much of a nuisance. Then I will send you both home. Do we have a deal?"

Arix's face took on a suspicious cast. "How do

I know you're not going to just slap collars on us both and keep us as slaves?"

Karina smiled. "To be honest, demon, I would send you home right now if not for that warlock. You've proved yourself to be more of a hindrance than a help."

"I'll take that as compliment."

"Please don't." Karina turned and began to walk back to the camp. "I will see you and the figurist at my tent," she called over her shoulder.

"Hey!" shouted Arix. "We're not done negotiating here!"

Karina didn't bother to answer. As far as she was concerned, the deal was already done.

25

[MARK]

"Mark?"

He stopped in his tracks and ducked behind a wall for cover.

"What's wrong, Sid?"

"Place me against the stone."

Mark did as he was bade.

"Yes, I thought so. We're being followed."

Mark peeked around the edge of the crumbling bricks. "Where?"

"See the bell tower?"

There was only one building tall enough to be a bell tower, but it was weathered and eroded beyond recognition.

"How did you know that's a bell tower?"

"The bell's still inside it. The ropes have long

since rotted away but the breeze is blowing across the bell, causing a faint vibration."

Mark peered up at the tower's summit and could just make out a dark, shaggy silhouette. "Oh shit. It's the werewolf."

"Werewolf? What is that?"

"A shapeshifter. Someone who can shift between human form and a wolf-monster thingy. Arix and I saw it near the reiver camp."

"Is it going to attack us?"

"I don't think so. It didn't before, and surely it would've had a go by now."

As he watched, the lycanthrope moved into view, allowing the sun to fully reveal her sinuous form and the silver-grey of her coat. The thing looked straight at him, her bestial face impassive. Mark wasn't quite sure why he thought the creature was a she. Maybe there was something about her stance or her features that was feminine.

Mark stepped out from behind the wall and offered the werewolf a tentative wave.

"Mark? What are you doing?"

"Establishing contact."

"You think it's friendly?"

"She hasn't proven herself hostile yet."

"She?"

Mark shrugged. "Just a hunch."

"Need I remind you that Vari is in the clutches of the despicable Arix the Damned and that we have little time to be dallying with the local fauna?"

"This might be an opportunity we can't afford to pass up. It's not like we have an oversupply of allies right now."

"Forgive me for pointing this out, Mark, but your last attempt at an alliance didn't work out so well."

The werewolf waved back, a jarringly human gesture. She then descended the tower, crawling down its sheer wall on all fours like it was the easiest thing in the world. Mark was reminded of the scene from Gary Oldman's *Dracula* when Keanu Reeves sees the vampire scampering like a lizard across the castle wall, his crimson cape trailing behind him.

"She climbs even better than Arix."

"And that is a reason to trust her because…"

"Oh, I'm not about to trust her, Sid." He followed up the assertion by casting "Second Skin". He would save Obsidian Plate for when the werewolf really wanted to have a go.

The werewolf approached across the courtyard until Mark raised a gauntleted hand. 'That's close enough."

She stopped and cocked her head. Mark was surprised by how cute he found the gesture, like she was a friendly dog wondering if it was walk time.

"Can you speak?" asked Mark.

"Yes, I can speak," the lycanthrope answered.

She sounded like someone trying to talk while chewing a large chunk of steak. The image wasn't terribly comforting, and there was something unnervingly familiar about her voice.

"Do I know you?"

The wolf shook her head. "But I know of you, warlock."

"How?"

"I was human, a Garlander. I heard things before the corruption did this to me."

Mark had tried to keep abreast of the troubling news that poured into Citadel these days, and he'd never heard of lycanthropy among the tales of woe. He attempted to bring up the creature's stats but only managed to access the basics.

Level 6 Wardog

"Do you have a name?"

"Greta."

"Right then, Greta, what is it you want?"

"To help you."

"Help me with what?"

The werewolf's smile was more of a snarl, but Mark could see she was trying. "I heard you travel with a dark-skinned woman. A healer? Where is she now?"

Mark felt heat gather around his eyes. "You know where they are."

"The healer and the axeman. Yes."

He took a step forward, his hand now gripping Volcanic Bastard. "Tell me!"

The werewolf raised her long-clawed hands. Contrary to folklore, her palms were hairless and Mark noticed heavy calluses at the bases of her fingers. They were more pronounced on her right hand. Was it from wielding a hammer or sickle, or was it from a sword? His grip on his own sword tightened.

"They are in the reiver encampment."

"Fuck! That slimy, traitorous-"

"She is alive," the wolf cut in. "Do you want her back?"

"Of course I do."

"Then follow me."

The werewolf trotted away on all fours. Mark followed her through a series of winding streets and shattered buildings until they reached the base of a spiral staircase. Greta motioned for Mark to wait, then scampered up the steps. A few moments later she returned, her claws now glistening with blood.

"Come."

"Who or what did you just kill?"

Greta ignored him and headed back up the stairs.

"Now would be an opportune time to leave," suggested Citadel.

"I want to see where this goes."

He ducked into a nearby chamber and found a secluded spot where he could lay down a resurrection point. Then he followed the stairs upwards until masonry and dust gave way to sky. The stairs ended prematurely on a landing. The top section of the tower had been cut clean off, presumably during the cataclysm. There was just enough room for him to share it with the werewolf and the dead reiver archer at her feet. Her smell was pungent but not unpleasant. It reminded him of his mum's old cocker spaniel, Biddy. At least it covered the stink of freshly spilled blood.

They were on the opposite edge of the encampment from where he and Arix had launched their initial attack against the reivers. They were just a stone's throw from where the altars had been arranged in a triangle. A woman in black stood at the head of the triangle. The palm of her left hand was pressed against the Altar of Solmora. She held Ishka's book open in her right. Vari was nowhere to be seen, but Arix stood nearby, leaning on his axe. Somewhere inside Mark, a bucket plunged down into the well of his emotions and came up brimful with hatred.

Out of the corner of his eye, he saw the werewolf looking at him. "You can have the demon," she growled. "The inquisitor is mine."

Mark assumed she was talking about the woman in black and that rang more than one alarm bell for Mark. Once again he gripped the handle of his sword. "How do you know she's an inquisitor?"

Greta's blue eyes bored into him. He was sure he'd seen those eyes before. "My village was attacked by reiver slavers. I escaped, but not before the inquisitor among them practiced her 'arts' on me."

"I thought you said the corruption changed you."

Greta growled. "Other arts, warlock. The painful ones."

"Was it her?" asked Mark, inclining his head in the direction of the camp.

"No. Another."

"Yes, you can have the inquisitor, but not before she sends Arix back where he came from."

"Arix? That's the axeman's name?"

"Yes. Arix the Damned. And I need to see what that book she's holding says first. I might still need Karina alive, at least for a little bit."

"That's a lot of conditions," the werewolf complained. "I was just thinking I'd bite the inquisitor's throat out, maybe disembowel her first though."

"Well, there's a ritual that needs to be completed and Karina is a vital part of it."

"What ritual?"

"See those altars down there? They can cause something called the Breaking Dawn, and from what I've read in Ishka's book, that could either spell really good news or bad news for Garland."

"What's the bad news?"

"If Karina completes the ritual, she would be able to command the chasms and the corruption that lies within them. She could open up new chasms in Garland and overwhelm it with creatures of *her* creation and under *her* control."

"That *is* bad news."

"It gets worse. The ritual requires a blood sacrifice. A human being of Level 6 or higher."

"Your dark-skinned woman?"

Mark squinted and gritted his teeth against the anxiety that was welling up within him. Every moment they hesitated was one moment closer to Vari's death. But the more he thought about the task ahead, the more daunted he felt about attempting it alone.

"Then what's the good news?"

"If *I* complete the ritual then I can close the chasms for good. No more corruption. With luck, it might even cure your lycanthropy."

The werewolf sniffed and scratched at a spot behind her ear with a long claw. "You'd still need a sacrifice?"

To Mark she didn't seem all that taken with the prospect of a cure. "Yes, that's where Karina comes in."

The werewolf ran a long tongue along her sharp teeth. "You have a deal."

"Any idea how we're going to fight our way through ninety reiver soldiers?"

"You seemed to have no trouble yesterday."

"So that *was* you watching us."

"Yes. You fought well."

"That was with Arix, and we had Vari supplying us with healing and essence potions." Mark quietly cursed the fact that he'd cannibalized Avalar's Leech. "You don't happen to know any healing spells, do you?"

"No, but I heal quickly."

"I don't."

"You can come back to life."

"Saw that too, did you?"

"Yes."

He realized just how lucky he and Arix had been. If this werewolf had decided to make their lives difficult last night, it could have staked out their resurrection points and griefed them as they respawned.

"If I die, I'll need you to collect my gear." He patted the pommel of Volcanic Bastard. "Especially my sword. We'll designate a meeting point each time." He wasn't about to let Greta see his resurrection point this time around. He would wait until she was engaged in battle before setting it.

"Might I interrupt this planning session with a little suggestion?"

The werewolf gave a start and stared at the amulet around Mark's neck. "What is that?"

Mark offered a wry smirk. "Sid the Talking Building, meet Greta the Talking Dog."

"Hello, Greta."

Greta sniffed, as if trying to catch Citadel's scent. "If it's a building, then why is it in a necklace?"

"It's complicated," excused Mark. "Sid? You had something you wanted to add?"

"Indeed. I noticed it during the attack yesterday, underneath the campsite. I didn't mention it yesterday as it didn't seem relevant, but today it could prove rather helpful. Mark? Would you do the honors?"

Keeping the amulet on, Mark pressed the ruby to the closest section of wall while Greta watched. Her ears twitched with curiosity.

"As I thought, there are sewers running beneath the campsite. Most have collapsed and are impassable. A couple remain intact. There's an entrance to one of them nearby."

Mark laughed, drawing a growl from Greta. "What's so funny?"

"No adventure is complete without a sewer run."

"I don't know what the fuck you're talking about," was her response and Mark was once again struck by how familiar her voice sounded to him.

"Nevermind," he said, shaking his head. "Sid?

Is there some way we can pop up into the camp from the sewer?"

"Yes, two places, and one of them is quite close to that marquee."

"Good, then we need to sneak in and get Vari out of there first."

Yet as soon as he said it, something felt off. There was a key piece of information missing.

"I'll bite some throats out then."

The statement startled Mark out of his reverie. "What? Why? As a diversion?"

"No, for dinner." The lycanthrope's mouth gaped into what Mark assumed was a smile. "Yes, a distraction. Give you a better chance of nabbing your lady friend without getting overwhelmed."

His instincts were waving red flags again. Mark had learned to trust them over his years of gaming. His brain invariably picked up far more than he was conscious of. As if summoned by a spell, a memory fluttered up from the depths of his subconscious. Tiles glowed brightly in the Chamber of Solmora. A secret room that only Arix could find.

"Shit!"

"Something about this plan vexes you, Mark?" asked Citadel.

"Shit, shit, shit!"

"A triple vexation. This must indeed be a terrible plan."

"Yeah, sorry, but it's not going to work."

"Why not?" demanded Greta.

"Arix has a spell called Truelight. It allows him to detect traps and secret doors. If I was him, I'd use it all over that camp to make sure some warlock doesn't pop out of a trapdoor and jam his Volcanic Bastard sword up my treacherous ass."

"Although I do enjoy the image," commented Citadel, "I must disappoint you there, Mark. The executioner's anus is remarkably reliable. His motions were regular and of an even weight and consistency."

Mark's mouth opened but no words came out.

"Arix's brain," continued Citadel. "Now that's a different story entirely. His face too. If you were to jab Arix in his treacherous-"

"Sid?" Mark interrupted.

"Oh, sorry. Yes?"

"You're nervous, aren't you."

"I'm rambling?"

"Yup."

"Alas, yes. A little anxious, if I'm to be honest."

Greta snarled, startling them both. "Do you two fucking mind?"

"Right, yeah," agreed Mark. "We need a new plan."

"And before you mention it, that hard-to-see spell of yours won't work either."

"Shroud of Shadow? Why not?"

"Karina has a spell called Sparks of Sentience. It lets her sense anything with a decent-sized brain in the surrounding area."

Mark eyed her with suspicion. "How do you know that?"

Greta shrugged. "I was shackled but they didn't blindfold me or block my ears. Had to stay sharp so I could find a way to escape."

Mark couldn't quell his anxiety any longer. "Can I really trust you, Greta?"

"We both want the inquisitor and we're more likely to do that if we work together. Trust has nothing to do with it."

Mark wished he could believe that. "Fine. In that case, I think I have another plan forming. I've got another way I can get in that might sneak me past Karina's brain-sense spell. But after that I'll need a full thirty seconds worth of distraction so I can make my escape with Vari."

"Can I help in any way, Mark?" asked Citadel.

"Yeah. If I got us close enough, do you think

you could pinpoint Vari's exact location based on her weight and shape?"

"Yes, I believe I could."

"In that case, my friend the talking building, and my new friend the talking dog, we are about to ruin Inquisitor Karina's day."

26

———

[VARI]

"You know this is nothing personal, yeah?" asked the executioner. "Like literally. You're not even a person and Mark needs to realize that."

She could read the guilt clearly in his dark brown eyes. He was struggling with what he was doing, but Vari doubted it had anything to do with her. She was a non-player-character to him, an illusion created by the great brain of metal and lightning that had forged her entire world. No, Arix's guilt was about Mark, and what her death would do to him.

But Vari had a few ideas of her own on that front. Mark would try to rescue her, of that she was sure. Whether he would succeed, now that was a different matter entirely.

"I've seen FIVR addiction plenty of times," continued Arix, regardless of whether Vari wanted to hear him or not.

She sorely wished her spell commands could be activated mentally instead of verbally. She'd Rend Flesh that annoying tongue right out of his mouth.

"I did a few videos on it during VR addiction awareness week. Views were through the fucking roof. You're dangerous, Vari, and people know it. A drug." He drew closer and stared into her eyes, like he was trying to see the strings and wheels inside her head. "It's the feedback loop, innit. He thinks he's in love with you and you're programmed to give him the right feedback so that he keeps on projecting those feelings. But it's all a lie. You're no more capable of love than my iPhone is." He chuckled. "People say they love their iPhone but no-one ever expects the fucking thing to love them back. I'll be having a few words with the *Reign of Blood* devs about this. They're facilitating FIVR addiction. Greedy, callous bollocks if you ask me."

Vari was *not* asking Arix and rather wished he'd shut up so she could concentrate. While a gag effectively disabled her spell casting abilities, it could do nothing about her skills. He'd need to gag her brain to stop those. In particular, Vari hoped that her theory about Physik Perception was going to pay off.

Arix the Damned
Class: Executioner - Level 9
Progress to Level 10 = 3022/5000

Body: 18
Modified Body: 19 (+1 from Dusk Leather Armor)
Mind: 15
Spirit: 15

HP: 162/162
Modified Body: 171
EP: 135/135

Skills
Axework (Tier 5)
Horse Riding (Tier 2)
Arbalist (Tier 4)
Acrobatics (Tier 3)
Climbing (Tier 3)
Buzzard Eyes (Tier 2)

Fox Ears (Tier 2)
Hound Scent (Tier 1)
Enduring Will (Tier 1)

Spells
Chopping Block (Tier 3)
Truelight (Tier 1)
Clean Slate (Tier 3)
Justice Prevails (Tier 3)
Righteous Fury (Tier 2)
Blood Retribution (Tier 1)
Suspended Sentence (Tier 1)

Her first analysis of Arix only won her the basics. Vari could now see his full character sheet, but she needed more. Karina was living proof that this world's magic could reach into Mark's 'real world'. The inquisitor called out to the metal brain, asked for a demon and got Arix the Damned for her troubles. Vari wondered what else could be asked of the marvellous machine.

"So here's what's happening," continued Arix, heedless of the fact that Vari was now picking him apart with her eyes. "I capture Mark when he shows up to save you. And he will. He's balls-deep in love with you, poor deluded bastard."

Her Physik Perception bored into the executioner, tunnelling under the skin into the viscera beneath. She could see how his Acrobatics skill was linked from the muscles in his arms, legs and back to the section of his cortex that managed proprioception. His Arbalist skill was a series of strong cords linking his hands to his eyes via a part of the brain that handled depth perception. His Axework skill was a latticework of fine threads that covered almost his entire body.

"Karina will cut you open and bleed you all over them altars so she can do her Breaking Dawn thing. I'll make Mark watch that. Not because I'm a cruel bastard," Arix hastened to add. "This isn't fun for me, yeah? It's supposed to be a fucking game. I like Mark. He's a good gamer and his heart's in the right place."

Your Physik Perception skill has reached Tier 5.

**Congratulations!
You have unlocked a new skill.
Meta Sight (Tier 1)**

You have earned 200 XP for unlocking a hidden talent.

Vari found herself going deeper, passing between the fibers of Arix's flesh and blood into something else. The sensation was both shocking and exhilarating. She likened it to the flight of an albatross as it soared out over the low-hanging clouds. How it then dove and broke through the concealing vapor, revealing the grey-bue vastness of the Karajan Sea beneath. Symbols flowed before her, an ocean of glistening iconography.

"Actually, scratch that. His heart's in totally the wrong place right now, but that's going to change, innit. Once you're dead, Mark's got nothing keeping him here. Yeah, he'll kick and scream for a bit, probably call me every name under the sun, but he'll come around eventually. He'll see what a nutjob he's been. Bit fucking embarrassing, yeah? You can love your algorithms. You just can't *loooove* your algorithms." He laughed at his own joke. "That's a bit of a laugh. Must remember that for my first show back."

At first the symbols coalesced around Vari, swamping her with incomprehension, but then she noticed the patterns. Taking a deep breath, she calmed herself enough to focus on one thick stream of letters and numbers. Words popped up, begging to be read. Binocular Vision. Magnification. Depth of Field. Terms associated with vision. She followed the stream to where it tumbled like a waterfall into a swirling pool of text. Extensor Carpi. Flexor Carpi. Grip Pressure. Muscle Tension. She was looking at Arix's Arbalist skill now in its most fundamental form, a tapestry of pure information.

Your Meta Sight skill has reached Tier 2.

"Anyway, I know you can't understand any of this, Vari. Not really. You're just a lump of machine code and script. I'm pretty much talking to myself, but I guess that's okay, innit. Better to talk it out than bottle it up. That's what I tell Krissy when she's having a bad one." Vari could see how the code changed as he rolled his eyes, as the symbols simulated his extraocular muscles. "Sometimes she tells me to shut up and leave her alone, so I respect that. She comes right. She always does."

Vari pulled back, soaring upwards until she had a birds eye view of Arix's information. She could feel her own brain making sense of it now, forming all that abstraction into a human shape. Head, torso, arms and legs were all there like a man-sized sculpture made from trickles of liquid metal. It was frustrating. She could see a thousand different ways to kill Arix right now, a multitude of strings she could slice through with her mental scalpel. If only she had one. She was the observer this time, not the surgeon. But there was one thing she could learn about Arix the Damned, one thing she could replicate for herself that might make all the difference.

"Damn, I miss my Krissy. Can't wait to see her face once I finally wake up from this virtual shithole." His mouth twitched into a sneer. "Can't wait to see those dev's faces when I sue their asses for this whole 'no logoff' bollocks. I could probably retire on the proceeds of *that* court case. But then...what would I do with myself? Probs drive Krissy nuts if I slacked around the house in my underwear all day. Drive myself nuts too."

Like a hawk sweeping the area for prey, Vari glided over Arix's data until she found what she was looking for. It was tucked in beside his cardiovascular biometrics. Whoever had written these codes had a poetic sensibility, clearly. This was very close to Arix's heart.

"Actually, will probs be too busy patching Mark back together. He'll hate my guts for a bit, but he'll come around eventually. Geeza's got potential, you know that? Nah, of course you don't know. He's got the brain of a pro gamer and I'm going to help him train it. I'll be the first to admit that I'm not the best gamer in the world. Don't have the patience for it, to be honest. But Mark, he could really go places, yeah? Just needs the right kind of management."

Vari studied the symbol and the shifting seams of code within. Arix would talk himself out soon, she could see it in the tides of his brain. The numbers associated with guilt had steadily dropped while he'd been monologuing. They were almost at comfortable levels. She didn't have much time left.

"It's all for the best, innit. Sacrifice is a necessary thing if you want to make something of yourself in this world. Mark will come to realize that." He smirked and patted her on the head. "Nice talking to you, Vari. Best chat we've ever had."

Arix stood, looked like he was going to say more, but then simply shrugged, pushed the tent flap aside and walked out.

You have cast your line into the river of consciousness and fished up a glistening talent!
Your Personal XP Reward = 150 XP

Vari bit down on her gag, struggling to contain her excitement. A squeal of delight would only draw the wrong kind of attention right now.

Mohkash wonders if you will release this prize fish into your own Flowing Waters?
This will enable you to activate your acquired Core Ability once the conditions are met.

Y/N

Yes! thought Vari.

She felt her new talent sink into her belly like a warming draft of mulled wine. Vari grinned behind her gag. Arix had said that sacrifice was necessary if you wanted to make something of yourself. The executioner was going to find out just how right he was.

27

[MARK]

The reivers worked under torchlight as they prepared the Breaking Dawn ritual. Inquisitor Karina was at the black heart of it all, drawing her runes and performing her incantations. From what Mark had seen in Ishka's book, he understood that the ritual was a lengthy process, as any bit of world-changing should be. Harnessing the power of the Chasms of Corruption, that wasn't something you wanted an apprentice inquisitor to accidentally trigger while she was goofing off on a Sunday afternoon.

But he also knew that Karina would need to have everything ready before dawn, and that she would sacrifice Vari as the first rays of sun touched the altars. Mark planned to strike just prior, in the narrow window between the end of the inquisitor's preparations and the beginning of the new day.

Of course, Arix was down there too, lurking about, observing the proceedings. The executioner had an impatient air about him, never settling in one place for too long. He was clearly excited about going home. Mark honestly couldn't think of anything worse.

"Mark?"

"Yup, Sid?"

"I just wanted to say that you are the finest Warlock I've ever worked with."

Despite the chill of the night air, Mark felt a flush of warmth inside. "Thank you, Sid."

"Now please, promise me something."

His inner warmth give way to a clammy dread.

"Depends what it is."

"I'm not sure how to put this delicately…"

"We're not going to fail here, Sid. We'll get Vari out and-"

"If things don't turn out quite as we hoped," interrupted Citadel gently. "I need you to promise me that you'll go through with the Breaking Dawn ritual, that you'll banish the corruption so that Garland will be safe."

He didn't want to go there. He didn't want to think about the gaping emptiness that Vari would leave behind. Instead, he focused on making a promise that he dearly hoped he would never have to keep.

"Yes, I promise," he rasped. "Even if Vari..." The words caught in his throat.

"She would not want her death to be in vain," urged Citadel.

"Even if Vari dies, I will complete the ritual. I will protect Garland just as I vowed."

"Thank you, Mark."

"But that's not how it's going to be."

"Of course not. I just needed to hear the promise."

He cast his gaze back down to the reiver camp and caught sight of Karina before she disappeared into her tent. Although he'd only read through the ritual's instructions once, a quick survey of the preparations told him that the inquisitor was finished. The night sky was brightening too. It was time to move.

Mark looked over to where Greta was curled up into a furry ball, sleeping peacefully. If he shook her awake he'd probably get his throat slashed open. Instead, he picked up a pebble and tossed it so it landed next to her head. Her eyes snapped open. Mark's hand went to his sword as a savage fury flickered across her cold, blue orbs. But then she yawned and her ferocity faded away as she stretched like a dog.

When she was done, Mark nodded his head towards the camp. "Ready?"

She greeted the question with a sharp-toothed grin. "For breakfast? Fuck, yes."

Under other circumstances, Mark might've laughed. "Let's just focus on the task at hand, eh? Lots of distraction and plenty of smoke, please."

The wardog nodded and slunk off into the shadows. He only had a few minutes before she would launch her attack.

"Ready, Sid?"

"As much as one can be under these trepidatious circumstances."

"Same. Let's do this."

The first scream went on for a long time. Mark tried not to picture what Greta had just done to that poor reiver. A shout followed, meat and metal hit the ground with a thump. A torch flew end over end through the gloom and landed on the roof of a tent. The canvas burst into flames. The occupants tumbled out shortly after, shrieking and burning.

The Wardog has slain four Level 3 Reivers.
Your XP reward per party member = 60 XP
Your party consists of two members.

He shuddered and looked away as he murmured "Ethereal Flesh". His vaporous body poured across the packed earth of the camp. As best he could, Mark hugged the shadows whilst keeping an eye out for Arix. The executioner was the only one who might recognize his mist form, having seen it during their previous assault on the reivers. Soldiers tore through his vapor as they ran to put out the fires and do battle with the wardog. Greta howled as she burned and butchered with unsettling enthusiasm.

The Wardog has slain three Level 3 Reivers.
Your XP reward per party member = 45 XP

Having reached a large pile of firewood, Mark solidified and cast his next spell, Lurking Inferno. He set it to explode on command rather than contact, then checked his EP count.

EP: 102/144

This was going to be tight, especially since he

didn't have one of Vari's essence potions to top him up. He didn't have any health potions either. Arix had stolen most of Vari's potions before leaving Citadel, and smashed what he couldn't carry.

He melted away again and this time followed the line of tents that Greta had conveniently set fire to. There was enough smoke billowing up that even Arix would have trouble picking out what was natural and what was warlock.

Speak of the devil, Mark thought to himself. The executioner now stood with Karina outside the inquisitor's marquee. The inquisitor's expression was impassive, but there was a smile on Arix's face that would've sent a shiver down Mark's spine had he possessed one in that moment. The bastard was enjoying this. Mark silently wished he'd chosen to upgrade Ethereal Flesh so he could melt that smug smirk right off his lips.

Mark settled in behind a stack of food crates and returned to solidity. He was within a knife's throw of the marquee. He laid down another Lurking Inferno before rechecking his EP count.

EP: 60/144

The Wardog has slain five Level 3 Reivers.
Your XP reward per party member = 75 XP

"Greta is keeping herself rather busy," whispered Citadel.

"Better yet, she's keeping the reivers busy too." He took the amulet from his neck and pressed it to the ground.

"Can you sense where Vari is?"

"There's a small tent to the right of the inquisitor's marquee. She's lying on her side so I imagine her feet and hands are bound."

Mark gritted his teeth. "I'm going to seriously fuck Arix up for this."

"And let me be the first to congratulate you when that transpires."

Mark popped the amulet's chain back over his head. "Sooner rather than later is what I have in mind. Ethereal-" He stopped and watched as Karina ducked into her marquee. At the same time, Arix set down his crossbow and walked towards the smaller tent. Vari's tent. "Shit, what's he doing? We've got a good hour before daybreak."

"What did Ishka write about the timing of the sacrifice, Mark?"

"As the sun kisses these sacred stones, the living waters shall rain upon them."

"Is that the exact wording?"

"Yes, I memorized it." Then he felt his own living waters run cold. "Change of plan, Sid."

"Why? What's wrong?"

"The blood needs to be poured over the altars as the first light touches them. Ishka didn't say that it needs to come straight from the victim."

As if to confirm his fears, Karina reappeared from her tent, a large steel bucket in her hands.

"Oh, my," exclaimed Citadel as Arix returned from the smaller tent with Vari slung over his shoulder. "What do we do?"

"Kill Arix before he can pick up that fucking crossbow of his!" He drew Volcanic Bastard as he growled "Obsidian Plate!" For the briefest of moments, Mark was surrounded by a wet fog of glimmering black. The vapors coagulated like blood cells to an open wound, scabbing over Mark's body from head to foot.

EP: 49/155

He didn't wait for it to finish. He was already charging at the executioner, another spell lashing out from his tongue. "Terrifying Manifestation!"

EP: 34/155

Arix shrieked like a little boy. "Oh the horror, the terror of it all! Mummy!" Then a grin broke the executioner's mock expression of fear as Mark stopped in his tracks, dumbfounded. "Come on, Mark," oozed Arix, his voice oily with smugness. "I seen you use Terrifying Manifestation on them reivers, remember?" He nodded his head in Karina's direction. "Got some help from my new BFF over there. Bit of mental protection."

As Mark's mind raced, searching for his next best move, Karina calmly set down her bucket and raised a hand. The surrounding tent flaps opened and vomited reivers. Archers loosed arrows that bounced off Mark's obsidian armor. Men-at-arms charged at him, their gauntleted hands gripping large shields, their heavy armor rattling and clanking with every hurried step.

"Mark!" Citadel's voice was shrill with panic, the ruby on the amulet flaring brightly. "I couldn't feel them. I didn't know they were-"

Mark ignored him as he closed the last few meters to Arix and brought Volcanic Bastard sweeping around in what he hoped to be a leg-severing arc. If he could cut the bastard's legs out from under him, there was still a hope that Mark could scoop Vari up and outrun the reivers. But the executioner was ready for him. He shifted Vari to his arms and performed a graceful front aerial over Mark's simmering blade.

Before he could recover and strike again, the first reiver hit him with a ring of steel against stone. The shield knocked him sideways, and before he could regain his feet, the man was on top of him, thick arms wrapped around his legs. A woman joined the man, her weight crushed the breath from his lungs as she threw her own body across his. A couple more like these two and Mark would be completely pinned down. Helpless. He had to get clear. "Ethereal Flesh," he wheezed in desperation.

The sense of burden lifted from him as he melted away from the grasping soldiers and rose up in the air.

EP: 16/144

Mark aimed for his first Lurking Inferno, hoping to draw the reivers into his trap, but his progress was stopped short by a strong gust of wind. He tried to move again, only to be buffeted backwards. There was another gust behind him, then a third to his right. Mark tried to still the rising panic within him. The soldiers had formed a circle around him, their shields dropped in favor of thick woollen blankets they fanned toward him, his own vaporous form used against him. Such was the turmoil of air movement they created, he couldn't move upwards either. It was like trying to climb a ladder during an earthquake. He was trapped and he could see that the reivers were going to keep this up for the full twenty minutes of the spell's duration if they had to.

His only choice now was to take the fight to the reivers. He needed to fight his way over to Vari, free her, and together they'd kill the reivers and make a run for it before Arix resurrected. He was practically out of essence so he wasn't going to be able to terrify the executioner this time.

As fast as he could will it, Mark solidified and went for his sword. He expected the reivers to shy back, to draw their weapons, but that's when he realized that none of the soldiers had weapons. Uttering a shrill warcry, a heavily tattooed woman charged at him, arms curved outward in a fashion he knew all too well. He'd watched enough rugby games back home to recognize a tackle when he saw one. He sidestepped into a crouch and sliced the legs out from under her. She went down screaming. He straightened and drove his sword into the chain-clad chest of the next charging reiver, a big man with a wild mane of black hair. The man dropped like a stone and dragged Volcanic Bastard with him. Before Mark could pull his sword free, another reiver tackled him from behind, driving him down onto the man he'd just killed. He thrashed, trying to throw the reiver off, but the soldier was joined by one heavy body after another. Mark roared in frustration and fear, helpless against the crushing weight. An absurd image flitted through his panicked mind, of playtime at primary school when someone shouted "pile up" and Mark had been designated as the 'lucky' recipient.

Moments later, Mark felt his booted feet being bound together. The weight was lifted mercifully from his back as his hands were roughly grabbed and tied. A cloth gag was forced into his mouth. Finally he was hauled to his feet and brought face to face with a grinning inquisitor.

"You're just in time, warlock," she purred, "to witness something truly glorious."

Karina clicked her fingers and two men-at-arms took Vari from Arix, flipped her upside and held her between them. Still smiling, Karina knelt down beside Vari's upside-down face and gently tied her hair into a ponytail so that her dangling, black locks were tidied away.

"For what it's worth, Mark, I am sorry about this," offered Arix. The executioner knelt beside Mark and gently removed the Amulet of the Citadel. He held it to admire the workmanship. "This is much prettier than the last one. Like what you've done with the sword, Sid."

"You really are a piece of work, Arix the Damned," said Citadel with as much venom as he could muster in his voice.

"Honestly, Sid. I wish there was another way." He slipped the silver chain over his head. "But Mark just has to understand that you're not like him and me." He gestured at Vari and the gathered reivers. "None of these fuckers is." Arix stood and looked down at Mark. "Flesh and blood. *Real boys*, that's what we is. None of this Pinnochio shit. We're players in a game, and she," he finished, pointing at Vari, "is just one of the fucking pieces. You'll understand that once she's gone. It'll all make sense again once you get the fuck home."

"All very interesting, demon," remarked Karina. "Now kindly shut up while I kill this traitorous little bitch."

Vari's eyes met Mark's and he was taken aback by how little fear he saw in those warm, dark orbs. It seemed she had resigned herself to her fate. No whimpering. No begging. She was going out with dignity.

"Vari!" he tried to shout, but the gag turned it into a incomprehensible bellow. The sound of a terrified calf facing the slaughterhouse.

Vari closed her eyes as Karina unsheathed Blood of the Lost and drew its blade across the figurist's throat.

28

[VARI]

Vari clamped both hands over her mouth to stifle the screams that threatened to burst from her throat. Her nostrils flared as she breathed in and out against the memory of the pain - the hot line of fire across her throat and the hungry darkness that followed.

This is what Mark goes through every time? she wondered. It wasn't something she ever thought she could grow used to, not like he had. It wasn't the pain. She'd suffered plenty of that in her life already. She knew how to weather suffering. No, it was the darkness that terrified her. A roiling mass of uncertainty that promised everything and nothing. It was a beshadowed mirror, reflecting her every hope and fear, taunting her with her own imaginings of what happens beyond the predictable boundaries of life.

Her chilling thoughts were mercifully interrupted by a notification.

Congratulations!
You have harnessed the power of Resurrection and respawned from your first death.
Your Personal XP Reward = 150 XP

She stood, did her best to shake off those chilling thoughts and focus on the task at hand. She'd successfully stolen the power of resurrection from Arix. Now she had to hijack the Breaking Dawn from Karina.

After repairing her pentagram, she searched the walls of the tent until she found a peg at the back that was looser than the others. She worked it loose some more, checked that the coast was clear, then slipped out under the canvas.

Vari crept towards the rear of Karina's marquee as she puzzled over how she was going to get past Arix and free Mark. She figured that her best bet was to retrieve his gear from the inquisitor's quarters, assuming they'd been stored there with her own cloak and staff after the warlock's capture.

Rather than let the situation overwhelm her, Vari focused on putting one foot in front of the other. Perhaps she got a little too focused, because she almost ran headfirst into a urinating reiver as she rounded the next tent. The startled man spun about, almost splashing Vari in the process. Unfortunately for him, he chose to prioritize the tucking away of his privates over drawing his weapon. Vari lunged forward, clasped her hand around the soldier's throat and whispered, "Rend Flesh". Skin and muscle parted beneath her fingers, only to begin knitting together again as his Vigorous Healing ability took effect. Vari wasn't about to make the same mistake twice. Had she taken into account the sergeant's Vigorous Healing ability back at Citadel, Dayna might still be alive. "Rend Flesh," she repeated, and this time blood gushed over her hand and down the reiver's armored chest. He sank to his knees, gurgling quietly, his cry of alarm drowned in exsanguination. She gripped him with both hands as he toppled to the ground, softening the impact so that his jingling armor wouldn't give her away.

You have killed a Level 3 Reiver Man-at-arms.
Your XP Reward = 30 XP

She heard another gurgle behind her and raised her hand to direct Rend Flesh at the fresh reiver target. The reiver was already dead. Bloodied claws lowered the woman's corpse to the ground as steel-blue eyes regarded Vari with wary curiosity.

Level 6 Wardog
Aka Captain Maribella of Credence

The class didn't mean anything to her. Neither did the name. But Vari would have recognized those blue eyes anywhere. She'd seen them glaring over Dayna's shoulder as their owner drove a dagger into the ranger's brain. Now Vari knew how that must have felt and her stomach clenched at the thought of Dayna's experience after that, of plunging into the vortex of the unknown.

She felt her lips curl into a snarl. The wardog recognized where this was going and raised both of her claws.

"Now isn't the time," she whispered. "Your warlock and I, we're together in this."

Not only was she a murderess, she was a turncoat too. Then again, Vari knew what the inquisitors were, what it was like to suffer under their yoke. She couldn't exactly blame the woman for that. But she didn't need to trust her either.

"Does he know who you are?"

The wardog shook her head.

Vari frowned and pointed at the marquee. "Get us into that tent. We need our gear, and whatever alchemy Karina has been cooking up."

The wardog glanced over at the marquee and turned back briefly to smile before striking out. Two Level 4 reiver archers guarded the back of the marquee. Vari's Rend Flesh wasn't enough to kill them, not from a distance, but she managed to drown their cries in blood as the wardog finished them off in silence.

You have killed two Level 4 Reiver Archers.
Your XP reward per party member = 40 XP
Please note: Your party currently consists of two members.

After yanking out a few tent pegs, they were inside the marquee. Out front, Vari could hear Karina as she conducted the Breaking Dawn ceremony, reading out lilting words that hadn't been spoken in centuries.

Vari donned her cloak and leaned her staff against the workbench as she perused the inquisitor's stock of potions. There were some nasty biomancy concoctions that she didn't recognize, and wanted nothing to do with. She had no wish to become another of Karina's monstrosities, not like the wardog behind her. Nor did she want to unleash some horrendous malaise either. She unclipped the clasp on a small wooden box and gave a sigh of satisfaction at the twinkling vials within. Essence potions.

"What's your EP like?" she whispered at the wardog.

"Fuck all left." Vari tossed her one of the vials and motioned for her to drink it.

Maribella downed the brew in one gulp and then grinned through a predator's teeth.

Vari ignored her as she sipped at her own essence potion and felt her insides tingle with the replenishment. She was just tucking a couple more potions into her belt when a voice interrupted her.

"Now here's a couple of freaky ladies. A werewolf and a zombie. This is turning into an episode of Buffy the-"

Vari didn't care what Arix thought about anything. "Rend Flesh!" she shouted, focusing on his throat.

He winced and slapped his hand to his neck. "Ow!" he whined. But when he lowered his hand there was no blood, just a long and ugly bruise stretching across his skin.

Too much HP and too many defensive buffs for her to make much of an impression on him. She looked to the murderess for help but the wardog was already on the move, lunging at Arix with teeth bared and claws outstretched. She was fast. The executioner was faster. He dropped, rolled, and headed straight for Vari. She didn't have time to think before she found herself flying into Karina's workbench. Pain seared across her back as her ribs cracked against the bench's edge.

"Blinding Malaise," she wheezed from the floor.

A milky film spread over Arix's eyes. "Fucking hell!" he growled and began to swing his axe back and forth, establishing a defensive perimeter. The wardog crouched and watched with deadly intent, waiting for her moment to strike. That moment came at the end of an axe swing, while his hands were still being dragged away by the momentum of the follow through. She dove at him before he could correct his weight, dug her claws into his leather armor and dragged him down to the ground.

"Hey!" came a shout from the door flap. Sergeant Gunder stood there, mace in one hand, heavy shield in the other.

"Sculpt Bone!" she hissed and was rewarded with a loud crack as the big man's tibia snapped. He went down with a roar of pain. Now she had to do something about her own fractured bones. "Sculpt Bone, Mend Flesh," she muttered in quick succession. Pain shot through her side has her ribs realigned and fused back together. Then the warmth of healing followed, melting the agony away.

Vari stood, took up her staff and gave the groaning Sergeant Gunder a once over with Physik Perception. He had Vigorous Healing at Tier 3 and would be back on his feet in a few minutes if she didn't do something about it.

She looked to the melee that was raging between the executioner and the wardog, and momentarily considered using Sculpt Bone to break one of Arix's legs, to give Maribella an advantage. Although the wardog had received a number of deep gashes from Arix's axe, they were healing up fast, even more rapidly than Vigorous Healing would enable. This was Karina's biomancy at play.

Before Vari could act, the executioner gave a growl of frustration, flung his axe behind him and raised his silver gauntlets.

"Righteous Fury!" he roared. "Time to eat silver, bitch!"

His body was bathed in a steel-blue aura as he moved in on Maribella, fists lashing out with blinding speed. The wardog ducked under the first couple of jabs but was then caught by a right hook that sent her sprawling. Smoke puffed from singed fur where the silver knuckles had connected with her cheek.

"Justice Prevails," purred the executioner through his triumphant sneer. Once again his body glowed with steel-blue light and Vari watched in quiet horror as three separate claw wounds healed away to nothing.

It seemed the wardog wasn't going to be able to take the executioner alone, and Vari knew she wouldn't last two seconds with Arix once Maribella went down. They needed Mark, right now.

She looked down at the reiver sergeant and sighed with frustration. He was hiding behind his shield now. She wasn't going to be able to finish him off with her staff and he had too many hit points to bother with Rend Flesh. She broke his other leg with a Sculpt Bone and then cast Blinding Malaise on Arix again, if only to slow down his assault on the wardog.

"Fuck! You are so motherfucking annoying, Vari! When I'm finished taming this mutt, I'm going to chop you into doggie treats! Then I'm going to-" The rest of his words were cut short by the claws that raked across his face and split his lip open. With a feral howl, he lunged for Maribella and drove her to the ground. Even without his eyes, he seemed to be able to sense his opponent's position and strike back accordingly.

Your Sculpt Bone spell has reached Tier 5.

Your Blinding Malaise spell has reached Tier 2.

Vari waved the notifications aside, drank down another essence potion, gathered Mark's gear from where it lay in the corner, and got out of there before the executioner made good on his threats. She stepped outside and was greeted with the sight of her own blood being tipped over a set of sun-kissed altars. Her welcome was made even warmer by two reiver archers, bowstrings drawn and arrows nocked.

She closed her eyes and shouted, "Illuminate!", willing her Ring of Radiance to flash at maximum power. She opened her eyes again when she heard the yelps of pain and heard the arrows swish past her, missing her by a hair's breadth. Two Sculpt Bones later and the archers were flat on their backs, clutching at their sundered legs.

You have neutralized two Level 4 Archers.
Your XP reward per party member = 40 XP

Karina turned and fixed her with a baleful glare even while she continued to chant the words of the Breaking Dawn. The altars were glowing now, brighter than the sun that touched them. Vari looked from Karina to Mark. He stood bound to a post with a gag wrapped around his mouth, his face a mess of blood and bruises. Vari longed to heal him, to ease his pain and enfold him in her arms. But first she needed to halt the ritual.

Vari knew she wouldn't be able to touch Karina with her spells. The inquisitors trained figurists. Karina would have a natural resistance to anything Vari could throw at her. So she did the only thing left to her. She threw down Mark's gear and jumped onto the closest altar. She raised her staff high, stepped off the altar, and brought her weapon down onto the inquisitor with the full weight of her descent. With a shriek, Karina raised one arm to block the staff while the other went for the sacrificial dagger on her belt.

Hardwood connected with bone and Vari felt the latter give way. The inquisitor's forearm snapped like a branch under a woodsman's axe and her shriek turned to a scream of agonized rage as she drew her dagger and thrust it at Vari. The figurist didn't bother to dodge. Physik Perception told her that the blade would pierce her just to the right of her belly button and cut a hole in her lower intestine. It would be painful but not final. She stood her ground and drove her staff into the woman's face. Through the pain that swept across her belly, Vari heard a satisfying crunch as Karina's jawbone cracked.

The inquisitor tumbled backwards, hands clutching her face, her curses reduced to slurred, incomprehensible squeals and grunts.

You have neutralized a Level 9 Inquisitor!
Your XP reward per party member = 45 XP

A jolt of agony shot through Vari, so violently that the world around her narrowed to a small, white pinprick. She took in a deep breath, despite the further pain it caused her, and willed herself to remain conscious. As the blackness receded, she whispered "Mend Flesh". Spasms gave way to mere aches and Vari was able to bend enough to pick up Blood of the Lost from where Karina had dropped it in the dirt.

You have interrupted the Breaking Dawn ritual!
Your XP reward per party member = 150 XP

Warning!
If the Breaking Dawn ritual is not continued and completed within the next 300 seconds, the ritual will be abandoned and the altars will go into a one week cooldown period.

She looked up to see other reiver soldiers now closing in fast. She grabbed Karina by the hair, hauled her to her feet, and pressed the dagger to the inquisitor's throat. The approaching soldiers stopped in their tracks.

Holding Karina close, Vari made her way over to Mark. So sharp was Blood of the Lost that it cut through Mark's bonds like they were cobwebs. Then the dagger was back where it belonged, hovering over Karina's jugular like a vulture over a fresh corpse. The reiver soldiers continued to watch her, their hands on their weapons, but they dared not make a move.

Mark shook off the ropes and pulled the gag from his mouth with trembling hands. "Vari, I-"

She shook her head. "Take one of the essence potions from my belt, get the book, and finish the ritual."

He smiled, pride glinting in his bloodshot eyes, and drank the potion down in one go. Then he pronounced "Cunning Linguist", slowly and clearly, as he walked to where Karina had laid down Ishka's tome, its pages open to the last rites. He placed a bloodied finger on the yellowed parchment, finding the place where Karina had left off, and spoke the words, lilting and arcane.

Congratulations!
You have reached Level 9 as a Figurist!
Progress to Level 10 = 3024/5000

You gain 2 Attribute Points and may upgrade two spells and/or skills by one tier each.

Please note that the spell upgrade may not be applied to spells or skills of Tier 5 or over.

You have gained one new spell!

Grow Afresh
The caster may regrow body parts that have been lost.

Tier 1: Applies to a single body part no larger than a human middle finger. The part will regrow within one day. The part must have been lost within the hour.

Tier 2: Applies to a single body part no larger than a human hand. The part will regrow within one day. The part must have been lost within the hour.

Vari didn't need to think about it. She upgraded Grow Afresh to Tier 2 and Alchemy to Tier 4. Then she dropped both attribute points into Spirit, took a deep breath, and then channeled her flush of excitement into a whisper of unadulterated menace.

"I love that man," Vari hissed into Karina's ear. "You made him watch me die. Now you're going to watch him destroy *everything* you've worked for."

The inquisitor whimpered. Whether it was from the pain of her broken bones or the agony of watching her life's work destroyed before her eyes, Vari really didn't care. Pain was pain. It didn't matter where it came from. It hurt just the same, and the woman in her arms had dealt out more than her fair share of it.

Mark recited the final line and closed Ishka's tome with a satisfying thump. His eyes took on the faraway look of someone reading a notification and Vari let out a sigh of relief. It was almost done.

29

———

[MARK]

You have successfully deciphered and completed the Breaking Dawn ritual.

Your Cunning Linguist spell has reached Tier 2.

The Breaking Dawn awaits you! The Chasms of Corruption are yours to command.

A map filled Mark's vision, a bird's eye view of the lands affected by the corruption. Each and every chasm was shown as a slash of glowing red against the brown of the Barrens, the greenery of Garland

and the mottled shades of the Reiver Empire all the way to Credence.

The latter came as a shock to Mark. Not once had he thought about the effect the corruption was having on the reivers. After all he had said to Arix, after everything he claimed to be real about this world, not once had he considered that these reiver soldiers could have family and friends back home. They too might be hiding in their lords' keeps for fear of Cave Ghasts and Mist Wraiths. They too may have seen their people dragged by lurking horrors into those fetid depths. Karina was here to take control of the altars, to wield corruption as a weapon. But perhaps most soldiers were simply here to stop bad things from happening to the people they love.

He tried to calm the churning emotions in his belly, stave off the bewilderment that threatened to paralyze him. His mind was a honky, stinking traffic jam of thought. His heart beat a ferocious tattoo against his ribs. Not because he was afraid of the ritual, the altars, the corruption or the Breaking Dawn. Because Vari was alive.

He'd seen Karina cut her throat. He'd seen that bitch bleed Vari out into a fucking bucket. He'd seen the soldiers discard Vari's exsanguinated body like it was just another sack of rubbish. He'd seen the inquisitor pour Vari's lifeblood across these altars with the calm of a gardener watering her plants.

Yet Vari was alive. More than just alive. She was saving his ass. She was the reason he was now standing here, his fingers poised to heal the first bleeding wound on this magical map. Had she been a player all this time? She couldn't keep *that* a secret from him, could she?

Mark shook his head. He had a quest to complete. He reached out and touched the closest chasm. It rose up before him, pulling close so that he could make out the fetid, writhing life within. Mist Wraiths beyond count, undulating gently as they lay there, dormant, ripe for the awakening. A few had risen of their own accord to circle the chasm, to protect it. The forest around them had withered at their presence.

Do you wish to unleash the contents of this chasm?

Y/N

There was a foresters' settlement nearby. A half dozen huts clustered together in a clearing. He could see them going about their daily chores, children, women and men, oblivious to the anni-hilation that awaited them only a few kilometers away.

"No," he whispered.

Do you wish to close this chasm?

Y/N

"Yes."

If you do this, the chasm's contents will be destroyed. Are you sure you want to close this chasm?

Y/N

"Yes."

The lips of the chasm drew together like the seams of a ziplock bag, pulverizing the mist wraith swarm in a vice of earth and stone. A few wraith scouts flitted away and Mark quietly hoped that the foresters would be able to handle them on their own. He looked to the village and saw that the people had paused in their daily chores. They were gazing in the direction of the rift. Some had knelt down, others had taken hold of a post or a wall for support as the earth trembled beneath their feet.

A tall man hurried out of one of the huts, his grey hair tied back into a ponytail. His leather armor was old but well cared for. As were the bow in his hands and the quiver of arrows on his back. A retired ranger. Mark gave a sigh of relief. The village would be alright. An experienced ranger like that would be more than a match for the few surviving mist wraiths.

"Close the chasms," he told the map.

Please indicate the chasms you would like to close.

"All of-"

The wardog's limp body crashed out of the marquee and landed next to him. It was followed by a swearing executioner.

"Fuck me! You bastards are *really* pissing me off now!" When he saw Karina, cradling her arm, her broken jaw set off-kilter, he went an even darker shade of red. "Oh that's just fucking terrific! How's she supposed to send me home if she can't even fucking talk?"

In his peripheral vision, Mark saw Greta rise to her feet, her teeth bared.

"Fuck's sake," whined Arix, sounding more like a tantruming teenager every second. "Learn when to lie down, doggy!" The executioner shouted in Vari's direction this time. "And you, Figurist! Fix that woman's jaw. If you fuck up my ride home then I'm going to introduce you to a whole world of hurt. Even better now that you can resurrect. I don't know how you did it. You're sure as shit not a player. But you're going to wish you could just die by the time I'm finished griefing you!"

"No, Arix the Damned," Mark calmly assured him, "you're not going to do anything of the sort. Mind over Matter."

EP: 6/144

The Amulet of the Citadel unclasped itself and flew into Mark's hand. Then he turned his attention back to the Breaking Dawn map, zoomed in on the Barrens and tapped on the appropriate spot. He took a quick look at the list of monsters on offer and added a Siren for good measure.

He then lay the amulet down on the Altar of Solmora and gripped the bloodstained stone with both hands. "Vari! Brace yourself!" As if in answer, the earth rumbled and gave a jolt that threw Greta and Arix to the ground. The reivers around them followed suit, tumbling over with a series of startled yells and colorful curses.

Over the sounds of panic came the roar of sundering turf and an "Aaaarrgghh!" as Arix tumbled into the resulting rift. Mark winced as he turned to see a pair of silver gauntlets clutching the hole's edge. Of course. The executioner had preternatural reflexes. Arix's twisted and reddened face appeared and soon the rest of him would follow. Greta moved in to attack but Mark stopped her with a barked command.

"Greta! Wait!"

The wardog turned to him, eyes narrowed with anger. "I may look like a dog, warlock, but that doesn't mean you can..."

Her voice trailed off as she noticed the thick tentacle rising up behind Arix. It was joined by a second, and then two more. The siren was awake and looking for breakfast. The executioner only just got a leg up onto the surface when a tentacle lashed itself around his thigh. The others struck just as quickly, wrapping around his arms and face. Arix's scream was muffled by slimy sinew as he was dragged down into the abyss.

"Fuck," huffed the werewolf. "That was unsettling."

Mark looked over at Vari. The figurist had reacted immediately to his warning, grabbing onto the pole that Mark had been tied to. Her free hand still held the dagger to Karina's throat. She said something that he didn't quite catch, then the soothing warmth of Mend Flesh spell swept over him. He smiled his thanks and turned back to the Breaking Dawn UI.

"Close all chasms," he told the UI.

Closing all chasms is irreversible. You will not be able to reopen them.

Please note: you can still open new chasms as long as you possess the three altars and can fulfill the requirements of the Breaking Dawn ritual.

Are you sure you want to close all Chasms of Corruption?

Y/N

"Fuck, yes!"

The earth shook again, more violently this time. Stones and mortar cascaded from the ruins around them as chasms right across the Barrens closed in on themselves. The land was healing, just as Mark's own cuts had healed moments before under the influence of Vari's Mend Flesh spell.

Mark watched with grim satisfaction as a geyser of blood erupted from Arix's rift as it shuddered shut. Siren blood, mixed with a healthy dose of executioner blood. Around them, the surviving reivers either huddled together, scrambled for cover, or simply held onto something for dear life.

Then it was over. Almost.

Congratulations!
You have completed the Mountains of Corruption Quest!

You have sealed the **Source of Corruption** and the **Chasms of Corruption** in The Barrens, Garland and the Reiver Territories. **Monsters of Corruption** still roam but their numbers will not be replenished.

Your reward per party member = 1500 XP
Please note that you currently have 3 party members.

Congratulations!
You have achieved Level 10 as a Warlock.
Progress to next level = 5297/8000
You have been awarded 2 Attribute Points.

Spell Selection
You have 7 magical spells available for selection.
You have 2 spell slots remaining.

Brain Leash (Cast cost = 7 EP)
Crippling Lethargy (Cast cost = 9 EP)
Contagious Fervor (Cast cost = 9 EP)
War Cry (Cast cost = 10 EP)
Wave of Despair (Cast cost = 11 EP)
Fortress of Fire (Cast cost = 12 EP)
Rift of Corruption (Cast cost = 12 EP)

Please note: Rift of Corruption has been unlocked because you have completed the Mountains of Corruption Quest.

His eyes met Vari's. "That was quite some XP payload."

That got something between a pant and a chuckle from Greta. "Yeah, thanks for the level-up, Warlock."

He shrugged. "I think you earned it, don't you?"

Karina slurred something bitter yet incomprehensible through her broken mouth. Mark ignored her as he donned his armor and picked up Volcanic Bastard. The other reivers had recovered their collective nerve and were closing in.

He dropped both attribute points into Spirit, bringing it up to 18, then slotted Rift of Corruption along with Fortress of Fire to continue with his general fire theme. Then he let out a sigh as he eyed the approaching soldiers. "I've got two fire traps out there I could set off but I *really* don't feel like killing anyone else today."

"Don't think you'll have to." The wardog pointed at Karina with a long and wicked claw. "With her out of action, I'm the ranking officer around here."

"What?!"

Then he realized where he'd seen those cold, blue eyes before. His sword was halfway drawn before Vari's shout stopped him dead.

"Mark! No!"

He looked to Vari, incredulous. "You knew about her?"

"As soon as I saw her, yes."

His next question was cut off by a savage

howl. He drew his sword the rest of the way, expecting the murderess to be on him in moments. There was no need. The wardog was on her knees, her face a mask of agony. As he watched, a bizarre and disturbing transfiguration took place. Her teeth withdrew and flattened. Her claws retracted. Her fingers shortened. The thick wolven fur sank back into her flesh, leaving pale skin and tattoos behind in its wake. In under a minute, a platinum-haired reiver knelt before him, naked as the day she'd been born.

She stood and flashed him a grin. "Maribella of Credence, at your fucking service, warlock." Then she vaulted onto the Altar of Khorlvah to address her troops.

"Right you asswipes! Party's over! Gather your shit and let's get the fuck out of this shithole before any other poor bastard has to die."

"Begging your pardon, miss," growled a deep voice from the marquee's entrance. Gunder had recovered and was watching the proceedings with open suspicion. "It was you doing most of the killing of late."

Maribella shrugged. "You were following that crazy bitch's orders. And I know you, Gunder. You wouldn't have liked that one bit but still you sucked those commands down like a good little soldier." She turned back to the reivers. "The way I see it, you've all got a choice. On one hand, you can fuck off back to Credence and sign up with the next inquisitor nutter you come across. Of course, they'll torture the shit out of you first to make sure you're telling them the truth about what happened here. And they might hang you as a deserter since Karina isn't going anywhere without me and my dagger at her back. *Or* you follow me, the Wardog of the Barrens, and help me gut every fucking inquisitor we can find."

Perhaps it was the stirring speech, or perhaps they were just afraid of being slaughtered by a savage wolf woman, but they cheered like someone had just announced it was free beer o'clock. Whatever the reason, Mark was glad to see them all sheath their weapons and set to salvaging what remained of their camp.

Mark looked at the naked reiver woman and tried to summon the hatred he needed to avenge Dayna. Whether due to time or exhaustion, it just wasn't there.

"One day, sergeant-"

"Captain," the reiver interrupted.

"One day, *captain*," he corrected through gritted teeth, "we're going to meet again. And when we do, I'm going to cut your head off."

"For the ranger?"

"Yup."

"Fair enough, but don't expect me to hand it to you on a fucking platter. I'm a bit attached to it."

Mark couldn't help but smile. Dayna would be calling him every name under the sun right now, if she were here. Perhaps she was watching him now from some other instance, doing exactly that. She would just have to deal with it. He was done killing for today.

The captain saluted and hopped down off the altar. "Before I go find something to cover this bare ass of mine, what are you planning to do with that piece of shit?" She was looking at Karina, murder in her eyes.

"She needs to send the executioner home," Mark reminded her.

"And after that?"

"She's all yours."

The captain grinned and Mark was reminded of the wolf she'd been only moments before. "I reckon I'm going to develop a taste for inquisitors. Makes me feel like changing back in time for lunch."

Karina's look of fear was all Mark needed to know that the wardog meant every word of it.

30

[ARIX]

Arix plucked a battleaxe from the hands of a dead reiver and tried not to think back on his own recent demise. Tentacles and slime, followed by fatal claustrophobia when small places got even smaller.

He gave the dead man a kick, just for being an NPC in a world filled with *really fucking infuriating* NPCs. Everything was right royally fucked as far as he was concerned. All his plans flushed down the loo. No way was he going to be able to drag Mark back to reality now that his dream girl had risen from the dead.

He still couldn't work out how she'd done it either. She weren't no player so it had to be some sort of glitch. Some really unlucky quirk in the code.

Nah. That weren't it neither. She had to have done something. He didn't know what and that gave him the screaming willies. NPCs were *not* allowed to change the rules of the game. Yet another reason he had to ditch this nuthouse, sooner rather than later.

He rounded a newly fallen building and strode towards the inquisitor's marquee. He found Mark and Vari sitting outside with Karina. The latter was tied to a pole. He heaved a sigh of relief.

"Oi! Bastards! I want a word with you lot!"

Vari looked up as he approached while Mark stood and rested his hand on the pommel of his sword.

"Maybe put the axe down first," suggested Mark.

Arix eyed the warlock for a moment or two, trying to judge where he was at inside that delirium he called a mind. Mark had his full gear on while Arix's axe and armor were buried ten meters underground.

"I can tell by his stance that Arix is conflicted as to whether to attack you or not," informed

Citadel. "He keeps shifting his weight from left to right."

"Oh for fuck's sakes! Can I not even contemplate a bit of quiet fucking murder without some NPC giving me a running fucking commentary?" He looked to the grey-mantled sky and imagined a row soft, bearded heads looking down at him. "Oi you devving fuckfaces! Get me the fuck out of this asylum before I sue you for every motherfucking cent you have!"

Then he turned back to Mark and fixed him with the baleful glare that he usually reserved for addressing troll commenters on his YouTube channel.

"You might be a lost cause, Mark, but you're standing between me and my imminent salvation." He raised his battleaxe and prepared to charge. "I don't care how many runs this takes. That reiver bitch is coming with me."

"Sid?" Mark's voice was unnervingly calm. "Do you think you could locate Arix's resurrection point?"

"I already have, Mark. It was remiss of him not to move upon awakening this time."

Arix felt the hot winds of his fury drop away, leaving his sails limp and lifeless. If Mark got the better of him this time, and he probably would, the warlock could then grief him at leisure. He took a deep breath in a vain attempt to still the roiling frustration in his gut. Then he feined a nonchalant shrug and tossed the battleaxe aside.

"Fine, fine. Have it your fucking way then. I'm done with this shit-assed game anyway."

"Good choice," answered Mark.

"Fuck you."

For the first time, Arix noticed what the reivers were up to. The few that remained were roaming the camp, salvaging, packing and taking orders from…

"Fuck me. Sergeant Maribella?"

"You two have met?" wondered Mark.

"Yeah. We was introduced during my stint as a slave."

Mark smirked. "Notice anything familiar about her?"

Arix wrinkled his nose. "Nah, It…"

Actually, there *was* something about the way she moved, and when she turned to look at him with those frosty eyes of hers the realization rushed at him with claws and slavering jaws.

"Fucking hell! The dog?"

"That's Captain Dog to you," corrected Mark.

Hearing this, Maribella gave Arix a wolfish grin and then turned back to her work, swearing colorfully at a couple of soldiers who were looking to crack the beer keg they'd just salvaged.

Arix folded his arms and looked to Karina. "That your doing, luv?"

Karina burbled something and Mark gave Vari a knowing nod. Vari stood, placed her hand on the inquisitor's cheek and murmured "Sculpt Bone" and "Mend Flesh" in quick succession.

Karina spat blood at Vari, narrowly missing her, and opened her mouth to let rip. Mark silenced her with a glare. "You say one word that I don't tell you to say and Vari breaks your jaw all over again."

The inquisitor clamped her mouth shut and returned the warlock's glare.

"So now what, Mark?" wondered Arix.

"Time for you to go home, Arix."

"You know that I'm going to be talking to the *Reign of Blood* devs, right? It won't matter what I say or don't say about you. They only need to look at their data to see what's what. They might just pull the plug on you."

Mark's eyes hardened. "No, they won't. Because you're going to talk them out of it."

"And why would I do that?"

"Because Vari here has seen into your selfish little soul."

"What the fuck are you talking about?"

"Physik Perception," Vari answered for him. "I used it on you while you were busy assuaging your own guilt by talking too much. Once I reached Tier Five, I unlocked Meta Perception and that allowed me to see what you really are, Arix the Damned."

Arix felt a chill go down his spine. "And what am I, Miss Scripted-bot-lady?"

He'd meant it to come out nice and smooth, with just the right seasoning of vitriol. Instead his words sounded sluggish and sticky because his mouth had gone dry all of a sudden.

"This version of you is just a construct of words and numbers that exist within the confines of a brain made of lightning and metal. In Mark's world you're a real person. This," she said as she looked him up and down, "is just a puppet."

"Same with your boyfriend there, luv."

"I know. His body is somewhere else, in another world that I'll probably never see." She rested her hand on Mark's leg. "But he tries to be more. Mark is here, spirit and mind, because this is where he wants to be. You don't care about this world, Arix, and that's why you'll never belong here."

"Of course I won't. It's not fucking real!"

"No, Arix," said Vari gently. "I think it's *too* real, and you don't know how to deal with that."

There was a shadow of a doubt now. Faint, but it was there. He weren't no AI expert, but bog-standard game bots couldn't think like that. Vari was not only recognizing the difference between his avatar and his real self, she was accepting, in her own terms, that she too was a construct inside a computer. He wasn't very up on his consciousness philosophy, but it sounded scarily like self-fucking-awareness to him.

"Vari?" he croaked.

She looked at him, her dark eyes blank of emotion, like she was trying to work out which species of cockroach had just crawled onto the seat of her toilet. He cleared his throat and pushed the reluctant words out of his mouth. "For what it's worth, I'm sorry."

Vari's expression didn't change. "Just go home, Arix."

He looked to Mark. "Guess this is goodbye, innit."

Mark's smile almost reached his eyes.

"Goodbye, Arix."

31

———

[MARK]

Two days went by and Mark was still in *Reign of Blood*. Perhaps Arix hadn't talked to the devs like he claimed he would. Perhaps the devs were happy to let sleeping dogs lie. Or perhaps they would pull the plug any second and he would wake up in his hospital room. Too many 'perhaps' for Mark's liking. If a hospital bug didn't kill him then the suspense might.

It was cool in the fortress this evening. Most of the villagers had lit their fires. Earlier in the day Calder had gathered everyone together to hear how Mark and Vari had completed the Chasms of Corruption quest. Some asked after Arix the Damned and seemed happy with Mark's 'gone' response.

Whether he was dead or simply off on other adventures, no-one seemed to care. It appeared Arix had successfully alienated everyone he'd interrogated.

The rustle of her robes announced Vari's arrival. She joined him at the battlement and followed his gaze down into the courtyard.

"Still worried that you'll blink and find yourself back in your old world?"

Mark sucked his bottom lip before answering. "Did Meta Sight tell you that?"

She laughed. "No. That anxious look on your face did."

"If it comes to that, I'll find a way back in, I promise."

"I know you will. What would these people do without their great Warlock of Garland?"

He quirked an eyebrow at her. "That's right. 'These people' would miss me something wicked."

She drew close and slipped her arm around his waist. "Yes, 'these people' certainly would."

"Well, at least we managed to solve their corruption woes. But do you think I did the right thing, burying the altars like that?"

Having slotted the Rift of Corruption spell, Mark went ahead and opened up a chasm right under the three altars. He'd close it again, straight away, ensuring that several dozen tons of rock and dirt stood between some ambitious inquisitor and another Breaking Dawn.

"It was worth it to see Karina cry," Vari assured him. "It must have been difficult for her, seeing her life's work slip through the cracks like that."

"Not as bad as what Captain Maribella was going to do to her," observed Mark.

"I hope she meant what she said," said Vari.

"What bit?"

"About developing a taste for inquisitors. Dayna would shoot me in the face for saying this, but Captain Maribella might actually turn out to be worth a thousand rangers when it comes to keeping Garland safe."

"I'm still going to kill her the next time I see her," stated Mark matter-of-factly.

"But not yet?"

He smiled. "I think we deserve a holiday, don't we? Travel around Garland for a bit. Actually see this beautiful country that we've fought so hard to-"

"Evening, geezas!"

Mark yelped and Vari shouted "Rend Flesh!"

as she pointed at the smiling apparition. Arix just kept on smiling.

"Sorry, luv. Thought you might do that so I asked the devs to give me temporary God Mode."

A fearful shot of adrenaline spiked through Mark's gut. Arix with God Mode was a *terrible* combination, but the executioner clocked his alarmed expression and waved away his concern.

"In the words of Douglas Adams, Don't Fucking Panic. I'm not here to break your toys. Far from it, in fact."

"Would you like me to fetch the cockroaches, Mark?" asked Citadel from somewhere near Mark's feet. "Judging by his current weight, Arix appears to be unarmed. I would wager that a dozen or so could tear him limb from-"

"No need to release the bughounds. Fucked if I'm hanging out with you nutters any longer than I have to anyways." He winked at Vari. "No offense, luv."

"The feeling," said Vari, "is totally mutual."

Arix grinned and turned back to Mark. "Anyhow, I got you a job."

Mark sighed. "I'm not fucking working for you, Arix. Now or ever."

Arix feigned shock. "That hurts, that does." Then his grin returned with full force. "But I'm not the one paying you. I just organized it. It's the *Reign of Blood* devs what want to hire you."

The spike in his gut dissolved into something akin to a hundred scuttling spiders. "What sort of job?"

"User Experience Analyst they want to call it. Basically, you're just a glorified Beta Tester."

It was then that Mark registered that Arix wasn't in his executioner garb. He was wearing a bomber jacket, a black Resident Evil t-shirt and black jeans. Arix took a pen and a sheet of folded paper from the inside pocket of his jacket and handed them over. Mark opened the paper and read over the contract while Vari glared and Arix grinned.

"They want to shift me to a private hospital, cover my medical bills and pay me a salary," Mark summarized. "In return, they get to observe how I interact with the world and its inhabitants."

"Not your most private moments, don't worry," Arix assured him as he clicked his fingers at Vari.

"Sid?"

"Yes, Vari?"

"Did I leave Blood of the Lost in the bathroom?"

"I'm afraid not. It's in the armory. Would you like one of my cockroaches to fetch it for you?"

Arix raised his hands. "Hold the fuck on, stabby lady. As much as it pains me to admit this, Mark was right." He pointed at the ceiling. "Those fuckers set this all up and then just let it run for six months on hyper processing. They weren't looking to crack the lid on it for at least another six. Then I comes along, tells them I've suffered no-logoff and VR torture for several days and that they'd better crack that lid before I sue their company into fucking bankruptcy."

Mark's eyes narrowed. "You got a payout?"

"Not nearly as much as I'd have got if I'd gone public." He leaned against the battlements, a conspiratorial smirk on his lips. "But then I wouldn't have a first week's exclusive when they do finally release."

"Release?" squawked Citadel. There was real fear in his voice. "I've been managing my existential crisis rather nobly, I thought. Yet it's one thing to realize that your world was created by some otherworldly mages with frankly unfathomable powers, quite another to learn that these mages intend to turn your home into a playground for a horde of Arix the Damned types. How many everborns are we talking about here?"

"Everborns?" wondered Mark. "Like Zevryn the Everborn?"

"Yes. Zevryn was the first warlock with the power to resurrect. Everborn was the moniker I offered up and he rather took to it."

Mark mentally tried it on for size. Mark the Everborn. It had a nice ring to it.

He raised an eyebrow at Arix. "One of the devs, trying this world on for size?"

Arix shrugged. "Or an alpha tester under a non-disclosure agreement."

"He was summoned by the druids," interjected Citadel. "Like you were, Mark."

"What happened to him?" Mark asked him.

"He did his duty, fended off a reiver invasion, and then the druids sent him home."

Arix's brow wrinkled with suspicion. "Don't think them devs are telling me the whole truth yet."

Mark didn't think so either. "Sid. You said that it was Ivara of the Dancing Flame who took you under her wing?"

"Indeed. She was an 'interesting' mentor."

"Was she born in Garland, like you?"

"Not that I recall, no. Then again, my migration from body to building was less than smooth. I lost more than I gained, I'm afraid."

"What about Garridar?"

"He was rather tight-lipped on the subject of his background, but I can assure you that he was neither Garlander nor reiver."

"The devs assured me that they'd left this world alone," interjected Arix. "They wanted it to be completely independent. In fact, they were pretty chuffed to learn it was populated and relatively nice, not some post-apocalyptic dust bowl."

"Interesting." Mark sighed. "We're not going to solve this mystery today, but it looks like we're not the first outsiders to come here, Arix."

"And as I said, we won't be the last neither. A full player influx is going to happen sooner or later," concluded Arix. "At least you'll get fair warning now. And the devs have promised to profile everyone right down to their proclivities. No sick fucks allowed."

"Sick fucks like you?" snapped Vari.

Arix winked at Mark. "You need to tell Vari a bit more about our world, yeah? Especially the internet. There's bastards out there what make Karina look about as evil as dearly departed Braemar."

Vari visibly shuddered and looked to Mark for confirmation.

"Sorry, Vari, but Arix is right about that." He

tapped the contract with his index finger. "What's with this clause about 'special quests'?"

"Alright, you're a little bit more than a Beta Tester then. Resident Bug Hunter too. Like, for a start, they want you to go have a word with the druids. Can't have them summoning anyone else here. They was lucky they got you, Mark, and not some-"

"Asshole like you?" Vari finished for him.

Arix groaned. "Really, Vari? *Every* fucking opportunity?"

Vari pointed at her throat. To his credit, Arix was quick on the uptake.

"Alright. Point taken." He turned back to Mark. "At some stage you'll have to go sort out them inquisitors too."

"Give Maribella a few weeks," said Mark, "and there might not be any inquisitors left."

Arix shrugged. "It might be just a mop-up job, but the devs need to be sure."

"Can't they stop the summonings themselves?"

"Not from the outside, no. It's something these AI..." He paused and checked himself. "These 'people' have come up with on their own. Got the devs scratching their heads."

This was an "ah ha!" moment for Mark. As

he'd suspected, the druids and the inquisitors had somehow turned their rituals into code and hacked systems completely external to this version of *Reign of Blood*. It was dangerous, but it was also bloody fascinating.

"Anyways, you'll get to the bottom of it, assuming you sign that contract."

Mark waved the papers at Arix. "What happens if I don't sign? What happens if I don't want to be their Bug Hunter?"

"You'd be a muppet, that's what. They won't kick you out so no need to get your bollocks in a twist. They'll make sure you can log off. Whether you do or not is up to you." Arix looked at his watch. The flashy black and gold device was an affectation twice over. Firstly, because this was FIVR, and secondly because no-one wore watches these days. "Right. Time for me to piss off. I promised Krissy dinner and a show at the West End this evening." He pointed at the contract. "The devs said to take your time thinking it over. Me, I say sign it and live happily fucking ever after in La La Land. Means I don't ever have to worry about meeting your spotty ass on the street some day." He stood, straightened his jacket, and gave them both a wave. "Toodles and here's to never meeting again."

"Something we can all agree on," offered Citadel.

"That goes double for me," agreed Vari.

Arix blew her a kiss and vanished without even a puff of smoke.

Vari turned to Mark, her dark eyes full of questions. Only one made it to her lips. "Well?"

"Well what?"

"The gods are offering you a pact. Are you going to pledge them your undying service?"

"They're not gods, Vari, they're-"

She shushed him with a kiss and then firmly cupped the sides of his face as she stared into his eyes. "Are you going to live happily ever after with me in La La Land?"

"Ahem, I think I'll leave you to it," offered Citadel. "I have cockroaches to muster and an existential panic attack to stave off."

"Any time you need to talk about that, you just say. Okay, Sid?"

"Thank you, Mark. I will."

Mark felt Citadel's presence fade away, like the air settling after a door is closed. Without breaking eye contact with Vari, he scribbled his signature on the paper and tossed both it and the pen onto the floor. Out of the corner of his eye, he saw them vanish just like Arix had done.

"I'm not sure it's always going to be 'happily', Vari. There's inquisitors to deal with."

"Their monsters too. Worse things than Captain Wardog."

"That's right. And The Barrens is still full of creatures and secrets."

"And it'd be nice to free Karaji from reiver slavery at some point."

"Outsiders coming in and causing trouble as well." He smiled and drew her closer. "So, I guess what I'm saying is that it might not be the healer slash children's entertainer scenario any time soon."

"That's okay. I can wait."

"Ever after?" asked Mark.

Vari answered him with a kiss.

End of Book Two

Congratulations!
You have completed the "Weighty Tome"
quest.
With your piercing eyes you have slain the Epic Boss that is Book Two.

You are a ruthless executioner of reading material!
Your XP Reward = 500

If you enjoyed *Executioner: Reign of Blood* and have not already taken on the **"Signed in Blood"** quest, simply follow the link below and you will be teleported to my mailing list signup.

And this quest comes with a loot drop as its reward.

Were you wondering how Citadel came to be the spirit-in-the-stones of the Warlocks' rightful fortress? Having completed the **"Signed in Blood"** quest, you will receive two FREE short stories.

Here's the link…

https://www.edmcrae.com/free-short-stories

In **Old Flame** you will learn how Citadel and Ivara of the Dancing Flame fought to the bitter end against the forces of oppression, and how Sid gave up his body to become the guardian and keeper of the Warlock Way.

In **Bloody Minded** you will hear about Dayna's experiences during her nightmarish expedition into The Barrens and why she was the only ranger to return with Wayfarer's diary.

Also, reviews are the Notifications that keep us LitRPG writers questing and leveling up. If you could please consider leaving a review at Goodreads or Amazon that would be truly awesome.

Thank you again, Lorekeeper! If you want to check out my other stories, learn a bit more about about me, or hear my thoughts about LitRPG and video games, you're most welcome to stop by www.edmcrae.com.

Cheers!
Edwin McRae

CHARACTER SHEET: ARIX THE DAMMED

Class: Executioner - Level 9
Progress to Level 10 = 3022/5000

Body: 18
Modified Body: 19
(+1 from Dusk Leather Armor)

Mind: 15
Spirit: 15

HP: 162
Modified Body: 171
EP: 135

Skills
Axework (Tier 5)
Horse Riding (Tier 2)
Arbalist (Tier 4)
Acrobatics (Tier 3)
Climbing (Tier 3)
Buzzard Eyes (Tier 2)
Fox Ears (Tier 2)
Hound Scent (Tier 1)

Enduring Will (Tier 1)

Spells
Chopping Block (Tier 3)
Truelight (Tier 1)
Clean Slate (Tier 3)
Justice Prevails (Tier 3)
Righteous Fury (Tier 2)
Blood Retribution (Tier 1)
Suspended Sentence (Tier 1)

Gear (Buried in The Barrens)

Solmora's Bite
Two-handed Battleaxe
+50% to base axe damage.
+25% attack speed.
50% chance of inducing a melancholy that reduces the victim's damage dealt by 25%.
20% chance of inducing crippling despair that paralyzes the victim for 5 seconds.

"Despair is the fertile soil from which delight may sprout and bloom." - Ishka the Devout

Dusk Leather Armor
+1 Body.

+5% movement speed.
20% reduction to torso damage during daylight
or darkness.
40%reduction to torso damage during twilight.
5% chance to prevent total damage during daylight or darkness.
15% chance to prevent total damage during
twilight.

"Dusk watches from the shadows as night mur-
ders the day."
- Vaydn the Merciful

Jaravir's Handshake
Silver-forged Gauntlets
40% reduction in damage to the hands.
10% reduction in all physical damage received.
10% increased accuracy with two-handed
weapons.
10% increased damage dealt with two-handed
weapons.

"I make a promise with a handshake and keep it
with a fist."
- Jaravir the Bloodcoin

Kren's Tempered Cuisses

25% reduction to damage sustained to the
upper leg.
25% chance to prevent all damage to upper leg.
15% reduction in upper leg muscle fatigue.
+10% to knee attacks.

"I don't care if you've got balls of rock. I've got a
knee of forged steel." - Captain Kren of the Imperial Guard

Kren's Tempered Greaves
25% reduction to damage sustained to the
lower leg.
25% chance to prevent all damage to lower leg.
15% reduction in lower leg muscle fatigue.
+10% to kick attacks.

"They say not to kick a man when he's down.
What a wasted opportunity." - Captain Kren of
the Imperial Guard

CHARACTER SHEET: MARK THE EVERBORN

Class: Warlock - Level 10
Progress to Level 11 = 5297/8000

Body: 18
Modified Body: 20
(+2 from Jaravir's Icy Resolve)

Mind: 16
Modified Mind: 17
(+1 from Jaravir's Icy Resolve)

Spirit: 16
Modified Spirit: 18
(+2 from Amulet of the Citadel)

HP: 160/160
Modified HP: 180

EP: 160
Modified EP: 180

Skills

Swordplay (Tier 5)
Horse Riding (Tier 2)

Spells
Terrifying Manifestation (Tier 4)
Second Skin (Tier 4)
Arcane Edge (Tier 4)
Ethereal Flesh (Tier 3)
Mind over Matter (Tier 1)
Ivara's Ignited Exhalation (Tier 3)
Forge Anew (Tier 1)
Shroud of Shadow (Tier 2)
Cunning Linguist (Tier 2)
Lurking Inferno (Tier 3)
Obsidian Plate (Tier 1)
Fortress of Fire (Tier 1)
Rift of Corruption (Tier 1)

Gear

Garridar's Ironhide
35% reduction to damage caused by hits to the torso.
20% reduction to damage to arms.
25% chance to prevent total damage.
10% Fire Resistance.
10% Cold Resistance.

"One must grow a thick skin to survive this harsh world."
- Garridar Stoneye

Volcanic Bastard Sword
A blade of living lava bound by thermal enchantments.
100% bonus to base sword damage.
150% bonus to base armor penetration.
30% chance of inflicting burning damage for 1-6 seconds.
25% chance of breaking a base weapon when sparring.
75% chance of cauterizing organic material.
Ambient heat can be transferred into metal and stone with 80% efficiency.
"Our petty angers are puffs of steam to the mountain's molten rage." - The Infernal Marakor

Jaravir's Icy Resolve
Silver-forged Helmet
+2 Body.
+1 Mind.
40% reduction in damage to the head.
10% reduction in all physical damage received.
Contains 'Petina of Frost' to keep the wearer cool during battle.

"Either your head stays cool or you lose it."
- Jaravir the Bloodcoin

Amulet of the Citadel
+2 Spirit

"Magic is the essence of a warlock. Loyalty is the essence of a friend." - Citadel

Cuisses of the High Legion
20% reduction in damage caused to the upper leg.
20% chance to prevent total damage to the upper leg.
10% reduction in upper leg muscle fatigue.

"An empire begins with a pair of sturdy legs and a willingness to march." - Commander Ezra of the High Legion

Greaves of the High Legion
20% reduction in damage to the lower leg.
20% chance to prevent total damage to the lower leg.
10% reduction in lower leg muscle fatigue.

"Forget ceremony. A soldier stands on tender

flesh and brittle bone."- Commander Ezra of the
High Legion

CHARACTER SHEET: VARI OF KARAJAN

Class: Figurist - Level 9
Progress to Level 10 = 4524/5000

Body: 12
Solmora's Blessing +1 Modifier: 13

Mind: 17

Spirit: 19
Solmora's Blessing +3 Modifier: 22

HP: 108
Modified HP: 117

EP: 189
Modified EP: 216

Skills
Alchemy (Tier 5)
Physik Perception (Tier 5)
Horse Riding (Tier 2)
Meta Sight (Tier 2)

Spells
Mend Flesh (Tier 5)
Rend Flesh (Tier 5)
Puppeteer (Tier 4)
Sculpt Bone (Tier 4)
Purify Blood (Tier 2)
Blinding Malaise (Tier 2)
Cleanse Infection (Tier 2)
Grow Afresh (Tier 2)

Gear

Solmora's Blessing
+25% reduction to damage received.
+1 to Body.
+3 to Spirit.
+50% resistance to magical manipulation of the wearer's Mind.

"With clarity and purpose we find our way through the mists of despair." - Ishka the Devout

Ebon Staff of the Dusk
20% increase in casting speed.
+20% to staff base damage during daylight or darkness.
+50% to staff base damage during twilight.

"Day and night are stale illusions. Everything changes and dusk has the truth of it." - Desir the Leaden Heart

Blood of the Lost
+20% to base dagger damage.
30% chance of inducing internal hemorrhaging in an organic enemy.
+30% accuracy when thrown.
Will return to owner if in line of sight.

"We might be lost yet our blood will always find its way home."
- Ishka the Devout

Ring of Radiance
Produces a white light with a radiance equivalent to a burning lantern.
The wearer can invoke the radiance effect by uttering "Illuminate" and stop the radiance with an utterance of "Extinguish".
The wearer can strengthen or weaken the radiance through force of will.

Breastplate of the High Legion
20% reduction in damage to the chest.

20% chance to prevent total damage to the chest.
10% increase in lung capacity.

"Can't terrify an enemy with wheezes and gasps."
- Commander Ezra of the High Legion

ABOUT THE AUTHOR

Edwin has been a screenwriter and narrative designer for over 12 years now. After four years of writing for television, he started with Grinding Gear Games in 2010. He became lead writer on the creative team that took their online ARPG, Path of Exile, from 80,000 players to 20 million players and a 100 million dollar buyout from Tencent. During the last eight years he's worked with numerous Indie game developers, helping them turn their ideas into stories that players can experience and enjoy.

Edwin has recently fallen in love with LitRPG, a genre that beautifully incorporates his twin passions of video games and science-fiction.